NICOLE GLOVER

DEATH BY CHRISTMAS CAKE

DATURA

DATURA BOOKS
An imprint of Watkins Media Ltd

Unit 11, Shepperton House
89-93 Shepperton Road
London N1 3DF
UK

daturabooks.com
twitter.com/daturabooks
The cookie crumbles

A Datura Books paperback original, 2026

Edited by Ella Chappell
Cover by Karen Smith
Set in Meridien

ISBN 978 1 91741 5 378
Ebook ISBN 978 1 91741 5 361

Printed and bound in the United Kingdom by CPI Group (UK) Ltd, Croydon CR0 4YY

9 8 7 6 5 4 3 2 1

MIX
Paper | Supporting responsible forestry
FSC® C013604
FSC www.fsc.org

For my favorite aunt.
Aunt E, your love, support, and encouragement
has the strength of ten Grinches plus two!

Chapter 1

My kitchen looked like a crime scene. Or maybe it was something worse than mere crime, given the spray of flour, dripping jam jars, dented pans, broken candy canes, and the pungent smell of burnt sugar. The whole place looked like the result of a fight against an intruder with nothing more than a batter-covered spatula – and it wasn't that far off from the truth.

I *had* been in a fight for my life when the blades of my hand mixer hit the edge of the bowl and sent its contents flying, splattering me in the face as I stumbled back, nearly bumping against a stovetop loaded with bubbling brown butter.

Bubbling *burnt* butter, I corrected myself, as I prodded the crisp and crackling edges.

This was what I got for trying to make two of Shirleen Foster's cakes at the same time, even though the cook herself always said cakes were not meant to be juggled.

Shirleen was going to be insufferable once she found out. I was never going to be the chef she was, but I got the job as her recipe developer because I had proved to be a decent enough cook.

The kitchen door moved open a few inches, as one of my cats squeezed in, her whiskers trembling as she sniffed about. The orange tabby was always the bravest and most curious of the trio, as Lola had the courage and wisdom of a cat on her fifth life.

She delicately walked through the mess, and then pausing at the batter spilled across the tiled floor, she raised large brown eyes at me, in almost human-like disapproval.

"I'd like to see you do better," I grumbled, but the cat had already twisted around, heading back to report to Decker and Poppy.

Cut by the dismissive tone, I turned off the stove and slid to the ground with a sigh. My apron tented before me as I looked down at the flour dotting the gingerbread cats on my socks.

I was not eager to start cleaning up, but this mess had to go if I was going to have a cake ready to bring tonight. I had talked too big of a game to show up empty-handed.

As I lamented, my phone began vibrating against my hip, bringing me to deeper despair.

There was only one person who would call me at this hour. With a groan, I brushed the flour off my apron and tapped my headphones. In the screen for the incoming video call, I could see I had more flour on my nose which I hastily wiped away. My face – slightly angular with dark brown skin, and shiny from perspiration – flickered out of view to be replaced by Shirleen who scowled as she looked over her glasses into the screen.

Forcing a smile filled with rainbows and sunshine, I said, "Hello, Shirleen."

"Are you trying to juggle cakes?" Shirleen's voice still had the twang of South Carolina Low Country to it that was soft and comforting even when sharpened with disapproval. "How's that working out for you?"

I surveyed the dripping batter that plopped onto the tiles before me. "It could be better. Though it seems I won't be able to bring two cakes to the party after all."

"I said you couldn't," Shirleen replied, smugness seeping into her words. "I thought you knew better by now."

"I overestimated my ability," I admitted, even as I squirmed like a student whose volcano science project had only gurgled instead of exploding.

Although we had been working together for the last few months, Shirleen tended to treat me like an assistant instead of a colleague.

I might have been a bit to blame.

From the very first message I'd gotten regarding the contract to work with her, I had been starstruck. My grandmother had frequently referenced Shirleen's first cookbook, *Season by Season*, and even gifted me a copy when I moved into my first apartment.

The bold golden yellow of the cover was still etched in my memory. Featuring Shirleen's smiling face, she held up a buttercream frosted cake with sprigs of rosemary and thyme to the reader. Her glorious afro was now sleek silver braids and her coke-bottle glasses had become round wire spectacles, but she was otherwise unchanged. She was still Shirleen Foster, the woman whose cookbooks had a place alongside *The Joy of Cooking* and *The Ebony Cookbook* in the kitchens that raised me. A bold and unapologetic dark skinned Black woman, who redefined the art of cooking and Mid-Atlantic foodways, and made a name for herself across radio, newspapers, and television by bringing good food to all. She was also the Christmas Cake Queen, as she had twelve cake recipes that were forever linked to Christmas and other festivities.

"It's always good to try," Shirleen remarked. "So don't feel too terrible, Keisha."

I waited for her to point out the mess I made. She liked video chatting, mainly so she could see exactly what I was working on and provide feedback on the spot for the days I worked from my kitchen. Obstinately hired as a recipe developer to give a modern voice to the book, I had only been given free range on the recipes that Shirleen didn't give two figs about. I had once been a data analyst at a local tech company, who lived out my true self as a food blogger by night. I never went to culinary school, never cooked for anyone beyond my friends and family. I had never even worked in a restaurant (nor did I desire to after the horror stories I heard!). Even now, I wasn't sure how Shirleen had seen my blog, but somehow she learned I was remaking her recipes and then asked if I'd be brought in to assist revising *Season by Season* with her.

Months later I still pinched my arm to remind myself this wasn't a strange and bewildering dream.

"Keisha, I want you to bring the Caramel Pecan for the party," Shirleen said. "I didn't make that one because you've proven you can make it adequately, just don't add your family's little twist on it. While most people think you can splash just about any amount of vanilla in and it'll be fine, I specify measurements to allow for certain delicate flavors to stand out."

I bit down the reflex to apologize, and murmured words of agreement instead. "I'll make the cake for tonight."

"Good, be there an hour early like we planned." She paused, and the next words lacked her usual bite as she continued, "Unless you can arrive even earlier to the manor."

"You need help setting up?" I asked. "I thought that Naomi–"

"Naomi has not been answering her phone all day. She's fired, even if she doesn't know it yet. How could she, today of all days! Everyone will be there tonight, including my ex-husband!"

I sat up, startled at this news. I had never met her former husband, but Shirleen's divorce over a decade ago had resulted in a court battle that was all over the news and had become one of the ten biggest food media scandals. From just the news coverage I could hardly believe Shirleen would ever willingly invite him anywhere. I didn't always like passing judgment on people, but Glenn Dupont needed to be judged like potato salad with unnecessary raisins.

"I thought you didn't want him there?"

"I don't. Naomi invited him by mistake. Now I can't even boot him out – once my publisher got wind of it, they thought it would look nice, especially as some of the early cookbooks had been dedicated to him."

"I'll get there earlier," I announced, "and make sure the staff knows not to let him in."

"Thank you." The rush of relief behind those words nearly bowled me over.

This party was the biggest public event Shirleen had held in many years, with all eyes on her. I'd had my share of bad breakups, so I knew what it was like for an old boyfriend to step out of bad memories, but I was lucky I had never had one intrude on an important night.

"I have an interview with a reporter before the party," Shirleen continued. "I don't know how long it will take, but it will cut into my prep time. You will have to convey some final notes to the caterers as well. Oh, and remember to dress up. It's quite the festive party with some very important people I want to introduce you to, and I don't want you to be mistaken for a waiter like the last time."

Shirleen cut me a look that sent me cowering from the concentrated disapproving energies of generations of elders past, present, and future. It was bad enough that I showed up once in busted sneakers and faded jeans at a major event, but twice was a bad look since I was a professional circling my 35th birthday.

"I have something nice to wear," I protested weakly.

"Then that's one less thing to worry about."

The phone snapped off and I grudgingly got to my feet.

First, I'd needed to clean these pans and bowls before I started the pecan cake.

I also needed to check what else I might be expected to do for this party. There had been a number of emails going around, and I'd ignored most of them, but I knew I was handling the prep work and some smaller details. There was probably more (there always was). Shirleen, as the star of the show, would be extraordinarily busy, but I hadn't expected her to ask me to get there even earlier.

With a new cake in the oven and my kitchen cleaned enough to make me happy, I headed up to my bedroom. I pulled out options for the night, as I basically had to start over. I didn't have much in the way of formal attire and the blazer that had seen me through many tech networking events was oddly both too casual and too stiffly formal for the party. I was considering the cowl-necked green sweater dress my sister got me last year when my phone vibrated once more.

I tapped my headphones to answer and didn't realize it wasn't Shirleen until too late. Before I could hang up, I heard the squeak of metal and the sharpening of a knife against a cutting stone.

"Hello?" I asked.

Sound vibrated along the phone, and the call clicked off.

I glanced at my phone. What was that about? A wrong number? A skittish telemarketer who didn't expect me to answer?

Just as I was looking at the unknown number, several text messages bubbled up:

YOU BETTER WATCH OUT
YOU BETTER NOT CRY
I'M TELLING YOU
SHE MUST DIE
YOU KNOW SHE'S BEEN BAD
SO DO GOOD FOR GOODNESS SAKE
IF YOUR BOSS DOESN'T CHANGE HER WAYS
SHE'LL BE DEAD BEFORE THE EVENING IS OVER

Shirleen Foster's Twelve Christmas Cakes

1. Cinnamon Roll Cheesecake
2. Red and Green Velvet Cake
3. Pistachio Apple Cake
4. Cinnamon Spice Apple Cake
5. Orange Chocolate Cake
6. Caramel Pecan Delight
7. Festive Black Tea Cake
8. Peppermint Cheesecake Marble
9. Brown Butter Pounder
10. White Chocolate Pomegranate Layer Cake
11. Gingerbread Layer Cake
12. Christmas Eve Black Cake

Chapter 2

I stared at the message ready to dismiss it as a joke, but the more I stared, the more a chill fell over me.

Shirleen was beloved by the public and well known for her cookbooks, her recipe column, and her short gig as a radio host. She still had a PO Box people could send letters to, and mainly had hired Naomi to help her with the fan mail she still regularly got. Given how easy it was to contact her, a prank call wasn't a surprise.

In fact, spam and scam calls were perfectly regular too, but they were never specific as this.

Or mentioned death for that matter.

This was an actual death threat and it was directed at Shirleen. It even mentioned tonight… the party!

What if this threat was related to it?

I screenshotted the text, and quickly looked up information for someone to call. The police non-emergency line didn't seem like the best option. Something about it didn't seem urgent or timely. But… Shirleen wasn't in immediate danger as far as I knew (and hoped). This would have to do.

The first time the phone rang and rang until I got bounced to an overstuffed mailbox. I stopped pacing the second time it happened as my panic was overtaken by annoyance, but on the third time I finally got someone on the line.

"Yes, what is it?" snapped a rather brusque male voice.

Startled that I actually got a human on the line, I stammered, "I like to report–"

"If it's an emergency," interrupted the voice, "call 911. If not, call in the morning."

"This is important!" I cried.

He sighed. "Is someone bleeding, injured or in immediate danger?"

"No," I admitted, then sensing he was ready to hang up I added quickly, "I got a death threat. Not me personally. It was a text to my phone, about my boss."

"Have you checked on your boss to make sure he or she is not in danger?"

"No, but–"

"For unidentified threats, call back in the morning when the office is open so you can file a report. If the threats become life threatening, please call 911 instead and dispatch will handle it from there. Thank you."

With that perfunctory note, he clicked off the line.

I stared at my phone, not sure if I wanted to throw it or call back in fury.

Both were equally tempting. Before I could make up my mind how petty I was feeling, an alarm flashed on the screen.

The cake was done.

It was probably a joke, I tried consoling myself again as I returned to my kitchen. A terribly bad joke, and nothing to worry about.

It was a short text that had very little detail, and no specifics for me to do anything more than worry. The number was obviously a spoof and could have been spam.

I mean, the call and the text had gone to *me*. Not Shirleen's phone. I'd been getting a lot of spam lately since

I'd been introduced as Shirleen's recipe developer. Most of it came through my blog. But my work number was widely available.

Finding I was having a hard time reassuring myself even in my own mind, I turned on the podcast I was in the middle of, and let my anxiety about the death threat be dampened by the recounting of a cold case that began with boots containing chopped-off feet washing up on the Michigan shore.

Riveted and revitalized by the detailing of how Edwardian-era forensics found a man's body three miles south of the lake, I got the cake out and prepped the finishing glaze. I changed out my batter-splattered clothes for a new outfit to wear in the kitchen at Tully Manor, and packed both a fresh apron and the sweater dress I would find time to change into when the party was at full swing.

With my cake decorated and in a clear carrier, I took the light rail to the manor. There were only a few people aboard and I was able to find an empty seat easily enough. I broodily stared out the window, watching as the aging brick homes shifted to modern condos and apartment complexes to the business district of downtown Hunton Bay, until we finally chugged along into the historic section.

Dropped off at the edge of cobblestone streets, I only had to cross a couple of them to arrive at Tully Manor. Built in the 1890s with robber baron money, it was functionally a museum when it wasn't the premiere venue in the city due to its ballroom. A visit to Tully Manor made me feel like a time traveler for, beyond a few modern renovations, it was little changed since its earliest days. Dressed up for the party and all its festive flair, every window facing the street had a candle, and garlands wrapped the house from the roof to its foundation. All it needed was some snow for the full postcard friendly vintage Christmas feel, but the pine and cinnamon that tickled my nose as I swept inside was more than enough.

I hadn't seen the ballroom yet, despite my visits earlier this week, but I got a glimpse of what it was becoming from the large vases left in the hallway filled with poinsettias and candles that – upon testing by me expelling a breath – were revealed to be LEDs instead of actual candles.

"We're not open to – oh it's you, Keisha!" From around the corner strode Austin. Already dressed for the party, he wore a red suit with a sparkling red tie and a lapel pin of Christmas trees glinted on his jacket. His hair, although graying, was still full and curly when it wasn't slick and shiny with gel. A white man with tan skin from an ardent love of the outdoors, from first glance it was hard to pin down how old he was, but his jokes and references to certain movies and music placed him in his mid-fifties with plenty of experience to back it up. Austin was Shirleen's fearless publicist and event planner, and had overseen everything that would occur tonight. He had been fretting for weeks because the guest list was a who's who list of major food media stars, donors, entrepreneurs, magazine editors, respected chefs, along with old school and new school influencers.

"You're here earlier than expected, did Shirleen send you?" Austin swung around with his phone, as if the older chef was hiding behind me. "It's too late to change anything. The caterer is at work and the last of the decorations are being set up as we speak."

"No, no, she's been very happy with things." I held up the carrier. "Shirleen just wanted me to set up the cakes."

Austin's eyes darted along my cake and his eyes narrowed slightly.

He had been full of smiles throughout the last-minute meeting Shirleen called to change a good portion of the party, but his one bone of contention was her insistence on making the cakes outside of the catering kitchen. He had all but begged the chef to make the cakes on site, in the interest of health and safety.

Shirleen had refused.

I squirmed at the disapproval in Austin's eyes, even though I was just a cog in the great wheel that was Shirleen Foster.

"The cakes are in the pastry kitchen," Austin said. "We've been collecting them as her nephew brings them here, with instructions to leave them alone until we get her express approval. I assume you have it?"

I barely nodded before he turned away to answer his phone. "Take care of it, why don't you?" he called.

I wasn't sure if he meant me or not, but I didn't linger to find out.

I took the chance to scamper away, working my way through the ornate hall until I pushed my hip against the door into a utilitarian but modern kitchen.

Arriving to the sweet tune of sizzling pans and clicking knives, I took a steadying breath as the last of my worries melted away.

To outsiders, the kitchen was chaotic, but in my view a busy kitchen was a sanctuary. Here, all the major pieces at play finally came together as everyone and everything had a role to take on. One of the assistants was tossing a chickpea salad, while another was furiously making a cranberry basil punch. In the staging area, crostini were being carefully prepared with smears of cream cheese and salmon layered like a cake. Each recipe, of course, came from *Season by*

Season, with modifications for the sensibilities of the event. While Shirleen had provided guidance, I was given credit for two of the appetizers as a nod to my role with the new cookbook.

I didn't know how this evening would go, but the food would be excellent.

One of the catering staff left his station to head toward the freezer, and as I stepped aside, I spotted a man holding a podcasting microphone chattering into the ear of a cook as she chopped up vegetables. I could only see him from behind, but the microphone and the backpack with patches from different destinations around the world were more than enough to tell me who he was, even before he turned around.

What was *he* doing here?

I took a hasty step back, and nearly got skewered through the shoulder by a butcher's knife.

"Watch it!" bristled the chef, who shuffled left, and the knife nearly sliced my nose off. The shout was hardly the loudest thing in the room, but it caused Virgil to spin around, his muted interest turning into delight at the sight of me.

"Just the person I was looking for," Virgil Sullivan called. "Keisha, can I have a few words?"

"I have cakes to prepare," I said, leery of the red blinking light on the microphone, despite the eager smile splitting his face.

When I first met Shirleen's nephew back in June, I didn't expect he would be so close to my age, and I had mistaken him for her intriguing and overly friendly yard guy. Sitting on Shirleen's back porch scrubbing an old pot she wanted me to clean, I pleasantly chatted away as he trimmed the hedges, the company and conversation making the worst of the tedious task fade away. While he warned me when my grumbling turned into complaining when Shirleen was near the window, he didn't say who he was until Shirleen mentioned it. Granted, few would see the relation at first. They shared no similar features, and Virgil with long dreadlocks, an irreverent air, and honey brown skin presented a stark contrast when he stood next to his aunt. At times I couldn't tell if Shirleen even *liked* him, for she was constantly complaining about what he was doing or not doing.

Virgil ran his own moving company, a small outfit where he often worked alongside his employees. Since I started working for Shirleen during his busy season, I didn't see him too often, but each time I did I got the impression of dimples and the smile of someone prone to laughing at his own jokes.

He had taken to fluttering around his aunt's house more often these days, due to the new cookbook. Apparently, he was doing a podcast about the updates. I bet he had pitched the idea himself, clearly aiming to keep riding his aunt's coattails. I knew Virgil was the only relative Shirleen saw regularly, and the knowledge he'd one day inherit a food media empire didn't mean he wasn't trying to grease the pig before it was ready. He was a nuisance and a distraction as he went around thrusting microphones into people's faces – or worse recording without permission.

That he hadn't got kicked out of the kitchen was the measure of his aunt's influence, his affable charm, and an ability to talk his way out of most situations.

"I can help with the cakes," Virgil insisted, and then uttered the words that set my teeth on edge. "It'll make great content for the podcast!"

Because I didn't dare say what I was truly thinking, I walked away. Virgil followed me into the pastry kitchen, making commentary like this was some overwrought documentary, until he stopped short.

"Where are all the cakes?" he asked, looking around at the shiny and bare metal counters. "Aunt Shirls was working on them for days."

"They're in the walk-in," I said. "Most need to be kept chilled until we serve them, although a few can be taken out now to get to room temp." Seeing as I wasn't going to get rid of him, and might as well make use of the extra muscle, I asked, "Will you help me?"

I had hoped by doing this he'd put the microphone down, but instead he rammed it into his backpack.

Eleven cake carriers were on the shelves, and the chill of the walk-in had frosted over the covers, making the cakes look like oversized snow globes. Shirleen had helpfully left in her elegant handwriting labels for each cake, so I directed Virgil to grab #7 and #10 while I put down the carrier I brought and went to pull on an apron.

I opened the carriers and, while the cakes were warming up, I collected and arranged bowls of nuts, caramel sauce, and whipped cream for the added toppings. As I drizzled caramel over the pumpkin spice loaf, Virgil rearranged the cakes for me, matching toppings to the right cakes as he followed his aunt's instructions. While he didn't stay quiet, I found him easy enough to ignore as I got to work.

Mostly, that is.

"Aunt Shirls never expected to be famous for the cakes. She just used to make them for all the parties that happened out in Red Oaks. I guess it was good PR when people started singing their praises, because it helped make them a tradition for many people. She made me the Cinnamon Roll Cheesecake each year and it's not Christmas without it."

I was about to agree and say my family was similar, when I saw the microphone he held close to his mouth.

I couldn't stop myself from scowling, and when he caught sight of me Virgil fumbled with the device, nearly dropping it onto one of the cakes.

"It's off," he said quickly shoving it into his jacket. "I know you don't like it."

"I didn't even realize you noticed," I grumbled, avoiding the genuinely contrite expression on his face. "You wave it around all the time."

"It's all for the podcast… for the new book… and you're part of it. It's in the contract." He had the grace to sound embarrassed as he said the last bit.

I didn't trust he was sympathetic to my feelings. Someone had said something to him, most likely, and he was worried about the content for his silly podcast.

"I know what my contract says," I said, gripping the spoon. "I just didn't realize you'd be recording everything,"

Virgil gulped. "I told you I'll cut the argument you had with your father–"

"We need to get these cakes ready," I interrupted. "I hate to ask the staff to move them."

"There's a cart somewhere, I saw it earlier," Virgil added, eager to please. "Follow me."

Although there was a number of things I'd rather do instead (including plunging my hand into a bubbling pot of oil) I followed him anyway, leaving the bustle of the kitchen behind for the quiet and shadowy corners of the manor.

A few turns through the corridors led us to the cart, just as he said, but I couldn't put any of the cakes on it.

"It's a utility cart." I had to force myself to keep my tone flat and even, although I was ready to rip something apart. I'm not sure why I expected him to actually be helpful. He had never been before, why should that change? "Look at those paint stains. I wouldn't put *anything* on it, especially cakes."

Virgil scratched the back of his head as he looked at it sideways. "I swear it was–"

A door slammed along the hall, overshadowing his words. "The guests will be arriving soon, so get that out of sight!"

They could have been event staff talking about anything, but there was an edge to the words that made me think otherwise.

The voice was too angry, too bitter... too ready to do mischief.

I walked down to the corner and stood as close to the edge as I dared. Virgil moved right next to me. By silent agreement we both stood there, straining our ears to listen.

Despite my best efforts I couldn't hear what the second person was saying, but the first speaker's voice was loud and clear.

"Don't worry, we won't start until Shirleen is here. Trust me, she'll get more than what she bargained for!"

Reminded of the strange message I received earlier, I gasped and nudged Virgil.

"Turn the microphone back on!" I hissed.

He grabbed it, but by the time the microphone switched on, a pair of footsteps retreated down the hall and the corridor's lights flickered out.

In the near darkness I stared at Virgil, the blinking red light illuminating his equally startled face as he asked, "What was that about?"

Chapter 3

I didn't have an answer for Virgil, at least not one I was willing to voice. Not when I felt like I had slipped and was falling in an endless tunnel with no bottom.

I might go to sleep with the dulcet tones of true crime host Gabriel Hugo in my ears, as he waxed poetic about brutal murders and crimes, but the last thing I wanted was to be in such a story.

At least unwillingly.

"I don't know," I answered him with a shrug. "Maybe it's just someone putting together a surprise for the evening."

"Nothing about that," Virgil cried as he waved his arms about, "sounded like a good surprise!"

"It's nothing," I said, grateful for the darkness to hide my expression. I shoved my hand into my pocket for the tiny flashlight I kept with my house keys. I flipped it on and turned my back on Virgil as I went looking for the cart.

"You told me to turn on the microphone!" he called as I danced the light over the boxes. "Aren't you worried?"

Keeping a breezy tone I replied, "I only thought we should record if they said something terrible, but they said nothing else interesting."

"Everything is interesting! Number one rule of podcasting: you never know if what you capture will be useful. So never stop recording!"

My tiny light drifted over hairline cracks in the wall. "I thought the number one rule was to always be recording, no matter if anyone consents or not?"

"Key," Virgil began.

I swung around and flashed the light right into his face at maximum brightness. "Don't call me that! We're not friends. I just work for your aunt, and I'm not obligated to be a subject of the podcast!"

"Geez," he hissed as he lurched backward, "how many times do I have to explain or apologize?"

"Until you actually mean it," I replied. As I spoke that was, of course, when I spotted the pastry cart. It was right behind him half hidden under a cloth. "Do me a favor though. Keep an eye on your aunt. She was upset that Glenn got an invitation for tonight."

I could feel the air around Virgil chill at the mention of that name.

"He was invited?" Virgil snarled. "How did he get one after everything he put Aunt Shirls through?"

"It was an accident, I heard. I don't know if he'll appear or not. But Shirleen seemed worried he would. Could you kick him out if he showed up?"

"I'll do it myself if I have to," he grumbled, hardly answering my question and leaving me more than a touch worried. I knew he didn't like his uncle, but I clearly had underestimated how much. "I can't believe this, of all nights!"

Virgil dashed off in the darkness, his sneakers squeaking across the floor as he hurried off. Before he left, he flipped the switch and light poured once more in the hall.

As I guided the cart back to the cake room, I kept my ears open for any more of the brash and rude voices, but heard nothing other than the catering staff getting ready.

I was taking pictures with my camera when the doors swung open and Fatima, the caterer for the night, entered with her green-haired assistant. While the younger woman waved at me cheerfully as she adjusted a diabetic pump at her side, Fatima sighed in relief as the furrow between her brows lessened.

"There you are," Fatima said. "No one could give me a straight answer about where you went."

"I had to get a cart," I said.

"A cart?" the assistant echoed as she stared at me. "You couldn't find one? But I brought them all here!" Her pale skin became even whiter as she twisted her head towards the kitchen. "Have they all gone missing?"

"I doubt that's what happened," Fatima said gently to the young woman.

Like froth on a peppermint latte, Fatima rose above small and petty dramas. Effortlessly cool, she had creamy brown skin and curly hair that could barely be contained by the strongest hair ties. Known for riding her motorcycle cross-country to support research for childhood cancers, she had been a pharmaceutical researcher who switched careers to open her own café and recently began a catering business on the side. While Shirleen's publisher was paying her the big bucks for the party, the prospect of getting her food onto the plates of some rather influential movers and shakers didn't hurt either.

If it wasn't for Fatima, I might not have been allowed to make the cake at all, despite Shirleen being in my corner. However, a month ago I made the Brown Butter Pounder for her, and Fatima carefully tasted the slice of cake, declaring it to be better than what her pastry chef could whip up and that I could handle the cakes for the evening.

"All the cakes are ready," I continued. "I got started earlier because Shirleen was anxious."

"For good reason," Fatima huffed. "I just got word we'll have to hold for an extra half-hour. We got major traffic delays because of the Reindeer Run plus the Hanukkah celebration in Port Walker, atop of the usual tunnel traffic."

"People need to schedule better," the assistant mumbled. "I never understood why they have a 5K on a Friday evening!"

"It got pushed because of other holiday events," I said. "Who's important that's coming late?"

"Everyone, it seems," Fatima said, "so wait for me to give word about what cakes to take out. Shirleen said something about most of them being for display."

I nodded. "They're all edible, but half are headed to a few soup kitchens and the YWCA."

"Good," Fatima said. "Make a note of which ones."

"What's your number?" the green-haired girl asked, whipping out her phone. "It's easier to keep you updated by text. Although I don't think you've gotten anything from us."

I got out my phone, and found out why. I had left it on airplane mode again, as I didn't want the Edwardian Christmas Murder podcast I was listening to interrupted by messages from the group chat with my friends, spoiling tonight's *Grinch or Not?*

I turned airplane mode off and my phone angrily rattled. So many messages poured in, I was afraid it might fly out my hand.

Fatima chuckled, only to stop when a hiss of oil caught her attention and she darted across the kitchen.

In contrast, the assistant stared at me in horror. "You had your phone off like that! What happens if someone needs to contact you?"

I could only shrug. "If it's really that important, they'll track me down. What number is Fatima's?"

Given the number, I made note of it. Before I could ask the green-haired girl more about the carts, another catering emergency got her attention and she hurried off, leaving me at my station.

As I had my phone still in hand, I skimmed my messages in case buried in them was something urgent. There were a dozen messages about backups that had put the HRBT tunnel traffic to a standstill yet again, although it was looking to be a bad night all around, as even the other tunnel, the MMBT, had major delays.

It was as I was exiting my messages that I spotted the email from Maxine Roberts of *Hunton Bay Journal,* wanting the scoop about a possible reunion between Shirleen and her ex-husband.

How did the press get the news already?

I grimaced, suspecting that if Naomi had gotten fired just like Shirleen had vowed, that might be one source.

I deleted the message, although Maxine would likely try again, especially if Shirleen confronted Glenn in front of dozens of eyes and cameras tonight.

As reporters went, I liked Maxine, and was willing to play nice for the upcoming cookbook, but I didn't like it when people tried to extract personal details they shouldn't know about. Maxine knew I got hired after all this went down, so why come to me at all? Did she really think I knew something, or was she after something else?

I went through the last of the messages and notifications, pausing at the unknown phone call that I had gotten that afternoon.

Unknown number, unknown location, and not long enough to track, even if I had the ability to do so.

Maybe I didn't have to?

My finger hovered over the unfamiliar digits, and before I lost my nerve, I tapped the screen. I watched my phone, listening to the soft rings as it sought the unknown caller. I was about to hang up thinking this number was a dead end when there was a click. I hastily put the phone to my ear, but I heard heavy breathing and then a burst of noise that could be music or a voice. Just as I heard the sound, the phone clicked off before I registered what it was or wasn't.

The door swung open and a hush went over the kitchen like a foreboding storm.

"Why did you all stop? There is a party to get ready for!"

I hastily shoved my phone away as the tall and slender form of Shirleen Foster swept into the room.

In deference to the party, she had dressed up for the evening, trading her usual uniform of khakis and boat shirts for a smart looking pantsuit. Festive green, its lapels had glitter elements that managed to dress up her black sneakers. Her themed brooch for the evening was a candy cane, and her braids were swept into a high bun that needed no adornment. I don't know where she found glasses with peppermint-striped frames, but I was envious of the spunky air it lent her. She was deep into her seventies, but Shirleen still moved fluidly in an exacting stride across the room.

"Keisha," Shirleen said as she approached. "I knew I could trust you with the set up. This looks lovely. What about the cakes we're holding back?"

"Ready to travel to the charities after the party is over."

"Wonderful," she said tersely. "Could you take them yourself? Of course I'll pay for your taxi." Shirleen gave me such a bright smile, it stretched across her face until I could see the cracks. "Come with me." Shirleen grabbed my arm with a surprisingly strong grip. "The party hasn't started yet, but I wanted you to meet someone before things get too busy."

A list of VIPs and their food preferences flashed in my mind. While there were many important and interesting people I'd have loved to meet, Adrienne Blake was the first. A consultant and a recipe developer at Kitchen Atelier, the only thing that I enjoyed more than her short-form videos sniffing out the latest food mystery was the fact her company had recently moved right here to downtown Hunton Bay, a short bicycle ride away. All of which made the chance of me working there more than a pipe dream.

"Sure," I readily agreed. Even if it wasn't Adrienne that Shirleen wanted to introduce me to, there was still a chance we might cross paths. I'd been trying for months to meet her as I attended other events with Shirleen. Perhaps lucky stars would shine on me tonight.

Letting Shirleen pull me along, we left behind the soothing busyness of the kitchen for the brewing chaos of the ballroom.

Walking through the door, I passed by the looming evergreen trees that sparkled in all their multicolored fancy. The furthest corners had touches of fake snow with miniature reindeer and snowmen.

Tables were decorated with red tablecloths with golden foil plates and silverware. Each of the centerpieces were made of frosted glass to resemble ice sculptures. While they were not all Christmas related, the winter theme was prevalent with miniature snowflakes, frolicking reindeer, groups of snow people, and even an ice skater. In a far corner, copies of all Shirleen's cookbooks were set out on a table. This, strangely enough, was the one thing out of place in my eyes, as it seemed like a museum exhibit.

Event staff swirled around the space holding trays of appetizers and cider in slender flutes. While the caterers were in discreet black, the event staff wore bright red vests and pants, paired with crisp white shirts and black bow ties. One moved to offer us a drink, but Shirleen walked right past the woman, as if she didn't even see her.

As Shirleen took me between the tables, we passed guests nibbling on appetizers and swirling cider in flutes. I spotted a few people I knew by the virtue of being in Shirleen's orbit: Javier Navarro, who owned three very popular restaurants. Carmen Hollingshead, a retired chef. William Billups, who started a licorice empire in his basement. Loren Gaffney, a celebrated food historian with a popular blog that hosted snippets of mostly forgotten cookbooks from around the world. Even DJ Oscar Fantom was there, whose soothing voice made rush hour in Hunton Bay somewhat bearable. Any one of them I'd have loved to have a few minutes with to just say hello, but Shirleen walked past them all.

Framed by the ballroom's windows was Austin, who was as tense as if he was stuck in bridge traffic alongside the esteemed guests for the evening. Then I saw his companion, and thought maybe he had a good reason for such panic.

If there was one name everyone knew these days it was Winifred Chan, a long-time food editor and critic who was recently named editor-in-chief at *Ladle* magazine. Her influence was legendary and so crucial to so many careers that I was surprised to learn that, like Shirleen, she had never planned to go into food media at all, but found her way to it by chance. While I could go on and on about all the work she had done to uplift various Asian cuisines and celebrate the nuances of Chinese and Chinese-American food, she was best known for her personal essay about the boba tea that made her finally understand her grandfather. Winifred was a dainty woman, in a neatly matching gold and silver cardigan and shirt, with her jet-black hair cut in a trendy bob. Her only acknowledgment of the festive theme were delicate silver earrings that appeared like tinsel at first glance.

"Winifred," Shirleen said. "This is my recipe developer, Keisha Scott. She's helping me update my recipes for the anniversary edition."

Winifred's eyes trailed across me as if I were a prime cut of meat. "That's not a name I know." She turned to Shirleen, her voice light and airy, even as her brown eyes remained quite cool. "Are you sure you want to have her assisting with your book? I know plenty of other recipe developers more than up to the task. You need all the help you can get with the update. Many things have changed over the years."

"I trust Keisha to know it. She was already making smart adjustments, as seen on her blog. I was rather flattered when my nephew told me there was someone doing excellent revamps of my recipes."

"Oh." Winifred's tone took on surprise, and her chilly disinterest melted away. "You're *Waffles, Shirleen's Way*."

Something of a smirk took over her face, and I felt ice start to make its way through my veins. Because after being introduced to so many important people in the food world, I knew that look.

I prepared myself for polite disinterest at best and a cutting rebuke at the worst, before a smile crested along her face.

"Shirleen, why don't you ever lead with the important parts?" Winifred laughed. "I know that blog quite well. It's quite a marvel given the high engagement was on par with site traffic. Not only did you share your experiences with the recipes, you encouraged people to submit their results from any of Shirleen's cookbooks in a monthly post that became quite an event. One of your recipes even went viral, I think?"

"Keisha's bake of Snickerdoodle Banana Parfait," Austin said, jumping in.

I was surprised he didn't drop the stats related to the post too. They were all over the media kit he had shared out, and were my strongest credit as a cook – beyond Shirleen's personal endorsement. I found myself wishing he had mentioned them, as Winifred was now considering me with a great deal more interest and approval.

I was debating how to casually slip in engagement metrics when Shirleen replied.

"The banana parfait brought Keisha to my attention." Shirleen favored me with a smile as warm as her decadent double chocolate muffins. "I saw not just an inventive take on old recipes, but how she made updates that show how differently we cook these days. It's amazing how certain staples grow in and out of favor. We used to be so afraid of salt when I was getting started."

"I never was," Winifred said proudly, "but some folks don't know how to properly season their food or their pans!"

The pair startled me with their bright laughter.

Austin checked his phone and slipped away from our group, whispering into the device without a word more. As he passed me, I watched his face tighten with a flash of anger, but I didn't hear what he said as his words were muffled as he turned away.

"I'm curious, Keisha," Winifred said, drawing me back to her and Shirleen with a small lift of her eyebrow, "why didn't you stay with the blog? With the right backing, you could monetize and get your own cookbook out of it."

"I was just doing it for fun," I admitted. "I didn't even think anyone would see it. Or if I wanted to work in food. I was just rambling about the food I was cooking for myself and my friends."

With an amused chuckle, Winifred remarked. "I think I've heard this before! No wonder you chose to work with her, Shirleen! You did that as well!"

"I'd rather work with someone without official training, like me. These cookbooks are for the home cooks, and while being a culinary whiz kid certainly isn't bad, I didn't have this knowledge when I first wrote *Season by Season*, and this new book is a modern update, not a revision."

"You should have just introduced us ages ago! If you had, I wouldn't have been so cross at you at Whisk and Kettle Fest." Winifred took a bite of the balsamic cranberry crostini, nodding favorably as she took in the flavors. "This is a nice shindig. I can't even get the accountants at *Ladle* to consider dishing out to celebrate the magazine's 90th anniversary."

"I wouldn't say it's a lot." Shirleen twirled the toothpick that had held the bacon-wrapped shrimp. "I'm getting seasonal parties for a book that won't be out until the end of next summer because they want to capitalize on the Christmas cakes."

"You're remembered for that." Winifred swung around to me. "Keisha, before she hired you, how many times did you make any of those cakes?"

"I've made all of them two or three times, though there's one I made every year," I replied. "It's not Christmas if there's isn't a slice of Caramel Pecan Delight washed down with a mug of peppermint hot chocolate."

Winifred snapped her fingers. "See, they're memorable!"

"Peppermint hot chocolate… I suppose that would pair well together," Shirleen said distractedly.

"Hot chocolate goes well with anything," Virgil interjected.

Suddenly appearing out of the crowd, he joined our little group, and he wasn't alone. With him was a woman with a light brown complexion whose features spoke of a vibrant mix of Caribbean and Latin influences. Dressed in dark plum, she didn't appear to have gotten the same message everyone else had about dressing for the festive season. With her hair pulled away from her long, narrow face, her austere look was dispelled only by the heart-shaped locket at her throat and deep purple lipstick. I wouldn't say her whole look aged her drastically, but it was hard to believe she was only fifteen years older than me.

Especially when Lucia Espinosa arranged her features carefully to not sneer at me.

Currently a teacher at the culinary program at Hook College, Lucia had once been Shirleen's student and mentee. We had crossed paths several times since I started working with Shirleen, and from the moment Lucia learned that I didn't even start seriously cooking until a few years ago, I was willing to believe she was eager to make me a featured victim on *Drawn to Murder*. I knew that getting to work with Shirleen Foster was a big deal, especially in the tightly knit food scene in Virginia, but I didn't realize it was *that* big of a deal. Especially to someone like Lucia, who was still nursing wounds from her failed restaurant.

Lucia held out a hand to Winifred, speaking to her without even greeting Shirleen or myself. "I don't think we've met before – I used to work with Shirleen. Big fan of your work. I teach at Hook College, and I know the students would enjoy having you come."

"I would enjoy it too," Winifred said politely, as she quickly shook Lucia's hand. "Oh, Shirleen, look, there's Javier. Should we say hello? I need to ask about his new restaurant."

"Aunt Shirls." Virgil began reaching for his aunt's arm. "I need to talk to you."

Shirleen gently shook him off. "Later, Virgil, I'll be right back. You just keep an eye out for the scum of the earth."

Lucia raised an eyebrow, but she waited until both Shirleen and Winifred were gone before she asked, "I suppose that means Glenn is here?"

Virgil sighed. "He's supposed to be coming. I don't know why!"

"Because he's part of the reason the book got made in the first place," Lucia said simply. "He encouraged her to share her recipes at that newspaper which began her column. The first edition was dedicated to him. Shirleen strongly hinted that part of the reason for this new updated version is simply to get him and his recipes off the page."

Lucia looked at me significantly, as if I should be upset. As if that was ever going to happen. Getting to work on this cookbook was a lifeline I desperately needed when I was drowning at a job I hated. It hadn't mattered to me why she decided to do an update, but maybe I should have asked.

"I suppose any update brings changes," I said.

"For the best," Lucia declared. "It's always better to move forward than talk about the past."

Her words were directed at Virgil who gasped as if jabbed in the ribs. "I only wanted to capture your experiences of learning at my aunt's side. It's all part of the podcast."

"I thought your podcast is about *Season by Season*," Lucia said. "That book came out long before I worked for Shirleen."

"Yes, but it's about the legacy that sprang from it. You're needed to talk about past meeting present, and you're not the only one." Virgil turned to me, waggling his eyebrows once more, playing a clown just to get sympathy.

I held up my hands, refusing to be used as a pawn to convince Lucia to take part in this. I didn't care that Virgil said he'd keep his questions limited to recipes. I knew that wasn't going to be the case.

"I'll think about it," Lucia said, lying through her teeth as she smiled politely. "I'll let you know later how my schedule looks, as it's nearly finals."

"You should take part, Lucia."

The energetic voice that boomed from behind us came from Davis Packer. He held a flute of cider and wore a gray suit with a matching sequin tie. With thinning brown hair and jarringly white and straight teeth, he was the last person I expected to be the former producer of Shirleen's old show, *Shirleen Foster's Kitchen Wisdom*. He was every bit a stereotypical Midwesterner, including having pale skin that needed sun, a deep fondness for all forms of casseroles, and a willingness to drive anywhere instead of flying. Surprisingly though, he could tolerate spice at very high heat levels, and when I cooked for him at one of Shirleen's dinner parties back in September, he called me out for downplaying the heat notes in a very parental tone.

I didn't expect to see him here tonight, but this just showed how many different people Shirleen worked with over the years.

"This podcast," Davis went on, "is a great way to talk about the book. Although it has nothing like the saturation TV used to have. Which is the excuse Shirleen is using this time."

"My aunt said no to a new show?" Virgil asked.

"She's said she's getting too old for such a grind." Davis smoothed out his tie. "But it wouldn't be a weekly format like it was back then. Times have changed. We'd do short format videos instead."

He looked at us, clearly expecting someone to jump in with ideas.

I avoided his gaze though, as I didn't even enjoy viewing those rapid-fire 90-second videos to begin with, and merely *thinking* about making content sent a shudder through me.

After a moment of hesitation, Virgil replied, "Aunt Shirls says she's at the age where she gets to do what she wants. I don't think I can convince her if you haven't been able to. But she does have a few TV spots coming up – if they go well maybe she might think differently."

"Really?" Davis asked eagerly.

"At WVHB," I said, wishing I knew more. With Naomi no longer working for Shirleen, I supposed handling all details like that would fall to me, even though Austin had been golden making all the arrangements otherwise. "It's the first she's done in a while. Shirleen's been excited–"

"How dare you show up!"

Shirleen's voice shattered the conversation in the room, bringing everything to a lull as her voice grew shrill.

Heads swung around to find the celebrated chef shaking in rage as she jabbed a finger, not at her former ex-husband like I had feared, but Ruby Walton.

Ruby, a fellow cookbook writer who worked with Shirleen on *Season by Season*.

Ruby, Shirleen's old friend who rose up in the food world with her.

Ruby, who stole Shirleen's recipes and tried to sue her for it.

Chapter 4

I knew about Ruby Walton long before I even started working for Shirleen, because the crash and burn of their friendship had been the subject of many gossip sessions for my grandmother and her friends. For Granny, this was her OJ Simpson trial, and she was 100% on Shirleen's side. The gossip had made such an impression on my young mind that I was astonished to learn Ruby still had a decent career afterward. Although I learned, as I grew older, time can soften just about anything, even the reputations of the most vicious people. In Ruby's case, it certainly helped that Shirleen's messy divorce and retreat from the spotlight in her later years allowed Ruby Walton to ascend higher than she might have otherwise.

New Orleans born and bred, Ruby didn't let a few minutes pass without reminding folk she worked for Leah Chase (although there were rumors that Leah hardly liked her). Her collaborations with Shirleen established Ruby as a consultant and recipe developer, and she would go on to contribute recipes to several Creole cookbooks, but she truly made more of a name for herself as a judge at various cooking and baking competitions. As a featured judge on *Whisk it All,* her facial expressions while tasting some of the more inventive concoctions the chefs whipped up were often the most widely shared images of the show. Gently plump and known for her signature red shoes and russet red wig, she was TV's tart and sweetly vulgar granny.

Ruby and Shirleen hadn't been seen in public together since the funeral of their editor Birdie Bailey nine years ago. Given the comments in the paper at the time, no one expected them to meet in person like this for another nine years or more.

This was going to be the big news of the night – especially if they continued to argue.

Even more so if there were photos, or audio clips, or, worst of all, video.

If anything unflattering leaked no one would even be thinking about the new cookbook.

Virgil swore under his breath, and without apology he vanished into the crowd.

I made to follow, but while the crowd had parted with ease for his broader form as he barreled through, they jostled in my path like branches in a forest blocking my way forward.

Voices rose to a fever pitch as Shirleen and Ruby continued to argue. The crowd tightened and closed ranks as they gawked, making it harder for me to get a glance.

Craning my head to see, I could only get a glimpse of Ruby Walton and her red wig. I couldn't even hear an odd word from them, as the crowd added their colorful commentary to the hubbub.

"...I thought Ruby might show up tonight!"

"I bet it's been years since they talked, ever since she stole the recipes..."

"Does it really matter who did?"

"Why would Ruby Walton show up? I thought *Whisk it All* was still filming?"

The crowd tittered and chattered and wouldn't budge, and I was forced to move around hoping that Virgil would be able to stop things from getting worse, or at least make sure it wasn't captured on the phones that were popping up.

Where was Austin?

Wasn't it his job to keep Shirleen looking good no matter what?

I craned my head around trying to look for him, but in my haste, I bumped into a woman who was busy dumping wrapped chocolates into an oversized purse with *Starry Night* splashed across it. I looked at her and she looked back at me, and she tipped the rest inside without averting her gaze and kept it moving.

I walked right on past, about to get around a knot of people, when I saw a sight that could only make tonight worse, if that was possible.

Glenn Dupont, Shirleen's terrible and no good former husband.

Of all the people not stuck in bridge traffic *he* managed to get here!

Glenn saw me before I got close. He didn't move or make a scene, but waited for me to approach.

A red cardigan and a bushy stark white beard made him look like Santa, if Santa had ever worked in a used furniture store for a commission and jumped on any hapless person who came their way. He wore tinted green glasses and an earring glittered in one ear. When he smiled, I could see why a younger Shirleen had been interested in him, and why she had finally cut ties.

"Did Shirleen send you to shoo me off like a wasp on a fine summer day?" Glenn asked.

"No, but she has quite a few things on her mind," I said firmly. "Try not to add to them."

"I recognize you from the pictures of her in the press. You're the one helping her with the new cookbook. Have you taken up the bulldog role since she just fired the other one?"

"The other one? You mean Naomi?"

"I guess that's her name," Glenn said. "I gave up learning her assistants' names since Shirley goes through them like Kleenex. I'm surprised the girl lasted this long."

I held my tongue, as I saw that tee up a mile away.

He flashed a smile at me. "I'm not here to speak bad about Shirleen."

"Then why come to a place you're not welcome?" I countered.

"To celebrate." He gestured to the poster of the original *Season by Season* cover placed so prominently in the ballroom. "Shirleen started writing on a typewriter at our kitchen table. Everything she wrote about, I ate first, and my opinions guided her recipes. I'm in every word and every sentence of the cookbook. Even one of the Christmas cakes is a recipe of mine."

"Your mother's recipe," I said, thinking of the six cakes that were not to be served, and how the White Chocolate Pomegranate Layer Cake was the first earmarked for charity. "Or so you claim."

"I didn't come here to start anything," Glenn protested.

"You weren't meant to be invited," I said.

"I'm not the only one," Glenn said, "but don't worry, I won't cause trouble. The embers of the year is a time for making merry... and setting things right with those we've wronged."

His gaze moved away from me, darting across the room towards Shirleen and Ruby. As far as I could tell, they were no longer at each other's throats, but several people were still watching them as if they were the most interesting things around. When Glenn spoke again the faux jovialness in his voice was gone, and his tone was low and soft, speaking more to himself than me. "When you get as old as I am, there's very little time to set things right."

As if knowing she was being spoken about, Shirleen turned in our direction, and her gaze sharpened. Glenn melted into the crowd, passing by the lady whose *Starry Night* bag must have been full with all the food she could manage to pilfer.

If Shirleen had seen her ex-husband she didn't show it. She imperiously waved me over.

Standing near a glistening Christmas tree, Virgil had strategically placed himself so no one could get a decent picture of Shirleen and Ruby without him somewhat rammed in the middle.

The tension between the older ladies needed a serrated knife to divide them. I was ready to flee at my first whiff, and nearly applauded Virgil for stubbornly remaining nearby. Although a glance at his resigned features suggested that this wasn't his first choice.

"Ruby, this is Keisha Scott," Shirleen said. "I suppose I don't need to tell you about Ruby Walton, do I?"

"I'm well familiar. Nice to meet you." I held out my hand, but Ruby looked at it as if I had a glob of cake batter on it before I hastily withdrew. "My grandmother had the tie-in cookbook you did for *Whisk It All*. She adored your buttermilk chicken, said it made a great base for the tweaks she made."

Ruby's lips curled up slightly. "If she did that, then she truly didn't make it."

"Well, not as written," I stammered. "But aren't recipes meant to guide?"

"No," Ruby snapped.

"Ruby will be staying for the rest of the evening," Shirleen said to me, ignoring her one-time friend. "Could you bring a slice of the Festive Black Tea Cake? It's her favorite."

"I'm surprised you remember," Ruby huffed, but the harsh lines of her face had softened.

Shirleen, however, remained quite cool. "I remember everyone's favorite foods."

Virgil cleared his throat. "Aunt Shirls," he said firmly, "I really do need to speak with you, and it cannot wait."

"I suppose it cannot," Shirleen agreed. "Keisha, I leave Ruby in your capable hands."

Shirleen and Virgil withdrew, and I could only imagine what Virgil had to say as he vigorously gestured in a hushed tone. Would it just be about Glenn, or would he mention the voices we heard too? Or maybe even something else?

Ruby stepped away from me and I hastened to follow before I lost track of her.

While I kept my gaze averted to avoid the whispers, Ruby held her head high, and walked right to the side table where what was left of the appetizers remained. She picked up a glass and took a sip of sparkling cider as she studied the food. From this angle, I could see a small purse pressed against her side, as if she rode a packed train and couldn't risk letting it be jostled. Red, to match her shoes, the purse bulged slightly with a spiral notebook that barely fit.

I couldn't help but think it was a favorite purse of hers. Why else shove a notebook in it? Unless the notebook itself held something she didn't want to leave behind.

"You don't have to keep eyes on me," Ruby declared, abruptly. "I'm not a spoiled child about to cause a scene."

I said nothing, and Ruby picked up a plate and a napkin as she continued. "I'm also not here to see Shirleen. I have settled everything I needed with her long ago. You needn't worry about me bringing trouble"

"You don't need to explain to me!" I nearly squeaked.

"Oh, but I must. You're going to report this to her, good little worker bee that you are. Which number assistant are you? Are you aware that she changes assistants as often as walking shoes?"

"I'm not her assistant," I protested. "I'm working with her as a recipe developer."

Ruby's brittle chuckle cut through the air around us. The ambient chatter fell away and my ears burned as the only thing I could hear was her voice and the faint mockery that followed each word. "That was what *I* was. I was her tester and her co-writer. I listened, I tasted, and I shaped the recipes that gave Shirleen trouble. My suggestions created dishes that made her famous. How did she repay me? By claiming I stole her recipes and making such a fuss, we ended up in court! If you aren't careful, she will do the same to you."

"I'm here to help update the recipes."

Ruby tsked and gazed upon me with pity that ground against my pride. "Then it's worse than I thought. You're already pushed into the shadows."

"It's our book. We're working together."

"For now." Ruby gestured at my clothes, which, while they weren't chef whites, certainly emulated them. "I nearly took you for staff, and the way Shirleen just summoned you over… You may not be her assistant, but that's how she views you. You're not unique, she does that to everyone. She will do it to you. So don't trust anything she tells you."

It was almost with relief that the crackle of a microphone filled the air. Oscar Fantom kicked off the festivities with a purposely out of tune rendition of Twelve Days of Christmas, replacing the iconic gifts with Shirleen's cakes.

The crowd laughed, but I couldn't even enjoy the puns as I stared at Ruby.

TV's favorite granny was mean and bitter. Maybe she was right to be, given all that had occurred with Shirleen, but there was no reason for her to tell me all of this, even under the guise of a warning.

"Why should I trust you?" I asked. "We just met."

"True, but I know you. You are me."

"I didn't study cooking under Leah Chase," I said.

"No, but you have your whole career before you. Don't settle for the scraps Shirleen gives you. I had to reinvent myself several times over just to gain some success."

First Glenn, and now Ruby. What was it about me that made near strangers so eager to say such things to me? Shirleen was a grouch, a grinch, and I even witnessed her unironically declare "humbug" just last week, but I was starting to see she had her reasons. There might many guests here tonight, but very few ranked as her friends.

Instead of responding to this advice Ruby shoved at me I muttered, eager to end this encounter. "I'll get your cake."

Escaping into the kitchen, I found Fatima had already got her staff ready with the final preparations. All twelve cakes were already on festive little trays, with pear trees, swans, gold rings, and more decorating each cart. The cart I found matched the three others that were already there, and I wondered yet again why it was elsewhere, and why no one told me where those carts were in the first place.

"Any last-minute requests from Shirleen?" Fatima asked as she dabbed her face with a towel.

"No, I just need to get a slice of the tea cake cut for a special guest," I said.

"I'll take care of it." Shirleen bustled through the cake room door, her face set in stubborn lines.

"You said you wanted me–"

"Forget what I said," Shirleen snapped. She strode straight to the cakes and placed the tea cake onto the counter with a thump.

"Keisha, go and get changed. You did bring a spare set of clothes, didn't you?"

"I did, but if you need me for anything else…"

Shirleen waved me off. "Fatima is here to help. I can manage this part." She took out a knife as she spoke. It was sharp enough that it glinted in the light, and she held it not like she was about the slice the tea cake, but as if she was going to stab it in its center. She adjusted her grip, but the stern resolve on her features remained, as a warning.

My protests and even my questions withered away.

What had happened in the brief moments I had stepped away? Was this from Virgil's conversation with her? Was it possible he made things worse?

I tried one more time to ask, but Shirleen had begun cutting and you never interrupted someone with a knife.

Asking Fatima's green-haired employee for the changing room, I was directed down the hall. I pulled on my sweater dress with great haste, fearing a disaster developing in my absence.

I stepped out of the changing room to find Virgil waiting for me with a fretful expression and none of his usual good humor.

"What else has gone wrong?" I cried.

Virgil blinked and then rushed to assure me. "Nothing that hasn't already. Which is why we should talk."

"There's no–"

"There is time," he interjected. "All the planned jokes and speeches are happening now. Aunt Shirls will do her thing with cutting the cakes right after, which means you can stay right here and tell me why you weren't bothered at hearing threats related to my aunt, and even tried to shove them aside."

"You're still upset about that?" I attempted to laugh him off. "You're seeing shadows where there's nothing to fear."

I made to step around him, but Virgil quickly shifted right, blocking me. I stepped back, and he slid over, with a challenge in his eyes and growing frustration. "You're saying it's nothing, but your face is telling me something else. You are worried, and I'm supposed to be a buffer for something more than old ladies ready to throw hands."

Virgil was doing what he usually did – making jokes and quips. But the stubborn set of his chin told me a different story. I wasn't going to get rid of him no matter what I said.

I thought over my options before I asked, "Have you gotten any strange messages about your aunt lately?"

Virgil considered me with a slight tilt of his head. "Be more specific. You won't believe the weird stuff I get in my inbox these days."

"Not weird," I said, "but a death threat."

It was the first time I had admitted it aloud, and the word felt too clumsy and loud. Silly even, because who goes around talking about death threats if you weren't a bodyguard to a celebrity?

Yet Virgil's expression did not alter. Instead his gaze considered me with surprising sincerity.

"What number did it come from?" he asked. He took out his phone, readying himself to take notes.

I gasped, as the slight pressure at my temples went away, and the quiet lifting of a burden I didn't realize I was shouldering just vanished.

"It's not just me," I whispered, going nearly lightheaded from relief. "You got one too!"

Virgil chuckled. "You shouldn't look so happy to hear that there are multiple death threats."

"I'm happy knowing I'm not the only one."

"I can't say the same," Virgil sighed. "I've gotten some strange emails over the past few months, especially once the book was announced. Aunt Shirls just says it's part of being well known, but she had never received death threats before. Did you contact the police?"

"I tried," I grumbled. "They told me to file a report in the morning."

Virgil blinked. "Did you not tell them what it was?"

"I did!" I blustered, outraged by the question and the memory of my ill-fated attempt. "What about you? You got one too! Why didn't *you* file a report?"

"I only just saw it, but I might have checked earlier if you told me."

"Why would I tell you?" I scoffed, and he didn't even look offended. He might be Shirleen's emergency contact, but between his bad jokes and how he floated in and out these past few months he never quite seemed like someone I could confide in during a moment of great distress. "Besides, I might just be worried for nothing. It could be a prank. It might even be Naomi behind it all."

Virgil blinked, quite baffled. "Naomi? Her assistant?"

"Haven't you heard? She's not working for Shirleen anymore. I think your aunt fired her, or perhaps got her to quit."

"Both are the same," Virgil said rather grimly. I must have done a poor job hiding my surprise, for he added, "My aunt has done so much for me, but I won't lie, the difficulties of the past few years largely started with her. I wouldn't be surprised if someone wants to kill her."

Maybe it was finally talking about all of this after bottling up my concerns, or perhaps it was the soothing tone he took that reminded me of my favorite true crime podcasts, but I found myself asking, "Who do you think would make such a threat? What names come to mind?"

Instead of dismissing my words, or worse laughing, Virgil weighed my question with great care. "A few, but as for who I would think could try, that number is more precise. I've been interviewing and reaching out to many people Aunt Shirls knew or worked with over the years. Many are here tonight. At least one person tried to get their interview struck down over some very raw comments they made. I don't think they realized I'm her nephew when we conducted the interview."

"People are that candid with you?"

"Given a microphone and a listening ear, you'd be surprised by what people will tell you of their own accord. I try to capture it all, as you don't always realize what is important until later."

"Is the microphone on right now?" I asked. He had got rid of his backpack of course, so there hardly seemed a place for him to carry a microphone. But I had forgotten men's clothes came with functional pockets, and he pulled it out to show.

"It can be," Virgil said. "And perhaps it should be given all that might occur tonight."

These clever words were far too prophetic. On the heels of his words, shattering glass – and a scream – cut through the chatter in the ballroom.

It echoed horribly for several moments before more voices rushed in, causing a clamor that pressed all around.

Goosebumps prickled along my back as blood pounded in my ears.

Something dreadful had just occurred.

Please let it have nothing to do with the threats I had tried to forget!

"Aunt Shirls," Virgil whispered, but he shook off his shock faster than I did and led the way out of the corridor.

We burst into the ballroom. Very few people were moving, as guests, catering staff, and more stood still in shock or confusion, unsure what had even happened. Because of her green suit, I spotted Shirleen at once. She was shaken and supported by Fatima, who got her into a chair, but the attention in the room wasn't on Shirleen.

Oscar Fantom rushed back to a microphone, and his voice boomed over the crowd even as it shook. "Emergency services are being called right now, but if there's any medical professional around, please come forward. One of the guests has taken ill and needs immediate medical attention."

"I'm a nurse!" An older red-haired woman hastily removed her brocade jacket as she hurried forth. "I can help!"

The crowd shifted forward to allow the nurse to come through, and Virgil and I drew closer in her wake.

That's when I saw Ruby.

I saw her shoes first.

Those signature red pumps were askew and half off her feet. The rest of her lay sprawled untidily on the ground. Her eyes were round with panic and fear as one hand clutched at her throat and the other stretched out to keep death at bay.

While the sight had sent the people around us scurrying backward, Virgil and I surged forward.

Virgil went to his aunt's side at once. "Aunt Shirls," he said, reaching for her hand. "Are you alright, do you need your medicine?"

Fatima, who was rubbing her hands against her apron, turned to me, as if she expected me to have any medicine on hand.

"I'm fine." Shirleen grasped his hand, her voice sharp and rasping as it broke. "But Ruby, oh Ruby!"

Not far away, the nurse had placed Ruby's head in her lap and was trying to keep her from hurting herself as convulsions washed over her body like tumultuous waves. Helping her was a male guest who looked like he only got involved because he was nearby.

As for Ruby, her limbs were still twitching as she lay on the ground, writhing in pain. Ruby's face was slightly flushed with hints of pink, and short grunts and odd sounds emerged in spurts. Terrible as they were, I wanted them to continue, as with each passing second those movements and sounds slowed and softened.

Unable to focus on Ruby, I let my gaze go around her. She had managed to get her slice of Festive Black Tea Cake. Now, it lay mostly eaten on the floor next to her, smashed like the shattered flute of cider nearby. Remnants of both the liquid and the cake were splashed along the front of her blouse and skirt, and were spreading as the nurse and her volunteer helper assisted the woman.

While Ruby was fading, she still resisted the nurse's efforts to keep her still. Her left hand desperately twitched toward her purse. It was just as fat and overstuffed as I saw it last. I picked it up and her notebook fell out, as did several pens, breath mints, a bedazzled phone with ruby gemstones, a floral printed wallet, and a slew of loose papers and receipts. I grabbed what I could, shoving it all back into the purse, my ears ringing in embarrassment at making such a mistake.

I was still putting stuff back in when the EMTs arrived.

I got up and out of the way, as Ruby was moved onto the gurney, with the nurse quickly detailing her state.

"Her pulse is weak, but steady," was all I managed to hear as the nurse and the rest of her words moved out of earshot.

One of the EMTs stood on the edge. It took only a moment to recognize my friend Eden. Because of all her texts in the group chat, I forgot she was on-call tonight. I was glad she was, as she might be able to fill me in on the details I couldn't witness.

Eden didn't approach me, but she nodded as our eyes met before she joined her coworkers, miming that she'd call me later.

"Keisha," Shirleen's voice brought me back to my surroundings. The shock had rolled off her, and Shirleen rallied like a commanding officer ready to give direction to her troops. Her voice wasn't as crisp as usual as she said, "Give me Ruby's purse. I need to call her brother and tell him Ruby got sick."

She glanced at my hand and the purse I still held. "I could do it for you," I said.

Shirleen shook her head. "He doesn't know you, it's best to get the news from a familiar voice. Virgil is taking care of things out here." Although in the middle of talking to the bystander, at the sound of his name Virgil half-spun and even pointed to himself as if this was news to him. Ignoring him, Shirleen kept her eyes focused on me as she continued. "I'll need you to help out in the kitchen."

"But Fatima–" I began to turn, looking for the caterer.

"Has her own work. I need you to pack up the cakes for me, since I'll be taking them back. If you see Austin, send him to me. Why is it when I don't need him, he's underfoot, but when I do need him, he's nowhere to be found?"

Thus, given my tasks, I collected the cakes and retreated to the kitchen, which was now as chaotic as the ballroom, as Fatima was busy elsewhere. I could barely even answer the young green-haired employee's questions about what happened in the ballroom. I said what I could and then left her and the others to gossip.

Boggled as I was to be sent to do this, I appreciated being able to do *something,* even if it was a small task like this. I boxed up each cake, placing them aside for the charity they were intended for.

Belatedly, as I recalled these were meant to go on the cookbook's social media account, I got my camera from my bag and took photographs. I snapped images from all angles on autopilot, trying not to see Ruby lying there on the ground, her hand stretched out as if asking for help.

My phone vibrated in my pocket, once again from my friends' group chat, as Romy sent a link to a news update about the incident.

Key isn't this your party?

The texts filled up with various reactions from everyone commenting, even Pascal, my elderly neighbor who generally went to bed early, had urgent queries.

I scrolled along the growing list of messages, touched by their concerns even if I didn't know how to answer their questions. How could I, when I didn't even know what just happened?

Did Ruby take ill? Did she have some condition that would trigger such violent convulsions?

I put down my phone and went back to photographing the twelve cakes because I didn't know what else to do.

I blinked, and counted the cakes spread across the table just to be certain.

At the start of the evening there had been twelve cakes but now there were only eleven.

One was missing.

The tea cake that Ruby had been given!

The Cookbooks of Shirleen Foster

- *Season by Season* (1977)
- *Shirleen's Kitchen Wisdom* (1979)
- *Shirleen Foster's Christmas Baking Treasury* (1982)
- *Rise and Shine: Recipes for Breakfast in Bed, Brunch, Breakfast for Supper, and More!* (1996)
- *Dear Shirleen: Advice and Recipes from the Vance Post and Courier Years 1974–1985* (2000)
- *Heart Healthy and Tasty Kitchen* (2003)
- *Bring the World to Your Kitchen (Over 400 Recipes from Austria to Zimbabwe)* (2009)
- *Season by Season Revisited* (2027)

Chapter 5

After all my running around last night, on top of the various shocking events, I crashed, collapsing onto my bed after begrudgingly washing away dirt and despair.

I felt like I had barely shut my eyes before my phone rang, shattering my misshapen dreams with shrill notes. I shot up, disturbing my cats who had nestled around me.

Scrambling for my phone, I blinked in the near darkness, barely registering HUNTON BAY POLICE DEPARTMENT flashing on the screen at first.

"Hello?" I asked. Lola slipped into my lap and I absently scratched behind her ears as I wondered what I had done to merit such a call. I didn't even have a car anymore to get stolen.

My wondering was cut short by a cool voice. "Keisha Scott, you need to come down to the police station and submit a statement for the incident last night involving Ruby Walton at Tully Manor."

"Incident, Ruby Walton?" I asked. As it all clicked together, I jolted awake as if ice had been dumped on me. "What happened, is she okay?"

"Were you not there last night?" the voice asked.

"I was."

"Then at your earliest possible convenience please come down to the station. Your eyewitness statement is required."

The phone call ended before I could get another word in, let alone ask why they wanted me there in the first place.

They say morning makes things clearer, but as sunlight trickled in my bedroom, I found my memories were muddled and jumbled with images of Ruby lying on the ballroom floor.

Was there something else I could have done? Something more useful?

I kept seeing the contents of her bag falling to the floor, as I dropped it at the worst possible moment.

Why had I panicked so?

All I did was consume true crime and mysteries. I'd listened to so many hours of podcasts, watched so many procedurals with quirky detectives, and my bookshelf sagged with dog-eared mystery novels and books on true crime and criminology. I knew five different knots, memorized a dozen obscure rules in states I would never live in, and could stitch up a knife wound.

Yet I'd done nothing.

I'm not saying I could have jumped in with CPR and commanded the scene, but I could have done more than stand and dump a poor woman's purse onto the floor.

My phone buzzed with a new message, and with a sigh, I skimmed through the texts and voice notes from my friends, which ranged from curious to concerned. I would get to most of them later as I didn't have anything new to share.

My younger sister, Aisha, who communicated with me mostly in gifs and memes, sent a text message filled with several sentences conveying her concern. And my father *called* me from the West Coast at five o'clock in the morning my time and didn't even leave a message or text about why.

I dialed him right away.

"What's wrong?" I asked brusquely, ready to cross whatever distance to get to California in a timely manner.

"Key." My father's groggy voice filled my ears, only dulling some of my garbled panic. "Why are you–"

"You called me. Did something happen?"

"I hoped you'd tell me," Dad said. He shook off the cobwebs of sleep as he continued, "I saw the news, or rather Aisha sent it to me. What are you going to do now? You can't keep working this job. Not that you should give up on cooking, but a career change is always good..."

Upon hearing no one I was related to by blood was dead, severely injured, or missing, regret from calling rolled in right on cue. "Dad," I grumbled, "I'm not getting a new job. This one suits me just fine."

"Are you sure? I was looking at the news. It doesn't look good for your boss." Dad said, and this time I heard genuine worry in his voice, and not just the parental worry that I was somehow ruining my life for quitting a semi-stable career for one even less so. Although it was far too early for another critique of my career choices, the worry entwining his words reminded me that if I let him, he'd travel across the country to make me soup, clean my house, and fix that creaky step on my stairs.

"What did Aisha tell you?" I asked, switching over to the message my sister had sent, wondering if she alluded to freaking out our father without giving me a heads-up.

"Some news clip," Dad said. "About an arrest, because someone died."

"Died?" I echoed, as my finger landed on a link Aisha had sent me earlier:

Acclaimed Cookbook Author Shirleen Foster Arrested, Suspected of Murdering Former Friend and Colleague.

I swore loudly and vehemently enough that my father berated me as if I was in high school again.

"It's terrible news," Dad said, "but no need for such language!"

"This is horrible," I bemoaned. "I don't know why they are accusing Shirleen of this!"

"You didn't know?"

"I just woke up!"

"You mean," Dad drawled, "you just turned your phone on! I don't know why you do that. What if I was injured when I called you, what would you do?"

"I'd still be several hours late, since there's a whole country between us."

"No one told you to move to the East Coast," my father huffed. "Us Scotts keep moving forward, we don't look back."

"I don't have any news to share," I said. Torn between worrying him further and spilling all the details, I decided to add, "I have to give a statement to the police, because I was an eyewitness."

"Call me the moment you leave the police station," Dad said, leaving no room for argument. "Even if you don't think you have important news. *Especially* if you don't think it is."

After saying goodbye to my father, I fed my cats and scarfed down a quick breakfast. Grabbing the first clean leggings and shirt I could find, I pulled on my winter coat.

While the bright red might be too much for a police station, there was no time to look for something else. Luckily, I had my gloves already in my pockets, so I jumped on my bicycle and headed for the downtown police station.

I wasn't worried about being questioned.

I had recently listened to the *Penny Drop Affair* which reenacted several police interviews, so I felt confident I wouldn't do anything that would be foolish or make things worse.

No, my worry was all on the major news.

Ruby was dead, which was a shock to read, but not a complete surprise given how she had appeared as she was taken into the ambulance. I was no doctor, but anyone could tell it didn't look good.

But why would they arrest Shirleen?

She wasn't exactly a sweet old lady, but being brash and difficult at times didn't make her a murderer.

Was it because of their fight at the party? Did police gather statements from eyewitnesses and decide Shirleen was to blame for Ruby's death? The article didn't say much. But I was perturbed by all manner of terrible outcomes.

I had seen too many true crime documentaries where the police arrested innocent people just to keep a case neat and tidy. There were even a few where it was all an accident and they ruined someone's reputation just thinking there was foul play.

This had all happened in less than a day. There couldn't be any real evident to merit Shirleen getting arrested, could there?

What if there was? a voice suggested in the back of my mind.

I considered what I knew of Shirleen and my memories of the night before. My reaction was the same as when

I first saw the news blast. There was no way Shirleen would do this. It wasn't about her being on the cusp of a return to the spotlight. I just had this feeling she didn't do anything to warrant being arrested. Shirleen was prickly and frustrating but her hard shell hid a genuine kindness. It didn't compute. Why did she get arrested? Were the police arresting her to make it seem like progress in the case? I didn't like the thought of that at all.

Arriving at the police station, I left my bicycle at the nearby rack and swept inside, giving my information to a very bored person manning the front desk.

As I signed in, I saw Virgil's name right above mine and finished adding the rest of my information in a rush. If Virgil was here, so were answers.

It was too early in the season for holiday brawling, and the traffic of the previous evening must have limited some of the usual Friday night antics, so the faded and worn chairs in the waiting room were nearly empty. In a far corner was a young man who reeked of vape smoke snoring his night away, an older woman knitting mittens, and an old man in an elf costume splattered with droplets of dried blood. The last person in the waiting room was getting coffee from a machine that shuddered and rattled as it spat out lumpy brown liquid. I walked past him, settled into a chair, and ignored him until he said my name.

I looked back in barely concealed astonishment. It was Virgil that I had overlooked. Unlike me, he must not have managed to go home as he wore the same clothes I last saw him in, except that the ugly leather jacket I had associated with him was gone, allowing his fitted blue sweater to make more of an impression as it highlighted his broadly built frame. He had also at some point put on heavy dark framed glasses, which along with a hint of stubble, was enough to alter initial impressions of him.

"Sorry, didn't realize it was you," I said as nothing better came to mind.

Something of a smile eased his expression, and he held out a cup of mud-colored coffee before he sat across from me in a nearby chair.

He had his backpack and recording equipment with him, and this time I wasn't annoyed to see the protruding microphone and its blinking light. His tendency to record for content was an evil power, and one I hoped to put to good use.

"You heard the news?" Virgil asked.

"I saw pieces, but not enough to know what's going on." I looked at him hopefully.

"I hardly know either," Virgil replied. "My aunt's been arrested, but they haven't filed charges so she'll be let go soon. As if there was anything to begin with." He huffed and lifted the coffee cup to his lips. "All the police have right now are a few eyewitness accounts from the party about her fight with Ruby and the cake."

"The cake?" I echoed, a bit lost. "What about it?"

"It's a small and silly thing." Virgil's foot tapped nervously against the floor. "Ruby was older, but she was relatively healthy and had no major health conditions. There's also the anonymous tip – came in even before Ruby died. It mentioned poison in the food. The police took the cakes from us right there at the hospital and from what I heard from the caterer, samples of food from the party as well."

"I understand why they did," I remarked. "Ruby was flushed pink, convulsing, and short of breath. It's very likely she was poisoned with arsenic or potassium cyanide.

Hopefully toxicology and the autopsy they'll perform will prove what occurred."

Virgil blinked at me. "How do you know that?"

"True crime podcasts," I answered.

"Oh," he said, and managed to brighten as he tried to interject some humor. "You're one of *those* people. Is that why you're not a fan of my podcast?"

"Don't be ridiculous," I said.

Although he wasn't far off the mark.

Virgil's podcast was a series of interviews with the people his moving company had helped, so it was half advertising and half public interest stories. Not the sort of thing I went for usually. I'd listened to a little of it when I started working for Shirleen out of sheer curiosity, but I soured on the idea of listening to more once I caught Virgil recording my private conversations.

"While I'm not a criminologist," I said, returning to more important matters, "based on the evidence, I think it's cyanide poisoning."

"Would you rather be right?"

"I'd rather Ruby not be dead," I answered honestly. "I like listening to true crime, not being part of the show. You don't always get answers about what occurred."

"Well then, what if this is a mystery?" Virgil asked. "You always get your answers then."

"Not always," I said. "Neatly tied bows don't make a good story."

"Because we don't expect them in our lives." He tapped a finger against his coffee cup. "They only arrested Aunt Shirls because it's convenient. We were leaving the hospital when it happened."

"Do you think they did it because of the tip, or was that an excuse?" I asked.

Virgil's expression turned curious as he paused before answering. "Aren't you going to say trust the process?"

"The process got Shirleen arrested when her hands weren't even covered in blood," I said. I forced myself to keep my voice low, so it wouldn't carry in the room. "Sure, she might be a person of interest or even a strong suspect, but this is too fast and too soon. It doesn't sit well with me. I mean, has there even been time to conduct a proper investigation?"

"I'd advise to keep that opinion to yourself," Virgil whispered.

Startled by the crisp authority in his voice more than his words, I was about to ask what he meant, but he discreetly pointed to his right.

Crossing the room toward us was a police officer. He had closely cropped brown hair, freckles, and a few lingering acne bumps that reminded me of how long I had been out of college. His spiral notebook creaked as he opened it. "Good you're both here. I'll take your statement first, Ms. Scott."

The officer brought me to a small room that must have often seen informal questioning like this, didn't have a two-way mirror or even tables with handcuffs slots on them. Just four chairs across from each other with a long table in between, like the worst sort of meeting room.

I sat across from the officer and answered questions about everything between my arrival at Tully Manor and until Ruby was taken out of the ballroom. They were basic questions whose aim seemed to be placing my set of answers against others with little excitement other than to find out how I measured up.

"You worked for Shirleen Foster, and you handled the cakes," the officer stated.

"I made *one* cake," I said. "The Caramel Pecan. I made it at home and it was sliced up for the party."

"Did you see Shirleen Foster around the cakes?"

"Not directly before," I said. "I was sent to give a slice of a cake to Ruby, but someone else gave it to her. It might have been Shirleen but it could have been someone on the service staff. I had stepped out of the kitchen by then." I didn't add that Shirleen had sent me away, or the manner in which she did.

"The rest of the cakes, how were you involved? Reports said you did the final touches."

"I finished them, but I didn't handle the cutting or serving."

He nodded, took a few notes, and turned the page in his notebook. "The tea cake?" He asked. "Who made that one?"

I swallowed. "Shirleen," I said. "But I was there when she made it. I don't recall her adding any poison to the cake batter."

"No one said anything about poison." The officer's tone was flat and almost bored. "Nor is anyone accusing Shirleen Foster, for that matter. We just want to get the facts about what happened."

Until the toxicology report came in. Then we'd know if it was cyanide, arsenic, or something worse. Because if there was one thing I knew, this was no accident.

"The fact you need to know is that last night before the party someone sent me threatening messages, saying Shirleen would be dead before the evening is out." I paused, letting my words echo in the tiny room.

If I thought I might have better luck with the officer, I was sadly mistaken.

The absurdly young man blinked at me. "Did you make a report?"

"I did, I meant to… I thought I could do it now?" I concluded weakly.

He sighed but turned a page in his notebook. "Tell me about the threat."

Repeating the message left me feeling silly, but the officer wrote it all down without comment, and more infuriatingly, without concern.

He asked me more questions about how long I had worked for Shirleen, what was our working relationship, and how well I knew Ruby.

I told what should be useful, but pulled back on the warning Ruby gave me about working with Shirleen as I didn't want to add further fuel to the fire. I did try to tell him about Ruby's purse, but the young officer had stopped being so diligent in his notetaking. He didn't even write a word down when I tried to tell him about the missing cart, and cut me off before I could even mention what I overheard with Virgil.

"I think I have more than enough," he interjected.

I tried to squeeze in a protest. He concluded the interview. I was quickly led back out, and Virgil was taken in my place.

I sat there in the slightly fuller waiting room, where idle chatter around me and mounting tension only increased my anxieties.

I didn't track how long my interview was, but Virgil's didn't seem to last nearly as long. He returned in no time at all with a scowl and frustrated confusion.

"Where is my aunt?" Virgil asked the young officer.

"She's still being questioned, but she should almost be done," the officer said. "We have a few questions for her, as she was close to the deceased."

"As were a few others," I couldn't help but point out.

"We've talked to them already," the officer interjected. "You two were the last of the statements we required."

Yet I doubted that was true, given how few hours had passed. There were so many people to talk to, not even including those who had gotten a front row seat to the main event like I did.

"All we're doing is–" the officer began, only to stop at the arrival of Shirleen and a plain clothes detective.

Even at this early hour the detective was attired in a neat striped pantsuit with an all-weather coat, as if she was about to go out on her rounds. Although her hair was steel gray, her golden tan skin was quite youthful, with only a few gently creased wrinkles around the corners of her eyes. While my true crime obsession didn't encourage me to gain an intimate knowledge of the police department, I knew who the detective was, due to a recent article celebrating the city's first Filipina detective. Just like her photograph, the detective struck an imposing image in her signature striped attire as she loomed with quiet authority.

She held out her hand to Virgil for a crisp, professional handshake. "You're the nephew then, Virgil Sullivan? Pleased to meet you. I'm Detective Constance Dimaandal, and I'll be overseeing the Ruby Walton case. I'm sorry about this sad business and appreciate you and your aunt coming to give your statements."

The detective turned to me. "You must be the recipe developer. Ms. Scott, I'm so pleased you were able to come here. Any information you provided will help us conduct our investigation." She turned her gaze to the three of us. "While I cannot share updates, I will say that you should remain in the area for the time being. You are important witnesses and persons of interest, so until the investigation has reached a conclusion, please inform my office of any travel, no matter how frivolous it might seem."

I wanted to ask about the tox report, and if we could be updated on it, but the detective and officer had already departed, sweeping into the hallway.

"Keisha."

I turned back to find Shirleen buttoning up her coat with certain urgency. "Would you mind stopping by the house?"

"I'll follow behind, I'm on my bike." I tapped the helmet dangling from my bag.

As I got on my bicycle, my phone buzzed. Pulling it out, fast-flying messages from friends filled the screen, but it was the new message from my sister that I opened first. No words for helpful context, as typical of my sister, Aisha had just sent a link to a social media post.

With a headline related to Ruby's death, below it was a clip of an old interview with Shirleen from the 1980s. Caught in the middle of laughing at a joke Ruby just said, Shirleen suddenly stopped and looked right into the camera, and said in an entirely deadpan voice:

"That's why folks, I'll be the one to kill her."

Chapter 6

Over the next few hours, a number of interviews, both television and radio, started popping up all over social media. They were very old, coming at the height of *Season by Season*'s popularity back in the 1980s. But the one that was the most widely shared was a painfully short clip, with all the context stripped away, taking what had been at the time ribbing between good friends and twisting it into grim foreshadowing.

Worse were the comments underneath these clips and the rampant speculation that stirred up more than a few judgments.

"This is what I dislike about the anonymity of the web," Virgil said, as he scrolled through his aunt's tablet as if his feed was covered with rotting fruit. "People think they're prosecutor, judge, jury, and executioner all in one. Ruby's death was just announced, how could the thought of foul play even have entered the discussion? Not a single thing has been confirmed."

"Foul play – you make it sound like it's one of those old timey mysteries." Shirleen wrapped her hands around a mug of elderberry tea. She attempted to smile but it trembled at its edges. Usually robust, she seemed to be shrinking right before my eyes under her cardigan. "You know those mysteries with rich British people in a country manor, and a dreadful number of bodies that pile up from all the murder that occurs, but yet are oddly comforting?"

"Aunt Shirls," Virgil began, "what happened–"

"Is an accident. Misunderstanding," Shirleen interrupted. "It's not murder. Why would someone want to kill Ruby? She's annoying but not that annoying."

"Please," Virgil said in a strangled voice. "Tell me what happened. All of it, and not just the pieces you're forgetting to tell the police."

I turned sharply to my employer, ashamed I had not thought of this occurring. Shirleen famously skimped on the most innocent of details around her prized recipes, so why would she not hesitate to do the same for more important matters?

Shirleen sipped her tea for several moments longer, before she carefully placed it on the counter. "Are you recording for your podcast?"

"And for the record!" Virgil bristled. "You heard the detective, you are a person of interest. Just because they couldn't charge you this time, doesn't mean they won't if they find just cause."

"Ah," Shirleen said quite unkindly. "There is the money I spent for the law degree you're wasting!"

Virgil didn't even flinch.

He pushed forward his microphone so it was aimed right at Shirleen. "Berate me, tease me all you like, but tell me what happened. I can't untangle things otherwise. You went to get the tea cake to smooth things over with Ruby. What happened next?"

Shirleen sighed and played with the ends of her cardigan. "I cut the cake in full view of the staff, and placed the slice to the side. Then I asked about bringing the rest of the cakes. The whole schedule got delayed because we were waiting for Bianca Rossi. I wanted to hold things as long as I could, since the event only occurred at Tully Manor in the first place because of her generous donation. I had brought the cake out to Ruby and was going to speak with Bianca. I handed the cake to Ruby. We exchanged a few words, and I left. Bianca wasn't that far away, and we were chatting when I heard a scream."

"What did you say to Ruby?" Virgil asked.

Shirleen adjusted her glasses and then leaned forward to speak directly into the microphone, her face holding traces of gentle mockery. "I told her she had some nerve showing up here without telling me, but that I could not deny she wasn't an important part of the book. I said I was sorry I didn't invite her to help with the new version, but I thought she wasn't interested anymore. I said that I wanted to talk more when I got the chance." Her voice trembled. "Ruby sampled the cake, and she gave me her opinion on it."

"What did she say about it?" I asked before Virgil could. "It was her favorite, I heard you say."

"Well known to be her favorite," Shirleen answered. "The tea cake was a tribute to her mother who came from the UK, by way of Jamaica. The cake has cinnamon and vanilla to compliment it. I don't know why she said she could detect almond in it. I never used that except in specific cases."

"Almond?" I cried.

When aunt and nephew both turned to me, I struggled to keep my face neutral as I feebly added, "What an interesting note to pick up."

Interesting didn't cover half of it.

If I was interpreting Ruby's symptoms right, the almond flavor just about cinched it. I was 90% certain Ruby was poisoned with potassium cyanide. Although how it got into the cake, I had no idea. I wasn't lying to the police when I said I watched Shirleen make that cake. We'd made it in this very kitchen, with the ingredients from her pantry. At the party I didn't even touch that cake, as that was one meant for charities and never intended to be given away.

So how did that particular poison get into the mix?

"Why did they arrest you?" Virgil asked his aunt for the benefit of the recording.

"Suspicions around the tea cake. Eyewitnesses all mentioned me offering it to her. Once that tip came in about the poison, that's all the zealous police needed. They couldn't keep me there because all I did was cut up a cake. I put the slice down when I went to help Fatima. Anyone could have come by and tampered with it before I gave it to Ruby."

"Do the police even know if it's really in the cake? Could it have been on the plate or fork?" I asked.

"I didn't even consider that." Shirleen tapped her chin. "That would have been awfully clever of the murderer!"

"Who do you think would have been that clever?" Virgil asked.

Shirleen waggled a finger at him. "I'm sure the police have teams looking for that answer as we speak, but the pair of you are asking an awful lot of questions."

"We're worried about you," Virgil said. "I've been getting death threats related to you. Keisha got them too. Probably anyone connected to you got them as well, so we must check with Naomi."

He said this to shock her, but Shirleen only rolled her eyes. I knew we had lost her then. No matter what either of us said, she wasn't going to give a cooperative answer.

"I've always gotten that sort of thing." Shirleen remarked. "Make a name of yourself in this country, no matter what year, people say an awful lot of things to cut you down."

"Someone texted me that you'd be dead before the evening was over," I said with a touch of outrage. "Just before the party started, we heard people talking about you, and it wasn't good. What if Ruby wasn't the intended target?"

"My dears." She favored us both with an indulgent smile, ready to pinch our cheeks and press candies into our hands. "No one's going to bother me. These threats are just that, threats. The police know about them and Ruby's death might even stop any further attempts of mischief – not that there were any in the first place. So, Virgil, you don't have to stay here guarding my door. I'll be fine, and if there's a single questionable thing, I'll call you."

"But–" Virgil and I began, only for Shirleen to cut us off once more.

"What can you do, that the police can't?"

Well, she had us there.

Virgil scowled, as did I, unable to give a proper answer.

Shirleen cackled and then held out her hand for the tablet Virgil begrudgingly returned to her.

"Keisha, while you're here, let's work on the pumpkin cheddar bread and the spicy black bean soup. Today seems like a day for all the comfort a person needs."

"Aunt Shirls," Virgil protested.

Without even looking at him, Shirleen said, "If you want to help, get an apron. Although before you do that, I need you to go to the store, as I don't have everything I need on hand."

Shirleen went to her well-stocked pantry and when she started calling out ingredients, Virgil grabbed one of the many sticky notes scattered on the counter and scribbled everything she said down.

Because I was pulling up both the original recipe and my updates in my notebook, I could already tell that half the ingredients she listed weren't even for the recipes she wanted to make today – or even the ones planned for the next week.

Judging by the slight eyeroll he made while he jotted down a few of the more egregious ingredients, I knew Virgil noticed that as well.

"I'll be back," Virgil said loudly and then shoved the microphone into an arrangement of fake flowers. The sponge mic cover couldn't help but pop against the bright blue petals in the bowl.

Catching my eye, he lowered his voice to plead, "Please try to get her to explain the recipes. The last few recordings have been idle chatter that won't suit the podcast."

"She knows you're recording," I said, refusing to agree. "She's just going to talk about the Christmas cakes again."

"Then get her to go into greater detail if you can. Because so far, I've gotten better content for a true crime podcast!"

Although he wasn't serious, I found myself mulling over the idea.

True crime was about investigating and examining the facts to find where the truth lay.

While Ruby's death was a terrible thing, for this to spark such backlash and scrutiny of Shirleen couldn't be by chance… unless Shirleen was being framed.

It wasn't that far of a stretch. I had listened to four very good podcasts (and two very poor ones) that involved someone being framed for actions they had nothing to do with – it was only made plausible because people expected bad behavior from the framed individuals.

Just as some people expected the worst from Shirleen.

While the police would do what they could, they wouldn't look at things the right way.

Not the way they needed to.

Not like *I* could.

Why else did I spend all these years devouring stories about brutal murders, abductions, and serial killers?

Yes, part of that was to be prepared in the very unlikely circumstances that I or any of my loved ones became the victim of murder and various violent crimes. But another part was that I liked a good puzzle.

Right now, I had three assumptions to work with:

1) Ruby was murdered, most likely by poison
2) Someone framed Shirleen
3) Whoever poisoned Ruby was likely present at the party or had someone act on their behalf

To figure out who did it, I needed to find out who had the opportunity, which pointed directly to the party list.

First things first, I needed the guest list from Naomi or Austin. Speaking with Naomi to get her side of the story about the events that led to her getting fired was also important. I also needed to see the night from Shirleen's eyes, even if Shirleen would probably evade my questions as nimbly as she did Virgil.

But I would succeed where Virgil failed. He might be closer to her and knew her quirks, I could speak the same language as her.

"Shirleen," I called when she came to check on my progress, "last night, did–"

"I forgot the sourdough starter. I never really like sourdough, it's so fussy." Shirleen handed me a new bag of AP flour. "Did you want some of the starter? You said you're having a holiday party with your friends."

"The week after next," I said, jostling the container. "Since a few of us will be headed away to see family or making other trips, this week coming up is the last regular dinner of the year."

"It's good you have weekly dinners." Shirleen said. "It can be tricky and a hassle, but when it's a habit you can make beautiful memories."

I took a stab at getting her talking. "I remember you started hosting dinners when you first moved to Virginia."

"I was quite the little hostess," Shirleen snorted. "First, it was with my husband to help support his work. Then it was supporting mine. Then to show I could still manage it." She banged the bowl across the counter with a thud. "You said you tested out the vegetable tart at your last dinner. How did it go?"

"Thumbs up from both the vegetarian in the group and the vegetable-averse person," I said, dredging up the memory. "They said I should have made it for Friendsgiving, but my neighbor Pascal said you never try something new on a holiday unless you're willing to face a chorus of disappointment."

Shirleen laughed, and it was the first genuine laugh I had heard since yesterday. "He's right about that! My mother always said it was bad luck, but I think she was trying to avoid my aunt getting creative with the types of cheese she put in the macaroni."

"Was there something you wanted me to try out with my friends?"

"Well," Shirleen began, and then paused, shaking her head. "I can't do that to you. You probably have a menu already set."

"I have a list of ingredients, but I'm in need of a menu," I said.

Shirleen gasped. "You haven't made a menu? You're braver than me!"

"It makes it fun," I said, taken aback at her tone. Even more so at how open her expression was now, when I was so used to the stern taskmaster. "What did you want to do with the soup?"

"We're going to try it in the slow cooker today," Shirleen said. "My last go around turned to mush, so I wanted to adjust the time and add more starch. What do you think of a handful more garlic?"

I tweaked the recipe as we worked, writing in my notebook the changes against the original recipe, translating Shirleen's mutters about handfuls into teaspoons or tablespoons as appropriate. She could figure it out if she was sitting down writing, but because I was here she could focus on getting the flavors right while I took notes. With the adjustments finished, I started peeling carrots, and the smallest sweet potatoes I could find.

As I leveled the peeler against the root vegetable I asked, "I need to know your schedule for the week. I usually ask Naomi, but since she's no longer working for you..."

"I'll share it with you, but I can manage. My generation was the one that made computers useful after all. I just like having someone handle the devices so I can cook."

"Then why did you fire Naomi? I asked as I peeled away the knobby skin of the sweet potato.

"Because she couldn't do even the smallest bit anymore!" Shirleen declared hotly. "These past weeks have been filled with missed messages and her telling people the wrong things. It's a miracle the party last night even happened in the first place. It wasn't supposed to be at the manor, but at the arts center. But there had been a fire in their kitchen and we ended up moving it."

"I didn't know that," I said, filing this tidbit away.

"Oh, this happened at the end of summer," Shirleen said dismissively, as she sifted the beans in the bowl, plucking out the imperfect ones to drop onto a nearby dish towel. "The damage was extensive enough that it couldn't be ready in time to host such a group. I didn't want to rush them, so we went with the manor, which should have been perfect."

"It was perfect," I said. "And Naomi, how was she part of it?"

"She did arrange things of course, but if it wasn't for Austin, it wouldn't have come together. Before, there were just so many things Naomi could have done better, and I let it slide because I needed her and didn't want to interview new assistants again." A sigh rattled through Shirleen and she studied a cracked bean between her fingers as if it was delicate porcelain smashed beyond repair. "It's going to be rough without even the little help she did manage to give. If you're able to step in that would be wonderful."

As if I had a choice when she still bore the weight of the previous night.

Shuffling the whispered advice Ruby had given me into a dark cupboard, I asked. "What do you need me to do?"

Virgil returned from his errand as we were cutting into the first loaf of pumpkin cheddar bread.

"Looks gorgeous, Aunt Shirls," Virgil said as he placed several pounds of butter and shallots onto the counter.

"Need you to test it." Shirleen held out a plate to him. "That's how I know it's good."

Virgil broke off a piece of the bread and took a bite without any fanfare. He chewed, he swallowed, and shrugged. "It's alright, but I can't taste the pumpkin."

"Well, it's not supposed to be strong," I bristled. "It's supposed to be a hint."

"Let's try again," Shirleen cut in. "We'll do extra sharp cheddar. Did you want to try rosemary or thyme? Or should we try for a kick?"

"We have enough to try both," I said, hunting around for more canned pumpkin. "One more herb-forward, while the other has a touch more cayenne."

Once I sorted out the measurements from Shirleen, a call on her personal phone had her abandoning me in the kitchen with Virgil.

While sent off on an unneeded grocery run, he had taken a moment to shower and change clothes, but that wasn't enough to shove him back into the tidy box I had first put Shirleen's nephew in. Something I did on instinct when I recognized how much of a distraction – in every way a person could be a distraction – he was. He was not a cook, he made diverting conversation about any topic, and it was easy to share a laugh with him when he wasn't secretly recording private conversations. I could easily ignore tolerable good looks verging on handsome, but an affable nature was much harder.

This time, however, he wasn't as much of a distraction as I feared he might be. In addition to cleaning up some of the dishes left in the sink, Virgil had turned off the microphone and was more concerned with checking the recording than pestering me.

It gave me time to think as I shredded up cheese once more, mulling over a very delicate question.

"Have you finished the first podcast episode yet?" I finally asked.

Clicking sounds answered me first. "Not yet," he said. "I've done mainly interviews and I'm trying to figure out how to cut the story. It's meant to be a look at the cookbook revision, but it's also my aunt's history."

"With all the interesting people who played a part," I added, hoping to affect a lightly curious tone. "I was wondering if I could hear some? I think it might be helpful as I work with Shirleen to get better knowledge of her past."

"It would help you to understand the original stories behind her recipes," Virgil said before he added with a smirk, "unless you just want to live out your deepest true crime fantasies?"

I shook the cheese grater at him, sending pieces of cheddar flying about the table.

"For your information, my ideal true crime fantasy is to find out what really happened in the elevator Lillie Van Buren vanished from. This, however, is far from it. Because there's trouble afoot with Ruby and everything."

"Yes, trouble with the cookbook." Virgil remarked. I wasn't sure what it was about his glasses, but they gave him a sharper look, making it hard to recall the goof I had grown accustomed to thinking of him as. Or maybe it was just knowing that he had a few mysteries of his own. No matter what it was, people always had a reason to quit something, especially if it was being a lawyer.

"The publisher might push back the book, or even cancel it, due to Ruby's death," Virgil continued. "Since you quit your job for this, that is reason enough for you to play investigator like one of your favorite podcasts."

The light wasn't blinking on the microphone, so it was the only reason I didn't shut him down completely.

"This would make an *excellent* podcast series," I enthused, "or even a side story. Especially if the news doesn't find a new scandal to focus on. People will want to know Shirleen's story, and you have direct access."

"My aunt doesn't easily share her private life."

"Yet she talked freely into the microphone when given a chance. She'll want to set things right."

"I want that as well," Virgil said.

"If you want that, and I want that, and so does your aunt, why won't you let me listen to the other interviews?"

He gripped the microphone protectively.

"It's not just audio I need to cut. I've been listening to the interviews again anyway, because even without last night happening there's something odd in what they told me, but I don't know everything. Some people assume I had knowledge in places, while others assumed I knew nothing. Maybe you might know something." Virgil flipped on the microphone as he spoke, waving it before me, its blinking light both an invitation and taunt. "Because you're right, this could make an excellent podcast. You're probably the only person I know who wouldn't want to frame my aunt. If she gets arrested your plans are disrupted big time."

"Likewise," I said meeting his gaze. "Relations aside, she is the central figure of something you are already investing so much time and effort into."

His smile was wry. "My losses are less than yours, but I don't see why I shouldn't help you with this."

"You're not helping–"

"I am," he said firmly. "If you want to listen to my recordings. We're working together or not at all." I scowled, but he showed no signs of faltering. "My aunt is either the next victim or being framed. I'm part of this. I know Aunt Shirls's history, her quirks, and the people in her life. I'm also, if you haven't forgotten, in the middle of interviewing people for the podcast, which gives me a very plausible excuse to meet any particular person of interest... or even possible suspects."

With a feeling I might come to regret it, I said, "Let's work together to solve this mystery." Before he could interject, I continued. "I need to talk to Naomi and Austin. They knew the schedule and who might have been at the party. I have a planned meeting with Austin on Monday – would you like to come? I can say you're standing in for Naomi."

"I was actually planning to do her interview that day."

"She hasn't canceled yet?" I couldn't help but ask. I knew if I was fired in the way Shirleen described, I wouldn't even bother.

"Even if she had, I need to speak with her anyway about Aunt Shirls's calendar," Virgil said. "You being there shouldn't cause too much trouble. Also, I agree, getting the party guest list will help. It would get the full picture of who was there as a guest – or who was there to cause mischief. With a little finagling I might even be able to get interviews from most of them too. After all, we have a person contacting us, plus the people we heard in the hallway. It could be connected or something separate."

Because he broached it first, I asked with trepidation, "You've known Shirleen and her world much longer than me, who do you suspect?"

Virgil took several moments before he answered. "Frankly anyone at the party is likely, but there are some more likely than others. I don't recall seeing Naomi there at all that night, but Austin to me seems very much like the sort to say there is no such thing as bad publicity."

Introduction to *Season by Season Revisited* podcast

> Virgil Sullivan: *The funny thing is that no one ever thought* Season by Season *would gain such a devoted following. Seen as a young housewife who just contributed to a column at a small-town paper, the proposed cookbook was viewed as a project that coasted off her youth as much as the Soul Food movement. Shirleen Foster didn't have the expertise of Vertamae Smart-Grosvenor or Edna Lewis, but the goal wasn't to teach as much as it was to provide advice and a different way to view cooking for oneself and others. Not the best way, but one way you can view food and everything else around it.*

Chapter 7

The partial interview Virgil had done with Austin was a quick listen. On my bike ride home, I was able to get through the entire piece, including the outtakes and narrative segments Virgil used for the intro and outro. I didn't learn anything useful about Austin. Most of what they talked about were things I already knew or saw occur. Austin told no personal stories and kept things focused on the work. It was nice, I suppose, to hear Austin talk when he was giving a single moment his full attention.

This time of year, my ride through Hunton Bay was filled with elaborate Christmas lights and displays that presented a feast for the eyes and sometimes ears. Some cropped up shortly after Halloween at the first hint of a chill, but most people had the decency to wait until after Thanksgiving to decorate their yards with candy canes, reindeers, presents, trees, giant ornaments, snowmen, and even Christmas mice, as they counted down to the big night.

Not Christmas, by the way, but Hunton Bay's Twinkle and Tinsel Showdown, where the winner of the best holiday display gets named. You don't win anything more than bragging rights, discounts to local small businesses, and the choice between season tickets for either the local baseball or hockey teams, but from the way people decorated their homes you'd think there was real cash money in play.

My neighbors were determined that the winner should come from our street this year, so from the moment I turned the corner, I was dazzled by lights of every color draped along roofs, windows, bushes, and trees, to celebrate winter and the festive season. There was so much illumination I didn't even need to have my porch light on when I got back to the house, as I could see pretty well without it.

This also had the added benefit of being able to see from the corner that my friends were standing on my porch.

"Key!" Romy called as she leaned against the banister, the bells on her hat jingling. "About time you showed up! Did the chef you're working for get arrested or not? I've been waiting for you to say all day!"

"Don't worry, we haven't been out here that long," Eden added. "I decided to wait for you at Romy's place and when we saw you go past, we booked it over. You really should take a different route to get back, that's how you get stalked."

I chuckled at the advice I'd given her once now being thrown back at me. "Well, it seemed to help you out this time," I said. I placed my bicycle on the porch and looked at my friends. Holding up the leftovers I added, "You can pester me with your questions over dinner."

Luckily enough the leftovers matched my friend's food preferences.

Eden didn't like mushrooms and Romy was allergic to nightshades, and I let these two factors guide the meals I shared with them. By cooking for my friends, I'd learned to make adjustments, and found a certain enjoyment that leaned into the strengths of what others called restrictions. To me, if someone was lactose intolerant or allergic to eggs, or wanted to eat a great deal of protein, these didn't restrict my cooking but were preferences that encouraged me to try different things.

Eden had been a friend of mine since high school debate class. As a fellow Black nerd, she first introduced me to the world of ren fairs. While we kept in touch, mainly meeting up to go to the renaissance fairs out in Maryland, an old boyfriend brought her to Hunton Bay. Five years later, the boyfriend was gone, she stopped perming her hair and went natural, and our friendship evolved to bestie level. She worked as an EMT, restored classic cars for fun, and was still trying to convince me that my love of running translated into a willingness to run a marathon.

Romy was a cello player with a seat in the Hunton Bay orchestra, and her playing had been featured on well-known soundtracks for films and video games. Freelance work as a web developer kept her from returning to the terrible office job we first met at some years ago. She had quit first, giving me the strength to do so as well when my manager breakdanced on my last nerve. Romy's family was mostly centered in Virginia Beach, and my deep appreciation for Filipino food had me a frequent visitor to numerous celebrations.

As I heated up the food I brought back with me, Eden turned on my Christmas tree, making comments on its Gothic style, because it was chocolate black with purple ornaments.

"She's never going to let you live it down." Romy teased as she stepped onto a footstool to reach my upper cabinets. "You kept saying that black Christmas trees were tacky one year, and then the next you brought one home."

"I don't even remember," I scoffed.

"Don't worry, I'll remember for both of us." Eden returned to the kitchen with a playful scowl. "Stop keeping us in suspense, Key, what's going on?"

"Come on, tell us!" Romy added.

"I will," I countered, "but first you tell me what you saw."

Because Eden had been at the scene, there wasn't too much I had to explain. As I dished out soup and stacked on a plate three types of bread, she interrupted with details from her view from the ambulance.

Ruby had been in rapid decline from the moment the EMTs were called. That she died wasn't so surprising to Eden, who often said many of the rides she took ended with the patient dying either on the way or in the emergency room. Ruby had fallen into a coma while en route and died shortly after arriving, showing signs and symptoms of an acute allergic reaction. Eden wouldn't say more than that, no matter how much I prodded.

"I probably shouldn't even have told you that much," she said. "It's against the rules."

"What are you even asking?" Romy shoved her plate aside. "Your boss wasn't arrested, was she?"

"She's a person of interest, mostly because of the cake," I said, so focused on chewing over what Eden said I avoided the rest of my plate. The police had asked a lot of questions about the cake, and if toxicology proved it was cyanide like I suspected, it was only marginally worse. If there wasn't poison, the police might think Shirleen deliberately included an ingredient that she knew Ruby would be allergic to – even though Shirleen had no clue Ruby was going to be there.

Realizing they were waiting for me to say more I added, "It's just speculation, I'm sure the police will find out what happened and take care of things."

My friends exchanged glances, and I wondered if they knew lying. I didn't want to worry them, but I couldn't let things settle on their own. I wasn't convinced the police were going to do this without trying to arrest Shirleen for real. While Detective Dimaandal was clearly competent, I didn't trust the rest of the police. I was still irked by calling in the threat earlier and later getting the brush off when I tried telling the young officer about the same threat. His lack of notes did not restore my confidence that this wouldn't be a rush job to get a pat answer. Not helping were the dozen true crimes stories I had consumed recently that featured police incompetence in other major and minor ways.

If I wanted to know what happened, I had to find out myself.

"We've got this week's dinner settled. It's sheet pan meals," I said, shifting gears. "I have somewhat of a plan for our party next week, but what about the week of Christmas? You guys said you were going to figure it out. While I love you dearly, I'm not doing weekly dinner and Christmas Eve dinner just days apart from each other, even if not all of us will be there. We talked about skipping."

Our weekly dinners never had the same number of people. While my core friends were there every week, our numbers fluctuated with the addition or absence of old coworkers, neighbors, mutual acquaintances, and temporary strangers. As the holidays chugged along, showing up for the dinners had mostly been my true and blue. Given how I usually cooked the main courses each week, I didn't mind a temporary reduction in numbers.

"I like the idea of combining them," Romy said, "instead of skipping it. Out of the usual folks, Brendan, Shauna, and CJ won't be there. Jessica and Sunil will try to make it, depending if they really are going to Seattle or not. Jamal is still a question mark."

"He said he'll show," Eden added. "His cousin's wedding got moved to the week after, so he'll be in town for the party."

"Adding in Jamal, that makes it a small group, so we should just go to a restaurant," Romy said. "You do so much for us, Key, that my gift to you is that I got reservations at High Note Harmony, and the rest of us will chip in for a nice dinner at Magnifico."

"So fancy," I laughed, unexpectedly delighted. Magnifico had a whole fleet of desserts that could be set on fire in different ways. "I've been wanting to go there again. We'll be doing karaoke too?"

"It's essential fun for the holiday," Romy said innocently. "Do I need to lay on the guilt that I can't go to Manila with my family this year?"

"You just want to have redemption for the disaster from the last time!" Eden jeered. "Who does karaoke featuring showtunes?"

"It's not a competition," I intervened as they both started to point utensils at each other. "We don't keep points."

"Not in the way that matters," Eden grumbled. "That makes us, Jessica and Sunil, Jamal, and who else?"

"Will Pascal come?" Romy asked me.

"Let's ask him."

I went to a window in my living room and flipped on and off the lights.

It took a few minutes before my doorbell rang for the kitchen door. Waiting out there in an argyle cardigan and a knitted cap hastily pulled over his shiny bald head was the short and pear-shaped form of my neighbor.

Pascal Norwood had retired three times only to get back to work out of sheer boredom. He was currently an adjunct at Hook College, the president of the neighborhood league, and a longstanding member of the Friends of the Library and personally recruited me, Romy, and Eden to join. Deeply involved with the community, there were about a dozen small projects and activities that he often roped me and my friends into each year. A widower with no children, and a big empty house, he was the de facto host for our dinner parties, because he had space and enjoyed every aspect of hosting. While we didn't always eat every meal together, I shared a lot of my food with him. We often got mistaken for grandfather and granddaughter by strangers. I was embarrassed about that until I realized how much Pascal boasted about me to all his friends. As for his food preferences, while he was open to many cuisines, he only ate about three vegetables and stubbornly refused to try beets. But he had a sweet tooth and made short work of any cookies lying around.

"I didn't think you were home long enough to cook," Pascal said sniffing the air, his brown eyes alight with lively interest as he licked his lips. "I was going to defrost one of the soups you made me but…"

"There's plenty left over," I said, escorting him in. "Eden and Romy are here. I've been telling them the latest news."

"News about what?" he asked innocently, as if he hadn't been blowing up my phone as well.

"Oh, you know, the dead woman at my party. I don't know why everyone is so eager to hear about it."

Pascal just smiled. "It's not so often we have something exciting like this in our little circle. Most of the time we're living vicariously through CJ's travels around the world. Did you see the video of him doing karaoke with those K-pop girls he met?"

"I think that might be why Romy reserved space at High Note," I muttered.

"Well count me in," Pascal hooted. "We can do some Christmas karaoke. I've been practicing!"

"Looks like we got our answer," I called to Eden and Romy. "Pascal is in!"

He joined us at the table and polished off what was left of the food, adding his comments for me to take back to Shirleen about what made an impression or not.

I always enjoyed cooking for my friends, but since I started working with Shirleen, they got excited that their comments and opinions, either good or bad, made them a part of the cookbook. I hadn't told them yet, but they were going to be acknowledged as the Whaley Street Supper Club.

This was what I loved about food, what had me in the kitchen mixing, measuring, stirring, even after a long hard day.

Food allowed me to be creative, to think, to reach out to others. I was never the most social animal, and it was only the company of a good friend that allowed me to survive any size gathering. But, ask me to cook a meal, to bake any sort of dessert, or give opinions on a dish, and I was in my element.

It was also a good way to learn about people.

To learn their preferences and their dislikes. To get a window into their past and what they were worried about currently.

Food also provided a good way to start up a conversation. I would certainly need one in the days to come for this investigation I was planning.

"What do you like better, my peppermint bark or cookies?" I asked. "I think I may need a peace offering for some of my meetings next week."

Interviews for the *Season by Season Revisited* podcast

1. Alberto Torres ✓
2. Fatima al-Said ✓
3. Davis Packer
4. Austin Hammond ✓
5. Carmen Hollingshead ✓
6. Ewing Charles ×
7. Loren Gaffney ✓
8. Winifred Chan ✓
9. Roselle Pierpoint ×
10. Malcolm Demetrious Freeman ✓
11. Bianca Rossi ✓
12. Weyland Stone ×
13. Javier Navarro ✓
14. Brandon Morton
15. Margot Baptiste ✓
16. Naomi Fleming
17. Lucia Espinosa
18. Merle Banks ✓
19. Oscar Fantom
20. Ruby Walton ×
21. Keisha Scott

Chapter 8

The best place to start a mystery was always at the scene of the crime. So, the very next morning I hopped on my bicycle and headed back to Tully Manor.

The manor's social media had been flooded the day before with visitors, who had arrived once the police rolled up their caution tape and departed. Mainly local reporters and curious civilians had been there, although a few social media posts had been people who wanted to spice up their content with holiday mayhem.

Those accounts were ghoulish, but very useful, as it allowed me to determine what and who to expect around the manor.

The police were gone, and it was too early for visitors as the manor wouldn't open for a few hours, but not so early that staff wouldn't be around. I wanted to snoop, not break in. Although if given the chance, I wasn't going to rule out sneaking around the grounds.

Dismounting, I wheeled my bicycle around the corner so I could at least be discreet, only to find someone else was at the bike rack.

"What are you doing here!" I cried. Virgil looked up from locking his bicycle. I startled him, yet he didn't appear surprised at all to see me.

"I was exploring the neighborhood," Virgil stood and swept a hand about. "It's a nice little place, isn't it?"

I eyed the microphone poking out of his coat pocket. "Just exploring?" I echoed. It wasn't lost on me either that he was once more the bespectacled version of himself, one that was slightly more serious and the ghost of the lawyer he apparently had been.

He met my glance with one of his own that pinned down my wiggling words.

"Yes," Virgil remarked, "I was just exploring the area. Weren't you? How odd that we both were struck with the same idea to come back, even though it's the site of a great tragedy."

I wasn't in the mood to play games even if he was. "Fine," I declared. "I wanted to return to Tully Manor. It's closed now, but the police are gone."

"What did you expect to find?" Virgil questioned. "Any trace of evidence or clues might have been trampled over since that night."

I shook my head. "I'm not looking for clues; I'm looking to see how this could have happened in the first place."

Without a change of expression, Virgil nudged the microphone closer to me. "Could you repeat that, I didn't quite catch it?"

I rolled my eyes but indulged him all the same as I leaned towards the microphone. "We're going to retrace our steps that night to see how a killer could enter and leave without being noticed!"

Leaving our bicycles at the rack, we walked up the front toward the manor. Virgil narrated our approach, painting the scene with his words, and remarking on the details I was keen to overlook. As I lifted my eyes to the turrets on the roof, the trimmed gardens, and the gravel path that led to a small parking lot, I found myself enjoying the Victorian-era decorations.

Virgil went on further to describe what he had seen that night, until I interrupted him.

"You remember the exact number of cars lined up along the road?" I asked, quite amused at such a boast.

"I took a picture of it," Virgil said."Don't you take pictures to remember exact details?"

"Yes, but," I began, and then remembered I had moved the pictures I took with my camera onto my phone. Pulling it out, I quickly flipped past assorted images to show him the cakes.

"Look!" I declared.

Virgil absently adjusted his glasses and his eyes darted from my face to the phone screen. "What am I looking at?"

"The cakes! There's eleven in this picture because one is missing! The tea cake that Ruby ate!"

"Well, didn't the police take it?" Virgil murmured. "They took samples of everything else."

"It was taken *before* we knew about the poison. Before the police charged in to take all the food. The only sample they have is the slice found with Ruby," I said.

Virgil frowned, but all he did was point to a far corner on my phone. "What is that?"

I turned my phone back to me and had to squint at first before I saw it – a bit of person in a bright red outfit that didn't match the sedate uniforms of the catering staff.

I tapped the image, zooming in. "It could be a person," I murmured. "The venue staff wore red uniforms that night."

"Were they let into the kitchen?" Virgil remarked. "Did they let anyone in?"

"No idea, but they did let you in," I said. "You were poking about. There was no bouncer keeping people from coming."

"Maybe there should have been."

My phone vibrated and the notification that flashed on the screen was for the latest episode drop for a local history podcast.

"Sorry about that," I said, spying the surprise on Virgil's face. As I took back my phone, I added, "Do you think we can view the house? Or should we go around the grounds?"

"To do what? Peer into the windows?"

"Of course, I want to see the inside too!"

"Is that what you're doing here? Or are you trespassing?" A stern-faced, pudgy older man stood on the steps of the manor. In his red vest and pants, and trim beard, he looked like a very angry Black Santa Claus. The docent badge attached to his lapel called him Marcus.

I turned to Virgil, but he had already turned to me with deep entreaty in his eyes.

"We are..." I began, drawing out the words as I looked in vain for a flying reindeer to help guide me out of this trouble, until I settled on something that was spotted with the truth. "We are doing a podcast about unsolved mysteries and little-known historical facts."

I didn't get much further before the man stopped me with a groan. "Another one! Georgina was right. We should start advertising this, we've gotten more foot traffic this weekend than we did all fall!"

"How many people have shown up?" Virgil swung the microphone to the docent.

"Worried about beating people to the punch?" The docent pulled at his vest, absently straightening himself as he looked into the blinking light. "You don't need to worry;

we haven't been able to let anyone inside because the police have only just finished their search."

"Could we take a look?" I asked. "We won't touch anything and we'll be sure to mention the history of the manor, the hours it is open, and any special events coming up."

"And the gift shop?" the docent asked after a moment.

"Of course," Virgil reassured the older man. "Won't take more than an hour. You can keep an eye on us with any cameras you have."

This got a dignified chuckle out of him. "I trust you, since you're trying to come through the front door. You needn't worry about us recording you. The cameras there are just for show – it was too costly to make the renovations to get them hardwired."

I laughed along with him, even as this news only brought in dismay.

No recording cameras meant no footage for the night other than what people may have taken with their phones.

Marcus must have been bored after all the excitement of the weekend, for he chatted with us for longer than I expected. The staff had not been told much about the current state of things, only that if there was just cause for further investigation the police would return. Although he wouldn't let us have free range, he was happy enough to show us through the parts of the manor that had been open for the event.

Ropes and locked doors kept people on the main floor in the East Wing, which was where the ballroom, the kitchen, and a few smaller meeting rooms were. Most of the updates to the manor were focused here, compared to the rest of the house which had been preserved as close to the original as possible.

Without the fuss of the party, I was able to really appreciate the manor. Free of that haze of the night, I couldn't shake the feeling I was walking about a movie set for a period drama. As I turned the corner, I expected to see ladies in fabulous walking dresses and high collars strolling past sipping tea.

Despite beams of late morning light drifting in from the windows, it felt dimmer in the hall given the earthy browns, sage green, and dark gold that was not only in the wallpaper but the heavy curtains as well. Every table we came across was loaded with at least ten items of various sizes, and there was even a hallway where bookcases spilled out lining the wall, their shelves stacked with books, small statues, a globe, ornament trinket boxes, a typewriter, and a fleet of ships in glass bottles.

While there were so many things that nearly caused me to stop in my tracks – including an old-fashioned lantern sitting on a windowsill decorated with stars – what finally did the trick were the stiffly posed portraits on the walls. I don't know why it never dawned on me that the Tullys were Black. Not the passing for white, Talented Tenth Black. But unambiguous Black. The Black of jazz, joy, jubilation, juke joints, and journeys. The Black of boldness and pride, and hair shaped and styled to display a range of hair textures. The Black that I could see echoes of my family in, as this was a place I would have belonged. Their portraits were in several groups, with some of the larger ones focused on the matriarch and patriarch of the family, although their children and their grandchildren at various ages covered the remaining walls.

Marcus paused next to me, and I realized he had been waiting for me to look as there was a chuckle tucked in his words. "Because the cities are different these days, we forget that Norfolk, Port Walker, and Hunton Bay all had strong, vibrant Black communities where we were like piano keys with our white neighbors, side by side. Our homes were as rich as the stories we tell. I suppose that's why your aunt chose the manor as the place for her event."

Virgil wasn't even fazed as the older man turned to him. "You knew who we are?"

"I did, but she wasn't so certain." Marcus pointed to what I thought was a painting, and I suddenly understood where the ghost stories about the manor came from. A middle-aged Cuban woman's face peered out. Her dark hair was piled atop of her head in a bun, and there was a pencil behind her ear. The manager of Tully Manor smiled at us with great mischief, but then retreated from sight, leaving behind the empty frame of a faux mirror.

"Georgina says it's fine for you to venture about in the ballroom. I wish you luck." Marcus added, "I don't think you'll find anything useful. It's been cleaned up very well."

Marcus opened the door to the event space, and retreated into the hallway, leaving us to explore as we wished.

The ballroom curtains were drawn, so the only light came from a chandelier. Virgil flipped the switch and rays of light spilled over the cloth-covered chairs and tables stacked against the wall. The decorations that filled the ballroom were there, the red ribbons and flowers loud in the quiet elegance of the room. The space was cavernous with it empty of people and conversation, and it seemed to take me twice as long to cross the space to where Ruby had fallen. I thought it would be tricky to find the spot since it had been in such an open area, but there were scuff marks left on the floor and faint dings from the EMT's gurney.

Taking out my camera, I took pictures, snapping quickly in several short bursts.

Just as Marcus had said, it was clean and tidy and I could see nothing there I hadn't already, but I was looking for something that was never going to physically be there.

I knelt on the very spot where Ruby fell and walked myself through the memories of when I crouched down next to her in a vain attempt to help.

I could see her again. The flushed face, the convulsions, the vivid fear on her features. Ruby had pointed to her purse, and I picked it up hoping to ease her distress.

There had been no time to look in her notebook, but I wished I had spared even a moment to glance at a single page. I had dropped the bag and been too panicked about shoving everything back to take note, but I had held it. I should have looked at it when I had the chance.

What had been in that notebook that concerned her so greatly?

I remained crouched on the floor letting the feel of the notebook pass over my hands.

"What are you doing?" Virgil stood above me, hardly hiding his puzzlement.

I'm surprised he let me go this long, but then he had been pacing around the ballroom doing his own thing.

I remained where I was, turning to look at the room. "Spooling back memories," I answered. "That night, Ruby pointed to her purse, I dropped it trying to bring it to her."

"I heard it fall." Virgil said.

"I tried to put everything back, and finished up just as the EMTs arrived." I mimed the action, and as the memories played, I saw myself slipping what was left in my hand into my pocket – not into the purse – in my haste to help.

"My pocket!" I patted my empty coat pocket thinking of the clothes I wore the night of the party. "It's in there!"

"What's in the pocket?"

"Don't know," I said, jumping to my feet, "and luckily enough I was too tired to do the laundry. I'll update you later, but it wasn't noticeable enough for me to feel it. You're not the only one with questions. What about you?"

"What about me?"

"I gave Ruby's purse to Shirleen. I assume she gave it to you. If you have it..."

"Then what?" Virgil interrupted quite testily. "You'll think my aunt is guilty after all?"

"I'm doing this because I think she *isn't* guilty," I said, unsure at this swing of his opinion. "Unless you lost it."

"I didn't lose anything!" Virgil sputtered with such heat, the faint chill in the air of the ballroom fell away. "The purse ended up with Ruby's brother."

"Did it have a notebook?" I asked, as I discreetly pressed record on my camera. I trusted Virgil enough that I didn't think he'd poisoned Ruby Walton, but that he might help cover up murder and assist his aunt, or another unknown perpetrator, wasn't entirely out of question. He had been in that kitchen that night, without even a half-hearted excuse about why. His usual goofy and unserious air didn't mean much. People held multitudes, and I knew from a steady diet of true crime and unsolved murders how a genial air could be a well-crafted mask. Instinct was telling me to trust him, but I had trusted my instincts before and ended up with shattered illusions and a broken heart. Better to think the worst of him now than get a nasty surprise.

"I remember a book sticking out of the purse," Virgil said after a moment. "I didn't look at it closely if that's what you wanted to know."

"Darn," I said, hoping I spoke lightly enough to dial back the temperature. "I hoped you had. Ruby had said she came to the party for a reason that had nothing to do with Shirleen."

"You never mentioned this before," Virgil said.

"I forgot," I replied, wishing I'd kept quiet. I didn't like how astonished he was that Ruby spoke to me at all, no matter if he had a good reason to assume or not.

"It was a busy night," Virgil grunted. "Shall we move into the kitchen?"

I agreed without much enthusiasm, as I knew there would be little for us to find. I followed him anyway, turning off the recording on my camera as I did.

"In here," Virgil said, going by the cold stoves. "The catering staff was getting ready to flip to serving the cake. I poked my head in looking for you before my aunt shooed me out."

"After everything that happened, when I returned, I found they had just started cutting up a cake." I said taking another picture with my camera. "I walked back in here–" I entered the cold storage, looking at the now empty shelves and getting a faint whiff of sugar, "–and got the rest. I had the door shut, and couldn't hear or see anything, until Shirleen told me to leave the cakes alone."

"Then they went to me, and the police got them," Virgil said. "Although they tracked us down at the hospital."

This place was busy that night, but not that many came in and out. Fatima had a small staff of five. The manor staff, plus five others who served food and drinks to the guests.

Shirleen, Virgil, and I had popped into the kitchen more than a few times.

Had there been anyone else?

"I should talk to the caterer," I mumbled.

"I think the guests might be more useful."

"Can the guests tell us what happened to the carts?"

"The carts?" Virgil echoed.

I pointed to one that was left in the corner of the cake room. "Why were they misplaced?"

"Were they misplaced? It seemed the caterers found them rather quickly?" Virgil said.

"How do you know if they were?" I ventured. "The catering assistant was quite confused that I couldn't find anything. One of them was hidden in the hallway where we heard those people."

"Coincidence?" Virgil said.

But I wasn't listening to him.

Surrounding the cart tucked in this space, I took several pictures of it, especially as it still had some decorations on it for the 'Twelve Days of Christmas' theme. Three others were in the kitchen, and I photographed those as well.

Virgil's unspoken skepticism washed over me, and I was ready for him to say something, but instead he pointed to the bit of ribbon.

"This cart was out on the floor when Ruby collapsed. I remember the odd-looking faces of the pipers."

Was it? I searched my memory neither doubting nor believing him. "It could have been brought out earlier."

"There wasn't a cake on it," Virgil said. "I remember that because when Aunt Shirls was bossing us around like chess pieces, I grabbed the cart to get it out of the way, and it was near the wall."

"Completely empty?"

"I loaded up those cakes without even thinking about it." Virgil frowned. "You know, it's odd. I visited the ballroom the day before with Aunt Shirls and somehow everything was reconfigured slightly."

The kitchen door opened before I could ask him more about that. The manager was in a red sweater dress with a cowl neck, and sensible flat boots, looking very much like Mrs. Claus with a clipboard.

"I know you are looking around for your podcast, but I was hoping you could take back with you the things you left behind. I'm not sure if it's still good, but you might want to have the carrier at least."

Virgil mirrored my confusion, but as Georgina looked at me, I asked. "Cake carrier?"

"And a cake knife." A hint of a frown entered her face, with a touch of worry and fear. "These do belong to you and Shirleen, right?"

I gathered my remaining wits to stammer out, "Why yes," and before she could say more, I added, "I didn't realize I left them behind."

"I found them this morning tucked in the staff refrigerator. The police didn't check in here since the door was locked. Shirleen must have left them behind. I allowed her to use the staff room earlier that night." She looked so hopeful, I couldn't disappoint her.

"I'm glad you kept them." I said, and meant it. Georgina must have thought Shirleen had nothing to do with Ruby's death, or this cake and the knife would have gone to the police.

Georgina took us to the staff room. She unlocked it and turned on the light.

It was what you might have expected. A small windowless room, with a sagging couch, a card table, and some chairs. The kitchenette included a midsize fridge, along with a hot plate and an electric kettle. The door to what must have been a bathroom was closed and there was a coat rack adorned with a few winter coats and scarves.

As I couldn't exactly take pictures with Georgina right next to me, I did my best to commit all I saw to memory. Georgina opened the fridge and sitting on the shelf was a domed cake carrier that I did not recall ever seeing, and sitting on the shelf above it was a slender case.

This is how I knew we got lucky. Because if Georgina had known anything about knives, she'd know just by the brand that neither myself nor Shirleen, nor the caterer, would ever have a knife that was so mediocre it actually dulled while you were cutting.

I took this excuse for a knife anyway, pretending they were something I recognized and thanking her, and vehemently hoping this wouldn't be mentioned to the police.

As I tucked the knife into my bag, I spotted deep skepticism on Virgil's face. He said nothing though, not even letting a whisper of suspicion appear as Georgina led us out.

"I hope you were able to see all you wanted," Georgina said. "We're about to open–" She stopped short seeing Marcus in the hall, for he wasn't alone. Detective Constance Dimaandal stood there scribbling in her notebook.

"Where are the people who showed up about this podcast?" the detective asked.

"They're right there actually," Marcus said.

She turned to look at us, and her cool professional exterior rippled just slightly, but it wasn't from surprise. It was the look of someone who had lost a bet – and a bad one at that.

"I'd like to talk to you," Detective Dimaandal said, with no pretense that she was asking this of us. "I'm curious about your podcast. Unsolved mysteries are one of my chief interests, especially around this manor." She glanced at Georgina. "Could you delay opening up? Not for too long, I just have a few words for them."

"You're welcome to use this room," Marcus said, opening the door to a room set up as a meeting space with a small table and few chairs facing a projector screen.

I placed the cake carrier and knives onto the table. While Virgil and I sat in the chairs, Detective Dimaandal walked around, never letting her eyes move from the cake carrier. "Tell me about this podcast. Which unsolved mysteries are you into? Are you curious about the death that happened here New Year's Eve 1928? Or something more recent?"

"You mean the rocking chair incident in 1965? It's more of a ghost story," Virgil said, his attempt at a joke going down like a lead balloon.

"No, I don't mean that, and you know it." The detective pointed at the cake. "Are you tampering with evidence?"

"Oh no," I said quickly, hoping the pitch of my voice sounded quite genuine. She didn't seem to buy it as I continued. "I haven't done anything. We just found this."

"After sneaking in here," Dimaandal said.

"We walked through the front door," Virgil said. "It's not a crime scene; the police are gone. Nothing was marked off."

"True," the detective said, but didn't soften the edge of her words. "Why are you snooping around? Ruby Walton's death is police business, and not the work of amateur sleuths.

Don't deny it. You've been *inspired* to investigate. With CSI this, true crime shows that, and all those cookie-cutter shows with quirky investigators, and don't get me started on the hundred different versions of Sherlock Holmes. It may seem like a good idea, but no matter what you think, I assure you, there is no crime to be solved here."

"Then why have you returned to the manor?" I asked. "Did you forget something?"

"I did, it seems," she remarked. "This cake, where did you find it?"

"The staff room," I said, "with a knife. The door was–"

"Locked," Dimaandal finished for me. "I didn't press for them to look as it was too far away from the ballroom. It didn't seem important at the time. Clearly a miscalculation."

"A cake's missing," I blurted out. "You collected eleven cakes, but the tea cake, the one that Ruby had the slice from, is missing."

"Missing." Now Dimaandal looked less annoyed and more surprised, even a touch alarmed as she pointed to the carrier. "What about this cake?"

I reached for the carrier, and after remembering to put on my gloves, opened it. Notes of orange and cacao floated around me. The glazed pound cake sat on a daisy-patterned platter. Orange peels were cut into spirals and flower shapes, and a few orange flecks of the fruit popped against the rich dark brown of the cake. While the glaze was smudged slightly from being rocked around, it looked quite innocent and unaware it was being considered evidence.

"This is not the tea cake," I said.

"I know that much," the detective said. "What is this then?"

"The Orange Chocolate Cake," I said, "but not how Shirleen makes it."

"How do you know that?" Dimaandal said. "Tell me without eating it," she added as I leaned toward the cake. Her brown eyes were fixed on me, like a hawk. "You don't know how many so-called experts taste test unexplained food before me to poor effect."

"People do that?" Virgil asked.

The detective nodded grimly. "More often than you think."

I didn't intend to lick the cake, but I did hover my face above it and took a strong whiff. "This cake is made with black walnut extract. Shirleen always uses hazelnut."

"What does that prove?" the detective asked.

"Ruby made this cake," Virgil answered. He wrinkled his nose and then shuddered. "She made it with walnut, and I always hated it."

"Are you sure?" I asked.

"She used to bring it around often, back when they were still talking to each other," Virgil replied. "I had to eat the whole thing by myself once – you don't forget that easily."

The detective pointed to the knife I had pulled out when I grabbed my gloves. "And the knife. Is that Ruby's too?"

"It can't be," I said, reaching for that as well. I turned it over, exposing the brand stamped on the case. "It's a cheap blade and will cut so poorly only people who don't know food – but like to impress other people – will get it. It's the sort of knife people expect chefs to use."

"Did you find the knife with the cake?" the detective asked.

"That doesn't mean it was put together at the same time," I quickly replied.

"I'll be taking both of these for testing all the same. Your assistance has been noted, but let's not make it a habit."

"But we've been helpful. I told you there's a missing cake!"

"The only cake that matters is the one that's being tested." Dimaandal shook a finger at us. "As far as we know, Ruby Walton died from an allergic reaction to a bite of cake. Tragic, but nothing nefarious."

"There's a reason you showed up here," I said. "I bet the tox report was inconclusive or doesn't explain the anomalies you spotted."

Detective Dimaandal blinked and let silence hold her answer.

"You know something is wrong," I said pressing my luck, even as Virgil kept shaking his head for me to be quiet. "Something is not adding up. This cake, the tea cake that went missing, and this knife could be connected or not. I swear there was poison in play. In the cake or elsewhere!"

"Then, Miss Scott," Dimaandal said, "find that missing cake."

Before I could answer, there was a knock on the door and a middle-aged, uniformed officer poked her head in. "Detective D, you got a call you need to take."

"Coming," Dimaandal said before turning back to Virgil and me. "As fun as it was to chat, I'll have to cut this short. Just remember, this is police business. It's not a game."

She left the room, speaking to an officer in hushed tones.

The moment the door shut, Virgil pulled out his microphone to stop recording, I got out my camera and quickly snapped pictures of the cake and knife.

"She ran out of here too fast," I said. "I wanted to tell her I suspected it was cyanide."

"I'm sure the detective would have *loved* to hear that from you," Virgil drawled. Although as he tucked the microphone away, he was not as dismissive as his words might seem otherwise. There was concern as he watched me take pictures, and there was his manner of giving counsel that was a mix of his old profession and pragmatism. "You heard her, she wants us to vanish like yesterday's news."

"Even if I was right? Wouldn't she confirm it?"

"I don't think so," Virgil said. "I imagine when the autopsy is public, you'll have a hard time gaining access."

"I'm just curious."

"Some would say you're meddling."

"Because this is a mystery I will solve," I said.

He stopped short. "I thought we're doing this together?" Virgil protested.

"When convenient," I said.

To my surprise he gave a small chuckle. "You mean convenient to *you*."

"Of course, why would it be any different?" I quipped. I took one last photograph before I put away the camera.

We walked out into the hall while the detective was carrying on parallel conversations with her officer and whoever was on the phone. Her eyes tracked us as we passed, as if making sure neither the cake nor the knife walked out with us.

Once more outside, Virgil fell into step with me. "I've been meaning to ask, what's with carrying around a camera? I've met enough photographers to know that it's a pretty spiffy one."

I glanced at the Fuji X100S that had been a gift from my father, as we often traded cameras based on our preferences.

Boxy yet compact with a classic and retro feel, I nearly always had it with me.

"You carry around a microphone," I countered.

"I never know when inspiration will strike."

"Likewise," I replied. "I like the camera as it keeps me engaged when taking photographs of the world around me. It's an old habit of mine I only just returned to."

I could see him gearing up again to ask for more details, but my life was not a book from the library he could check out, so instead I asked, "Tell me about the *Moving Day* podcast. It's the one that convinced the publisher that it wouldn't be a terrible idea for you to cover the new cookbook, right?"

Virgil took the change in subject with ease. "It wasn't their approval that mattered, but my aunt is very careful about media these days. For good reason."

"You had to convince her?" I asked, quite surprised, for I had not known that part. Yet it didn't come as a complete shock, given how Shirleen acted churlish around the microphone.

"Why is that a surprise?" Virgil said, as he rightfully guessed my line of thinking. "She's very stubborn, but Aunt Shirls liked *Moving Day* and agreed to let me do this."

"Which is about your moving company," I said.

"It's about people moving, not the company itself," Virgil clarified. "You'd know that if you listened, because I never run ads for the company, despite my friend saying I'm leaving nothing but money on the table."

"I have listened," I said. Seeing the glint in his eyes, I decided not to mention I had turned it off after a few minutes. "Okay, I haven't listened too much." I pulled out my phone. "Which one do you recommend?"

"You don't have to force yourself to listen," Virgil said, rather quickly. "It's not true crime, so I know it's not your favorite."

"I don't mind," I laughed. "After so many missing white girls, kidnapped white girls, and strange murders in remote campgrounds, I need a palate cleanser. I listen to other things too, mostly other people in food media I admire, and even some weird science podcasts. I got really into this local history podcast recently. I'm really jazzed about the new episode drop, because it's mainly about Hunton Bay and its neighbors. Although my bicycling club has traveled all over Hunton Bay, there are places I would have never found without listening to the pod. So *Moving Day* is a nice change of pace for me."

I looked at Virgil expectantly, less curious about the actual podcast and more about his backpedaling the whole thing. We all had our secrets, and unfair or not, I wanted to know his even if I kept mine locked away.

Because after all, I wasn't the one with an aunt who had everything to lose and gain from this murder.

"A good one," Virgil finally said, "is *Nine Empty Perfume Bottles*."

"What makes it good?" I couldn't help but ask.

His smile slowly unfurled, letting the dimples shine through enough to make me temporarily forget the strange cakes, the other encounters we had at the manor, and how annoying he could be. "There's a mystery in the middle of it."

Interview: Austin Hammond

Virgil Sullivan, voiceover: *Austin Hammond is the co-founder of* Flair Spotlight, *which started accepting clients ten years ago. Of the five publicists, he has the most experience, having worked for over two decades as a publicist for writers, artists, and even actors. He also brought to the company one of its biggest clients, Shirleen Foster, for the anniversary edition of* Season by Season.

Virgil Sullivan: *What does a publicist do that I can't do myself? Don't you just send emails and call people?*

Austin Hammond: *Anyone can send an email, but it's how it's positioned that matters. People want access, but they don't want easy access. They want mystery. They want people to be shrouded in secrets. They want to wonder. Pop stars don't reach out to a venue begging for a spot. They send someone in with a pitch they can't refuse. I do that for my clients, and a little more as needed.*

Chapter 9

Although I downloaded the episode Virgil had mentioned, plus a few others from his podcast, I didn't give it a listen as I spent the rest of the afternoon hunting down the knife and recreating the Orange Chocolate Cake. I made the cake mostly to pound out my feelings, as despite the brand name I couldn't figure out where the knife might have come from.

I knew it must have originated at the housewares section at a local grocery chain. As it was a regional chain, that limited the spread, but there were seventeen stores in Virginia, with double that number in North Carolina and even a few in Delaware and Maryland. Which didn't narrow things down or provide any helpful clues beyond the explanation the knife didn't drop out of the sky.

I still had Detective Dimaandal's warning echoing in my ears, but I also recalled how she listened and considered what we had to share. We found something she hadn't, and she considered it earnestly enough to challenge me to find the missing cake.

By the time I got my version of the Orange Chocolate Cake out and decorated, it was time for my weekly ride with the Cruising Hunton Bay Bikers.

When I joined the bicycle club, at the usual meet up spot at Mermaid Pier, I rolled up at the same time as Sunil and Jessica, who were bundled up quite well against the cold. Lights decorated their bikes bright enough to cut through the fast-growing gloom.

Married and a few years older than me, they were exactly the artsy friends I knew I'd make when I moved into the area. They were too busy with work to have pets, but they did enjoy looking after my trio of rascals when the need arose.

Jessica was the reason they were in Hunton Bay, as she was a graduate of Hook College, and the connections she had here brought her to the Hunton Bay Dance Academy, after her retirement from professional dancing. Although she traveled around with dance troupes at Alvin Ailey, she adored teaching children to love dancing. On my card of food preferences, it was often easier to list what she could eat instead of what she couldn't, as she had a laundry list of allergies and food sensitivities paired with an adventurous spirit to try what she could. Jessica was the reason we started weekly dinners in the first place, as I wanted to prove I could make tasty dishes that considered her allergies, and the best proof is an audience. Of all my friends, Jessica was often in the kitchen with me, assisting and helping me prep – and splitting the good bits of pan drippings before we brought out the food.

Sunil worked as a film and radio archivist at the local radio station, WVHB, that was collaborating with Hook College to document what he called the "loves and lives of college students" by looking at archival film and radio from decades past. A film buff and true movie lover, if I wanted to watch any film – be it anime with subtitles, comic book movies, romantic comedies, Oscar bait movies, films from Bollywood and Nollywood, horror films from Korea and Japan, and terrible adaptations of wonderful books – Sunil would only ask when and where. He adored film as a genre and enjoyed listening to my takes as much as seeing a movie. His food preferences were few, although he didn't like highly processed meat substitutes. Also, because he grew up with a Bangladeshi mother who went heavy on the spices, I had yet to cook a dish for him that made him pause to comment on the heat level, even while the rest of our friends rolled on the floor calling for milk.

"Now those are some bright lights," Sunil said. "You said you were going to razzle dazzle it for this ride. I had doubts, I had concerns, and I had fears that you would overload your bicycle, but I was once again proven wrong. You have outdone yourself once again, Scott."

"Thank you, thank you," I said affecting a short bow as I sat astride my bike. I had carefully strung up strands of battery powered multicolored lights along my handles and bike frame, so the effect transformed my bicycle into something extraordinary. "The only thing more fun than putting these lights together was planning for this week's dinner. You'll be there, right?"

"Of course, though we won't be there for Christmas Eve dinner," Sunil said.

"Once the final bows are done for my students," Jessica added, "we're dashing off to catch the train all the way to Seattle. We should get there before Christmas Eve."

"And if not?" I asked.

"We'll just turn back around on the train to avoid all the complaints," Sunil said, as he pressed a kiss to Jessica's cheek. "I always wanted to go all the way across the country by train, and this is a good excuse. What about you, when and where are you flying out to? I'm jealous, I wish my folks would fly me out for the holidays."

"We only do trips because my family stopped doing presents a long time ago, after we all got each other the same blender for Christmas," I said. "My dad's flying here and then we'll take the train up to Providence to collect my sister. We're going to Martha's Vineyard this year."

"Oh, it'll be lovely, but not as lovely as summertime," Jessica teased. "My aunt has a place in Oak Bluffs, and I adore the gingerbread cottages. Remind me to tell you all about the restaurants you must try." Her smile faded slightly. "I'm glad to see you in good spirits; we were worried about you. All that terrible news about the cookbook author you're working with. I'm glad she wasn't arrested. How are you holding up?"

"I'm fine," I said, hoping I could quickly brush aside their concerns.

"A woman died right in front of you," Sunil exclaimed. "You shouldn't be in a rush to let anything settle."

Bells jingled loud enough to stop our conversation, before the fearless leader of the bicycle club, James, whistled over the crowd and cried, "Let's ride, folks!"

I sped off on my bicycle before anyone could stop and ask questions, easily pedaling my way to the front of the group as we rode along the pier that was owned by Hook College's rowing club. This, as well as the brilliancy of the lights strung up across homes all preparing for the Christmas light competition, got me away from them easily enough, but not for long. Jessica and Sunil easily caught up the longer the ride went, as my bicycle was distinct enough they could keep finding it.

I tried to use the others in the club to block conversation, but as the nights had grown long and cold, there were fewer bodies to act as a buffer.

"You know, Eden said to keep an eye on you," Jessica remarked, as the pair finally boxed me in. "Has something happened?"

"Nothing," I said. "I was just asking questions and poking around. I'm sure you saw the news around Shirleen and her history with the victim."

"Quite a bit, mostly through the group chat. I think we're just shocked to be this close to such news," Jessica remarked. "A couple of the people I worked with even asked me if I knew any more, since I'd mentioned you're working with Shirleen in the past. It's an accidental death, isn't it? Heart attack or allergic reaction?"

I gave up then, as I didn't want to be chased all over town. "What did Eden tell you?"

"You're playing detective, even if you'd deny it when asked directly." Sunil leaned over eagerly. "Do you need help snooping around? Because I'm your man for that."

"No need," I said quickly as Jessica tittered.

"No, no, feel free to borrow my husband, I've neglected him this past month," Jessica cried far too gaily.

"I have help already," I insisted. "Shirleen's nephew wants to find out what happened as well. I wouldn't say we're investigating, but we're thinking that Shirleen might have been framed. Those old interview clips resurfacing were far too well timed. They must be hard to find."

"Actually, they're not," Sunil said.

The biking group had stopped at the end of the bike trail facing a blaze of red traffic lights. As we waited for the notoriously long light to change, I craned my head over to Sunil. "What do you mean?"

"You forget where I work?"

"How could I?" I said. "You were able to connect me with the producers for a segment Shirleen gets to do next week."

"Then you should remember I have access to archives, and that while the radio station that Shirleen did her call-in show doesn't exist anymore, WVHB has it all."

"All? How do you know?"

"Lots of people have been interested since the announcement of the new cookbook. Fans and her publisher mostly, but someone who wasn't either recently messaged the station wanting access to the files. It was sent around the end of November – 23rd or 24th, but I just saw it."

The light changed to green and we quickly crossed the street. Nearly a dozen bicycles streamed across into a neighborhood glittering with Christmas lights. Sunil and I fell back to the middle of the group as his words had excited my imagination. "Can I get access to the archives?"

"No. Not without putting in a request. Fair warning, it'll take weeks for it to get fulfilled, since we want to make sure you won't destroy equipment and steal records. If you get permission from either Shirleen Foster herself or her beneficiary, access can be granted easily."

"I don't think that will be a problem," I said, thinking the time had come to see how insistent Virgil was about us working together. "Just tell me when I should come by."

The next day, I arrived for my previously scheduled meeting with Austin with a tin of peppermint bark and the hope the candy would be enough to cover Virgil's unannounced appearance.

"I'm equal to peppermint bark, not even something like cookies or brownie bars?" Virgil quipped as he met me outside the coworking space where Austin kept his office.

Virgil was still wearing his glasses, suggesting this was a semi-permanent change. He had also ridden his bicycle over, arriving just as I locked my own. I didn't think he would show, but I was glad to see him and his microphone.

"Austin doesn't like chocolate or caramel," I said as I held up the snowman tin. "But mint is a flavor he has in frequent rotation. It's good to know everyone's food preferences, especially for times like this."

Virgil was still eyeing the tin with more than a fair share of amusement. "I'm more interested that you think he needs a bribe."

"Just because he barely told you a thing in the interview doesn't mean he'll do the same to me. It's not a bribe," I said, "it's just a way to ease into conversation."

"I doubt it'll work."

For all our concerns, Austin barely noted Virgil at all.

He was on the phone as we arrived at his tiny office, and he gestured for us to shut the door. The desk of his coworker was empty, so Virgil drew that chair over as I sat in the remaining chair across from Austin. He tapped several things on his computer, before he abruptly ended the call and gave me his full attention.

"You will have to make all of the food for the appearance at WVHB, not just the prep work," Austin said to me, hopscotching as usual over pleasantries. "Also, be ready to speak on camera or even do the appearance solo. It's the condition we had to meet to keep the taping."

"They want to cancel?" Virgil asked.

"They're worried," Austin said, dodging the direct question. He absently rearranged the pencils neatly lined up on his desk, pushing them in and out of order. "The internet chatter about Shirleen is about old drama. The allegations will fade. Since Ruby Walton has just died, we must tread carefully. I suppose the funeral will be soon. I heard it's already planned for the end of the week."

"That soon?" I cried.

"It's quick," Austin shrugged, "but I suppose at that age you're expecting death anyway."

It was a poor joke and neither Virgil nor I rewarded it with even a polite smile.

"Ruby Walton was only seventy-five. She was hardly expecting death so soon," Virgil said.

"Especially not at the party," I said and slipped in a lie. "She seemed very keen to talk to me about something she had planned."

"You too?" Austin asked, and his eyes snapped back from the screens, favoring me once more with his full attention. "She kept trying to pull me aside, asking me to help her with something. Although I'm not sure what she thought I could do. I merely arranged for meetings with the media who have the runway to spark attention I couldn't help her publish something."

"Publish?" I asked.

"I don't know, a cookbook maybe?" he huffed. "Either way, it wasn't important. The police didn't even ask about that, why are you?"

"I'm just trying to figure out what happened that night."

"You were running around quite a bit," Austin eyed the snowman tin I had placed on the corner of his desk. "What is this again?"

"Peppermint bark," I supplied. I nudged the tin even closer to him, jostling the lid so minty goodness drifted into the air. "You have a choice between milk chocolate, and white chocolate. I used peppermint oil, with pieces of peppermint candy in it for a nice crunch. No nuts."

"How lovely." Austin pulled out a sizeable chunk of white chocolate bark and took a hefty bite.

His nod and a sharp look of appreciation coaxed a smile out of me.

Austin relaxed.

"There was a lot going on that night," he said between bites. "I had been there since just before the museum closed for the day. There was so much to arrange, it's not really my job, but with all the chaos of getting it booked in the first place I wanted to be there."

"Because Naomi made such a mess of things?" I ventured.

"Mainly yes," Austin nodded. "Granted, I haven't had much interaction with her, but I'd never thought she would cause so much trouble. Things that should have been booked were canceled. The wrong guest list went out. I don't blame Shirleen for firing her, although I wish she was there that night, just so I could get answers out of her. The decorations were sent elsewhere and had to be brought here. Thank goodness I had handled the caterers directly, because that would have delayed us further, even if the traffic did it for us. I planned for a buffer of time, given we had some important guests. Still, we went right through it. We had barely even started before, well, *it* happened."

"Do you have the guest list for the evening?" I asked. "I was going to try to get it from Naomi, so I can make apologies for what happened."

"I have one," Austin took another bite of the peppermint bark. "I even have a list of those confirmed to be there, plus a few surprises. I don't think I ever expected to see Glenn Dupont, although to be frank, given what Shirleen told me, I expected worse. Mr. Dupont chatted with me for a short while, like we're buddies. He wanted to know about Shirleen's other events and how he can take part. Don't worry," Austin said before Virgil or I could interject. "I didn't say a thing. He's a charmer, but I never give my client's secrets away. I'm just glad he didn't run into Shirleen that night, although the damage was already done. She was so distracted. I could barely get her to follow the schedule, which was so frustrating. I mean if she didn't insist Ruby get that slice of cake, none of this would have happened, and the evening would have gone off without a hitch!"

I doubted it.

If the cake was poisoned with Ruby in mind, the evening would be ruined regardless, because such a cake would have gotten to her one way or another – or into someone else's hands.

"Are you blaming my aunt?" Virgil leaned forward, his words pointed enough that Austin's smile wavered as he retreated.

"I'm not accusing her of anything, but as I told the police–"

"You *told* the police!" Virgil pounding on the armrest may have been theatrical, but the blistering contempt in his voice was not. "You are her publicist, if you can't say a good word for her, who can?"

"I can't spin what was already seen by everyone else," Austin remarked, unabashed. "The feud with Ruby Walton is well known and she only added fire to the scene. Surely you know better than me."

"I was in high school when it peaked," Virgil fumed, annoyed at the finger of blame pointed at him. "You know teenagers, if it didn't affect us, we didn't care."

"Well, I suppose it's personal to you," Austin said, "and not all went public. I only know about it because Shirleen told me more when she hired me. Ruby said that Shirleen was an excellent cook, but she couldn't do a consistent bake."

"Couldn't do a consistent bake?" I pondered.

Virgil turned to me surprised. "But you and Aunt Shirls have been baking for weeks."

I had been doing the baking for the most part as she dictated to me. She had gone on about the recipes, and flavor profiles, adjusting things based on my suggestion and input for modernization. At the end of the day, however, I was doing the baking from mixing to the final touches on the cake.

"She is not as young as she once was," I ventured.

"I know she's been ill," Austin said. "She got very sick six years ago–"

"And is hale and hearty as ever," Virgil interjected. "This was just an accusation, probably tinged with jealousy."

"True, but it struck a chord." Austin took a big bite of the bark, and it loudly crunched in the room.

I hoped he chipped a tooth, but alas, he continued to munch on.

Austin handed over the guest list. I watched as he emailed it without further protest, buying my nonsense about sending cards of apology.

I left him the tin, although Austin promised to give it back to me, as it was such a lovely one.

Virgil and I rode down the elevator, and he opened his coat revealing the blinking microphone.

As he checked its battery I asked, "Did you know that about the feud?"

Virgil seesawed the air with his hand. "I've gotten pieces, as I reached out to old collaborators and their relatives. No one said anything too terrible, but I knew it was on the surface."

"Anyone in those batches we should speak to again?" I asked.

Virgil began counting on his fingers. "Nah, some of them don't live here, or have no reason to frame her. The ones I've done already are those that still like my aunt. Only one person called to ask to get the interview retracted given the news. There might be more in coming days, but we'll see."

"Who was that person?" I asked.

"Legally I can't tell you, but you haven't met them. This is someone who knew my aunt way back when she was working at the newspaper in her hometown. I was excited, it's very hard to get interviews with folks from her newspaper days."

"What about her radio days?" I asked. "Is that a bit easier?"

"Well, she was mostly in the 757 so it isn't so hard to find people still living nearby eager to talk."

"Especially with WVHB's archives?" I asked.

"Yeah, I suppose. Why are you asking about that?"

"I have a friend who works in the archives, and he said he can let me snoop around, if I get permission from Shirleen or a beneficiary."

Virgil snorted. "My aunt will not say no, if you're worried about that."

"I'm not afraid," I lied through my smile. "I figured you'd be the easier ask, and we could go look, as we are working together. You have such an eye for detail and could see something I might have missed."

"Now I know you're trying to sweet talk me!" Virgil laughed. "I mean it's true, but Keisha, you don't have to give it a spin. If you think there's something there in the archives, maybe it's worth looking into. That clip of Aunt Shirls and Ruby that was going around, I did some digging, it was newly uploaded, and somebody got it somewhere and sat on it for major impact. The archive will tell us how that happened. Do I have to sign a permission slip or is it just an email?"

As we rode the elevator down to the lobby, I detailed what Sunil had told me and what days would be best to go.

"If we're lucky," I said dashing ahead, "the archives might give us a match to whoever shows up on the guest list Naomi has."

"I get why you want to talk to Naomi, but is it worth the time spent?" Virgil said, darting away as a shopper bustled past with overladen bags. "Naomi was fired by my aunt; she's not going to want to talk to either of us."

"Did she cancel her interview?"

"No, I'm supposed to meet her at the library, but a no-show is still possible."

"Naomi will likely be very honest. She has nothing to lose and is probably rightfully angry."

"Will she talk?" Virgil ventured. "You gave away a good bribe."

"Peppermint bark was never going to work on Naomi," I scoffed. "Sympathy will!"

"Sympathy as in…"

"Nothing I want your microphone to catch," I said.

Virgil chuckled. "I can edit to make sure what rude things you say to loosen up Naomi's tongue won't appear. Talking to Naomi might be tricky. I don't know how she feels about you, but I always thought she didn't like me."

"Then you might as well go home," I said.

His eyes narrowed. "Why?"

"Because Naomi just ran into the Christmas market."

"What?" Virgil took a full 360-degree turn that did him no favors, until I steered him in the right direction. Across and further down the street a wooden sign with sparkly Christmas trees advertised the Holiday Fair in the Armstead Arcade.

I patted his shoulder and headed across the street. "Naomi's wearing a furry oversized candy-striped hat with a giant pompom. Can't be too hard to find."

Chapter 10

While most stores promised to whisk you into Holiday Town, the moment I stepped through the doors into the Armstead Arcade, I was smacked in the face with festive cheer. I didn't know what was stronger, the piped-in evergreen scent that tickled my nose or Mariah Carey's clear effervescent voice ringing through the air. Or maybe it was the aggressively green, red, and gold decorations, and fake snow décor that made it clear you weren't in Kansas anymore.

"Oh my," Virgil said as he staggered at the assault to the senses. The old-fashioned mutter seemed the perfect match for his wide-eyed astonishment. "There're so many people here already! How will we find her?"

"By splitting up. You take this fork and I'll go the other way. We'll meet up in the middle."

"Unless there's another exit," Virgil muttered, but he took a deep breath and plunged into the half of the arcade with toy vendors and a Santa Claus tinkering in his workshop to the delight of several children.

My side was only marginally less busy, as the crowd lingered longer between the vendors. The Holiday Market had stalls and tables for local pop-ups and other small businesses and organizations in the area. A sweet old couple had elbowed their way to the front for the prime real estate, not just to sell coffee and hot chocolate but advertise their downtown shop. From there, shoppers entered the market facing goodies of all sorts. One side oozed vintage and traditional vibes as stalls were bursting with wreaths, wrapping paper, mini Christmas trees, Santa hats, elf costumes, and candy canes all for sale. Vendors sold caramels and candies, popcorn dyed green and red, and boxes of gingerbread and gingersnaps. There were seven different vendors selling ornaments, but they all had different themes from local regional pride to classics. A blue and silver stand sold everything from chocolate coins and dreidels to mini menorahs. There was a table with several trains traveling through a snow-covered village, a candlemaker with a stand called "Stink, Stank, and Stunk" with unusually scented soy candles, and someone representing Refugee Voices sold beautiful handsewn tablecloths. I waved at Mandy from Mermaid Pirate Bookshop, and as I passed Tito's Spot, I promised Romy's cousin Liza I'd be back later to sample the lumpia.

It pained me to quickly walk past them both and keep short the polite chatter I usually made, but I didn't have time to linger as I needed to keep looking for Naomi.

My boast to Virgil was crashing down around my ears with each step.

I thought finding a white girl with brown hair in an outrageous Santa hat would be easy, but I passed by five as I walked into the market. After walking up to two people by mistake, I contented myself with lingering around various wares until I got a good look.

In the fleeting moments of my first glimpse, I had the impression Naomi had seen me. Shock had so comically rattled her face that I could see her eyes widen from across the street before she darted into the market, a sparkling red and green gift bag swinging from her hand as she ran.

I looked for that gift bag now, figuring that would be my best shot, and was rewarded when a glimpse of green led me to where Naomi lingered at a gourmet hot chocolate and mug stand.

As the younger woman read the label of a hazelnut blend, I strode right up and picked up a mug featuring a gingerbread man with his broken foot stitched up with frosting. Pretending to look at the mug, I made a great show of looking to my right and seeing Naomi.

"Ah, Naomi, funny running into you here!"

Naomi jumped with genuine surprise, and I mentally gave myself a pat on the back for being able to sneak up on her.

Freckled with curly brown hair often in pigtails, she had let her hair fall loose and only the hat kept it tamed. Her petite face and rounded features made her appear slightly younger at first, and peaches and cream skin often revealed the swing in her emotion as her flush of embarrassment, anger, or annoyance was quite prominent. She was just short of ten years younger than me, and going to pastry school at night. While Shirleen and Austin were quick to see her as a girl, I saw someone whose mistakes were not the fault of youth, but carelessness.

As I did most of my recipe testing in my own kitchen, I didn't get a chance to work with her often, but I met with her enough to not be surprised that her time with Shirleen was over. I had never observed major issues, but I could tell that Naomi was often overwhelmed by certain aspects of her work.

"Keisha," Naomi squeaked. "Are you by yourself?"

"Yes," I said waving the mug about like a hostess on a late-night infomercial. "I'm off for the day, exploring the Holiday Market. It's always busy, but it's going to be way more next week with all the last-minute shoppers."

"I ain't complaining," called the knitting vendor behind the stand. She beamed at me and pointed to a pyramid stack of tins. "I got some samples you can try if you like. Let me know what you fancy."

"Thanks," I said. Still returning the vendor's smile, I put down the mug I held to pick up another with a grouchy cat in a lumpy Christmas sweater. "What do you think? Will it be a good present for Shirleen?"

Naomi stiffened. "I'm not the person to ask about that."

"Well, Shirleen is a hard person to get a gift for."

"And hard to please," Naomi muttered. Louder, she added, "I don't know if you heard, but I'm not working for her anymore." Her words were followed by a grimace as if she fully expected me to know this already.

"I may have heard something about it," I said, and made sure to amp up the empathy in my voice, adding in a soothing tone, "But I'm surprised to hear it, and so sorry for that to have happened. I would have never expected Shirleen to do that."

"Shirleen's great, a genius, and really attentive when it comes to teaching. But tell her the wrong thing once, make one mistake, and she'll never let you forget it."

"What did you do that was so bad?" I asked.

Naomi adjusted her grip on the gift bag she still held, to select a pink mug with yarn balls stacked to appear like a snowman. She cradled the mug, her fingers tightening around it. "I accidentally invited her ex-husband to the party. That's the offense that got me fired, and I swear I meant nothing by it. I was working with a contact list that she *gave* me. How was I supposed to know that it was decades old? It was hard enough figuring out who was on it to begin with. Apparently, she kept every contact, but their importance was marked by a system of icons set up by a previous assistant that was often hard to decipher."

"A code," I murmured, thinking of some original recipes that Shirleen had shown me that used her particular brand of shorthand. It was like reading a coded message – you knew there was a way to unlock it but were uncertain of the key. I had brute forced most of the code but still needed Shirleen's help. "Didn't she use this system," I continued, "to mark out her friends and the people she wanted to be in touch with?"

"I don't know about that." Naomi put the mug back and swung her head to look unseeingly at the tins of hot chocolate. "Shirleen has enemies and rivals, some I guess she deserved, but sometimes to get by you need to be as sharp as your knives. Many of the names in the book were never even her friends, but simply those she was keeping close tabs on. I invited them all to the party by mistake without knowing that pesky detail. They didn't all show up. Some invites never even made it, some politely refused, but quite a few actually contacted Shirleen, which is how I got in trouble." Naomi rubbed her neck. "I may have tried to connect with Roselle Pierrepont, using Shirleen's name, and that didn't quite work out."

I imagined it wouldn't.

I also imagined flaunting Shirleen's name at Roselle Pierrepont was the burning house of cards that got Naomi in trouble in the first place, along with the subsequent invites to Glenn and Ruby.

Owner of the famous Pierrepont Café out in Indianapolis, Roselle Pierrepont had most recently been shunned at this year's Whisk and Kettle Fest, because Shirleen had been asked about the praline pies the café served. The question had come out like a summer thunderstorm during a quick fireside interview following the new cookbook announcement. Without missing a beat, Shirleen quipped, "Pierrepont's pies were a worthy substitute if you cannot find the time or inclination to travel to find something far more satisfactory."

How Naomi didn't remember this bit, I could only chalk up to the fact that she forgot older folks tended to go to the grave holding tight to their grudges.

Still, I was sympathetic enough that I wasn't going to drive the knife in deeper.

"I'd like to see a list of contacts," I said, gently nudging our conversation back. "I think I'm taking your place until the New Year and–"

"Don't do it!" Naomi all but grabbed my arm as she cried, her face bright with panic.

Only the reminder of a whole display case of mugs behind kept me rooted in place, and from throwing her off. I felt like one of my cats when a stranger tried to pet them. Except I couldn't wiggle away and dig my claws into the younger woman. I bit my lip to keep me from shouting at her to let go, and Naomi took my expression to mean something else.

The younger woman only tightened her grip. "Don't work for her as an assistant, that's a terrible idea!"

"I am already working with her."

"As her tester, you're working *with* her. Once you start doing her emails and taking her calls, you'll be working *for* her, and it'll only get worse! You should ask Janice."

"Who's Janice?" I asked.

"A former assistant, I think? I've seen her name in old papers. She went from being one of the co-authors of the early cookbooks to her assistant, after a similar mistake. If you do anything, don't do that!"

"Is that all you know?" I said, sniffing out something interesting. While I knew that Shirleen had other assistants before Naomi, Janice was not a name I'd seen or heard referenced before. Maybe there was a reason for that?

Naomi pulled back and shook her head as if she had a sudden change of heart. "Forget I said anything, I'm just causing trouble."

She turned and bolted from the stand.

As I still had a mug in hand, I was about to put it back when I heard her cry out in surprise not far away.

"Oh, Virgil, I didn't see you!" Naomi stumbled away, after nearly colliding with the podcaster.

I wondered if he had been lurking about, but thought he was staying back to let me do all the hard work. I nearly gave him a thumbs-up for excellent timing to prevent Naomi wiggling away.

Gently assuring the blubbering Naomi that no apologies were necessary, Virgil bestowed upon her a charming smile.

"I thought that might be you, what a fantastic hat," Virgil said.

"Oh, this," Naomi flicked it with a coquettish little laugh. "It's just a silly thing. My friend gave it to me as a White Elephant gift last year."

"Well, it suits you and it's perfect to go shopping in today."

Naomi's face turned bright red, and she averted her eyes.

"I don't want to intrude," he said hastily, "but I thought we were meeting today at the library. I know it's a bit early, but I was looking forward to talking with you."

"You were?" Naomi said with such enthusiasm, it was all I could do to keep from sighing.

I don't know where Virgil got the idea the girl didn't like him, because I could already tell it was quite the opposite.

It may have even explained the gift bag, which I was pretty certain held something she had painstakingly picked out for him.

Which meant that wasn't guilty panic that sent her bolting into the market, but a crush making her see what one would despair the most to view: the object of her affections out with someone that was not her.

The shock that had crossed her face when I first spoke to her had been her realizing the truth to that pesky problem.

"Shall we go somewhere quiet?" Virgil suggested, seemingly oblivious to the deepening of the girl's scarlet flush despite his glasses.

"Quiet would be best for the interview," I interjected.

Naomi gave a little start as if she had forgotten about me already.

I continued, "We won't take too much of your time asking about the cookbook and working with Shirleen."

"Oh," Naomi drooped. "You wanted to meet me for the podcast. I should have known." Puzzlement crossed his face, but before he could even ask, Naomi chirruped in a cheerful tone. "Why don't we go to the library like we planned?"

The downtown library was cool and quiet compared to the market. Walking past tropical potted plants looming over us and the benevolent painted face of the city's first Black librarian reading to a group of children, I went up to one of the librarians and got us a meeting room for the next hour. I didn't think we'd need all that time but given how Virgil set up the microphone on the table, I thought it might run longer than planned.

His first opening questions were about the cookbook and how Naomi first learned about Shirleen. Despite her bitterness about their ending, she couldn't hide the delight she had at meeting the famous chef and cookbook author.

As I sat pretending to take notes, it was interesting watching as warmth entered her face as she spoke of the earlier encounters with Shirleen.

Virgil, of course, did not ask about the party or the cascade of mistakes that got her fired. He did ask something that I did not get to ask. It happened near the end, where he had pretended to switch off the microphone, but he had left his hand to cover the telltale blinking light.

"Did my aunt know about Ruby being invited to the party before Ruby showed up that night?"

Naomi tugged at the handle of the gift bag. "She learned about it when we were going over the guest list the day before. The caterer wanted to check on food preferences since there were several last-minute changes to menus. It came out then, and I thought Shirleen was going to lose it as she was already mad about Glenn. Not," Naomi said quickly, "that she said she was going to do something. She was just upset enough to let others see."

"Then she fired you, I'm sorry about that." Virgil said.

The color rose once more in Naomi's face. "It's alright! I was thinking of going to pastry school full time. I did learn a lot from Shirleen, more than I realized."

"If I needed help with anything, how can I reach you?" I asked.

Naomi gave me not a phone number, but her contact information on a social media platform that I seldom used, with the handle @bakingonsunshine.

Naomi hopped up. With her face redder than Santa's hat, she shoved the bag at Virgil.

"This is for you. Merry Christmas!"

She dashed off but didn't leave the library, ducking around a pillar wrapped with tinsel.

"This is for me?" Virgil asked with great surprise.

"Open it," I muttered, "She's waiting for your reaction."

"What? She's still here? Then why–"

"Don't look," I cautioned. "She's shy because she has a crush on you."

Although I knew the word confounded, I had never had an example before me in real life, until Virgil stopped pulling out the tissue paper to stare at me as this news registered.

He had no idea, and this realization seemed so genuine it made it all the more amusing. I didn't quite understand it, but watching his astonishment grow, I had a glimmer of why Naomi had taken a fancy to him.

"What did she get you?" I asked.

Virgil pulled out of the bag a solar powered battery pack and a small, waterproof field notebook and pen, plus an assortment of wrapped chocolates.

"Wow, this is nice." Virgil twirled the pen around, delighting our little spy. "I only just mentioned I'd like something like that and she got it. Naomi is quite thoughtful and observant."

I glanced back over my shoulder, but Naomi had left, slipping out the library's automatic doors with a broad smile despite her pink cheeks. "I wonder if she knows more than she lets on."

"We all observe much, just need the right questions to make us remember." Virgil put everything back in the bag and put it aside as he considered me. "Before I found you two, what did you learn?"

"Just a few extra details." I quickly summarized for the still recording microphone's sake as much as his. "Overall, it's a bad look for Naomi."

Virgil emitted a soft whistle. "It's also not looking good for Aunt Shirls."

"You don't think she did it?" I ventured.

"Of course not!" Virgil scowled, betraying a flash of offense by my question. "It's just in the court of public opinion she's losing. She may have even already lost."

I shook a berating finger at him. "Talking like that is not helping matters."

Virgil shrugged. "Can't help it. I'm very much a 'prepare for the worst' type of guy."

"Well don't be." I turned my phone to him, showing off a series of positive social media posts, defending Shirleen's reputation and character. "Not everything is as bad as it seems."

"I wonder if it's the same with the others. I didn't get a chance to speak with anyone else from that night."

"Let's contact the guests," I suggested.

"Now?" He blinked.

"Why not, we have the list. I can get us a few more hours in the meeting room," I said. I paused, realizing I was making assumptions again about him and his time. "Unless you have to be somewhere else soon?"

"Nothing that can't wait," Virgil replied. "My interview is with Lucia tomorrow."

There were around 125 people who had been invited to the party. Of that group, around 43 had been delayed due to traffic. Many were local to the area, although a few traveled as far as from DC, Philly, NYC, and even Oakland. We started with a system, trading names and working our way down a list.

I got through my portion of the names quicker, as I had people that Shirleen didn't know intimately. On his side of the meeting room, Virgil explained the same story over and over again, to friends and old acquaintances who had much to say to him. In contrast for me, I had clipped and short conversations, and more confusion about why I was even calling in the first place despite me doing my best to echo Virgil.

"I could hardly see a thing," Loren Gaffney declared. "I was too far back when Ruby fell. I didn't even know something occurred until the announcement was made."

"I think the announcement was a mistake," William Billups said when I called him next. "Everyone started panicking. Sure, the screaming didn't help, but we didn't have a clue otherwise."

"Part of me isn't surprised," Carmen Hollingshead told me in hushed tones. "Things like this always happen when Shirleen and Ruby got together, though granted no one ever died before."

"None of this," Malcolm Demetrious Freeman declared, "explains why you are asking me questions better asked by the police." The dulcet tones in my ears reminded me that he used to be an opera singer before a lack of opportunity pushed him to diversify his interests. While many were eager to dine at one of his many well-renowned Brooklyn restaurants, I wanted to be invited into one of his super exclusive dinner parties.

I felt like shaking in my boots to even speak to him, but I wasn't about to let that stop me.

"I'm asking because I was right there," I admitted. "I saw Ruby collapse and want to understand the reasons around it. Since it's causing complications for Shirleen."

"You would know this quite well," Malcolm said, "for you are the recipe developer working with Shirleen. The former data analyst."

"You know who I am?"

"I know everything and everyone worth knowing, and you, darling, are a person worth knowing," the restaurateur drawled. "If you're doing this for Shirleen, I suppose I can tell you what I saw. I saw how the items in the room were arranged at an odd number. It didn't seem quite right given all the careful planning."

"What do you mean?" I prompted.

"The table and decorations, how they were arranged around the room. The ballroom was more of an oval, which made it hard to balance things evenly, especially when part of the room was taken over by staging and other equipment. I have put together many an event in challenging spaces, so I knew there were only a few ways that room could be set up, and something was off about it. It had clearly been set up one way and then changed rather abruptly."

"There were a lot of things that were still being settled," I said, thinking of Austin on his phone and how some of the decorations were still being moved into place.

"After some drastic rearrangements," Malcolm said. "I got there fairly early and they were was still moving around. It didn't look terrible. But the discerning eye always knows. Shirleen certainly wasn't aware of the changes, because she mentioned having to rethink part of a speech she was giving that night. She could do it but didn't like how the lights were set up. I heartily agreed with her, of course."

Malcolm shared a few more observations but couldn't chat longer as he had urgent business to attend to. I wrapped up my call as Virgil tossed his phone onto the table in a huff.

"People don't pay attention to anything useful!"

"Which is something all the same," I said. "That they told you nothing – assuming they were telling the truth – means we can count them out as suspects. How many can we strike out?"

"Quite a few, but there are several names I will have to keep calling until I get an answer. One of them I was trying to lock down for a while. Brandon Morton makes documentaries and has been interested in my aunt for ages as a subject for his next film. He should return my call, but he did say he was traveling. It sounds like an excuse."

"Why do you want to talk to Brandon Morton?" I asked.

"He was very close to everything happening – he was the man that helped."

"The man," I echoed. It took a moment, but I recalled the man who had been urged by the nurse to assist. His features were murky to me, but something else stood out sharper. "He was very reluctant."

"He was grabbed because he was the nearest," Virgil said. "I spoke with the nurse, who just happens to be a retired army nurse. She gave a very detailed description of everything she saw and did, including what she saw around Ruby. Which is good because very few people were able to do the same."

"What do you mean?" I asked. "I'd gotten several people to tell me what they saw."

"Did they tell you what they witnessed, or did they answer questions based on what *you* thought they might have seen?" Virgil asked.

That he might be close to the truth was very irritating, but it had nothing on the feeling that he might be right. That I had asked all the wrong questions in my zeal to get answers.

"What did the nurse say?"

"She tapped Morton to help because it looked like he knew what was going on, but when he spoke to me, he had no clue what I meant at first."

"Which is why you want to have a longer conversation with him," I realized.

"One of many reasons," Virgil replied. "One of many."

Interview: Naomi Fleming

Virgil Sullivan, voiceover: *Currently in pastry school, Naomi Fleming grew up without even realizing that Shirleen's recipes held such a major influence in her life. Her teacher had shared the Red and Green Velvet Cake one Christmas and a single bite inspired Naomi to pursue baking as a career, although she never would have dreamed she would get the chance to work with Shirleen Foster herself.*

Virgil Sullivan: *How did what you learned from Shirleen surprise you? Didn't she say that while you were an assistant you were also there to cook as well?*

Naomi Fleming: *Mostly in that I learned to do so much. She often told me to prep this, prepare that, and I often had to figure it out. Shirleen never went to any of the big culinary schools, and really just learned by observing all the other amazing chefs and cooks. That made her excellent in explaining what to do, but she often had bad habits. Shirleen often put off adding the finishing touches, leaving me to do it, especially when Keisha was not around…*

Chapter 11

Because Hook College was only a few blocks from Shirleen's creaky Victorian home, I went to her house the next morning, to make it easier to tag along with Virgil for his appointment with Lucia.

Alberto, Shirleen's home assistant, opened the door, cheerfully informing me that Shirleen had just gotten back from her morning powerwalk.

I wasn't surprised, as I had timed my arrival to accommodate this. On previous visits, I had seen her more than once in the neighborhood, vigorously striding with one-pound hand weights, a visor, and a fanny pack. She often cajoled me to come along with her, and the one time I agreed to walk with her, I had to maintain a half-jog to keep up.

"Does she always go by herself?" I asked as I hung up my coat.

"Virgil runs laps around the block while she's out. They have some system figured out that keeps them both happy and less likely to fuss."

"I doubt that," I muttered.

Alberto snickered. "They're going through a rough patch. Her doctor gave her some mixed news earlier this summer and they've been squabbling about it ever since. You being hired to help with the book is the only thing that stopped Virgil from moving back in again."

"Again?" I echoed.

"The first time was when he quit working at his fancy law firm," Alberto said, clearly anticipating me to follow up with a dozen more questions. I did want to ask, but I'd almost rather have the answers from Virgil himself even though I knew from the older man's glittering eyes he had *all* the tea. "You may only come in a few days out of the week, but you lessen a burden I don't think Shirleen is willing to admit is quite heavy. She'll be down shortly, maybe even sooner when I start cooking things up." Alberto went back to his pancake batter. "I'll be out of your way in a moment. Looks like it'll be a big cooking day."

On the whiteboard along the wall were eight recipes that needed working on, that I was somehow supposed to get made over the next few hours. More interesting, though, were assignments marked on the board that split the work between me, herself, Alberto, and Virgil. Virgil was mainly on prep, dealing with all the simpler tasks, but my eyebrows raised all the same. All these months I'd been coming and going, and he'd never helped with more than a grocery run.

"How has she been?" I asked.

"As good as anyone accused of murdering someone they used to be friends with." Alberto liberally poured vanilla into the batter. "I don't know about you, but I'd personally be a mess! I decided to come in all week in case Shirleen needs me more than usual, not that she would tell me, stubborn as she is."

"You think Shirleen isn't doing too well?"

"I think she is doing a good job of pretending," Alberto said as he poured melted butter into the batter. "She can't fool any of us, but she's managed to fool herself. She wants to go to her friend's funeral. I have half a mind to talk her out of it, even though it'll be good for her. When I went back to Puerto Rico for the first time in thirty years, I hated being back as much as I thought I would, but I got closure I wouldn't have gained otherwise."

"You think they were still friends?" I asked.

"No matter how it turned out, they started out as friends first," Alberto said as he fired up the griddle. "I'm hoping mainly it'll settle things around here for now. That's the one bit we can manage."

Right on cue, a bang from upstairs rattled and shook the house hard enough that I jumped to my feet, uncertain if I should give into fight or flight.

Alberto however just waved his spatula with little concern. "Virgil is up there, it's fine."

"Someone still could have been hurt," I said.

Alberto held up a finger.

Seconds later, arguing drifted down the stairs that was too vibrant and robust to cause concern. As I listened to it, truly listened to it, I found the squabbling reminded me of when my dad fell off my roof trying to fix the drains and after seeing he only had a twisted wrist, I started fussing about how he shouldn't have gone up there in the first place.

The arguing remained at such a loud volume I didn't quite realize they had come downstairs until aunt and nephew came through the door.

Shirleen blew through the kitchen, her phone wallet dangling from her wrist. She was in a powder blue velour tracksuit, and matching headband patterned with a blue cheetah print. In a huff, she let the swinging kitchen door strike Virgil, who followed with a beat-up cardboard box under his arm. He too was in athletic gear – a sweatshirt and basketball shorts over leggings – which seemed fitting as he appeared quite ready to run as far away as possible.

"Aunt Shirls, I turned over the entire attic, not just this morning, but last week too. It's not there. It's got to be in the storage unit. I'll go there this weekend and get it."

"You shouldn't have put it out there in the first place," Shirleen bristled.

"If I recall–"

Shirleen spun around waggling a finger right before his nose.

"Don't get smart with me, young man. Just because I told you one thing doesn't mean you're supposed to listen! I count on you rebelling!"

As Virgil was agog over this, I chuckled and hastily covered it with a cough as Shirleen whipped around at me, with venom in her eyes.

"Did you say something, Keisha?"

Panicked I blurted out, "Is something missing?"

"Just old Christmas ornaments that she doesn't even put on the tree anymore." Virgil placed the box down onto the table with a small thump. He pushed up his glasses as he spoke right to his aunt. "Besides, it's too late to bother. Everyone knows that if the decorations aren't up by the fifth of December, it's too late–"

"You're just miffed I had you poking around, but if you did it right the first time, it wouldn't be an issue." Shirleen drifted over to where Alberto was quietly stacking pancakes. "Those are coming out nicely, Alberto. Whose recipe? Yours or mine?"

"Hers," Alberto pointed to me. "I love a good recipe that goes heavy on the vanilla."

"Any recipe that doesn't isn't worth trying," I replied, both pleased and flattered at this. I had made pancakes a while back for an earlier section of the cookbook, and while he asked for my recipe, I never thought he would use it. "Shirleen, was there anything you wanted to prepare today?"

"I'm thinking Red and Green Velvet Cake," Shirleen said. "I wanted to do that one for the cooking demo at the TV station."

"There's Black Cake on the list," I said.

"Yes, but that's for the funeral. Not to bring," Shirleen said softly. "To make it in her memory, and how we learned that polishing off a bottle of Jamaican rum wasn't the best idea." Her words brought on a silence that allowed only the sizzle of the griddle to intrude. Then Shirleen clapped her hands together, declaring with forced cheer, "We'll start after breakfast, of course. Now hurry up with the next batch, Alberto, I like my pancakes piping hot!"

I'd had breakfast already, but I took a pancake to be sociable, especially as Shirleen brought out a small basket of syrups, encouraging me to dip and taste and note the difference between raspberry, roasted praline, and apple cobbler. I sampled all of them, her special touch tucked into each flavor, and at one point didn't bother with the pancake at all, pouring a small pool of sweet goodness directly onto my plate.

I couldn't remember the last time I had a home-cooked breakfast made by someone else.

My friends and I had such odd schedules that we never did brunch. Late night kimbap or a run for freshly baked cookies was far more likely. If we had gone out and then later piled up overnight at someone's place, I was up early making food for everyone. I also never got a chance to linger over a dish, because someone, usually Eden or Jamal, had to dash out.

Eating with Shirleen, who was my boss, and Alberto, who was like a coworker, was nothing like eating with friends, but it was comforting in another way. As if I was part of things in this strange little household, with all its inner workings and strange secrets.

Shirleen finished first and went upstairs to change. Alberto soon followed to help with her medicine.

This left me in the kitchen to start on the first of the recipes, while Virgil rummaged about.

He had not eaten the pancakes, but had quietly cleaned up the kitchen as we ate and then gathered ingredients for a smoothie.

The last person I had shared breakfast with had been my ex-boyfriend and it was hardly sharing when I had a stack of waffles while he drank chicken and spinach smoothies. He had been very into fitness and optimization of the human body, largely viewing food as fuel. Which I could have dealt with, if it wasn't for him belittling my enjoyment of cooking for others.

If I had any fear that Virgil might be the same, I soon forgot them as I watched him pour into the blender frozen fruits, yogurt, honey, and a few things my ex would have scoffed to see. Just one of the many ways they were a world apart…

The blender roared to life and I jumped, nearly dropping my pen.

"Did you want some?" he asked.

I turned back to my notebook. "No, I just wondered why you're letting the pancakes go to waste."

"This is my way of getting required fruits and veggies in. Word of advice: never make a smoothie with kale and fresh grapes, especially one with seeds. Terrible all around."

"I would have never tried that," I said honestly.

He shrugged as he poured the purple concoction out into a glass. "I like to try everything just once. The weirder the better. I think it came from Aunt Shirls raising me. Everything in the *Rise and Shine, Heart Healthy,* and *Kitchen World* cookbooks, I ate first, even if it was disastrous in the end. I think I liked knowing that no matter what I said about the food, she listened. It's a powerful thing as a kid. She even dedicated *Rise and Shine* to me."

"To you? Then you're the little boy on the cover?" I turned to the shelf where the cookbooks sat ready to be grabbed as a reference. Bright blue with a little boy gazing up in awe at the stack of waffles on the cover, I had noted the similarity to Virgil but had brushed it aside.

"I thought you knew that?" Virgil remarked as he stirred the smoothie. "It even says "dear nephew" in the book, and are there any other dear nephews running around here?"

"I didn't realize," I said. "I suppose the glasses threw me off." Pretending to study my notes for the recipe, I added, "Have you always worn glasses?"

The amusement that colored his voice with obnoxious oranges and yellows made me glad I didn't look his way. "I always have. I just broke a pair on a job earlier this year. I was trying contacts out for a while, but the other night I accidentally fell asleep wearing them and that reminded me why I hated them."

"Don't need your life story," I grunted.

He came around to sit down at the table so he faced me and taunted me with a half-smile. "You asked. What do you want to know?"

I looked away from him and the faint reflection of myself in his lenses, and decided to pursue a less dangerous topic.

"You're Shirleen's only relative, then? Around, that is?" I asked. "Most of the time when she mentions her family, it's siblings or cousins that have already died."

"I'm the only one around," Virgil deadpanned. "Because she adopted me and I won't inherit anything if I don't hang around here. Which includes running errands, fetching things, and even literally running after her as she powerwalks around the neighborhood."

His tone was too ironic for me to tell if he was joking or not. I also had the sense he was egging me on, daring me to ask something foolish. Instead I took a different tack, "What's this about ornaments?"

"Nothing. She's just looking for them." Virgil waved a spoon at me. "It has nothing to do with the case. She's just feeling nostalgic."

"Because someone she used to be very close to died, right before her eyes, and maybe before they could reconcile?" I suggested.

"What an idea," Virgil declared with wide-eyed pretend shock. "Such an idea had never occurred to me!"

I let this pass without comment, as I walked right into that one. "How has your aunt been? Do you think Ruby's death will impact progress for the cookbook?"

"You have a better view of that than me," Virgil said. "All I know is the podcast. And things are up in the air."

"You aren't doing it anymore?"

"No, I've been getting questions about optics." Virgil sipped a bit of the smoothie before continuing. "The first episode is very heavy on the history. A lot of it is all about Aunt Shirls's friendship with Ruby. I don't mention the feud to come, but it's there."

"It sounds fine to me, but I could listen to it and give you a better opinion."

"No need," he said quickly. "I'm overthinking it."

"It's no trouble," I said, puzzled at him once again backpedaling. "I'm more interested in the interviews for the raw data itself, but sometimes seeing things from another interpretation brings illumination."

"That's right, you were a data analyst before," Virgil said, strongarming the pivot in our conversation. "How terrible was that?"

"It was terrible enough I was ready to do something different." I shrugged. "But if I didn't have a very frustrating manager, I wouldn't have cracked open Shirleen's cookbook to start stress baking. The job however was quite good. I like data all the same, whether it's numbers or talking to people."

"Or learning about gruesome murders?"

"It does inform one of several things." I couldn't help but grin. "Which means I might hear something you might have missed."

"It'll be a rough cut," Virgil warned, "hardly polished."

I leaned my elbows on the table, meeting his eyes. "It doesn't matter to me. I'm on a break between podcasts. Oddly enough, even my favorite true crime shows aren't as interesting when a murder falls at my feet."

* * *

The rest of the morning was dedicated to recipe work. True to the board, we all jointly tackled a few tasks, even Virgil. His aid seemed to be the price for the placement of the microphone on the counter as Shirleen properly explained recipes.

While she made snarky and sly remarks about him editing out certain pieces from the final cut, her gaze was fond as it fell on him. When he struggled with peeling ginger, she laughed, taking it from him, saying he was no better than when he was a little boy.

Virgil left around noon to get ready for the interview with Lucia, and most of the chatter went with him. It became even quieter when Alberto took his break.

I was finishing up the last few recipes with Shirleen when a message flicked across my phone from Virgil with the first podcast episode for the cookbook.

I hid a smile, and saved it for later.

"What are you and my nephew plotting?" Shirleen asked.

I shut my laptop's lid before I realized Shirleen was still on the other end of the counter looking over my notes. I pretended as if I meant to put the computer away as I asked, "What makes you think we're plotting?"

"The whispers, the conversations that stop and start when I'm not in the room." Shirleen looked sharply over her glasses. "You talking to him first instead of the other way around."

"Shirleen," I teased, "were you eavesdropping?"

"I cannot eavesdrop, this is my house. Don't change the subject like Virgil does," Shirleen retorted. "I also didn't get where I am today by ignoring what people say and what they don't say. You think Ruby was murdered and that the police won't be any help, but what do you hope to accomplish?"

"Restoring your good name?" I suggested.

"I've given up on that." Shirleen rubbed a thumb along the typewriter brooch she had pinned to her apron. "A few good friends are all I need. Especially ones I can trust. Whatever you're up to, I trust you're making good choices, and not spilling the secrets of my recipes on this podcast thing."

"That won't happen," I said.

"Just be careful who you talk to. Some of those names ended up in my address book because I want to make sure I know what moves they are making next."

Interview: Fatima al-Said

Virgil Sullivan, voiceover: *Growing up in Queens, Fatima al-Said had plenty of people to learn to cook from. Her grandmother from Palestine, whose recipes were rooted in need and upheaval; her elderly neighbors from Pakistan, who told her about the history of the Partition as they made kheer and kalakand; and the mother of her best friend, a crafty Italian hairdresser who could make vegetables exciting to even the pickiest of children. There was also one other person: Shirleen Foster, on screen every afternoon on Tuesdays.*

Virgil Sullivan *(laughing)*: *Tell me more about the first recipe you tried, you said it was a disaster?*

Fatima al-Said: *Oh, disaster is probably too tame of a word! I overbaked it so much, I think my father was able to use it to keep our table from wobbling. I didn't know what I did wrong, so I wrote Shirleen a letter. And she was so kind! I got a nice long handwritten letter with tips and suggestions. I had it in a folder forever. That was the first time she contacted me. The second time was to cater for different* Season by Season Revisited *events. She remembered my name and hoped I was the same little girl who wrote to her so many years ago!*

Chapter 12

Hook College had started in someone's living room and – flash forward nearly ninety years later – it had taken over the original boarding house as well as a chunk of the neighborhood as the school expanded. Although, except for subtle signs tucked on corners, or even street names like College Drive or Griffin's Way, you didn't realize you were on campus until you passed the bust of the school's first teacher and namesake, Andria Hook. Then you would see the signs for the campus buildings, and the statue of Atticus the Griffin with his claws over the year 1899. Smaller than the other HBCUs in the area, it had a proud tradition of scholarship and was renowned for its literature program, turning out some of the finest poets and writers around.

I was somewhat familiar with the school's perimeter, as my bicycling group often wound around the area. It was also the same path I'd run on occasion, as the school was along the river path that meandered through the city. But I hadn't ventured further. So I was glad to see that Virgil waited for me right next to Atticus the Griffin. He had his backpack of equipment slung over his shoulder, but otherwise looked almost professional in a camel brown coat and beanie that was a slightly darker color.

"Would you really have gotten lost?" Virgil asked.

"I would have gotten turned around certainly, I'm not familiar with this building."

"It's fairly new," Virgil said. "But not that hard to find."

This turned out to be true. Following the winding path through the interior of the campus soon brought up the newly minted Darden Innovation Center, where technology labs and state-of-the art kitchens could be found.

Voices of lecturing teachers echoed in the hall in what must be the among the final sessions of the semester. However, instead of trying to squeeze the last bit of learning into her students, we found Lucia in her office. The door was ajar and the soft chatter of her mechanical keyboard filled the air as she muttered to herself.

When she looked up at Virgil's knock, I watched the expressions on her face change, and I wasn't sure if the scheduled interview was going to go off without a hitch.

Or even happen at all.

"You're coming today about the podcast," Lucia exclaimed. "I completely forgot!"

I'm afraid my skepticism must have shown on my face, for without a word from us she blathered on, "It's the end of the semester. While classes are done, there are still finals. I got asked just this morning to proctor a test tomorrow. I'm preparing for it right now."

"It'll only take a few minutes," Virgil assured her.

"No, I can't even spare that." Lucia shut her laptop. Hurriedly grabbing everything that appeared to be important, she even picked up a stapler by accident and shoved it into her bag. "I have to get across campus."

"We can talk as we walk," Virgil said. "I've come prepared."

"Not today," she said. "I'm much too busy. Also, do you really need to talk to me? What can I say about Shirleen that hasn't been said already? She was my mentor. She taught me things. I grew past it. Surely this is more than enough for the silly podcast."

Lucia pulled on her coat and made to get out the room, but I slid over to block her path.

"It'll just be a few questions," I said.

Lucia shook her head. "I don't have the time to spare."

I protested but at Virgil's nod, I reluctantly moved aside to let her pass.

We followed her out of the office, and she locked the door as if afraid we'd slip inside and wait for her return.

"When would be a better time for you?" Virgil asked. "Later this week? Or next week?"

"I'll have to check my calendar," Lucia said, avoiding our eyes. "Like I said, it's a busy time."

To complete the brush off, she turned her back on us and headed down the opposite end of the hall, her footsteps a continued rebuke as they echoed.

"Busy time!" I scoffed. "She's changed her mind, and is too cowardly to tell you."

"No doubt," Virgil said. "I wonder why she did?"

"Do you think she'll actually reschedule?"

"If her only reason to talk to me was to fuss about my aunt, I don't see why not," Virgil replied. As he concluded these words with a shrug, I squinted at him.

"Why aren't you more upset?" I asked.

He pulled a microphone out of his coat pocket with its blinking red light. "I didn't expect she'd actually go through with it, given I only got a weak agreement at the party. What I got isn't an interview, but a nice soundbite. I'd rather that than her ranting about the failed restaurant."

"All the more reason to try to get her to talk," I said. "I never knew that about the restaurant. Shirleen and Lucia seemed to get along well."

"From what I've heard, Lucia only got the teaching post because of her association with Shirleen," Virgil said. "Clearly she believes in not burning bridges that may have use in the future."

"What if it changed?" I asked. "All the more to reason to talk to her."

"You heard her. It'll be hard to catch up with her, given how busy she is."

"Then we try to find Lucia while she's busy." I pointed to the flyer on the wall. In bright colors was the announcement for a gingerbread house contest run by the culinary program, that was open to the public. "Lucia will be a judge and she can't make a scene."

"She still might not talk to us," Virgil cautioned.

"Not if I win the contest!" I retorted.

"It's this weekend, do you have time to make a gingerbread house?"

"It's more than enough time," I said. "I just need a theme."

"A spaceship," Virgil suggested with surprising enthusiasm. "Or dinosaurs." He paused before he continued with a sense of wonder that brought a certain glee to his face. "Or both!"

"Maybe." I couldn't help but laugh, taken in by such a wild idea. "I'll have to keep it simple."

Footsteps interrupted further brainstorming. I didn't expect to see Lucia, but I was surprised to recognize another culinary instructor, who stopped in the middle of the hallway upon seeing us.

Gloria Thompson had been at the party, and I had even called her the other day as I worked my way down the guest list. While Gloria hadn't hung up on me, she had quickly got off the phone when she realized my connection to Shirleen. I wouldn't say she made excuses, but she was in a rush to end our call.

I couldn't help but wonder if she would replicate that once again in person.

"Oh," Gloria Thompson said, "I didn't realize you came after all." She bit her lip nervously. "I thought I told your aunt that we didn't expect her to show up today. Not that I don't appreciate her generous offer, but the Dean thought it might be wise, especially with finals on the way, that she visits another day."

"I don't know what you mean," Virgil said. He glanced at me for answers, and I shrugged. Although I had gotten full access to Shirleen's calendar, I hadn't memorized it.

As Gloria quickly and awkwardly told Virgil all about the visit to the college that had been scheduled today with Shirleen, I discreetly checked my phone. I had recently been given access to Shirleen's work email but hadn't checked it. Waiting for me like an unwanted present were several reminders, and a very belated cancellation by the school.

"If it's about the death," Virgil said, bluntly cutting through the instructor's attempt to soften her words, "my aunt wasn't charged, nor will she be."

"I'm not saying she's guilty." A soft pink had filled Gloria's light brown cheeks. "It's that it will be a great distraction for the students. What happened might derail what the visit was supposed to be about. I thought your aunt understood."

"My aunt is not here with us." Virgil shoved his hands into his coat pockets, his voice calm, save for a small shake. "I was just making a visit to a place she's contributed to a great deal over the years, in both time and service. Hook

College has played an important backdrop in her career, and so of course I'm featuring it on my podcast."

"Would you like an interview?" I added tartly. "We're just here to record ambient sounds and chatter from the kitchens."

Gloria nearly stumbled over herself with platitudes, her eyes pleading from an attempt to course correct. In further apology, she even did an interview right on the spot, inviting us into her office with all the ease that Lucia should have done.

Gloria had not been teaching here at the college when Shirleen started, but Shirleen's presence at Hook as a lecturer turned what had been a few elective courses on home economics into a full culinary degree program that included food history and sociology.

"In a way, I owe my job to Shirleen," Gloria concluded. "Having her in the area has helped foster a culinary education that enriches both the college and the community."

"What a fine job it is," Virgil said.

"I don't believe she had anything to do with Ruby Walton's death," Gloria quickly added. "It's just a shame that people are quick to judge, all due to a few jealous rumors. Are we frozen as we are in a heated moment?"

"They say some moments, no matter how small, define us always," Virgil said. "What do you mean by jealousy?"

"Only that Shirleen left the staff just when she was offered tenure, due to nasty accusations about her work and recipes. I wasn't in the know, but I heard whispers of what it could have been. She could have stayed on as an adjunct, but chose to leave entirely, to keep those whispers locked away." Gloria glanced at her watch. "I must be going, the exam is almost over."

She walked us out her office and shook Virgil's hand. "Tell Shirleen I'm sorry, and that I hope to see her soon."

Once Gloria was out of earshot, I turned to comment to Virgil about this chance interview and information, and I found his gaze focused on the wall next to him. Although he had hid it well, there was stunned surprise in his face that he openly showed now that Gloria was gone.

"You didn't know that about your aunt?" I asked then, sensing I already had my answer.

"I knew she abruptly left, but I didn't know all this was occurring. Secrets, even then, were bothering her. I wonder even back then..." he began, only to stop.

His tone was so contemplative I couldn't help but ask. "Even then what?"

Virgil raised the microphone to his face and declared dramatically, "Even then, someone was trying to sabotage her!"

"Who would sabotage the Queen of Christmas Cakes is a question central to this mystery. Figuring out when this started may help us solve several other minor mysteries," Virgil said into the microphone, as we walked north the six blocks to Fatima's café. It was growing chillier as the shift to late afternoon began, but I shivered more from the question Virgil posed.

It was one thing for someone to plot against Shirleen due to recent squabbles but quite another to nurse a grudge nearly twenty years on. That was cold anger and bitter plotting, and I couldn't help but think poison would not be the last of it.

"If only you'd paid better attention when you were younger, you could be of help," I said. "Although if it was that easy, we'd have our answers already."

"You do know I'm recording this," Virgil said.

"Put it in," I insisted. "I'm the Holmes to your Watson, why wouldn't my thoughts be added in?"

"I never said I was *actually* going to make a murder mystery podcast. This is all just for the record," Virgil weakly protested.

I could only snort.

He was far too diligent in collecting soundbites for me to believe that!

"Then for the record, keep everything in." I said. "Didn't you say we must record everything to see if it's of use?"

"Well then, *Holmes,*" Virgil mocked, "you must inform me what would be useful."

"So far, everything. I'll give you notes later. You know, I always wanted to be on a true crime podcast."

I realized my error as Virgil surrendered himself to uproarious laughter.

"As a consultant and advisor," I said raising my voice to be heard. "This is better. I'm leading an investigation, dealing with clues, interrogating suspects, figuring out the timeline of the evening."

"Well then, Keisha, walk me through the evening." Virgil said, and he held out the microphone to me. It was the first time I didn't want to bat it away. As I raised my eyes toward him, something that could be called a smile lifted the corner of my lips.

"Give me a better line," I said.

Virgil leaned forward instead of pulling the microphone back. "Keisha, what do we hope to uncover through understanding this series of events?"

"Understanding begins with knowing when Ruby got here. She brought a cake that got shoved into a tiny fridge in a staff room and possibly brought a shoddy cake knife too, though she would know better than to get them. When did this happen? How much time between that and her encounter with Shirleen? Ruby also had shoved a notebook in her purse, with a few other things, including," – I withdrew a slip of paper from my coat pocket – "this, something I kept by accident in the chaos of cleaning up after I dropped her purse."

"It's a recipe." Virgil squinted. "Or part of it?"

"For vegan cheesecake brownie bars," I said. "At a party filled with so many movers and shakers, it's likely Ruby wanted to meet someone, possibly to share recipes, but it could be something else. She brought that notebook with her shoved into her purse. Could it be she's writing a new cookbook?"

"I suppose it's possible," Virgil mused. "She never produced one again, other than the tie-in cookbook for *Whisk it All.*"

"Then something occurred to make her want to try now."

The sign for Lemon Tree Bakery appeared, although as always, I saw the building first, with its bright cheery painted yellow brick. The large window up front displayed some pastries and cakes, with flyers papering a corner for everything from advertising Catered by Fatima to mutual aid meetings, protests against data centers, open mic night, immigration rights workshops, free whistles, a mental health seminar, writing clubs, and a flyer for the 14th Annual Great Hot Chocolate War.

A twinkling bell heralded our entrance. Other than a couple of older hijabi grannies in a corner working on a jigsaw puzzle, and a writer pretending to work away at his laptop, the only other customer in the shop was a middle-aged man, who was buying enough cookies that I could tell somebody was going to have a good time.

At the counter I recognized the short curly neon green hair, freckles, and diabetic monitor belonging to the assistant of Fatima's who was there the night of the party.

"Welcome to… ah." She blinked, snapping her fingers. "You're from the other night. Cake Lady and Podcast Guy!"

"I'm offended," Virgil whispered.

"I'm not, it's accurate," I remarked. "Is Fatima here today?"

"In the back office," the employee said. Then she leaned forward to ask, "Is this about," – she lowered her voice – "the dead woman?"

"Yes and no," I said.

"Unless you heard or saw anything," Virgil added.

The young employee looked between us, with hungry curiosity in her eyes. "Would I get featured on the podcast?"

"Depends on what you say," I said.

"I was in the room as it happened," she said in a rush. "I saw–"

"I'm not recording yet." Virgil was fumbling with the microphone as the back door opened and Fatima stepped out. She wasn't in chef whites, but in uniform all the same, with a long-sleeved tan shirt, slightly darker pants, and a dark blue apron with a snowflake pinned to the strap.

"I'll take their orders, Crystal, why don't you check the hot chocolate stock?"

Crystal pouted. "I was about to talk to them for a podcast. It could be good for business!"

"Go check the stock," Fatima repeated firmly, leaving no room for further protests.

Fatima took her employee's place, and as if we were strangers, asked, "That'll be two hot chocolates, right?"

"We didn't order anything yet," I said.

"This is the base price to get me to talk about that night," Fatima said.

I eyed the cabinet of gooey cinnamon rolls that were as fat as my fist and promised cream cheese frosting decadency. "And if I toss in a cinnamon roll?"

"You might even get some of my opinions. Although my information caps at a dozen pastries."

I bought not just cinnamon rolls, but gingerbread cookies, biscotti, scones, fruitcake, sugar cookies in the shape of snowflakes, and pâtes des fruits, all over Virgil's protests that this was unneeded.

Fatima just boxed up the treats as we fought over who would pay, and didn't even blink when I swatted Virgil's hand out the way with my credit card. She rang up the treats, and then started working on the hot chocolate.

At the corner where hot milk and other options were available, Fatima paused before asking, "How is Shirleen doing?"

"She is well enough, although she's very grateful for all the aid you gave," Virgil said.

"I did the best anyone could," Fatima said. "Although I was trying to make sure the finger of trouble wasn't pointed at me. Apologies," she added to Virgil.

"I understand," Virgil retorted. "You have your businesses and employees to think of."

"Two businesses," Fatima said. "The catering is a new thing, and right now the shop is covering its overhead. But I didn't really see anything. I watched Shirleen cut the cake and bring it out. We walked out together. Although I was distracted by the DJ's terrible jokes, there was never a chance for her to put any poison in the cake. That's what I told the police, although they weren't listening."

"The detective appeared diligent enough," Virgil ventured.

Fatima hesitated once more, as she mixed up the hot chocolate. "They didn't ask too much of my staff. The police only asked about what they wanted to hear. They want to arrest Shirleen. It's neat, it's tidy, and it makes sense with all the other accounts of the evening. Everyone heard their argument. The ones that didn't recalled the scandals."

"They wanted a neat story," I echoed.

"Just like in *Beaver Creek,*" Fatima said.

"Exactly!" I nodded. I knew I liked Fatima for a reason! She had excellent taste in naming an instant true crime classic.

"For listeners who are unaware," Virgil remarked into the microphone. "*Beaver Creek* detailed the grisly murder of seven campers in Utah. Famous not just for the cruel and unusual deaths, but for the fact the detectives handling the cases were so focused on making the park ranger the killer, that they managed to overlook more obvious clues. Will this prove foreshadowing for our investigation? Time will tell."

I scowled at Virgil, although it hardly fazed him, as he asked Fatima, "What did they ask you about that night?"

"What Shirleen did, regarding the cake. What they didn't ask," Fatima continued, "was if Shirleen even waited to *see* her eat the cake. Shirleen handed it to Ruby, and she went away." Fatima looked between us, her face aglow with excitement. "If you were going to poison someone, wouldn't you want to be sure, to get the timing right?"

Chapter 13

Settled at a table at the back of the café, Virgil played Fatima's parting words in a loop, as we lingered over a flight of hot chocolates.

I had tasted with care each shot's worth of cocoa goodness, but Virgil downed each one of them in a single swallow and blinked at me when I told him they were all different.

I sighed and diligently filled out his card too, as it was the least we could do for Fatima, since she'd told us something so important that it spun our investigation into a new direction.

"Why is it important?" Virgil said.

He had stopped playing the tape and resumed recording once more.

I took a moment to circle the last column on the hot chocolate card, commenting on the depth of flavor, before I put the card and pencil aside.

"That one word: timing." I said. "Shirleen frankly wouldn't be as famous if her timings weren't always on the money."

Virgil stared, still not understanding.

But that was okay.

He may have grown up around all of this, but he'd clearly missed a lot.

"You mean how she gets something made in the right amount of time? Hardly magic." Virgil scoffed.

I shook my head, insisting, "It's something that's quite important to her. When we're finally done with the cookbook, I'll probably remember some of my favorite recipes, and the ones that gave me the most trouble, but I will certainly recall her lecturing me about timing! The importance of it, watching for it, and making it clear as I described the transformations food undergoes." I held up my arm, twisting it so the watch's round face could be seen. I had started wearing the watch my grandmother gave me again, because Shirleen's eyes would narrow upon me when I checked my phone for the time. "Shirleen cares so much about timing that if she was going to do what they claimed, she would have spaced it out better. Not be so near when Ruby collapsed."

"What's the value in going on about her behavior? We know she didn't do it. We wouldn't be doing this at all if we thought there was even a chance."

"We know this," I countered, "but whoever poisoned Ruby doesn't. We're looking for someone close enough to Shirleen to have motive, but also distant enough that her habits and quirks can be overlooked or forgotten."

"Or the person is less than meticulous." Virgil frowned. "Doesn't change a thing."

"Because you're seeing it like you are tasting these hot chocolates and finding them all the same. You're missing the nuances of this case, whether it's murder, an accident, or a frame job. It's really quite simple."

A chuckle escaped Virgil. "Well then, I'm glad you're here to help me see that. Does this change the suspect list?"

From my notebook I took out two slips of paper. "Here's the full list of everyone invited and present at the party.

I checked it against the list of names in Shirleen's address book noting who she had marked as friend, foe, or business associate. I also marked out people who have history with Ruby and Shirleen." I pointed to the shorter list. "These are the likely suspects right now."

"My uncle is on this list," Virgil declared after a moment, his tone too carefully neutral. I couldn't tell what he thought, but I didn't think he disagreed with the inclusion.

"I spoke to him and he told me some rather alarming things," I said.

Virgil nodded and continued to read. "Austin and Naomi, I get. Some of the others – Davis? Lucia? You even got DJ Oscar Fantom on here?"

"They were there and all have a history with Shirleen," I said, defending myself. "While some don't have a clear motive, like your uncle, they have left me with a few lingering questions."

"No more than my uncle." In a gesture of what I was coming to expect when I broached the subject of his family, Virgil pointed to the box of sweets, not even pretending to make a smooth transition on topics.

"Why do you need so many anyway?" he asked. "Got someone special to give them away to?"

"I do actually," I said. I meant to leave it at that, but Virgil's face betrayed such deliciously sharp surprise which compelled me to add: "I got this for someone very close to heart – my friends who are going to love this assortment. We get together for dinner every week. Because I'm putting together a holiday party next week, it's sheet pan meals to keep things simple. I was going to make one of the Christmas cakes for dessert, but this has saved me, so I can focus on making a winning gingerbread house."

"I can come by and help," Virgil offered, as he absently tapped each of the tiny hot chocolate mugs, the twitch of his fingers betraying a hint of nervousness. "You are only doing this because of the interview."

I hesitated, thinking of the mess outside of the domain of my kitchen, my rumbustious cats, and the idea of Virgil Sullivan prowling around with his microphone. I had only just pulled him out of the column of disagreeable but unavoidable nuisance to a tenuous partner in crime. I hardly knew him, or even his food preferences.

"I said I'm going to make a winning gingerbread house." I slanted my voice into a taunt. "If you help, that won't be the case. I've heard stories that there's a reason you're only talking about the cooking instead of helping. Do the words 'Chicken Paprikash' ring any bells?"

Virgil put a hand to his chest and fell back against his chair dramatically, as he flounced about as if he had been struck from all sides by arrows.

I grabbed the hot chocolate cards and the baked goods with a roll of my eyes.

Let him joke. I wasn't wrong.

As I dropped the cards into the box, Crystal was back up front adding new pastries to the case. She cast hopeful puppy dog eyes at us, and Virgil took out the microphone and clicked it on.

"How well do you know Shirleen Foster?" Virgil asked the young woman.

"Not very well," the girl admitted. "I saw her only a few times, but enough to get good vibes. She's a pretty cool old lady, and helped me figure out the mistakes I was making with cinnamon buns."

"What do you remember about the night of the party?" I prompted.

The green-haired girl thought for a moment before she said, "We went over the allergy list, as there were newly added guests and Shirleen wanted to make sure everything was taken care of."

"Were there any surprises?" I asked.

Crystal shook her head with a slight frown. "Not that I remember."

"Let us know if there's anything you do," I added as I waved goodbye. "I'd love to hear it."

"You have an odd look on your face again," Virgil said as we stepped out of the shop. He held onto the pastries as I adjusted my scarf around my neck. "What are you thinking about?"

I didn't reply at first, my attention taken by a blue car with North Carolina plates that had suddenly backfired. The distraction the car created gave me a few moments to think about how to better frame what I wanted to tell Virgil. It still wasn't long enough for me to make the truth prettier than what it was.

"I want to get my hands on the autopsy report." I said.

"You'll just have to wait. The police don't really share sensitive details to persons of interest."

"You were a lawyer," I said.

"In family law, and my license isn't active. Won't be easy."

"But not impossible!" I cried with a confidence I had no business feeling.

The corners of Virgil's mouth went up in a smile. "I'll see what I can do."

I took the pastries from him and pointed left to the nearest train station. "I'm headed this way. I'll be working from my kitchen over the next few days, so I will see you at the gingerbread house competition."

"You're not going to the funeral?" Virgil asked.

"Ruby's funeral you mean? Should I? I hardly knew her."

"True, but my aunt would appreciate your company." He looked everywhere but me as he added, "Alberto can't come – not that I'm asking you to come being her assistant or aide. It's just that… well, the people who knew Ruby and Aunt Shirls will be there. I definitely want to speak to Ruby's brother Ruben, but if you're there, I can speak more easily–"

"We can find out if Ruby was poisoned!" I interrupted with great excitement for this facet of our investigation. "Maybe I should come after all, we can ask together. You won't think to ask for certain things on the autopsy form. Oh, and I wonder if I could get a word with the funeral director about irregularities when preparing the body!"

Virgil shuddered. "On second thought, forget what I said. Maybe you shouldn't come!"

A short train ride brought me home. My cats hardly stirred as I walked past, as they remained curled up in patches of late afternoon light like small furry mounds. Only Decker's eyes flickered open as I entered the kitchen.

I swear his hearing was sharp as any dog's, for I had just got ready to dish out their food when he led the charge with the others right at his tail.

I watched them eat, got in my ear scratches and allotted cuddles before, with a flip of a tail, I was given the brush off, and they departed to their chosen corners of the house.

Grabbing Shirleen's *Christmas Baking* and *Kitchen Wisdom* cookbooks off my bookshelf, because I couldn't remember which held the gingerbread recipe, I went back to the kitchen to get dinner ready… only to get to the cabinet and find all my pans were missing, as well as a select number of knives and bowls.

This couldn't be a robbery. It was too precise, and too odd, since they weren't even my good knives.

When I opened my fridge to find where Pascal usually left the groceries, I realized it was a good thing that the knives were taken because there would have been a murder otherwise.

I called Pascal, but it was Eden who answered.

"You're on speaker!" she sang out, her voice cutting over the background chatter and music.

"Hey, Key," Romy chimed in. "How's it going?"

"I've been robbed!" I spoke.

"And given a gift," Jamal's voice was flush with laughter. "We're cooking tonight. If it's not edible, Jessica and Sunil have generously offered to buy dinner."

"Maybe they should just order everything." I suggested with a sudden fright for next door.

There was a reason I cooked every week. It wasn't just because I enjoyed feeding people, or wanted to try different recipes, or had the most flexible schedule.

It was because most of my friends couldn't be trusted with a butter knife. I still had scorch marks on the ceiling in my kitchen from when I tried to teach Jamal how to make brownies, and I still don't understand how that even happened in the first place!

There was a rustling sound in the background as the phone shifted to a new person.

"Keisha, just come around at the usual time." Pascal's warm reassuring words filled the air. "We're all adults here, we can manage a meal between the four of us. Also, I'm not keen on letting them burn down my house."

Resisting the urge to switch to video to watch the possible disaster in the making, I ended the call and queued up my podcasts, adding in the file that Virgil had sent me from his cut of the *Season by Season Revisited* podcast.

My grandmother had owned all Shirleen's cookbooks, even if she hardly cracked open the *Heart Healthy* one. But *Kitchen Wisdom* and *Christmas Baking* Granny had lovingly brought out over the years. They had cracked spines, splatters and stains, and margins filled with copious notes. Most were related to the recipes, but others were just things she had jotted down because it was the nearest thing at hand.

I ran my fingers along the loops of her firm and crisp handwriting, reading once again her quick math to determine how many cupcakes she needed to bring to my elementary school for the Halloween party I had told her about literally the night before. Granny didn't raise me and my sister, but when I was in elementary school through my second year of middle school, my dad's ornithology research kept us on the East Coast, she could easily take the train down (or up) and did so as often as she could. The cookbooks were always tucked into her suitcases because that was the activity she did with me. My sister worked in the garden, which sprouted an interest in horticulture, and she currently worked in a large botanical garden and still donned Granny's floppy sunhat.

I turned pages now, recalling her making many of these notes right here in this very kitchen. This house was hers, and while it had been left to my father technically, it had gone to me when I took a job out here and Dad decided it was worth losing money on the rent to have someone in the family home again. While I was paying taxes on a house sooner than I thought, and had the mixed blessings of home ownership that came with endless projects, I found great comfort walking around the house on rainy mornings wrapped in Granny's favorite sweater.

The gingerbread recipe was in the *Kitchen Wisdom* book, and greatly modified with my grandmother's notes to adjust the oven and ratio of brown sugar. On a neighboring page, there was a blueprint for a fairy tale castle, with a moat of frosting speckled with sprinkles and gumdrops.

I still had enough pans to make the slabs of gingerbread, and I mixed in molasses, ginger, cinnamon, nutmeg, and the last bit of shortening. I had just enough, which surprised me with how little I used it in baking. Glancing back at the cookbook, I spotted my grandmother's note on how butter made weak gingerbread, and her raspy chuckle echoed softly in my ears.

I got everything mixed and was shaping the dough as I listened to the episodes Virgil had sent. It had started like he said it would, a look into the legacy and history of the cookbook, citing many accolades I hadn't even been aware of Shirleen having.

Most of the episode was about her newspaper column. In a soothing tone, Virgil related the many letters that slowly encouraged her to start sharing recipes and cooking advice. The episode ended featuring Shirleen's first editor, who back in the 1960s shepherded Claudia Mason's landmark book on French cooking into the world. The editor, Birdie Bailey, had a luminous career of her own, as she had a knack for selecting books out of the slush pile that transformed bookshelves. Working with Claudia got her interested in cookbooks and food writing, and Shirleen was just the first of many cookbook authors she added to that roster. Birdie had died some years ago, but for the podcast Virgil included an old interview of hers as she reflected on her decades-long career.

> Birdie Bailey: *Food tells us everything we need to know about people. Tasting another's food brings an appreciation to our differences. Working to develop cookbooks I have seen much of the world, and discovered places I overlooked right in my background. Working with Shirleen Foster, I, this New England Yankee, got a taste of not just Black American Southern cooking but the sensibility and understanding that still resonates today. Shirleen Foster might be known for the Christmas cakes, but it's through these cakes people find their way to her work and food, which remains astounding for how approachable it is and adaptable to changing times.*

As the episode ended, my hands were now kneading the gingerbread dough. I let things play on, and the file ended, flipping over to the podcasts I had downloaded earlier. Incessant ads played for products and services I would never buy, but I knew by heart, and then suddenly Virgil was speaking again.

> *"Wander off the beaten path, and you find a lighthouse with an odd history, involving prohibition smugglers, gangsters, and a school teacher who was caught up in the midst. Prepared to be shocked, because* Wow, It Happened Here*!"*

The lump of gingerbread fell out of my hands, crashing into the bowl.

I wasn't sure I heard right, but it was Virgil.

There was the same cadence to his words. He had introduced himself with a different name, but it was him.

I knew it, I could hear it, I couldn't *not* hear it.

It couldn't be possible, though.

My mind flashed to his odd look when the episode had appeared on my phone and his sudden reluctance to tell me about it.

Why wouldn't he tell me he was the host of *Wow, It Happened Here*? It wasn't terrible. Sure, some of the earlier episodes had sound quality issues as he hadn't got a proper microphone for the field, but it was good and solid. Why not tell me?

I worked the dough, slamming it into the bowl harder than I should, growing agitated.

Why not say anything and let me find out?

When did having a podcast become a deep, dark secret?

What did he think I was going to do? Make fun of him?

A knock on my back door saved me from making a mess of the dough.

"It's time for dinner!" Jamal declared as he swept inside with Eden.

Jamal was once a graphic designer at my old company, and we were work siblings, despite being in completely different departments. We hung out between meetings, grabbed lunch together, and commiserated over our workloads. After we both left the company, I saw him less often, because he was freelancing, but whenever he showed up for weekly dinner it was like no time had passed. His food preferences included a fondness for sprinkling hot sauce on every protein, beans included.

"Is there food to eat?" I asked as I separated the dough into smaller bowls so it could rise.

"Yes," Eden said, lifting the lid of the box of pastries I bought. "Because Sunil and Jessica just arrived with cartons, containers, and a jug of lemonade."

As I snorted, Jamal asked, "What are you making?"

"A gingerbread house," I answered.

"Why?" Jamal asked after a moment. "That wasn't on the list of goodies I gave you. Where are my Charleston chewies?"

"Not coming since you asked me," I said. "This gingerbread house is the ticket I need to speak with someone."

"That's a very vague response," Jamal remarked.

While he was willing to joke, Eden looked at me crossly. "Speak to someone about what?"

I saw no point in denying it, as I could see suspicions in my friend's eyes. The last time there had been an odd death in our orbit, she had also been a background player. We had been at ren fair when the newly crowned king of the day had toppled over. Although it would come out later that he had a heart attack, I had nosed around all over the fair in the mud like a bloodhound after a crime that didn't exist and had dragged Eden with me. And she never let me forget it.

"I was hoping to find out what they might or might not know about Ruby Walton's death," I admitted, avoiding her eye.

Eden scowled with that resigned air like one who had submitted to gravity. "You know this isn't one of your true crime podcasts, there's no murder."

"Yes there is," I protested. "I know there is, even if the police haven't announced it yet."

Jamal's head swung to Eden and then back to me. He was in my corner, because he also loved a good mystery, but Jamal liked to keep the peace when he could. "What does gingerbread have to do with this?" he settled on asking.

"There's a gingerbread contest and I'm hoping to ambush a person of interest there."

Eden sighed and pressed her fingers against the bridge of her nose. In contrast, Jamal blinked and asked. "Why not just ambush this person the normal way?"

"What would be the normal way?" Eden demanded.

Jamal threw up his hands in a shrug. "I don't know, murder isn't *my* hobby!"

"Have you got a murder board yet?" Eden said.

"Of course she has one," Jamal snorted. "We took a whiteboard from the office."

Eden stared. "You guys took an *entire* whiteboard from your old company? How did you manage it?"

"A screwdriver, gumption, and a man on the security desk who was willing to look the other way," I said. "We got odd looks."

"Even more so when you told them your big plans for it," Jamal added, with a grin. "Do you have your murder board set up in the front room?"

"No, I don't," I said.

It was set up in my *guest* room, and I had just added the names and photographs of our suspects as well as key moments in the timeline. It wasn't ready for primetime, and as much as my friends teased me, I wasn't going to show it to them. I just needed to sort my thoughts and get some connections going.

I used to follow along with my favorite podcast to track the crime's progress, so I was used to making these boards. With the podcast, even if I was listening to it weekly, I felt comforted that there were some sort of guardrails. I didn't have those right now. Just my assumptions, some intuition, and input from a podcaster who had already concealed one truth from me.

I didn't know how this case was going to unfold, but I knew what I found next could rearrange even my most careful of notes.

> Some of my fondest memories of Ruby are tied with food, the first bite of decadent chocolates, our last lingering swallow of wine, our hunt for an elusive pepper, the many attempts of making plain yeasted waffles, and the burst of tart strawberries that we devoured right in her garden. I remember her by the meals we shared, the ingredients we purchased at grocery stores and markets, and how when one of us tasted something truly good, we immediately ran to get to the other so we could try to replicate the magic.
>
> - From Ruby Walton's obituary
> written by Shirleen Foster for the *Hunton Bay Journal*

Chapter 14

The next couple of days clipped along. When I wasn't working on a few recipes for Shirleen, I was tending to the gingerbread house, which was more finicky than expected but became a way to channel my restless energy. Although Virgil sent a couple of texts lamenting that he was still unable to track down Brandon Morton, I hadn't really talked to him.

But I heard his voice.

Knowing that he hosted *Wow, It Happened Here* under a different name, I was able to find another podcast he had done. *It Was Law,* which talked about unusual cases, from famous ones involving a haunted house, to Louisiana allowing juries to convict 11–1 instead of a unanimous vote due to prejudices that sadly weren't so historical. It was more serious than the local history podcast, but his enthusiasm and interest was present enough to make even the dourest subject interesting. It had even fewer episodes than the local history one, and a much more irregular posting schedule. Yet no matter how different they were from *Moving Day,* they all had one thing in common. These were stories about people, with sharp insights that proved no matter how much he talked and rattled on, he was always listening and observing.

While working on the gingerbread house or even going for a nice long run, I burned through his back catalog of episodes. As I did, I got the impression that this was his truest self – not the goof he presented himself as or the lawyer he tried to be, but somewhere in the middle. The more I listened the more I was convinced I could be very good friends with this version of him.

On the day of the funeral, he and Shirleen picked me up at my place.

Despite being given a time to be ready, I was running late, as I had to hunt around for a sweater to wear with my black dress, and hastily tease my curls into a tidy bun. I managed to find my black wool coat, but I couldn't find any gloves other than my cherry and white striped ones.

My gloves got a wan smile from Shirleen as I dashed out to the waiting car.

"Those don't quite match," Shirleen said as I opened the back door.

"It'll be fine, won't it?" I asked.

"Don't worry, it's the right shade of red."

As I settled in the backseat, I caught Virgil's concerned glance in the rearview mirror.

He pulled off, heading out of my neighborhood and onto the major road without a word.

The radio was turned off, so a quiet filled the car for the most part. While the silence around Virgil and Shirleen was comfortable, I felt uneasy all the same. I knew I had been invited in a professional capacity, but this wasn't one of Shirleen's events. This was a funeral, and eager as I was for the chance to speak with Ruby's brother, I couldn't overlook that I would be amongst strangers, and even the people I would know the best, were still mostly that.

Unable to bear the sound of my own thoughts for much longer I said, "The funeral came together pretty quick."

"Most of Ruby's family is in Chesapeake," Shirleen replied. "The ones that lived far away were never coming to begin with."

"They know you'll be there?" I asked, suddenly curious about her attendance.

"I'm one of her oldest friends. I don't care what was said about me in the newspaper, the internet, the radio, or anywhere else. That fact does not change."

She directed this at Virgil, who said nothing as he put a microphone in the cupholder and flipped it on.

"Tell me how you first started working together with Ruby," Virgil said. "They didn't have blogs back then, so how did you find her?"

"Are you curious or is it for the podcast?" she asked.

"Yes to both," Virgil said.

I leaned forward as much as my seat belt would allow. "It also could be useful for the investigation."

"Keisha," Virgil muttered.

I waved off his concerns. "She knows what we're doing, and she's involved," I reasoned. "It's better to be upfront."

"You're darn right I am," Shirleen said with great vigor. "I won't be chasing after anyone, but I want to know what's going on. You're turning what's happening into a podcast, aren't you? I thought you wanted my input."

"I will if you wish." Virgil cleared his throat. "Aunt Shirls, how did you first meet Ruby Walton and decide to work on a cookbook together?"

"She found me," Shirleen answered. "We came to Norfolk because your uncle got a job in the shipyard that paid better than what he was doing before. I kept writing at the paper in Charleston, just had to send in my articles by mail. Around that time, I started sending in my recipes and taking questions. It gave me extra time to write. Sometimes I put in correspondence from readers. One letter was from Ruby, about correcting the timing of a cake of mine. It was the first of many letters featured in my column. She had been reading my column for a while, she was a new wife, and used the recipes to some success. She had a lot of opinions about the food that would impress our husbands and we came up with a measure to judge how good the recipe was."

"What was the measure?" Virgil asked.

Shirleen chortled. "I'll just say it was kisses, unless you think I need to say more?"

"No, you don't," Virgil said so quickly I had to swallow a chuckle.

"The cookbook started as a collection of recipes bound up together," Shirleen continued. "Mostly because it was a way to keep it organized. I never thought of writing an actual cookbook. I didn't consider myself a chef back then. The term home cook wasn't nearly as popular as it was now, but cooking at home was seen as nothing fancy. As it happened, Birdie Bailey tried one of my recipes on a lark. I won't claim she'd followed my column, since I wrote for Black newspapers, but word got to her somehow. Then word got to me asking if I'd considered working on a cookbook. I had no idea what to do, but I knew I needed to test recipes to make sure anyone could use them, so I reached out to Ruby, and she said she'd help. Neither of us could have imagined where such a question would take us. I still remember working in the kitchen, where one of her children was around to sample what we made. To think," she added softly, her words drifting into the edges of her memory, "it would end like this."

* * *

The day was too cold for rain, but not cold enough for the snow to stick to the ground. Flurries hung in the air, melting as they hit pavement. I helped Shirleen out of the car, so Virgil could park around the back. We weren't the only car doing so – one car ahead of us was still unloading its passengers while another car parked behind us to do the same.

Shirleen strode in through the open church doors with ease, but she gripped my arm as we swept through the door. Her brimmed hat had a small veil, but it didn't obscure who she was, and there were whispers at first as we walked down the aisle, until someone from Ruby's family strode up.

He introduced himself as Ruby's youngest son and he had a red kerchief tucked into his suit. "Thank you for coming," he said, loud enough that everyone around us knew he spoke to Shirleen. "This way, please."

Led to the front of the church, I recognized a few people like Winifred Chan and other locals in the food industry, but most were Ruby's family and friends. The son took us to a pew right behind the immediate family. We had what could crassly be called the best seats in the house, as we could directly see the open casket before us. Ruby lay there in a dress as red as the rubies she took her name from. Her hands were folded across her chest, clutching a handkerchief from her husband who preceded her in death. Her features were arranged peacefully but I grew uneasy, as she looked like a wax figure to me. I was about to have Shirleen move further away so I wouldn't have such a direct view when Virgil joined us and settled on the other side of me, dashing the chance for such a move.

I was embarrassed to say, but my attention drifted during the funeral. I didn't know Ruby that well, and most of the parts I cared about – her joint history with Shirleen or her cooking career – were glossed over in favor of the other facets of her life.

I also didn't like funerals.

My very first memory was being at a funeral, standing next to my father as relatives gave their condolences for our loss. Granny was across from us, seated in the pews and holding my little sister, who was the only one unaware how much our lives had changed. I was very tiny, but I knew that much. I still remembered how my father had held my hand and that while I was barely three, I was the one holding him up.

When Shirleen grabbed my hand as they closed the casket's lid, I nearly jumped to my feet. Virgil's head turned in my direction, tilting soundlessly in question. I shook my head, and stayed still as Shirleen squeezed. She held on to me, until the final remarks and hymns began. We rose when the pallbearers picked up the casket and carried her out the church.

Flurries swirled in the air as we drove in Virgil's car in the long chain of cars crossing town to the family plot.

Shirleen leaned on Virgil for this trek into the funeral grounds. As Ruby's husband had already been laid to rest, her plot was still in the older part of the cemetery. Here, stone angels and other figureheads appeared to be watching as we passed through. The flurries had stopped, but enough had clung to the statues in odd places.

It was as I stood around the graveside, my eyes restlessly drifting to the other gravestones and markers, that I spotted Davis Packer. I knew he was here because, as one of the few white men in attendance, I couldn't help but notice him.

His eyes were not, I realized then, on the grave where Ruby was slowly being laid to rest, but on Shirleen as she and Virgil stood on the edge of the group, near Ruby's grown children. He seemed surprised to see her, and I wondered if he thought Shirleen wouldn't even show.

I was wondering if we would have the chance to speak with him as well when I looked across the open grave at the other mourners, and saw lurking in the far back a shadow come to ruin the day.

A shadow also known as Shirleen's ex-husband.

I stepped over to Shirleen and Virgil, and tugged at Virgil's arm to get his attention. He turned, but so did Shirleen.

"Glenn," Shirleen hissed, her voice rising to a whisper loud enough that a few heads nearly turned in our direction. "Don't you dare let him near me!"

"We won't," Virgil said. I moved around to block Glenn's sight of Shirleen.

The outrage in Shirleen's face faded as she glanced at me. "What are you doing, Keisha? You're attracting attention."

No one was really looking our way as the pallbearers approached, but her words, for all their rebuke, held a different tone all together.

Even though Glenn vanished back into the ether he came from, I remained on lookout for the rest of the proceedings, well aware of what trouble he could stir up.

On the walk back to the cars, we fell into step with Winifred Chan. Accompanied by an older Chinese man I took to be her husband, we exchanged polite greetings.

"How are you holding up, Shirleen?" Winifred asked. "You and Ruby had such an interesting relationship."

Shirleen sighed. "At the end of the day, another one of my friends is gone."

"I know the feeling," Winifred murmured, and her husband added:

"I see my friends and family mainly at funerals these days, and fewer of them each time."

"I'm impressed they put this together so quickly," Winifred began. "But then again, Ruby always was a planner. I used to think she'd have everything planned, including her death."

"Are you saying she planned this?" Shirleen asked archly. "Because this was not how she'd wanted to go."

Winifred paused, but no one could have missed the exasperation on her face.

"At a certain age we come to accept not all plans turn out the way we would like," Winifred's husband gently intervened. With practiced ease, he managed to keep the conversation away from the mysterious death of Ruby Walton and back to reminiscing over shared memories with Ruby and the restaurant she cooked out of by accident.

"We were there for dinner," the husband said, mainly to me and Virgil. "There was about ten of us at the table, and it was Ruby's treat since it was Winnie's birthday. Well, the cook had quit seeing us, and the moment she heard it, Ruby jumped up to cook."

"What a firecracker she was," Shirleen said.

"Pity how the light's gone out," Winifred mused.

Returning to the church for the repast we found it draped in Ruby's signature red, from the tablecloths to the flowers. There was even music playing in the background, soothing but upbeat songs that would have been on my grandmother's playlist. I found myself absently humming along, but when a few people coming in scoffed at me, Virgil hummed along with me for a few bars before a rich baritone joined us.

"This is a celebration of life and we're doing exactly what my sister would have wanted."

These words sent the disapproval scrambling as a slightly rotund older man turned to me with a smile. He had wild salt and pepper hair, and a beard that needed a slight trim. With a bulbous nose and thick-rimmed glasses, I saw nothing really in his features that resembled Ruby, but I knew this to be Ruben Patterson, her younger brother. "My sister had planned her homegoing services down to the very last detail – and if there was a problem, take it up with her!"

This got a few chuckles, and more importantly seemed to give permission for the tension in the air to abate. People found seating or lined up to get food and conversation rumbled about in earnest. Even laughter peppered the crowd as a reminder that we were here to remember people as they were in the vibrant technicolor of life.

"Stay right here, Aunt Shirls," Virgil said, leading her to a table. "We'll get you a plate."

"Take your time." Shirleen tugged at his sleeve, bringing him closer for her to add in a hushed tone, "And try to speak to Ruben, he might know why he was allowed to bury his sister so quickly. Oh, and if she was poisoned, like you two think."

"Auntie," Virgil hissed, even as I shared a wink with the older woman.

Shirleen patted his arm before letting go. "I know everything, so don't try to fool me. It didn't work when you tried to hide the vase you broke and it certainly won't work now." She held out her hand, and in response, Virgil withdrew a small bottle of hand sanitizer that he squirted in her hands and mine, before using it on himself.

"Will Shirleen be fine on her own?" I asked, as we joined the quickly growing line.

"Didn't you hear her? She practically shooed us off," Virgil grumbled. "Don't worry, we were probably keeping people from talking to *her*."

This seemed to be true.

I looked over my shoulder. We had only just stepped away, but the other mourners approached Shirleen like they were petitioning a queen, forming a short line that snaked through the tables.

"We must appear intimidating," I remarked.

"Or at least a barrier," Virgil said with a shrug. "I don't think she wants us to come back right away. She doesn't like the food they tend to have at these things."

"Because she didn't cook it?" I asked.

"Well, we couldn't exactly ask her," Ruben murmured.

I hadn't been paying attention so I somehow missed seeing Ruben come back around the room to join us once more. "The obituary she penned was enough." Bushy eyebrows furrowed together. "Although some would say she did it only to silence whispers, I knew she meant every word. It was lovely."

"I will tell her so," Virgil murmured.

"I didn't get a chance to know your sister well," I said, carefully spinning my words to appeal to Ruben's sensibilities, "but she did give me some advice I've taken to heart, since I'm following in her footsteps."

"That's right, you are the new recipe developer for Shirleen's book. I'd admit I didn't realize how important it was at the time. I was still in school when *Season by Season* was published... I think Ruby would have liked to do another one, but life takes you to odd places." His eyes grew solemn and Virgil awkwardly added:

"I know you said that your sister had preplanned these arrangements, but it must still be a shock."

Ruben's gaze drifted to the smiling portrait of his sister. "I used to joke Ruby wouldn't go quietly in her bed with all the family waiting for her last rattling breath. But I never expected this."

"She wasn't sick?" I asked.

Ruben shook his head. "Just the usual aches and pains that made it hard to get around. It's why she was finally planning to sell her house and move in with her oldest daughter. Gayle had been trying to get it to happen for years, and now just when things were about to settle this happened. I wonder…" He paused, and there was just long enough of a break that it was a race between Virgil and me to ask the next question.

Virgil beat me by a hair. "Was there something she told you?"

"It's nothing, it's just, you know how things happen, and you remember something you dismissed earlier that you see in blinding clarity now." Ruben drew a hand along his chin. "I last spoke to her two days before she died. I called about what do to for Christmas, and that I wanted to get her pipes looked at before things got cold enough to freeze. She wanted to know about the forks."

"Forks?" I asked.

Ruben nodded. "Never got what she meant, but it didn't seem that important. I thought it related to a party. She had so many serving platters, and special cutlery she only brought out to impress people."

"Did she mention any unusual or unexpected plans?" Virgil asked.

"Not directly. She usually didn't tell me a thing until she had a task in mind for me."

Because this was likely our best chance, I took the gamble and threw my cards down. "I don't think her death was an accident."

Ruben looked at me long and hard before he said in a hushed tone, "I had the same thought when I learned there was poison in her system!"

Forgetting entirely about pretense, I asked, "What kind?"

"Something out of Agatha Christie. I can't remember details, but they found traces of something unexpected in the cake she ate. Some window of testing had passed so it's evidence, but not strong enough to be more than circumstantial. Something about the floor wax causing trouble. I didn't press the police to do a more thorough investigation. I guess I wanted it to be some sort of accident, so it could all be over… but why are you interested?"

"My aunt is one of the top suspects, despite very little strong evidence," Virgil said. "We think there is an angle the police are overlooking. Your sister was famous from her show. It's better to have a definitive answer to keep speculation down. We think there's more to the story."

"Like if someone wanted to hurt her?" Ruben frowned. "Can't think of anyone. She was leaving *Whisk it All* and was taking a small break. I hadn't heard of any trouble from her show or any place else."

"What about her past?" I asked, but a woman closer to our age approached.

"Uncle Ruben," she said quite apologetically as she interrupted. "They're asking about extra chairs. I don't know where they are."

"I have to take care of this," Ruben said.

"Go ahead," Virgil said. "Thank you for talking with us."

As the pair went off, I whispered to Virgil. "Did you get any of that?"

"Are you kidding," he tapped the lapel of his jacket revealing a small microphone as if he was a nerdier James Bond. "I was recording the moment we knocked the cemetery dirt from our shoes."

"You know, I had no idea Ruby was leaving the show," I said. "She was one of the most popular judges."

"Maybe it was time? She was on it for, what, ten years now?" Virgil paused before adding. "Aunt Shirls kept track of it."

"She did?"

Virgil nodded. "It was her way of keeping tabs. Aunt Shirls didn't watch the show or anything, but would ask me on occasion what I might have seen or heard."

"Yet they never talked to patch things up?"

"As far as I know the last chance was Birdie Bailey's funeral," Virgil said. "Timing wasn't right."

"I don't see how. What happened?"

Virgil hesitated and pulled at his collar, looking away from me, the tips of his ears going pink. "I can't tell you."

"Well now you *have* to," I said. "You know something!"

"I can't, not here." He lowered his voice to a whisper. "It's not right to say."

We were near the line for food, and people were standing too close for me to badger the truth out of him, so I said, "Don't say it, text it."

By the time I turned my phone on, I had several messages from Virgil waiting for me.

He didn't wait for me to look, diving into the food like a starving man.

It couldn't be so bad, I surmised as I opened his text, and my mouth fell open at the confession he couldn't utter aloud.

Love triangle gone wrong with DJ Oscar Fantom. S and OF dated first after the divorce. They broke up and OF moved onto R after her husband's death. Don't know the details, just that it blew up in a big way.

Well, that explained why the area's most famously booked and busy DJ was available to host Shirleen's little party.

I came up behind Virgil and when he saw my expression, he shuddered. "Don't ask me how I found out. She doesn't know I know."

I recognized the trauma in his eyes. In high school I had found out the hard way that my father had a new girlfriend when I came home early from a summer enrichment program. I asked instead, "Can we interview him too? Do you plan to?"

"I do," Virgil remarked, still wary about me reopening teenage traumas. "Oscar worked as a DJ at the same place that my aunt did the call-in show. He's been avoiding my calls."

"Because he knows exactly who you are. I'll handle it," I said, as I started filling a plate.

"I think he might know who you are as well," Virgil pointed out.

"Maybe, but not enough to care."

Back at the table, Shirleen's admirers were gone, but she wasn't alone. Chef Javier Navarro and his husband were at the table, as was an older woman whose name escaped me but looked familiar. Also at the table was Winifred and her husband, and Shirleen's former producer, Davis.

"Ah, the young people have returned," Davis declared. "We are saved from dreadful conversation."

"I don't know about that," Javier pointed out, "I'm sure Keisha would like to hear about the restaurant we started in the middle of a snowstorm by accident."

"You started it," his husband said reaching for his glass. "I warned him against it."

"It's a very good story," the chef said, smiling at me.

"I'd like to hear it," I said even as I squealed on the inside. Chef Javier Navarro knew my name! He could talk about the difference between romaine lettuce and arugula for all I cared!

Unfurling the napkin to spread across her lap, Shirleen winked at me, and said, "Fine, tell the story for the hundredth time, but just keep it short, Javier."

We ate as the chef regaled us with the perilous opening in a story I hadn't heard before, and was genuinely riveted by, despite everyone else interjecting their own comments. While I was curious about how the chef managed to source fresh produce in a storm that literally froze half the city, I found my attention drawn to the other end of the table. Virgil spoke to the woman I hadn't been introduced to yet with surprising warmth and animation.

I didn't catch what they were saying, until Javier's husband snapped his fingers and cried:

"*Moving Day*, I know that one! I started listening to it on my walks. That's you, my goodness, I love listening to how you tie objects to the reason for moving. My favorite one is about the suit of armor."

"He has other podcasts, you know," said the woman sitting next to Virgil. "*Wow, It Happened Here* and *It Was Law*, but they are under a different name, which makes them harder to find. But, once you do, you'll be in for a treat."

Virgil froze like an ice sculpture, and there was genuine panic in his eyes as he looked over at me.

I had planned to confront Virgil about this topic, but that desire fled as distress galloped across his features.

I forced a smile as I added. "I agree, they're quite good. Though I was really confused since there was a different name on them."

"The law podcast started from an old blog I began back in school," Virgil explained. "Charlie Montgomery seemed like a good way to prevent people at school from finding me and felt like a good enough name going forward. I kept the name for *Wow*, because I saw it as a spinoff."

"And also to keep people from finding it when you were an actual lawyer," Winifred said. "But it hardly matters now."

"Oh, it does," Shirleen cut in, "he wants to protect my privacy."

Her words were lighthearted but she stabbed the meat on her plate as she spoke.

"How many listeners do you have?" cheerily asked the woman who started this whole thing.

"Not many," Virgil remarked, and added, looking in my direction, "but as they say, quality over quantity."

"I didn't realize you were such an experienced hand at this," Davis said. "I just thought this was a little companion project because Shirleen didn't want to do any television interviews. How deep into Shirleen's history will you go, if you don't mind sharing? Will you talk about the feud?" The producer paused as he waited for protests, but when none came, he merely kept his gaze fixed on Virgil. "Well, will you?"

Virgil gripped the fork in his hand, but his words were smooth and unbothered as before. "It's part of the history, isn't it? There's no need to speak of it in great detail, as it happened later after many successful collaborations."

"You'll have only one side of the story," Winifred murmured.

"I can help with several details," Davis said hastily. "I was there, with a front row seat on the set."

"There's no need to dredge up all the past," Shirleen cut in. She twirled a fork around, her expression a mirror of her nephew's. "Plus, I trust Virgil will know better than any of us which parts will make a good tale. He's been interviewing a number of people from the old days."

"I spoke with him recently," Winifred chimed in. "It was a lovely conversation. Didn't you get a chance yet, Davis? I'm surprised you let a chance to run your mouth go past."

"I did send an invitation to you," Virgil added before Davis could chime in. "You might have missed it. But the offer still stands."

"I will have to think about it. Although I would like to listen to what samples you have, to know what to prepare for."

"I've only just started," Virgil said half truthfully.

"You must get to work soon," Chef Javier encouraged. "These days, if you're lagging behind you are in the dust!"

"Well, there's been so much to focus on," Virgil said.

"You'll figure it out, you always do," the woman seated next to Virgil said. She patted his arm and stood up, picking up her purse.

A large tote with *Starry Night* painted on it.

My staring at the tote – and the realization that I had seen it the night of the party – was noticeable enough that it earned me some chuckles.

"Why, Margot," Shirleen said to the woman, "I can't believe you brought that here!"

In answer Margot laughed and hitched the bag onto her shoulder. "Why not? One purse serves me well for all my needs. Besides, don't you remember Ruby gave this to me?"

Margot pressed a hand to Javier's shoulder and then blew a kiss at Winifred. "I will see you all later. Hopefully when we get to celebrate something a bit more cheerful."

I waited all of a few seconds before I got up to follow, grabbing my coat and purse just in case she headed outside.

Margot was not going around collecting food to shovel into her purse, but she did stop at a few more tables, saying a kind word or two before passing along a card.

Not wanting to be so obvious I was following her, I wound around in the opposite direction and caught up with her near the door.

She had pulled on her coat, but was taking her time with the gloves. She was moving between each finger, pulling them snug, and it was only as she was repeating the act did I know my furtive attempts were for naught.

"What do you want to ask me, Miss Keisha Scott?"

At a glance of her unamused expression I knew I had one shot before she walked away.

"What did you do with the dozen appetizers you snuck in your bag?" I began.

"Had a very hearty lunch the next day," Margot said. She tilted her head to the side. With smooth dark brown skin, and hair that showed not a hint of gray, I knew she was much older than me, but by how much was not something I could find out without asking. Nor did I dare as her eyes studied me as closely as mine did her. "Surely you didn't come all this way to ask me that. What do you really want to ask?"

"How do you know Shirleen and her nephew?"

I chose that question as it was a good way to ease in, and it was true enough. I did want to know as it explained her presence, and why I recognized the name Margot Baptiste from the list, but didn't know the face or her role in Shirleen's world.

"I'm a caterer. Retired caterer, that is. Just this past spring. I was the link that kept Ruby and Shirleen in contact these past years. One told me things hoping I'd pass it onto the other. I usually did because I loved the gossip."

"Who did you know longer?" I couldn't help but ask.

Margot exhaled. "I met them at a New Year's Eve party one year. It was late but not that late for the ball drop. I was having a hard time at the party, and they said to come with them to a better party. Then the next thing I know I'm sitting on a couch talking to an opera superstar and agreeing to cater Malcolm Demetrious Freeman's next party because his usual caterer was going on vacation. I never became famous or influential, but I made a nice life. I'm grateful for that and, if asked, I'm willing to do what I can for my friend who changed everything for me."

"Like invite them to a party in hopes to mend bridges?" I asked.

Margot's face revealed how close I landed to the truth, with a shocked but resigned expression.

"How did you know that?"

"I have been in the middle of friend squabbles before," I said. "I know no matter how wonderful my individual friendships are, as a group we are better. So I've meddled a few times."

Margot grunted. "You strike me as the meddling type."

"I'll take that as a compliment."

"Try not to, it leads to trouble. Take it from personal experience." She sighed even more. "Yes, I made sure Ruby was there. She told me she had gotten invited, wasn't sure if it was a joke Shirleen was pulling. I told her that was unlikely, as it came from Shirleen's assistant. I encouraged her to come. I saw it as a chance to force them to finally reconcile. The feud they had was really amped up by the media, but they just didn't know how to go forward. That's why I told her to bring a cake. It was their first collaboration together. I suppose I should have mentioned this to Shirleen as well. You heard her reaction."

"She didn't kick Ruby out," I reminded her.

"No, but she should have, it might have saved her life. Instead of being obligated to stay around and play nice. Ruby looked slightly unwell when I took the cake from her. I sat her down in an empty room. I put the cake up and went to get her some water, but when I came back, Ruby was gone."

"Did you take her cake knife too?" I asked.

Margot frowned. "No, why would she carry knives when there are some in the kitchen?"

"Forget about that," I said hastily. "What do you mean unwell?"

"I'm no doctor, but I didn't see her often, and there was change, that I couldn't fully name. In fact, I saw more of Ruby on her show and even those were filmed months in advance. Ruby once told me *Whisk* often held entire seasons back nearly a full year. Sometimes for schedules, but other times due to contract negotiations."

"Did that happen often?" I asked.

"Often enough that I wasn't surprised she mentioned it in one of the last conversations we had. Something about her agent messing things up. I think she was ready to leave the show and do something else. When you get to a certain age you really only want to put your energy toward the things that truly matter." Margot tugged at her gloves one last time and stroked her *Starry Night* bag. "Make time for your friends, Keisha."

"I will," I said.

Returning to the table, I found that Winifred and her husband had finished up and left but were making rounds around the room. Her husband held her coat and purse and looked impatiently at his watch. Davis, plus Chef Javier and his husband, were still talking to Shirleen, although a few others had filled the vacant seats, including Virgil's. Virgil himself was nowhere in sight. Shirleen, while nodding at what the chef was saying, discreetly pointed to the door that opened to the hallway and the rest of the church.

I was peering out into the hall, wondering if Virgil had gone back to the car, only to find him sitting on a wooden bench in the meditation garden.

A small space, it was slightly triangular, with the church's three walls wrapped around. In its center was a water fountain that was turned off for winter. It was a garden that, according to the signs, would sprout marigolds in the spring.

While others came here to take in the quiet beauty, Virgil had his eyes shut to it. He had slumped against the bench, hands folded against his chest, and long legs stretched before him. He must have heard the door open, for when I dropped down on the bench next to him, he didn't even react.

"So, this is where you went," I said.

"I wasn't going to stay out here that long," he muttered. "Just needed a breath of cold fresh air."

I fumed and tried not to sound too accusatory as I said, "I was invited not for Shirleen's sake, but for yours."

His eyes snapped opened, and he sat up like a windup doll. "For investigation stuff!" he sputtered.

"Yes, but if we weren't doing it, you'd still ask me along as some sort of buffer. As the fresh new face, they'll be telling me all the stories and asking probing questions about why I'm not half the success Shirleen is."

Virgil sighed. "I've been around this all my life, and Aunt Shirls didn't believe in babysitters. It was easier when I was still in school, as I could trot out a few classes and move on. But I became a lawyer and then I quit, and now people feel free to give opinions on what I should be doing instead. Usually it's not so bad, but there are people who'll get very rude."

"What makes you think I would bail you out?" I pretended to scowl at him. "You lied by omission about the other podcasts! Why not tell me? I was already listening to the new stuff."

"I was too embarrassed. I started them in what feels like another life."

"Because you were a big shot lawyer who decided to do a major pivot?" I said puzzled. "Virgil, I was a data analyst at major tech companies, and a darn good one too, before I quit everything to work on a cookbook. You at least did it because your aunt got sick. I did it because I had a really bad break-up. I had to do something. Before Shirleen contacted me, I was seriously considering dyeing my hair electric blue."

A laugh escaped him, not because I said anything particularly amusing, but because I tapped the valve for the release.

"You're right," he said once he composed himself. "I should have told you. What did you think?"

"In general, you got a good thing going on," I said. Although he smiled, something about it left me uneasy in a way I didn't quite comprehend. Pretending to cough I said, "Did Shirleen say how long she wanted to stay here?"

"I'm not sure, but we should head back inside. I wanted to speak with Ruby's children. I just don't know if they want to talk to me."

"But it looks like he does," I said pointing.

Davis peered out from the window. His nose wasn't pressed to the glass but he looked like a scientist peering at a brewing experiment uncertain about how it was going.

Taking my gesture as an invitation, he stepped into the garden, breaking the peaceful air with a burst of conversation from outside.

"There you are," Davis said. "I wanted a word more about this podcast of yours. What is the hardline of what you're putting in it?"

I bit my tongue to hold back a question. This was Virgil's podcast after all, but given Davis's earlier comments I wondered why the sudden interest.

"Hardline about what?" Virgil asked.

"The details about the past. The feud, I mean, between Shirleen and Ruby. It's important to talk about, but it's a very sensitive subject."

He had some gall to say that at the repast, where Ruby's loved ones were nearby, and it was no less galling here in the quiet of the mediation garden.

Virgil took out his phone, and made a show of turning on the recorder. "What do you know about their feud? I was in college when this all went down, and barely remember the finer details."

The flashing recording was a siren call to Davis. He walked over at once. Because he had forgotten his overcoat, he rubbed his hands and crossed his arms over his chest as he drew closer.

"The feud between Shirleen and Ruby came to the forefront fifteen years ago, but it had really started during the production of their show. It was the first time Shirleen and Ruby worked together."

"Not true," Virgil countered. "The radio talk show had Ruby on as a frequent guest."

"But that's the difference." Davis stomped his foot as he shuffled slightly. "She was a guest then, and the lines were clearly defined. *Today's Meal* put them on equal terms. They were co-hosts, partners, equal sides of a seesaw, and out in front of the camera together. While Shirleen can command the stage quite well, Ruby was a character that always drew attention given her vibrant and cheerful air. She also better matched the feminine air that a lot of the advertisers wanted to see. A soft soprano to Shirleen's brassier tone. Ruby was also a fresher face as she had stayed out of the limelight until then, and this changed their dynamic."

"You're saying Shirleen didn't like this shift?" I asked.

Davis took a moment before he replied. "I don't think she would ever put it that way, but I don't think she did. They argued before every taping, and even in production meetings, usually about the recipes. As the months went by the whole thing fell apart, and the crew was being asked to take sides."

"Choose between a woman who had become a household name with a landmark cookbook, or the woman who toiled behind the scenes who finally took center stage," Virgil said. "A tough choice."

"One that many refused to make," Davis said. "A portion of the crew quit or asked to work on a different production. As for the rest… while nothing ever made it to the show, there were things that went wrong when the cameras weren't rolling. Salt replaced with sugar, cue cards mixed up, counters moved just slightly in the wrong direction. I still have this vivid memory of a pile of bowls that fell on Shirleen. With a howl she snatched one up and threw it at the crew with such skill that the Cubs should have offered her a job." He waited for a reaction that never came, so Davis quickly added, "Production stopped shortly afterward. Ratings were decent, but not good enough for the execs when they heard about the troubles. Because of Shirleen's history I was able to produce her next show with her, which was a hit. Ruby walked instead of being part of it."

"She would be at *Dash* magazine for a while, and worked in film as a food stylist and consultant before joining *Whisk it All,*" Virgil said. "They remained friendly, it seems, for the next few years. I remember Ruby coming by when I was a boy."

"However, this is the moment the first cracks were made and grew until the friendship broke."

Virgil stopped the recording on his phone. "Thanks for this. When would be a good time for a more formal interview? I really wanted to hear more about the other shows you worked with Shirleen on. I'm happy to come by your office or another spot that is convenient for you."

"I will let you know, just need to get my secretary to check my schedule." Davis shivered. "Goodness, it's cold, isn't it?" He looked at us expectantly. "Let's go inside, shall we?"

Back once more in the church and embraced by the warmth, Davis shuffled off, and Virgil and I returned to the table to find Shirleen seated with a middle-aged woman who was Ruby from thirty years ago, except her hair wasn't dyed red.

"Gayle," Shirleen said, "this is my nephew, Virgil. With him, is Keisha Scott, who is working as my recipe developer, just like your mother did once."

"Nice to meet you both," Gayle said in a hoarse but warm tone. "I was just telling Shirleen how Mom was so excited to get invited to the party. I wish I'd been able to go with her. I remember the most about the cookbook out of all of us. I didn't go because my children wanted to watch that *Grinch* show, and Mom kept saying she wouldn't stay out late as she wasn't a spring chicken anymore and didn't like taking taxis so late."

"She took a taxi?" I asked. Gayle looked at me so defensively, I hastened to add awkwardly, "I thought there weren't any more of those things with all the rideshare apps."

Gayle relaxed with a nod. "They're still around. My mother stopped driving when my father died, and since the rest of us were at work or were too far away from most of her errands, she was a regular at Stringfield Motors. All the cabbies knew her, and she had a few favorites. They often waited for her if her errand wasn't too long."

"How interesting," Virgil said. "Can I have their number?"

Gayle blinked. "Why would you want it?"

"Because he's trying to get out of driving me around!" Shirleen jested. "If you won't drive me, I'll be like Keisha, bicycling around everywhere! I've seen three-wheeled trikes, I can manage that quite well, I think! Just picture me with a basket full of vegetables. Very French, or is it Dutch? I heard there are more bicycles than there are cars in

Holland." Shirleen rambled long enough I realized she was trying to distract Gayle, who frowned, at first in suspicion before bemusement took over, as Virgil chimed in with several disagreements.

As they did an amazing job of distracting Gayle, I quickly jotted down Stringfield Motors into my notes.

How interesting that Ruby was using cabbies! We might be able to get a sense of what she was doing the last few days before she died if we find at least one she rode with.

"I heard you have a moving company," Gayle said to Virgil. "I don't have a date or time yet, but I hope you can assist me in moving my mother's things from her home when my siblings and I decide what to do."

"Certainly." Virgil withdrew a business card with *Moving Champions* splashed on the front. "Take as long as you need to decide. When you're ready I'll be there with a truck."

After saying our goodbyes to Ruby's family and a handful of Shirleen's old friends, we departed at last to head back to Hunton Bay.

Shirleen waited until we were safely out of sight of the church before she did a giddy jig in her seat. "Wasn't I good? I managed to keep things from getting badly derailed! Keisha, if you're going to be an investigator, you must not ask questions that put people on high alert."

"Don't tell me you recorded that," I said to Virgil, as I slipped my feet out of my shoes.

"Sorry," Virgil said pulling out the microphone. "I'll cut it out. Aunt Shirls, did you know that Ruby went around in cabs?"

Shirleen grew less bubbly as she replied. "I didn't know all her habits, but she liked that sort of thing. She could take care of her business and not let her children worry. She liked to keep things close to her chest. Not secrets, but plans, until it was time to unveil them."

"Well, now we have a taxi cab company to question," I said. "I need to ask if the driver knew about the cake she brought."

"Ruby brought a cake with her?" Shirleen asked.

"To impress someone at the party?" I said. "It was her version of the Orange Chocolate Cake."

"No, it was for me," Shirleen's voice trailed softly in the car. "It was our apology cake. We made it when we argued. Big arguments, small tiffs, bets, disagreements, anything really."

"She didn't have it when she saw you," I said as delicately as I could.

"I wish I knew why not," Shirleen said as she turned to the window. "It would have changed the entire night."

The rumors are true! Shirleen Foster is coming to a television near you in Fall 1997. The new show, aptly titled *Shirleen Foster's Kitchen Wisdom*, draws upon the format that her long-time radio listeners will enjoy. She takes people's calls and letters, and provides a way to get out of the stickiest situations. Her producer, Davis Packer, sees it as a chance to bring Shirleen's work to a new audience looking for something they can't get elsewhere: "With so much noise and conflicting advice, people enjoy her straightforward approach. People want a partner in the kitchen, not someone issuing demands. Shirleen is unpredictable and prone to add twists you don't expect, but that's part of her charm and what make good television."

- From the *Hunton Bay Journal*

Chapter 15

Although Romy and Eden wanted to come to the gingerbread house contest, they couldn't make it due to work. I ended up asking Pascal to drive me, as my fairy tale castle was too big to wrangle on the train.

"Yeah, let that be your excuse," Pascal chuckled as he slid into his parking spot at Hook College. "I know you only asked me for the perks."

A former professor turned adjunct at the college, Pascal had enough influence to be able to park on the campus in one of the good lots. This came in quite clutch for various events the school put on and came with a guarantee of company. And for all that Pascal complained, he was more than happy to join me attending the various events Hook put on for the community.

"I wanted you to come, you're the first I thought of since I know how you are around sweets," I protested with a laugh. "Although the good parking spot doesn't hurt."

Unlike the last time I was there, the campus was much more alive, and it seemed the gingerbread house wasn't the only event as other holiday adjacent activities were occurring on the last weekend before exams began.

At first, I thought we were lost, but then little gingerbread signs began to crop up on the sidewalk, guiding us to the familiar building. Already, a short line had formed at the registration table.

Lucia was not one of the smiling people at the table, which was good since I entered under a false name.

Although I hadn't warned him, Pascal did not react at hearing 'KeKe Hardison' wished good luck. He just took the package and table assignment and murmured to me:

"I guess this might work after all, even if you don't have much of a plan."

After helping me get set up, Pascal took to roaming around the floor, in search for anyone handing out samples of gingerbread.

For something I put together in less than a week, I was quite proud of myself for how the castle appeared. I had just settled on the best angle to position it when Virgil approached. I had expected him, but not Shirleen as well.

Both were in better spirits than when I saw them last. Out of black and once more in her accustomed uniform with a brooch of a gingerbread man pinned to her shirt, Shirleen appeared less wan and had her usual spunk as she complained about how the competition was broken into tiers. Virgil nodded along. Although he had his bookbag slung over his shoulder once more with its frayed patches from his travels, he carried the nice camel colored wool coat over his arm.

"Good timing," I said. "I just got set up."

"Wasn't sure when it started," Virgil said. "I thought for sure you'd put it in one of those trailers on your bike."

"It's too small," I pretended to lament, "and the castle is too delicate."

"Then you could have asked me for help," Virgil said. "I would have come by."

As I was about to cobble together a good enough excuse, Shirleen interrupted.

"Goodness, you really did go all out to make one," she said as she walked around the table admiring my creation. My fairy tale castle stretched along the pan, with four towers with tiny windows and balconies. A small courtyard connected the buildings, and licorice gardens surrounded the castle. I built out the sugar moat, and placed gumdrops to stand in as jewels.

"This is amazing, but," Virgil added, a smile playing along his lips as he looked over at me, "I don't see any dinosaurs on spaceships."

"I didn't have nearly enough time," I said.

"If you wanted gingerbread dinosaurs, you could have gone around to help, I'm sure Keisha would have appreciated it," Shirleen remarked.

"She said the idea was to win, and she could do it without me," Virgil drawled. He stroked his chin as his gaze moved from the gingerbread back to me. "You really think it would draw Lucia out here? I haven't seen her yet."

"We can always break into her office," I said. "I got a lockpicking kit from off the internet."

"I'm going to pretend you didn't say that." Pascal's dry remark announced his return as he pretended to scowl at me.

"It might be defective," I said sweetly. "I haven't tried it yet."

He tsked, but his attention had moved away from me to Virgil and Shirleen. Especially Shirleen.

I don't think Pascal heard me at all as I made introductions. He just smiled at her, and she smiled right back.

"You're Shirleen Foster," he declared breathlessly. "I've heard a great deal about you from Keisha these past few months. Not that I didn't know about you before, there's your cookbooks and everything, but I'm a big fan. A very big fan."

"Always nice to meet another one." Shirleen grinned over this awkward exchange. "No need to be so formal. A friend of Keisha's is a friend of mine. You wouldn't happen to be that same Pascal she's been trying her recipes on?"

"I am. I live right next door. On my own. No kids and my wife's been gone ten years now."

"Sorry to hear that." Shirleen then pointed at Virgil. "I only have a nephew who's getting better at not hovering around me. I'm divorced though."

"I know, I heard, I mean–"

"Gossip has spread quite a bit about me already," Shirleen serenely interrupted. "Tell me what brings you here beyond helping out our young friend?"

"I am an adjunct at the college these days, because I can't really retire. As they say, when you stop moving–"

"The world just stops!" Shirleen declared.

They shared a laugh, and they turned to the other, off in their own little bubble as Virgil and I became akin to houseplants. "What do you teach? Keisha never told me that part…"

They strode off together, chattering away.

"Well, that'll keep them occupied and distracted as we do murder things," I said brightly.

"We'll see." Virgil took a picture of the gingerbread castle with his phone. "So, KeKe Hardison, do you think this plan will work?"

"It got us through the door." I put out the box where attendees could drop tokens to show how much they liked my gingerbread house. "Let's go look for Lucia."

The gingerbread house contest filled the large lecture hall, with several tables spilling out into the corridor, and some were even in classrooms. The houses were clustered by categories, so the ones made by elementary students and teenagers were separated from the adults. There were themes, for traditional houses, creative builds, edible builds, and even professional exhibitions.

The exhibitions were in a classroom; while there were only five, these were massive creations that stretched the concept of a gingerbread house to the very limits of imagination. From an abbey occupied by warrior mice and crafty badgers, to a ruined ancient moon castle, to a shipwreck split in half with archaeologist mermaids excavating its contents, to treehouses in a giant redwood forest where tiny gingerbread children ran along rope bridges. Each one was an art piece made by masters of their craft, and I could stare at any for hours. The biggest crowd had gathered around the leaning tower of Pisa, rendered in gingerbread and so cleverly engineered I kept walking around, wondering what non-edible items were used to keep it structurally sound.

"It's not just frosting, is it?" Virgil said as he turned his head to stare.

"A true master of the craft can do anything," I said even though I had no better idea than he did.

Another turn around the event brought us back to the room we started in. There were more gingerbread creations on the tables, as by now the event was in full swing. Some I wasn't quite impressed by as mine had quite a unique flair. As I surveyed them, I spotted Lucia standing front of my gingerbread castle, taking notes with deeply furrowed brows.

"You hooked the fish," Virgil whispered into my ear. "Shall we collect?"

He needn't bother.

As he spoke, Lucia looked up. Her eyes widened and she spun around and nearly bumped into the table.

"I think she saw us," I murmured.

Lucia clutched her clipboard to her chest, with her features set into a heavy scowl.

"I know that this is a free event," she fumed, "but you have some nerve showing up here!"

"We're here for the gingerbread houses," I said. "They're very cute. I even entered myself."

Lucia's eyes drifted toward my table and appeared even more miserable if possible. "The castle is yours?"

"Yes."

"What a pity, it's quite excellent." Lucia turned to Virgil. "I told you I'm too busy for an interview."

"It'll just take a moment. We can do it right now in one of the empty rooms." Virgil said. "I just wanted a few quotes about how working with my aunt influenced your career. You were one of her protégés and worked with her on her other endeavors too. I only need a little of your time."

"Give me a few minutes," Lucia relented. "Then maybe we can talk."

This was good… but Lucia agreed too easily. The last time we spoke she all but ran from us. So, what changed?

"I have to finish this section," Lucia said. "But if you set up in the kitchen classroom down the hall, I'll meet you there. It'll be the room next to a Christmas tree covered with kitchen utensils."

We found the tree easily enough given the ribbons around wooden spoons. While Virgil went inside to set up the room I went back lingered around the contest, keeping an eye on Lucia as she finished her round of judging.

True to her word, Lucia didn't take too much longer, she just needed to judge about five more houses. Once complete, she relinquished her clipboard and tucked her judge button into the voluminous pockets of her cardigan.

"I wasn't going to run," Lucia said, as I fell into step with her.

"I was just taking another look," I said airily. "This is a great turnout."

"Yes, it is," Lucia said proudly. "Most of the top prizes are bragging rights, but we managed to attract the attention of some serious gingerbread competitors. We expanded this year and I'm quite proud about the world class builders we were able to bring here."

Lucia rattled off the details of events as we got to the room.

The classroom had a dozen separate workstations with ovens, stoves, and shelves. With classes ended, the stations were empty of bowls and appliances I might have expected yet smells of rosemary and brown sugar lingered in the air.

Virgil had set up a pair of microphones at the desk a teacher would sit at and was fiddling with them as he gestured for Lucia to sit on the seat across from him. He pulled a stool from one of the workstations over for me, but it was not next to him. Instead, it was angled behind Lucia.

At first annoyed because I wanted to discreetly study her expressions, I found as I sat down I could see Lucia's face quite easily in the reflection of the shiny stainless steel stand mixer on the teacher's desk,

I caught Virgil's eyes on me, and I nodded as I opened my notebook.

"Keisha will be keeping time for us," Virgil explained before Lucia could even ask about my presence. He kept focused on the equipment as if Lucia herself was only secondary. "Don't worry, it's just a conversation. You can always tell me later if there's something you want cut."

Lucia swallowed, and her reflection in the mixer looked rather stretched. "Okay," she said.

He gestured for her to put on the headphones, and he did the same, before turning on the recording equipment.

The first few minutes were a fairly standard introduction. As it turned out, Lucia nearly dropped out of culinary school twice.

"To keep it simple, I will just say there was a lot of personal tragedy, including the death of my brother. He, my brother, always said I cooked too well not to share it with the world. In the last few months of his life, we watched Shirleen's shows. As it happened, I was able to attend a talk she was doing at the local culinary school, we got to talking, and she encouraged me to enroll. Even said to keep in touch. The program had an externship program and as Shirleen was opening a small restaurant, I twisted her arm to let me work for her. I stayed with her for the duration she had it, and it taught me more than I realized at the time. I learned several of her recipes from *Season by Season* because that's what the restaurant served mainly. I did my best knowing this could end as easily as it started, because she famously didn't take on students."

"Why didn't she?" Virgil asked.

"Because she was very much a self-taught cook. Her food was elegant, and she understood flavor, but her way of doing things was very unique. She also had certain expectations.

She was a taskmaster, which was why the restaurant didn't last for so long. Most of the staff quit to go elsewhere. While people flock to restaurants based on the chef, it's really the staff who keep you coming back."

"You stayed in the restaurant business for quite a while," Virgil observed.

Lucia's distorted expression hardly wavered. "I went from place to place to pick up skills, although I found myself focused on pastry. Shirleen gave me the foundations for it. She was about layering flavors, deepening them, or even using them to mask rather unusual things. She was very big on natural food coloring long before there was a movement for it. It was around the Christmas cakes mania when we crossed paths again."

Virgil glanced at his set of notes. "What started the Christmas cakes mania?"

"Tabloids." Lucia chuckled. "Some famous actress had one of Shirleen's cakes at her Christmas party. Everyone loved them, everyone wanted them, and the actress made sure the press shared the recipe. From there it started not just with that one, but all of them, as a reporter called them the "twelve cakes of the season". I was tapped to bake the cakes for show appearances. Doing those shows allowed me to finally raise enough money to get my own restaurant."

At hearing these words, I sat up on the stool, my wandering attention becoming razor sharp. I knew from gossip Lucia's restaurant had failed and failed in such a spectacular manner she vowed to never open a restaurant ever again.

I didn't know much more than that, but as my gaze drifted to Virgil, his dark eyes held a well of knowledge. "Was it just you running the restaurant?"

"I consulted Shirleen, took her advice on supplies, on a number of things – and well, most restaurants close after a few seasons, this is a business where we make an art of losing money. If not for Shirleen, I might have lasted a full year." Lucia's voice rose, rising in pitch, as she was nearly bursting to get the words out. "Shirleen is many things, but she doesn't know how to run a business, because it means managing people and getting people to fit in her neat little world. When they do not fit, when they go against her plan, it goes flatter than a soufflé in an earthquake."

"Perhaps that's why she stuck to cookbooks. Restaurant work was very short-lived," Virgil said.

"Food writing is where she excels," Lucia said. "Because no matter what she shares, people will make adjustments or blame themselves. It's also less work. Because there's only so many ways to make certain cakes, you end up with a familiar pattern and a few tweaks. You can say it's the secret to her success, she's very great at improvising."

"Sometimes a riff is what makes things work wonderfully," Virgil said. "As they say, all good artists steal."

"Exactly," Lucia leaned in closer to the microphone. "What they can't create, they steal."

To my surprise, Virgil didn't pursue further from here. He asked Lucia a few more questions, more about her favorites, and recipes from *Season by Season*, and what she thought should be updated or remain unaltered.

Virgil led the conversation so smoothly that when he suddenly reached forward to turn off the equipment, I didn't react until he said my name.

"Keisha has given me the signal, so that's all the time we have. You should head back, can't have you missing the event. Thank you so much for talking to me."

Lucia's chuckle was almost forced. "I'm afraid I went on a small rant. I haven't had a chance to talk like this to many people." Her face was rather bland as she asked, "Will Shirleen listen to this?"

"My aunt expressed an interest."

"Good." The bitter edge in Lucia's words could slice through molasses. "I hope she does. She ruined my restaurant. I wouldn't even be at this school, if it weren't for pity. Let this remind her of what she did!"

Lucia grabbed her bag and departed with stomps, a sound eclipsed only by the slamming of the door behind her.

"I thought she was suddenly very eager to talk, so this explains why," I began, only to stop as Virgil lifted a hand to show where the light for recording was still on.

"It was still running!" I exclaimed.

"I thought there might be more she had to say," Virgil said. "I knew there was a reason she was suddenly too eager. Didn't expect she'd unload like that."

"She cites stealing recipes, bad advice, bad tempers, and bad businesses," I said. "Everything to slander Shirleen's name and burn the proverbial bridge with it. Does she think you'll publish this?"

"I know she wanted Aunt Shirls to listen to what we recorded, but I think Lucia agreed to speak to us for another reason. She knows we're investigating."

Interview: Winifred Chan

Virgil Sullivan, voiceover: *Few people in the food world need an introduction to Winifred Chan, who at the time of this recording is the latest editor-in-chief at* Ladle. *A former dining editor at* Honolulu Chronicle, *she has written for* T Magazine, Chicago Reader, *and* San Francisco Chronicle. *While known to each other for some years previously, she and Shirleen didn't work together in a professional capacity until my personal favorite cookbook,* Rise and Shine. *Winifred contributed a few recipes to that book, as well as* Bring the World to Your Kitchen. *They also are co-founders of Clarify, an organization that provided cooking lessons to the community and gave teaching opportunities to immigrants, empty nesters, the formerly incarcerated, and others seeking a second chance.*

Virgil Sullivan: *What made the school interesting was that no two sessions were ever the same. Could you tell me more about that?*

Winifred Chan: *I would love to. Though I must say it was all Shirleen's idea. She was big on letting these women – it was and still is mostly women who taught, although not everyone was – decide their courses. They could teach their favorites, or the staples, or what they thought their students might want to eat. Some of them were never going to teach cooking outside of this, but for some of the ladies it gave them a sense of control. Shirleen was very adamant that we dictate nothing more than the cap of class sizes and what ingredients they can have. She still talks about the teacher who managed to get our poor admin to purchase an obscene amount of she-crab that mysteriously wasn't at all featured in the class!*

Chapter 16

I didn't win the gingerbread house competition, but I took a respectable third place. Which was always better than second, even though I knew there was some bias in the judging.

I did have a few children come back wanting to take pictures of my castle, and one girl, no more than nine with big round glasses rolled right up to me in a wheelchair with tinsel wrapped around the arm rests, a sketch book, and a keen look in her eyes as she asked me how I made it. She had a good grasp of baking terms and firmly told me she bakes with a real oven, with her daddy acting as her hands.

For the pair, I sketched out the entire castle and put down the precise measurements for each piece. The girl's grin grew wider with each passing moment, but her father was torn between grateful, amused, and worried, as I broke down how to put it together.

By the time I finished, Shirleen had returned. Standing at Virgil's side she gestured toward the gingerbread house and they exchanged whispers and chuckles about past ill-fated gingerbread houses.

Watching Shirleen, I could see the images that Lucia had painted. I suppose there was some truth, as Shirleen was famously hard to work with, but she was no worse than any other boss I had before.

I also could see how wrong I was about her relationship with Virgil. The prickly arguments and grumbling I'd been witness to were clearly anomalies compared to the affection that passed between them.

"What's going to happen to that cake?" Pascal asked as I began packing it up. "I heard only the winner will stay here."

"Maybe it can go elsewhere." Virgil turned to Shirleen. "Would the Moonhaven House take it?"

Shirleen nodded. "I'm sure they will. The kids would love it, let me call them." She whipped out her phone and dialed right then.

Before I even got the case over my castle once more, Shirleen called. "They'll take it today. Virgil will take you, Keisha, he knows the address."

Virgil narrowed his eyes at his aunt who looked far too innocent. "You make it sound like you're not coming with us?"

"I could, but it's way out the way, and I want to get home."

"We'll drop you off on the way."

"I could take Shirleen home," Pascal said quite easily. "You do live nearby."

"Very near." Shirleen waved off Virgil's grumbling as she smiled at Pascal. "I appreciate you offering. Where did you park?"

"Just on the other side."

"Show me the way. Oh Virgil, text me when you're back at your apartment."

As the pair departed, I looked over at Virgil, who appeared more amused than anything as he checked the directions on his phone.

"Aren't you going to stop them?" I asked.

"No," he replied. "I just remembered the cab company that Ruby used isn't that far away from the shelter."

The director at Moonhaven House was charmed when Virgil and I brought in the gingerbread castle over the threshold.

"Shirleen had said it was a castle, with a drawbridge and everything, and I thought she was exaggerating. This is wonderful, thank you for bringing it!"

"Where would you like it?" I asked.

"This way," the director said, taking us through a series of hallways and unlocking a pair of doors until suddenly we were in a large but warm room. The reading of some fairy tales were broken up as the first of the children saw us.

We were swarmed before we could even get the gingerbread house onto the table that the director had pointed out. There were nine or so kids who wanted to know where it came from or if they could eat it.

"No, you can't eat that," cried a young and tired woman who grabbed one of the smaller children. She looked at us with desperation for some greater authority.

"You can't eat it," I echoed as I leaned forward to get eye level with the child. "It's just for display. Santa sent it early."

"Santa!" one of the older boys huffed. He had eyes that had seen too much trouble for someone barely eleven. He adjusted the sling holding his broken arm. "Santa ain't no thing, other than made up! Where did it really come from?"

"She made it for a contest," Virgil explained as he pointed to me. "My aunt, Shirleen Foster, told us to bring it here."

"Miss Shirleen is your auntie?" a younger boy gasped. "Is she going to cook again?"

"Did she bring a turkey?" a girl cried.

"Or soup!" squealed another.

"Grilled cheese!" added another, and a cheer went up around the children as they began to chant Shirleen's name.

Before I knew it, I was peppered with questions about where Shirleen was and all the tasty things she made for them the last time they saw her. Even some of the mothers, who were drawn in from the kitchen, or the corners of the common room, asked no less enthused questions.

"Miss Shirleen is not here today," the director announced over the eager crowd. "But she will be here for our Holiday Party."

"Promise," the boy with the broken arm said, turning to Virgil. There was a desperate hope in his eyes even as he tried to act tough. "For the littles. I don't care what she does."

Virgil nodded. "I'll be back here with her."

Informing the children on how to care for the castle in the remaining time leading up to Christmas (and how to keep bugs from finding it) we left behind a great deal of cheer in the snug little room.

As Virgil took us out of the narrow driveway, I looked back at the disappearing house as trees swallowed it up. "I knew Shirleen donated and supported the shelter, but I didn't realize the other support she gave. The director said she does the big holiday meals for the residents."

"She's always done this," Virgil said with a shrug. "If she doesn't cook, she's finding a way to send food. Moonhaven is run by a friend, so she always does something. We'll be there for Christmas dinner."

"Will this go on the podcast?"

Virgil shook his head and got back on the main artery road. "That's the one thing she didn't want me to mention.

She doesn't want to make a fuss or invite speculation. She does it because she can and somebody should."

"You help," I said, for it wasn't lost on me how he was no stranger to any part of the place.

"I'm more than just a man with a microphone and a few podcasts," Virgil teased. "I have depth, I have layers. I have–"

"A kind heart, like your aunt," I interrupted.

He paused and recovered with a little laugh he always did when he wanted people to think of him as just a goofy podcaster. "Well, where else would I have learned it?"

The taxi cab company sat in a large shopping center where a beauty supply store, a discount grocery store, a pet supplies store, and a Chinese takeout were the last remaining tenants. In the wintry cloudy skies, the bold orange and blue of the company's logo stood out even more.

The door buzzed as we swept in to a mostly empty office. A radio dimly played, largely unnoticed by dispatchers fielding calls. One dispatcher, however, was listening as a middle-aged man talked about his son graduating college next weekend.

"This is the fruit of fifteen years of driving a cab all over the place. Front row seats to the best show in town." He paused and stopped recounting this anecdote to the dispatcher as he looked back at us. "Hey, we've got company."

"Can I help you?" the dispatcher asked.

"I lost my phone," Virgil rather sheepishly told the woman. "Left it behind earlier today."

"We can check to see if anything came in," the dispatcher said. "Do you remember who you rode with? Name or the cab number will be enough."

"Sylvester," Virgil said. "Can't remember if it's a first or last name."

"Either way there's only one," said the man who had been boasting about his graduation ticket. He jabbed a finger at his chest. "That's me. I might be able to help you. Just wrapping up my mandated break." He buttoned up his coat and rapped his knuckle against the counter. "Now you send me some good ones!"

"Why? You aren't paying for school anymore, I don't see why I should!"

Sylvester was chuckling even as we followed him out to the company parking lot, where taxi cabs charging at the electric ports waited.

"What does it look like? What kind of phone is it and did you have a special case on it? I might have seen it earlier, although I'm not sure if I did since I don't remember giving a ride to either of you today, or yesterday, or the day before that." Sylvester looked between us like a crafty old uncle of mine, who pretended he was less aware of things than he seemed.

So much for us being clever, we'd just got ourselves caught!

"He didn't lose a phone," I admitted, before Virgil could make things worse for us. "It just seemed like a reason anyone would actually come all the way out here."

Sylvester nodded as if he knew this already. "What really brings you here?"

"We heard that you often gave Ruby Walton a ride."

"I did," Sylvester said. "Although her daughter told you wrong. I wasn't one of her favorite cabbies, I was her favorite cabbie, period. Took her everywhere she wanted."

I gulped, understanding both what he said, and what he let dangle in the air unspoken.

Perhaps I wasn't as cut out for the detective business as I thought.

I did not notice him at the funeral, but then there had been so many unfamiliar faces yesterday, and no reason for him to stand out.

The same couldn't be said for him.

He continued to smile at us. Not dangerously, but there was a sense of being put on guard in fear of the worst. "I know who you are, so I know you don't mean me trouble, but if you're trouble or not, that I can't say. Either way I got a few more minutes left of my break, so best ask me what you want."

"You drove Ruby Walton to Tully Manor last week?" Virgil asked.

"I did."

"Did she have a cake with her?"

Sylvester tugged at his ear. "If you got questions like that, I'm going to need a fare."

We got into the backseat of the cab, hurrying in there as if it was raining and we had a flight to catch. Sylvester turned on the farebox and drove off.

Virgil had his microphone poking out his coat pocket, but if the cabbie noticed he didn't say a thing.

"I liked taking Ruby around. She was very considerate, tipped well, and every so often took me on a wild adventure."

"Where did you end up going?" Virgil asked.

"Port Walker Point – she liked looking at the water. She'd be out there for hours at a time, while I waited nearby. I asked what she was up to and she told me she was looking for treasure."

"You didn't mind any of this?" I asked.

"Why would I? I got paid, and it was easy work. It's nice to have a regular fare. It's why the night I took her to Tully Manor I didn't mind, despite it being last-minute. The night I dropped her off, at first she told me to wait. Then she called and said come back in an hour. I was leaving when I saw someone in a red uniform step out a side door, probably for a smoke break, as they walked a bit away from the building. I decided to see if I could get a quick fare, when I got a call. I was one of the last people Ruby had rung, so they called me." His voice shook. "I didn't even realize I was in her phone like that, not as some driver, but someone that could be mistaken for a friend."

His voice broke off, and we drove on in silence to let him compose himself once more.

"No one asked me about this, why do you care?" Sylvester asked.

"To finish the treasure hunt," I said. "Where else did you take her?"

"When I drove her most of the time, it was all about her errands. Grocery shopping, dry cleaning, getting presents for her grandchildren. Although she did have me drive all the way out to Richmond to get a writing desk."

"You got a writing desk in this car?" I asked.

Sylvester chuckled. "I rented a truck, and she paid twice my usual rate plus extra."

"Still should have had a professional handle it," Virgil grumbled. I shushed him before he could derail us, but Sylvester continued:

"This all happened not too long ago, just before Halloween. I remember thinking the extra I got meant we could get more of the good candy bars this year, plus some bubble wands." He was talking freely now and turned off the farebox, delighted to have someone eager to listen. "The desk was very important to her. She was fretting the entire drive up, acting as if it would be gone by the time we got there. Only when it was loaded up and we were on our way back did she relax. Even then she had me on the lookout for a blue car, as if this desk was valuable. She paid fifty bucks for it, and it wasn't much to look at. Guess there must have been some sentimental value. After that it was mainly the usual errands. The night I took her to the party, Ruby was quite chatty. She had brought a cake with her she intended to give as a gift. She was excited to be invited to the party. She thought Shirleen would never reach out in friendship again, so she was hopeful. There was also somebody very important that she wanted to meet, which meant her presence and the cake she brought wouldn't go to waste if her reunion with her friend didn't go well."

The cab company came back in view, and Sylvester pulled back into a parking spot.

"I wish you good luck treasure hunting," he said as Virgil paid for the talk and the ride. "Although I can only wonder what you will find."

Chapter 17

There was still plenty of daylight so Virgil drove us directly to Port Walker Point, as we both knew it and its nearby park rather intimately. It was, in my opinion, one of the prettiest areas in the 757, as the park stretched out the river providing an excellent view of the cozy waterfront homes and bungalows, and even the tiny library that sat at the water's edge. With the lapping waves and the occasional duck drifting past it was very easy to think Hunton Bay and the rest of the city was far away.

"I like to run out here," I said as we exited Virgil's car. I got my camera out of my bag as my shoes crunched against the gravel. "It's not too far, ten miles or so. A nice little run I always enjoy having."

"Ten miles?" Virgil sputtered. "You mean you go running ten miles for *fun*?"

"Most of the way runs by the river, so it's very relaxing," I boasted as if this was a regular occurrence instead of once in a while.

There was a muscle going in his cheek as he tried and failed to control his reaction.

"It's not very far," I said. "I thought you enjoyed going for a run?"

"Yes," he said hastily. "Ten miles is nothing. Nothing much at all." He cleared his throat, and we followed the winding path toward the park.

Port Walker Point ran along a residential area, but while usually there were a few people idling about, the winter chill must have kept many away, for the street was quite empty.

Looming fir trees blocked the homes that lined the street next to the park, turning it into a rather quiet sanctuary. The park was small and stretched like an upside-down triangle, so to get to the gazebo you were led through a narrow entrance between the trees that slowly widened into meandering walking paths.

When I ran this way, I would stretch and take a breather inside the gazebo. Most of the time it was occupied. Sometimes it was families with small children running about, or young teenage couples awkwardly flirting for the first time. Sometimes there were old friends catching up, or even some students who decided to do their homework out here. I'd seen artists using this as their perch to sketch and got glimpses of shy dancers practicing their first steps. I even saw a mime once.

On a cold, wintry late afternoon like today, it was empty. There was no one in the park and even the water was still, with only waterfowl drifting in the water.

"You suggested coming here," Virgil said as he stepped into the gazebo with his microphone extended to catch the ambient sounds. "Well, what are we looking for?"

"I didn't expect to find anything." I leaned against the railing of the gazebo. Brackish water greeted me, as well as the few reeds sticking out the water. "I think she was troubled about something and came out here to think. I do that too." I looked around the gazebo once more and caught sight of a historical marker. "What's the history of this area? You never covered it in your podcast."

"Not yet," Virgil said. "It's on the list I put out about episode locations, so I've done a little research. I can tell you the history of the neighborhood, and that this park was created in advance of Watch Night. Nothing too special. No accounts of treasure hunts here. Although this is the site of many Easter Egg hunts."

"Maybe it's personal history that brought Ruby out here?" I suggested, still grasping for an answer to put everything we knew into context. The detectives on my favorite podcasts made it seem so easy how they made the connections. I felt I was floundering despite my best efforts.

"I think it's more likely she was meeting someone," Virgil said. "The cabbie said she was out here for hours. He wouldn't have stayed put for too long, so likely he never saw if she was doing something more than just enjoying the waves."

"Then what did she do?"

"Met someone most likely, there are quite a few homes out here, and there's an independent living community in this neighborhood, maybe Ruby was visiting with someone at August Towers."

He pointed to the high-rise that we had passed earlier.

I considered it with new interest. "I think it's still early enough for visiting hours to still be on."

"I'm not breaking into a facility today," Virgil cut in.

Undeterred, I beamed with sunny promise. "How about tomorrow?"

"No," he retorted, far from amused. "Because you don't even know what we're looking for."

"But we do have some idea." I plopped down on a bench. It creaked as I did and rattled more than I expected.

As I adjusted the bench, my gaze rose to the rafters. I thought there was a cat up there at first, but as I squinted it didn't seem quite right.

"Virgil," I said, "do you see something too?"

He looked up, and frowned. "I think I do. Can that bench move?"

I tugged at it, but despite it wobbling, the other end was pretty secure. "No."

"I'll boost you up then."

Moving underneath the rafters, Virgil laced his fingers together and knelt down a bit so I could step up into his hands. I placed one hand on his shoulder, and with a tiny nod he raised me up to reach the rafters.

Bracing my hand along the wood, I looked ahead to a milky white object I had spotted.

"It's not a cat," I called down to Virgil as I reached forward. "It's a cake carrier. It's the one that went missing!"

"What!" Virgil called. His hand shook and I wobbled, losing my balance as I reached for the cake carrier. I fell, clutching the plastic case to me, but I didn't hit the ground – Virgil had lurched forward to catch me in time.

"Are you alright?" he asked as we remained there, close enough for me to see his glasses slipping along his nose. I could see my own reflection. It overlaid his suddenly serious expression and had me jumping back.

"Yes," I breathed, and then held up the cake carrier as both evidence and a shield. "Look, it's the carrier the tea cake was in. Right here, it's marked by one of those symbols Shirleen uses."

"It's empty," Virgil observed.

He swung me down to my feet, and I fumbled with the latches on the case. It was empty, with only a cake plate covered in a few crumbs and hardened glaze inside. Holding the lid, I placed my nose right over it and sniffed heartily. "Definitely the tea cake."

When Virgil didn't answer, I glanced back up to find his gaze trained on the rafters. "How did it get up there?"

"Obviously the murderer planted it."

"Sounds like an assumption to me," Virgil said.

"Who else would hide a cake carrier in a gazebo?" I asked. "To have it out here. This isn't the case of someone trying to hide evidence. They want it to be found, perhaps dramatically. With luck, we just cut into a plan that would have sent the police on a wild goose chase that landed here. Just like in *A Town Called Memorie*."

"What happens in that one?" Virgil asked as he held out the microphone.

"In that one, they plant evidence to accuse someone who was near the scene of the murder but had no connection whatsoever. The son of a major suspect, who was innocent, but whose arrest was used to force a false confession, and…" As I recounted the case my words faltered as something else struck me with a chill.

"And what?" Virgil asked.

"This was planted," I repeated myself, "but not to cast doubts on Shirleen, but someone close to her. Someone very close and who had handled the cakes that night."

"You mean me?" Virgil asked, more surprised than alarmed. "Why do you think that?"

Before I could answer, my phone vibrated. Ready to ignore it, I saw my sister's name flash on the video call, so I picked up.

"What's wrong, who's hurt?" I cried overdramatically.

Aisha only rolled her eyes. She lounged in her armchair in a hoodie and the fluffy pink blanket I had given her with cat faces. We didn't look that much alike, as she was short with rounder and softer features, while I was more like Dad, tall and lanky. We had our mother's hair, vivacious and curly, and able to transform it no matter what style we wanted. "Don't be like that, Key, it's not the end of the world if I call."

"It is when I don't have a flurry of texts first," I said.

"Here I was calling about you making Granny's gingerbread house. Where are you, I see water... and who's *that*?"

Aisha shifted around to get a closer look, but I turned my wrist realizing she got a glimpse of Virgil. My sister smirked as she pushed up her glasses, and a dozen thoughts flickered across her face.

"Don't be coy, Key, you're with somebody right now! It's a very handsome someone I haven't seen before."

"Aisha, you're seeing things!" I grumbled.

"No, he's right in view," Aisha called in a singsong voice. "He's come around. Hello there, stranger! What are your intentions with my sister?"

Virgil leaned over to peer at Aisha. He took her teasing without even a ruffle of discomfort as he answered her, "We're making a podcast together related to incidents of local history."

I hissed at him to be quiet as my sister beamed deviously. Any answer he gave was the wrong thing to do. We Scotts needed only an inch to go a mile.

"You're doing a podcast about the murder!" Aisha cackled. "That's so you! I don't know why you've never done it before. I guess you never had the perfect partner in crime."

"Knock it off," I said. "And it's never been reported that Ruby was murdered."

"That's why I called you," my sister said as she attempted to compose herself. "I was about to ask if you've seen the news. Ruby Walton's family just released a statement demanding answers for her death because they believe there is foul play. It's blowing up all over the place."

"What?" I exclaimed.

Virgil grunted. "Because we talked to Ruben. We must have sparked something."

"But to release a statement so soon?" I asked. "Aisha, are you sure?"

Aisha put a hand to her chest, echoing Granny. "I swear on everything and more, what I'm telling you is what I saw. Whether the information is wrong or not is another story."

"Aisha is right," Virgil said, scrolling through his own phone. "Ruby's family just put out a statement an hour ago. My aunt might not have seen it yet."

"Does it say anything bad about her?" I asked.

"No, but there are others who will, if it's not clear my aunt had nothing to do with it," Virgil said.

"What are you going to do about it?" Aisha eagerly leaned in.

She had jumped in to get ahead of me with that question, but I didn't have to ask Virgil, I knew exactly what he was going to do next, even if he didn't know it.

I waited until we crossed back into Hunton Bay before I asked:

"You're going to let me listen to the first cut?"

"First cut of what?" Virgil began, before he slammed his brakes, having nearly missed the sign for a closed road.

"The Christmas Light contest is going on," I said peering out at the pedestrians milling about the street. "Take a left, it'll take you all the way around. You'll still run into closed roads though, all the neighborhoods around me are doused with lights as they're taking part in the contest."

"That's terrible for birds," Virgil muttered.

"And will make a terrible time getting home tonight. The roads by your place should be fine. I know you're eager to get back."

"I left bread rising," he muttered.

"Very funny," I said. "You cut together an episode, didn't you? Not the one that was supposed to be the history of *Season by Season*. But something else entirely."

"Are you assuming or suggesting?" Virgil said testily. "Either way, tell me what I'm supposed to be doing!"

"Making a podcast for the investigation. You put something together, before the world points to Shirleen as the murderer."

"I'm not making a podcast about this," he protested, "it was a joke."

"Yet you've been dutifully recording for the past few days, collecting not just every twist and turn, but getting choice dialogue and facts," I said in disbelief.

"It was a joke," he repeated stubbornly. "I only even suggested it because of you."

I froze and sank back in the passenger seat. "Me?" I wondered, my surprise carrying the question out of me before I could even stop it.

But now it floated between us, the unsaid trailing after like gossamer butterfly wings.

Virgil kept his eyes on the road, his hands tightening around the steering wheel. "I had planned to go birdwatching that day I ran into you outside Tully Manor. I really had been joking about doing a podcast about what happened to Ruby. But when I saw you, I knew exactly what you were up to and knew you'd be resistant to the idea of working together. We hadn't gotten along well lately and, well, a true crime/investigative podcast was a good excuse to start over. But the more I joked about it, the more I realized how serious you were, it became more than an idea."

"An idea of what?" I said, somewhat lost in what he was saying and not saying. I turned to face him, and the tips of his ears were pink once again.

"An idea that there is enough for an investigative podcast."

Virgil was lying, but for the first time I wasn't that keen on getting the truth from him, since I didn't think I was quite ready for it.

"I don't have a full episode done. Just enough for a teaser, a taste of what to expect, that leads with one central idea: Shirleen Foster is being framed for a murder."

I nodded, taking in all of this. "You got a name for it?"

Virgil shrugged. "I have a few ideas, but I'm liking *Death by Christmas Cake*."

"Sounds good to me," I said latching onto this, on anything really to get over this awkward feeling. "I haven't made a podcast, but I have listened to enough to be a good editor. If we do it right this might scare up the murderer. Who's probably gotten confident they're getting away with this. I'm not going to let that happen."

"No, we're not!" Virgil agreed as he spun around the wheel.

Virgil's apartment was small and slightly old, but too new to have vintage charm. It was much like his car in that way. Neat and tidy, but very little worn as if he was hardly here. He led me in confidently as if he knew there would be no mess to quickly shove into a closet. Despite the steady temperature in the room, there was no warmth in any of the décor, until he opened a door to his office.

Here was life.

A messy room of someone busy and on the move, where his torn leather jacket was tossed onto a chair, and the baseball cap with his moving company hung from a doorknob. On the shelf were a few photographs of Virgil traveling around the world, often pictured with his aunt in a large floppy hat and binoculars around her neck, as they pointed and posed with all the small and big wonders they found. This felt like a long time ago, given Shirleen's hair wasn't so liberally gray and her face was a touch plumper, but a glance at Virgil made it seem it wasn't, as he was hardly changed save for his hair being much shorter.

Besides the recording equipment and lamp, on the desk was a stack of Shirleen's books feathered with sticky notes. There was a corkboard next to the desk, pinned with maps, copies of newspapers and magazines, as well as a few postcards and photographs. Pinned on the board were several different schedules for interviews, and odd scattered notes that made very little sense as I skimmed over them, for they were short summaries of the interviews and conversations we had with Naomi, Austin, Lucia, plus everyone we talked to at the funeral, including his estranged uncle. My name was on there as well, alongside a few observations about what I said or did.

Then there was a timeline of the night of the party with question marks where there were gaps and names where there weren't.

This guy.

If I let him, he'd try to solve the mystery on his own.

He wouldn't do so bad, but he needed help.

"Nice murder board," I remarked.

He looked up from turning on his equipment to blink at the board before he scowled at me. "It's a summary," he said.

"A very accurate summary with very detailed notes."

"As I've been editing *Season by Season,* splitting up segments and conversations made it easy for me to manage the files."

"You act as if this wasn't the plan," I said, going to the board with my notebook in hand. "You have things laid out better than I have. Can I?" I reached for the first card.

Virgil nodded and I started constructing the narrative.

"Ruby's death has two options. One, she was targeted and poisoned on purpose for reasons we don't quite understand. The second is that she was killed on purpose but with the aim to cause a scandal and even frame Shirleen. This is the leading theory we've been following since several factors point to someone having had it out for the pair – so it is revenge, with two birds and one poisoned cake."

"And a lot luck since Ruby wasn't supposed to be there," Virgil countered.

"True, but the invitations went out early." I tapped the card with notes from Naomi's interview. "According to Naomi, invitations went out in October, but not everyone RSVP'd until the very end. That's when Shirleen learned about Ruby, as well as the nineteen others who weren't supposed to be there at all."

"Some of whom showed up to the party." Virgil went to the board, pointed to the small list of the people we called and talked to. The mysterious Brandon Morton was on the list of the unexpected attendees, but he was still not on the list of those Virgil had spoken to.

"You still haven't talked to this guy?" I asked, spotting the ticks next to Morton's name indicating each call.

"I get his voicemail or he says he's traveling and can't talk."

"Are you sure he's telling the truth?" I asked.

"I don't know," Virgil admitted, "but he was there and the closest to what happened, and the only person I hadn't gotten a definite answer from. He hinted he saw more but wasn't eager to tell me over the phone."

"Then go to him."

"He lives in Williamsburg," Virgil said.

I winced. "That's too far."

"Still," Virgil continued softly, "I think he has something important to tell me, that's why I keep trying. There's something we're missing. I think he has a piece of it."

"What of the parts we do know?" I asked, turning back to the board. His timeline needed only a few tweaks from me, as there wasn't anything we knew from the evening. Even our ride with the cabbie just gave a few extra details.

I scrambled the list to arrange in no particular order the suspects we have given the most consideration:

1. Naomi, the fired and disgraced assistant.
2. Austin, the publicist who sees even death as good publicity.
3. Lucia, who still holds a grudge sharp as the day she lost her restaurant.
4. Davis, a TV producer who is connected to both and spilled the tea without compunction.
5. Winifred, a friend who held back telling the truth.

6. Margot, a friend who appeared to want to tell the truth.
7. Glenn, Shirleen's ex-husband who keeps popping up where he's not supposed to be.

Virgil frowned. "Are these our likely suspects?"

"Just people who are part of this." I reached over and nudged a few cards aside. "Naomi may have kicked all this off, but she couldn't be the murderer. Too young for all the drama, wasn't present at the party, and her motive came far too late. Austin did know about the guests, and was planning a great deal, so he's on the list."

"Lucia knows we're investigating and has a history with them both," Virgil added.

"As does Davis," I pointed out.

"Lots of people did." Virgil shrugged. "But only a few people in ways that matter. Which is why Winifred and Margot are on the list?"

"They both said things I find odd." I let my mind drift back to the repast, turning over the conversation. "They were friends, so I can't see them sitting so easily at Ruby's funeral if they killed her."

On the other hand, if you could do murder quite easily, you can do other things as well.

"Then there's my uncle," Virgil said. "He has motive and he never liked Ruby. As a murderer I can believe it, but as a poisoner, I'm not sure. But then he's always surprised me in the worst ways."

"Let's not forget the threats." I ripped a blank page from my notebook to add to the board. I wrote down the texts and messages, plus the gist of the conversation we heard while looking for the cart. "There were some credible death threats against Shirleen, but it was Ruby who died."

"But nothing happened to my aunt," Virgil said.

"Or did it?" I wondered. "What if Ruby's death stopped something?"

"Or was part of it. We have no idea. Let's just focus on what we know," Virgil said.

"What is that precisely?" I asked. I glanced at the cake carrier we had found, that now sat on the desk. The one thing I couldn't add to the board was the idea that Virgil was being framed. It wasn't as if the cake carrier had anything tied to him on it. It was just a guess. Like Ruby meeting someone at Point Walker Point. There was a frame of an idea but no hard evidence.

Or rather not the evidence that was helpful.

"The most important thing," Virgil said. I couldn't tell if he knew where my mind was meandering, but his reassurance was welcomed even if felt unearned since it should be happening in the reverse. "The podcast will get the murderer to show their hand."

Interview: Margot Baptiste

Virgil Sullivan, voiceover: *Margot Baptiste has catered dinners and parties for the biggest names around, although her name doesn't circulate beyond select circles. Now retired, she enjoys cooking for her community and relatives, and provides expertise and dollops of advice where needed. Her path crossed with Shirleen Foster on a fateful New Year's Eve, in a year she jokingly refuses to name. She says the idea to revisit* Season by Season *was her idea.*

Virgil Sullivan: *You never wanted to collaborate on a cookbook, not even one to talk about how best to entertain. You and Shirleen have thrown a lot of parties, for others and for yourselves, in a number of rather unique places. So, I have to ask, why not?*

Margot Baptiste: *Collaborations for a cookbook are tricky things. You have to trust someone with your vision and that they will support it instead of trying to derail or twist it into something else. I know myself. I work best alone, and I'd be more tempted to sabotage if it's just a cookbook. After all, it'll be my first shot with my name front and center, and perhaps the only shot, unless I got lucky like Ruby and get a TV show. Wait, can you cut that out? I didn't mean it like that. I mean, I meant it, but not in that way. Not like how it will sound. You know people always take things out of context.*

Chapter 18

Virgil didn't finish the episode that night, but I gave him enough notes to finish up without me. We were still hammering out the details as he drove me back to my place, arguing over what clips from the interviews to tuck in or if it was better to have clips of the night of the party. Because if we're going to come rushing out of the gate, it had to strike the right note, especially if it was going to pre-empt any attempt to arrest Shirleen.

In a perfect world this would be superfluous, but the police were already looking at Shirleen, especially as the poison was in the cake. A podcast wasn't evidence, but hopefully it would tap the brakes.

In the morning, I dropped off the empty cake carrier at the police station as an anonymous tip, with instructions to give it to Detective Dimaandal. I had shown up with a scarf wrapped around my face and a hat pulled down over my hair. The person at the desk scarcely gave me a second glance as they crunched a candy cane and typed up the report, although I scurried out as if I was in a spy thriller.

On the way to the WVHB taping on the following Monday, Virgil texted me a link to the final cut of the first three episodes of *Death by Christmas Cake,* which he had just uploaded. I didn't need to listen, but I did so anyway. I had spent the previous day practicing the cake I would make for the TV segment, as well as prepping the food intended for the dinner party with my friends, yet I couldn't get rid of my jittery nerves.

The taping wasn't happening at the TV studio, where I had originally planned to go into the archives with Sunil, but instead would take place across town at Kitchen Atelier, a fact that I found out very late the previous night.

Kitchen Atelier, a place where they tested recipes, provided tutorials and demos, did workshops, held classes... and was my dream job.

What had seemed once to be a far-flung dream was now a startling reality.

I tried to keep cool as I spoke to Shirleen about this as we sat in the dressing room. I wasn't doing a very good job, for she paused reaching for her lipstick, her reflection frowning in the mirror.

"Don't look so nervous," Shirleen said. "All eyes will be on me."

"I'm not nervous," I nearly squeaked.

Shirleen rummaged through her purse. "Take a breath and remember, you've always done prep. It'll be the same as always, except this time a camera will be trained upon you. Keep your eyes on me and forget everything else."

She pulled out a wrapped candy, and held it out to me. "Take it. It'll calm you down."

"What's in it?"

"THC," Shirleen said. She looked so sincere that my horrified face soon had her chuckling. "No, it's just homemade peppermint. If you need something stronger..." She shook her purse, and I heard the rattle of what could only be a flask. "Don't tell my nephew."

"I don't need it!"

"If it keeps you from walking on ceilings, I think you might want to try it."

"I'm not nervous about taping," I repeated clutching the candy.

"Then you're worried about Weyland Stone," Shirleen sneered. "He's not even in the building today. He still hasn't quite forgiven me for a literal noodle incident."

I couldn't help but smile, and Shirleen pressed another homemade peppermint into my hand. "Take a breath, Keisha. You're only cooking because they don't want me to start rumors up. Just do what you always do, and you'll be just fine."

I didn't unwrap the candies but tucked them into my apron pocket, alongside my notebook. As I got ready to put my phone in airplane mode, a flurry of supportive texts and messages floated up from my friends, with several gifs from my sister, and my father who helpfully texted: KNOCK 'EM DEAD, KIDDO!

A knock on the green room door brought in Austin. He looked more harried than usual, as he clutched his phone. His eyes flitted first onto me and then to Shirleen.

"Shirleen, did you approve of this? I know he's your nephew but that doesn't mean you can let him do anything he wants!"

Shirleen packed up her purse, feigning innocence. "Virgil posted the first of the podcast episodes. About time. I told him he needed to stop putting it off. Why are you upset? It's what you wanted."

"Me, want this?" he sputtered. "This is a disaster, and draws the wrong sort of attention!"

Austin tapped his phone, and Virgil's voice filled the small room. *"Ruby Walton's death needs to be further investigated, for it was not an accident that befell her, but a carefully arranged plan that snatched her life – all to frame and cast accusation on her friend."*

"This is not the podcast we discussed!" Austin declared. "And this nonsense about investigating. Bad enough Ruby Walton's family sent out a statement asking for more police attention, this is just more fuel to the fire!"

Austin continued to wave his phone around, but something about his ranting caught me off guard.

He was concerned about this, and not because this would make his publicity work hard. His panic, his outrage, even his annoyance at a podcast centering Ruby's death, it all went deeper than being surprised. He didn't expect this and it seemed to be upsetting his plans.

Or maybe exposing them?

Ruby's death being deemed an accident had meant there hadn't been closer inspection into the movement and actions of everyone that night.

Austin was one of my suspects, if only because he was floating in and around that night. He also knew the entire schedule and had ample opportunity. I hadn't stumbled across a motive yet, but his panic was provoking me to look deeper into him. Maybe even be wary about what he might do next.

"Why wasn't I told about this?" Austin swung around to me.

I shrugged. "Didn't you once say all publicity is good?"

"But this!" Austin said. "I should have heard about the podcast before it dropped! I have all these people calling me, and Maxine Roberts, that nosy reporter from the *Hunton Bay Journal* is here. You know her, the one whose nose twitches around for news. Don't know what she thinks she'll find. It's all in here already!"

Austin strode out the room in a huff, letting the door slam behind him.

I got up to follow, but I had just put my hand on the door when Shirleen sniffed behind me.

"Everyone's a critic," Shirleen said. "I wouldn't worry about him, he can't stop this podcast."

"What if," I began, "he tries something else?"

"Austin doesn't have all the happy power he thinks he does! I've gotten more positive responses from social media posts than any press release or article he got posted lately. Even if he doesn't like Maxine, she'll put out a good word or two. She certainly should, given she keeps asking to write a book about me."

"Is that why you were talking to her the night of the party?" I asked.

"I figured we'd talk once, and she'd realize everything is already in my books. But she wanted to talk about Ruby. I said no, and Maxine's been hoping I change my mind."

"You haven't, I'm guessing."

"I won't have someone spread gossip about me. They can do that when I'm dead – although they're doing it already, and people believe the worst."

"That's not true at all," I cried, coming to her side. "My friends enjoy sampling the food we've been making and hearing the tidbits I share about you, and would love to meet you." As this did nothing for her mood, I stumbled upon a brilliant idea. "In fact, why don't you come to my dinner party this week?" I said. "It's a holiday party, and Pascal will host." Watching her expression brighten at his name, I clutched at this as I said in my most persuasive tone. "I know he'd appreciate you being there, as he really enjoyed meeting you at the contest. He just can't stop talking about you."

Shirleen frowned. "I'm not sure, will it be a lot of people?"

"Not too many, I think. It's the last big gathering of all my friends before the holiday. You must come. Promise me you will!"

"I'll think about it," Shirleen said slowly. "I won't make any promises."

A knock at the door preceded the arrival of a production assistant, who brought us out to the soundstage. A small kitchen awaited us with the signage from the TV station placed prominently about. Around the size of a high school chorus room, about twenty people sat on a set of risers that wasn't very big, but they were very close, just right behind the crew. Many had won tickets to attend the taping, which came with the chance to sample the food I would make today.

As Shirleen stopped to say hello to someone she knew, I spotted Virgil near the back of the bleachers.

I didn't expect to see him, as he hadn't come to any of the other promotional events, but boy was I glad he was there.

Just catching sight of a familiar face shook off most of my nerves as I remembered the trick my father told me about doing presentations. Just focus on one person in a crowd, and forget everyone else.

I made to wave, but Virgil shook his head, as he ducked in his seat. As he did, I saw he was hiding from a two-pronged attack. On the left was Austin, seething as he tapped away at his phone. To the right, Maxine was scribbling in a notepad. I think the reporter may have spotted him, or at least was wise enough to attempt to block his way if needed. Or mine, given how Maxine sent a smile in my direction.

I smiled back, knowing I was her next target.

In her bright pea-green coat and electric blue glasses, Maxine had a youthful air, despite being a seasoned veteran of undisclosed years. While the *Hunton Bay Journal* was a long-running paper in the area, she had gotten her start in alternative and more grassroots papers, where investigative journalism still flourished. It showed in her articles now and her writings that might appear sensational, until you read close and saw the layers in which she was writing. That she was doing a book on Shirleen was news to me, but not much of a surprise given how often the reporter showed up to Shirleen's events. She had been at the party at Tully Manor, although I hadn't gotten a glimpse of her the entire night. While it was tempting to add her to the list of suspects, killing Ruby, or even Shirleen, before she got her full scoop didn't seem likely.

My pep talk with Shirleen had dampened my nerves, but I felt them rev up again as I recognized the pompadour of one of the most famous hosts at the test kitchen, Adrienne Blake. As one of the most popular segments of their media channel, she was known mostly for tasting food with a blindfold on, and being able to tell not just every ingredient that went into it, but how it was prepared, and what order the ingredients were added. Her recipes were great too, featuring unusually flavorful pairings.

"I'm so happy to finally get to meet you!" Adrienne cried as she greeted Shirleen. "We keep missing each other at all the big conferences. And you must be Keisha Scott. I've gotten the chance to taste your food at the Port Walker Tea Party and it was excellent."

Shocked she even knew my name, let alone ate my food, I nearly fell over. It was all I could do to keep from stumbling over my words. "I didn't know you were there."

Adrienne winked at me. "I like to go to events incognito. But that's not the case today! I was asked to guest host for today's segment. Some lovely folks are about to help you get set up. Look around the kitchen to see if there's anything you might want or might be missing. We procured the ingredients you mentioned, and there's a pantry with all the staples."

She pointed to the back room where larger glass jars and containers had various flours, several types of sugars and sweeteners, all the expected spices, and a shelf brimming with gluten-free and vegan options.

I poked around a bit and before I knew it, we were rolling.

Adrienne introduced us, before stepping aside for Shirleen, who introduced the recipes we would be making for the day, all of course drawn from her new cookbook with a mix of old and new.

As I prepped and cooked for the camera, Shirleen explained the reasons for the changes in a steady voice, about the decisions related to time, tastes, and texture.

The camera wasn't always trained on me, as Shirleen made eggnog. It did hover on me as I flitted about the kitchen from one station to the next, in a dance that had me moving between each course. The cake was first, since it needed to bake and cool off. Then the soup and small bites were next, arranged into individual servings.

Lost in the work, I forgot the crowd, Shirleen, Adrienne Blake, and even the cameras. It was just me and the food I was preparing, falling into a steady rhythm as I focused on the one thing that still made sense.

Filming wrapped soon enough, the cameras were moved out the way, and an assistant came up to take my mic.

Shirleen encouraged the audience to come up to eat and she was soon in a knot of people who were all happily asking her questions. While there were a few soup samples left, all the cake slices were gone.

"Darn, I should have come up here quicker," Virgil said. "I was trying to avoid Maxine." He gestured to where the reporter stood nearby. "She's asking about the podcast."

Although in the middle of talking to one of the audience members, Maxine turned and gave us a little wave. She remained where she was, but that wouldn't be for long.

"Don't we want people talking? You know," I added, "Austin was quite upset you posted the podcast without telling him."

"Oh, I know." Virgil rolled his eyes. "You should see the messages I got from him."

Instead of showing me though, he picked up one of the remaining eggnog mugs without his smile leaving his face. "Glenn is here."

I turned toward the crowd, looking for that specter of a man. Between the stage lights, the work ahead of me, and my own nerves, I had ignored the audience for the most part. I looked out further now and saw Glenn talking with Adrienne as they sampled the eggnog.

"How did he get in here?" I whispered.

"Don't know," Virgil said. "I didn't get around to asking. He's been crafty about it. Always around someone so I can't drag him out."

"I don't think that would be enough," I said. "He didn't come here on a whim."

"I want to know why. Once or twice is bad enough, but it seems he's everywhere he knows he can find Aunt Shirls."

I grabbed a towel to wipe clean my hands. "Maybe I can find out what he wants."

"That's not part of your job." Virgil said quickly, "This is a personal matter with him and my aunt."

I could see what he meant, but this is why I needed to talk to his former uncle. "What if it's not personal?" I ventured.

"He was at the funeral and he was there when Ruby died. He might know something."

Virgil inhaled sharply, and I thought he was about to refute me when he said, "Take the microphone."

He produced not the larger one I'd grown used to him carrying, but a smaller, no less powerful microphone.

I placed it in my apron pocket, and then I made my way over, where Glenn regaled Adrienne with a tale related to a restaurant he once worked at.

"Keisha," Adrienne said as she jumped on a break in their conversation, "I just wanted to say what a wonderful job you did."

"Shirleen knows how to find the keenest talents," Glenn added.

"I'm really impressed. I managed to get a sample of your cake, it's excellent of course." Adrienne checked her phone. "If this segment goes off as well as I hope, I'd love to have you back." She turned and grabbed one of her staff, launching into instructions for the next program.

I turned back to find Glenn studying me over the rim of his eggnog glass. "Have you come to run me off again?"

"If you know you have that sort of reception, why come at all?" I asked.

"Because this is the only way I can speak to Shirley," he said.

"She doesn't want to talk to you," I said. "Because the last time she did, you took her to court and tried to bleed her dry."

"She's getting me back for that by putting this new cookbook out. You're lucky, you know. You only got this chance because she wants to erase me from the picture. We never had children, so this was the closest thing we had together." He could have been an actor given how his voice quavered.

I steeled myself though. He had a reason for showing up, as well as a few motives to wish the worst for Shirleen.

"Why are you here today?" I asked. "You went through a great deal of trouble to get tickets for the event. She won't talk to you," I said, just to belabor the point. "You can keep showing up hoping she won't make an incident, but that won't help at all. Especially if you're after her money."

Glenn gripped the glass. "Listen here, young lady," he hissed. "Don't you dare speak to me like that. Didn't your folks teach you any manners?"

"They taught me not to force myself where I'm not wanted," I said, holding steady against his gaze. "I'm offering you one last chance. Tell me why you keep showing up like Jacob Marley and I'll pass the message along."

"Jacob Marley," he chuckled, amused instead of being annoyed. "Oh, that is quite fitting. I *have* come to tell her to change her ways, or all of this will be gone!"

I felt a chill down my back as he said it, and couldn't help but think of the text that had unambiguously threatened Shirleen with death. Was he the one who had sent the messages?

"Change how?" I asked. "What happens if she doesn't?"

His answer was lost in the shattering of a glass.

I spun to look, and saw a woman on the ground. Her blonde curls spilled along the floor as eggnog spattered the front of her sweater. Young, with freckles and a beauty mark on her chin, I thought she had just fainted until someone shouted, "She was poisoned!"

The room got very silent as if freezing water was thrown around, and then the whispers started.

Adrienne hurried forward. With the efficiency of a fire marshal, she cleared out the room and summoned an onsite medic to tend to the woman.

Unlike Ruby who had twitched and been heavily distressed, the blonde in contrast merely looked like she fainted and was hardly troubled beyond a slight frown on her face.

As whispers and titters grew louder, and people shot dirty looks over at Shirleen, I stepped forward and picked over the remains of the broken mug. I tapped my fingers against the eggnog instead and placed it on my tongue.

Out the corner of my eye, I saw someone flinch, but I focused on the flavors.

I had sampled the eggnog before as Shirleen needed to make a non-alcoholic version for the show. I was pleased to see there was no different notes in this flavor, or even a strong aftertaste of almond.

"Not poisoned," I declared loudly.

One of the audience members, who was twice my age, had the grace to look embarrassed. "We were just talking, it wasn't serious, just a joke that it was good that you made the food and that Shirleen only made the eggnog, and the girl, she–"

"You heard wrong," I said with as much patience as I could muster. "Ruby Walton died from a medical emergency. Nothing related to anything Shirleen did."

I could tell this wasn't convincing them, but I no longer cared.

I went searching for Shirleen and found her right behind me. She took the broken glass from me, and tasted it too.

As the women stared at her for different reasons, Shirleen declared, "No wonder she fainted, it needed more cinnamon." Shirleen turned her back on the audience and focused solely on me. "Keisha, can we talk?"

I followed her with a nod to the kitchen set, where Virgil sat on the stool. Placed there – I couldn't help but think – for he perched reluctantly on the edge and when he tried to rise to relinquish his seat, a single stern look from his aunt got him to sit back down.

"What did Glenn tell you?" Shirleen demanded of me.

"Nothing useful," I said.

Shirleen sighed. "Might as well tell me. I will hear it anyway. I don't need you and Virgil to protect me. Trust me, whatever that man has said, or tried to do, is nothing compared to what I have dealt with before."

This was directed to Virgil and Virgil alone.

"He didn't say much, just to change your ways." I said. "Glenn wouldn't tell me, said it was just for your ears. I said he was your Jacob Marley, and he took it as a compliment."

Shirleen's eyebrows knitted together. "Did you just call me Scrooge?"

"No, no," I stumbled over my words in a panic until I saw a faint smile on her lips. "He just wanted to warn you about something, but whatever it is, it's trouble and you shouldn't bother."

"Out of the goodness of his heart?" Shirleen scoffed.

"He's been very persistent," Virgil said.

"Oh, he's always been that," Shirleen retorted, "and it worked well on many occasions, but not anymore!"

"Aunt Shirls," Virgil said, even as the tips of his ears went pink. "He might be up to trouble again."

"I'll deal with it, as always." Shirleen sighed as she tapped the candy cane brooch pinned to her shirt.

"Did he do anything to you?" I asked.

Shirleen's expression wavered and I saw a flash of hurt on her face, before she brushed it aside. "Nothing that matters now."

"But if–"

"Leave it alone," Virgil grumbled. "That's none of your business."

"I only asked because of the case, if he's a suspect–"

Virgil lurched off the stool, and the annoyance on his face morphed into coolness that clued me in I was being too zealous.

The words to apologize were on my tongue when Virgil interjected. "This has nothing to do with you. You just work for my aunt."

Heat rushed into my face as I met his gaze, and never had I wanted more to be anywhere else.

It didn't matter if what he said was true or not, or even if what happened with Shirleen's ex-husband was a private matter, he drew a line and I had no say in anything. I worked for his aunt, but I liked to think I was a friend as well.

"Then I'll let you settle it," I said stiffly.

I stomped off back to the dressing room, where Maxine Roberts waited with a pen and notebook in hand.

The reporter's eagerness did not even abate when it became clear more interesting subjects had not followed me.

I wasn't in the mood to talk, but I didn't want to turn back.

"Just the woman I was looking for," Maxine declared. "I heard your podcast this morning. It was your idea, wasn't it? I knew you were into true crime. How does it feel to be in the center of a mystery?"

"I can't answer that," I said, grabbing my coat and shoving it on.

"Can't or won't?" Maxine said.

"Why don't you talk to Virgil? He put it all together."

"Your voice is on there as well, advocating for Shirleen and insistent that she's being framed. "What if people say you're only doing it to protect yourself and your career? No one would know who you are without Shirleen. You wouldn't even be here dazzling the folks at Kitchen Atelier, if Shirleen hadn't suggested this place over others."

Maxine had hooked me there, and I hated how such words caught my attention. "The truth about Ruby Walton deserves to be found. If the police find it before we do, that's wonderful."

"And if they don't?" Maxine asked.

"Then maybe our podcast can find what they can't," I said. Giving up on my gloves, I grabbed my bag, threw my scarf over my shoulder and walked off.

I was able to get out the building without anyone else trying to stop me.

I was in such a state, a blue car nearly ran into me as it zipped past. Or maybe I nearly ran into it as I plowed across the street. Who knew?

Either way, I was fuming at everything and everyone, and I was unwilling to be charitable. I walked at a fast clip, brushing past people, but I had to cool my heels at the train station.

As I waited for the next train, furiously deleting all the episodes from Virgil's podcasts, when his voice echoed in my ear anyway and I nearly dropped my phone.

"I shouldn't have said that," he began.

I glanced over, and saw Shirleen right behind him as if she dragged him over here by the ear. Virgil avoided my gaze, and I in turn was more than willing to ignore his apology since it was obvious he only said it because of Shirleen. Likewise, because Shirleen was there, I swallowed some rather crude words and curtly nodded instead of answering.

I had forgotten how close the station stop was to Kitchen Atelier, making it much more convenient for them to take the train as well, instead of driving over. Now we were stuck together through the next twenty or so minutes, unless I got off early and walked the rest of the way.

The train arrived with a squeal of wheels, and we stepped aboard a mostly full car, leaving few avenues for escape. Shirleen got a seat in one of the benches, but I was jostled right into Virgil. I looked up at him, and fought the urge to elbow him out the way. As the train rumbled along, we swayed in place. Virgil started to speak, but his words vanished under a cough as he turned his eyes towards the ceiling.

Vexed, I turned around, and that's when I saw Glenn through the window into the next train car.

He was looking in the opposite direction, but I saw enough to know it was him. Especially as he looked nervously over his shoulder before sitting down.

"Virgil," I whispered, "Your uncle just got on the train. We should follow him."

Chapter 19

"My uncle is on the train." Virgil began to shift forward, but I yanked him back.

"Don't look," I hissed.

"We're not in a spy movie," he rumbled as he shoved off my arm.

I scowled at him, ready to argue with him on several points about that.

"It might be best to pretend to be." Shirleen had pulled out a book, to hide her face. Although, given it was her cookbook that had a large blown-up picture of her on the front, I didn't think it would help much. "He keeps following me around, so let me turn the tables on him!"

Luckily for this slowly forming plan, Glenn didn't look in our direction, and kept his eyes locked on his phone the entire time. He remained on for two more stops before he stood and got off at University Hospital, and we followed.

Hosting a teaching hospital, a children's hospital, and a state-of-the-art neuroscience center, the area was a hub of activity, with a variety of shops, hotels, and entertainment nearby, in full festive swing. Because of the children's hospital, the decorations were the merriest around, with inflatables of cartoon characters, tinsel, multicolored Christmas trees, and decorative mailboxes for letters to Santa on display.

The crowd was thick this time of day on the sidewalk, and we just barely managed to keep eyes on Glenn, between shoppers and big fluffy Christmas hats blocking our view.

"Not so fast," Shirleen huffed as Virgil and I went ahead. "I don't have my powerwalking shoes on."

"We're going to lose him," Virgil complained.

"Maybe not." I pointed at Gleen's retreating figure. "Looks like he's gone into the hospital."

Glenn walked toward the visitor's entrance, first passing through a holiday fair with vendors selling crafts and food from their booths. There were vendors giving away free hot chocolate and coffee to the hospital workers and emergency responders. Employees from the City of Hunton Bay were there, with vendors to share information about city services. There were the usual carnival games, a small artificial skating rink, and loads of signs for various fundraisers.

Festive music was provided by a truck, from 107.8 WVPW. While kids enjoyed the mascot from the baseball team, Virgil's muttered swear didn't make sense to me, until DJ Oscar Fantom stepped around in a candy cane striped suit.

I gaped as well, because as much fun was that choice piece of gossip, I wasn't quite prepared to ask any questions about this particular bit of history.

"Now what's you got upset, did you lose sight of Glenn?" Shirleen asked. Her eyes flicked over to the radio station's van. Her face froze with the sort of sultry look that reminded me that age is not a limit on passion and gave further credence to the intel that Virgil had reluctantly given me. "There's Oscar. He was there that night. He might have seen something."

Before either of us could stop her, Shirleen headed toward the van.

Oscar Fantom, as far as I could tell, wasn't his government name, but I couldn't think of anything else that better suited the flamboyant older man, who was ambiguously tan and finely creased with wrinkles. Jovial with his young listeners, he faltered slightly seeing Shirleen.

Passing his microphone to his fellow DJ, he looked ready to vanish, but the open space left very few places to hide, so he remained accepting his fate with a wry chuckle.

"I don't suppose you're here to donate to our raffle?" Oscar said.

"I will, I just have a few questions for you first," Shirleen said. "Did you see–"

"I saw nothing that night!" he cut in, before she could say a word more. "I saw no one or anything at all!"

This incongruous answer to a simple question pinged my radar at once. While Virgil was too slow to react to get his microphone out, it fell upon me to ask:

"How did you see no one when you were the MC of the party?"

Oscar turned to me, baffled, but not baffled enough that he couldn't reply. "I saw no one of importance."

"But this must have been weighing on your mind as it's been over a week since," I said.

"What," Oscar began, glancing over to Shirleen and Virgil, "is going on? Why are you here, Shirleen?"

"By chance," Shirleen said brightly. "We stopped by for the fair. I could have sworn I saw my ex-husband pass by through here. Virgil thinks I'm seeing things, but I was hoping you might settle our dispute."

"Glenn, you mean?" Oscar seemed to relax at this news. "I haven't seen him. Don't tell me you're meeting up with him."

"Why ever should it matter?" Shirleen said with a syrupy tone. "You ended things when you started sneaking around with my friend. What I do now is none of your business. Did you even care about Ruby? You didn't even show up to the funeral."

"I couldn't." He rubbed his neck. "It wouldn't be proper."

"You know what wouldn't be right? Showing your face around Ruby's family!" Shirleen snapped. "Stop flinching as I say her name! You made a right mess of things!"

Oscar suddenly lurched forward. He didn't grab Shirleen, but Virgil moved to get in front of her in case the DJ did. "I had nothing to do with her death," Oscar hissed. "Don't come here accusing me of anything. I don't know what she told you, but if you go to the police to save your skin you'll find there's nothing."

"Except fear," Virgil said. "What do you know about Ruby and her death?"

Oscar's expression hardened into a polite mask, that was too aggressively cheery and could even seem pleasant to someone in a distance. But up close you could see the cracks. "This isn't an interview. Just because you ask doesn't mean you'll get answers."

I wasn't sure about Virgil, but to me that was answer enough.

I opened my mouth for a zinger of my own, but Shirleen got there first. "Which is just as well, you're terrible at giving *anything* of note."

She turned on her heel and stomped off toward the hospital's entrance. She didn't go in, but stopped by the wall leaning with one hand against the stone while her other hand pressed to her brooch.

"Aunt Shirls," Virgil began.

"I'm fine," Shirleen said. "Besides, we're in the best place for medical trouble."

Seeing his cross expression, she emitted a small laugh, and patted his arm. "Sorry, bad joke. Physically my heart is fine, but the metaphorical heart needs some care. I don't think I told you, but Oscar and I–"

"No need for details!" Virgil cried, but Shirleen continued.

"–had a very passionate love affair. It arose from the buildup of tension over years of working in the same studio while the other was married. A mistake, I learned. While he's part of the story of the cookbook and I know you planned to interview him, I'm asking you not to."

"Trust me," Virgil replied, "if I don't have to talk to him, that's fine with me."

"I think he'll refuse anyway," I murmured.

The aging DJ was all smiles once more as he greeted listeners, but given how he held his shoulders, I was certain he would run. Which was a pity because I *did* want to talk to him. He had been on the list for a while, and I had hoped he'd be like Fatima or even Margot: a witness to the event with tidbits of useful information. Yet it seemed that might not be the case.

Oscar had hosted the party in full view of an entire audience, and he was too well known to simply slip into the kitchen. He couldn't have poisoned Ruby, I thought, but maybe I was wrong. I did think for a second he had left the threatening messages, but he had threatened Shirleen to her face without pause far too easily. Why even bother with subterfuge if that was the case?

"No interview then," Virgil agreed, "but he knows something about Ruby, and that might be a motive. With your… history," – he barely got the word out without a stammer – "there's plenty to dig into."

Shirleen tugged at her coat and stood up straight. "You mean murder. I don't think so, the timing is not right. Not the timing of the evening, but in general. If he wanted to get rid of her, nearly twenty years later doesn't make sense. Not when the station's rumored to be getting rid of him. Why do you think he agreed to host? The money was just good enough."

"The station is firing him?" I sputtered, recalculating everything I knew about Oscar. "Do you know why and when it happened?"

"Not a clue," Shirleen declared. "Now that's enough about that bad decision, let's go find the one I used to be married to."

Going through the visitor's entrance, we found that the holiday fair continued inside. A large sign pointed further into the hallway to Santa's Workshop, with times for when the big man would be able to meet the kids. Further signs pointed to different areas for games, one that was mask required and the other that encouraged masking.

A young nurse in scrubs that featured snowmen in a marching band stood by a table with disposable masks and hand sanitizer. I thought for a moment about asking obliquely about Glenn but I ended up taking a disposable mask from her. I turned around to hand over some to Shirleen and Virgil, but they had come prepared, and already donned their own KN95 masks. Shirleen even had on a cloth mask with frolicking reindeer that lay over the top.

"You go that way," – Shirleen pointed toward the mask optional room – "and we'll take the other one."

I was so relieved I wasn't stuck with Virgil that I didn't question if letting them both confront Glenn on their own was better. We were in a hospital – it couldn't get too bad, could it?

I wandered into the larger room, floating past the games and vendor stalls. Unlike outside, which had been primarily for visitors and community members, for the inside fair I mostly saw patients at the booths with a cardigan or robe pulled over their starched hospital gowns. With jazzy music playing in the background, the room was warm enough I undid my coat and realized I still had my apron on.

With a jolt, I remembered the microphone Virgil lent me, and pressed my hand against the small lump in the large front pouch.

Was it still on?

It must be why Virgil didn't even fumble with a microphone while talking to Oscar. Me having it would be the reason I was sent here off on my own. I would be ready when I found Glenn.

"Are you here for one of the stalls? I'm afraid you'll have to go next door."

At a small table, a pair of women, one Hispanic, the other Black, sat playing chess. The Hispanic woman was in a hospital gown, wearing a cardigan with poinsettias as large as dinner plates across it, and a matching mask. The Black woman was dressed in outside clothes, but they sagged on her too-thin frame, and she had a pink knit cap over her head. While she was mostly dressed in gray and brown, her face mask was heavily bedazzled with pink and green sequins.

"I'm not here as a vendor," I said. "I just stepped in to see how the rest of the fair is going."

"There's not much set up, just a few places to hang out," Pink and Green said. "I was hoping you were selling something, as I'm getting whiffs of cinnamon and brown sugar even with this on."

"I just made a cake on television," I said.

"You can't just say that and stop," Poinsettia said as she waved a knight chess piece around, her eyes quite merry over her mask. "Do go on! What kind of cake and what show?"

"I was on *The Dish @ 9* and made a pistachio apple cake."

"That's the Christmas cake I used to make for my kids!" Pink and green cried. "I can't believe those cakes are still popular."

"I hear that Shirleen Foster lives in the area." Poinsettia added, "I can't remember if it's Norfolk or Hunton Bay. I know she got her start here."

"Well," grumbled Pink and Green, "it is nice that the area will be known for something more than military, bad traffic, and doomed to being underwater sooner than we think!"

"This is delightful!" Poinsettia said. "My nieces will get a kick out of it when I tell them I met someone famous from TV."

"I'm hardly famous," I protested.

"We can help with that!" Pink and Green declared. "We know everything that goes on here. Which reminds me." She turned to her friend. "Do you know where Emily is?"

Poinsettia shrugged. "She might be sniffing around – oh, there she is!"

Something – someone – tugged on the back of my coat, and it took every bit of willpower to stop myself from whirling around.

A girl who looked about ten, but could have been as old as thirteen, was sniffing my coat, her mask of pink candy canes pulled down. Her skin was dusky brown, and her nose twitched as her eyes were focused on my apron. She had a fluffy purple robe over her hospital gown, and hair was in four chunky braids with wooden beads at the end, and the tote bag she had slung across her body burst with books and pens. "You are the cake I've been smelling! Are you a baker?"

"I work for a cook," I said, thrown by the intensity in her eyes that overwhelmed her thin and drawn face. The amused chuckles from the ladies didn't fully put me at ease.

"Emily," Pink and Green said, "this lady made a cake on television! She's – sorry, I didn't get your name."

"Keisha," I said. "Keisha Scott."

Emily gasped. "You're Keisha!" She put her mask back on. "You're not as tall as I thought you would be, but that's alright." She imperiously grabbed my sleeve. "We need to talk about cakes!"

I let myself be pulled along, especially as it seemed the other patients and even the nurses just laughed and shook their heads as if this was a common occurrence, and not one they needed to intervene with. Emily took me through a series of hallways, through the double doors that connected Hunton Bay General with the Children's Hospital and into the brightly painted walls of the ward. I expected to be brought into her room, but Emily took me into a larger common room filled with toys waiting to be played with, and a few tables and chairs of various sizes. Emily sat down at the table and pushed me to sit in a tiny chair opposite her. With my knees bumping against the table, I sat still as Emily furiously flipped through her notebook.

"I need you to tell Ms. Shirleen Foster that this is how she can improve her cakes, by making them into cupcakes."

"Someone's done that before," I said.

"Yeah, but not the way *I* did it," Emily said, as she handed the sheet to me.

I didn't recognize the recipe, but I didn't need to, for she had neatly marked the date for it, and where she got it from. The radio show that Shirleen did way back when. I felt my eyebrows rise. How did Emily managed get her hands on this? Shirleen did this show back when *I* was a child.

"Where did you get this from?"

"I copied it." Emily shrugged. "I have every recording there is about Shirleen Foster."

"How?" I asked.

Emily leaned forward, her gray eyes earnest as a pound cake. "I got connections. I know everything about Shirleen Foster. Her cooking, her life, the people who have been there for all the highs and lows. I know she wouldn't kill her best friend. I can't believe anyone would think that."

"It's very easy to think the worst of people," I said.

"Because you won't get hurt." Emily nodded, her face filling with understanding. "Shirleen would never murder someone."

"She didn't do it," I agreed. Because I couldn't help but want to cheer up the girl, I added, "I'm hoping to uncover who did."

"I know, I listened to your podcast this morning," Emily said.

I had to bite back a laugh, because of course she had.

I smiled behind the mask as I asked, "Do you have a theory for me?"

"Just a few ideas," Emily said. "You're not wrong that someone might want to frame her. They're jealous of her new success with the cookbook. It's been a very long time and people are excited to see she is back." Emily turned to her notebook, and there I saw, between scrawled notes, printed pages of the recent articles and media coverage.

"The moment the new cookbook started it began. First, it was small chatter and comments on articles. The first rumors started even before Shirleen's friend was officially announced dead, and it's only grown. I can't do much to help, since I only get a few hours of screentime and that's mostly for schoolwork, but for Oreos my cousin is helping me remind people what good things Shirleen has done."

I stared at the fierce air radiating from the tiny form. "You're the one posting all the nice things about her?"

"My cousin has, I'm just feeding him the information," Emily said quickly, as if I was going to snitch on her.

I wouldn't dare, of course. But she was skittish, and something in her words sparked my interest.

"You said the bad rumors started early."

"They did." Emily narrowed her eyes, and then clutched her notebook to her chest. "Don't you know this already?"

"I do," I said quickly. "I've been trying to gather information to help Shirleen. Because somebody is trying to make things very hard for her. Since you know so much, could you help me figure out where to look?"

Emily loosened her grip on the notebook and considered my question with the thoughtfulness of a scholar. "Well," the girl finally declared, "you can always ask Janice O'Neal."

"Janice O'Neal," I echoed, trying to recall if I had run across that name before. "Who's that?"

"Her original best friend," Emily declared.

Before I could ask more, a heavyset blonde nurse dressed in scrubs decorated with festive desserts from around the world appeared.

"Emily," the nurse reproved. "I thought you were going to enjoy the party."

"I am," Emily said. "I enjoyed it and then I left."

"Well, there's someone here who wants to see you."

"I don't care about seeing Santa," Emily flipped the pages in her book and didn't noticed Shirleen slipping into the room.

Shirleen chuckled. "Would you like me to tell him that? It might hurt his feelings."

"It's you!" Emily burst into tears. They dripped along her face, soaking her mask as she shot accusatory eyes at me. "You didn't say she was here!"

"You didn't ask," I said.

Shirleen did not sit in the tiny chair I had sat in, but settled upon a chair meant for adult visitors, while Emily bounded over with her book. "I have several ideas for your next cookbook," she declared.

"Lay them on me," Shirleen encouraged with a wide grin. "This book still has room for one more recipe."

My eyes were prickling as they tried to hold back tears, and as I looked away from the pair, I found Virgil lingering in the doorway. Instead of being content to watch, he waved for me to come over.

I was still sore at him for his words at the TV taping, but I couldn't help but be drawn by the urgency in his gesture.

After a moment's hesitation, I sauntered over.

"I found Glenn," he said once I was near.

"Where?" I asked.

Virgil shook his head. "No, I have to show you, you're not going to believe me otherwise."

"I think I would," I protested, only to have to eat my words a few minutes later, as we entered the room set up to be Santa's Workshop.

Santa was in his chair and had in his lap a young boy, who was asking what reindeer ate and if they liked cookies. The bushy beard and oversized coat made it hard to tell, but I spotted an earring in his ear that proved it.

"Is that really…" I began.

"Yes," Virgil said from the depths of despair. "My uncle is Santa Claus."

A pair of twins, each wearing crowns and capes decorated with stars over their hospital gowns, turned around to look at Virgil, their jaws slack and eyes wide. "Your uncle is Santa Claus!"

They were loud enough that Glenn even looked our way. Under the beard, his grin grew merrier.

As Virgil nervously answered the demanding questions from the children, I tried to make sense of the vision I saw before me. Where had this jolly fellow listening to the chatty kid come from? It seemed so strange compared to the sleazy man I had encountered on several occasions.

Glenn had hurt Shirleen in the past. I didn't need the details or even a backstory to know he might try again. I wanted him to be behind this, but he was also a very obvious suspect.

The twins got their turn to badger Santa, allowing Virgil to resume our conversation.

"According to the person running the event, he interviewed here last week," Virgil said to me. "Based on the time of the interview, he had just enough time to drive to Tully Manor and join the festivities, but not to set up for poison."

"He could have planned ahead," I said.

"He's not a planner," Virgil grumbled. He looked around for any tiny humans with big ears, before he added in a whisper, "Otherwise, he never would have gotten in enough debt that my aunt had to publish that *Heart Healthy* cookbook, which still hates to this day."

Luckily the line for Santa wasn't long, and when the last child gave their list of wishes, Glenn took his break, and strolled over to where we waited for him.

"Well, now," Glenn said, hooking his thumbs along his belt, absently adjusting the padding that gave him the appearance of Santa's girth. "Who's following who?"

He beamed at us behind the false beard and for the first time in my life I wanted to punch Santa in the face.

"What do you have to say to Aunt Shirls and does it have anything to do with a death threat?" Virgil asked.

Glenn's smug expression deflated. "How did you know I got one?"

I hadn't, and neither did Virgil it seemed from how he blinked. But he recovered quicker.

"Because we both got one," Virgil huffed, irritation flashing on his face. "All these times you kept coming around, why not lead with that?"

"Because no one would let me get a word in," Glenn said. "Your aunt had poisoned you against me. You used to be my little buddy, and she–"

"She was dragged to court to pay for your debts," Virgil cut in. "She wants nothing to do with you."

"Tell her I'm a changed man." He pressed his hands against the rented Santa suit. "All the things that happened before won't happen again. I've been to therapy and worked out the issues. I'm just concerned about her. Those messages had a mean slant to them. With Ruby dying I can't help but think there was a mix-up. Keep an eye on her. Things ended badly, but at the start they were almost wonderful."

Virgil held up a hand. "Can I see the message you got?"

Glenn scrolled through his phone and showed us a very familiar unknown number. The message itself was similar to mine, but there were several more sent to him over a period of two weeks, with a few attempts by Glenn to write back demanding answers that never came – only more threats.

The whole exchange looked genuine to my eyes. Whoever was doing this knew Shirleen's history quite well. Because otherwise why contact him? Was it a mistake? Or was there hope that Glenn would distract Shirleen?

"I'll tell her about this, but not the content," Virgil said handing back the phone. "Maybe she'll take care since even you're getting them."

"Good," Glenn grunted. He took back his phone. "That podcast of yours, it's good stuff." With this gruff parting, he returned to Santa's Workshop.

Honestly, I was really torn by the thought of going in there and ruining several dozen kids' belief in magic. As much as I wanted to, I couldn't see him as a murderer.

"Think he's really changed? He didn't ask for money," I said to Virgil.

"Leopards never change their spots." Virgil cleared his throat and held out his hand. "Can I have the microphone back? Before you storm off with it again?"

"I didn't storm off," I said, "I was trying to catch the train." I handed it over with little protest anyway. "I don't know if it got everything."

"Something is better than nothing," Virgil said as he turned it off. He paused before he began. "What you heard from Glenn and even Oscar, don't bother with it."

"But it's related to the case."

"No, it's not."

When he didn't clarify or even explain, my temper rose up, hotter than before. How foolish I was to even expect an apology!

Just when I thought he might be different, he just went ahead and proved me wrong.

"Fine, then you know what else is not related to the case? Me!" I jabbed him in the chest and he backed away as if my finger was a fire poker. "If I can't have all the data, I'm not involved anymore! Good luck figuring it all out!"

I didn't even wait for him to respond, and strode out, pausing only to buy a bundle of chocolate before I got on the train to head home.

Slumped on the seat, I turned on my phone. An afternoon's worth of messages poured in and I watched as the number rose on my group chat, hoping I just missed out on gossip on the latest shows and nothing truly important, because I didn't have the energy for anything else. Luckily there were only a few I needed to reply to.

To Pascal, confirming the list of groceries for the party. A quick reply to my father, who asked for details about the train tickets to Providence even though I told him I was going to take care of that. As for the rest, Sunil and Romy both had questions about the *Death by Christmas Cake* podcast. Eden left cryptic notes saying not to do anything she wouldn't do, and Jamal teased me about updating my murder board.

Austin had also left several messages, continuing his grumbling about the podcast in my inbox. Apparently, we had cost him a whole day's work, because a mere mention of Shirleen's name brought the wolves out, including Maxine Roberts. I couldn't tell if he was upset about not knowing about this, or didn't like that we were investigating. Probably both, I figured.

It wouldn't hurt to find out. Maybe I could arrange a meeting to speak with him again? I did need to get the snowman tin back from him. Should I show up alone? What if he was the murderer? Would it be safe to go?

Leaving that question aside for now, I quickly conducted a search for Janice O'Neal. The way Emily had mentioned her made the woman seem so important. Another recipe writer? Or perhaps someone who owned a restaurant now and was writing a cookbook? The name wasn't familiar to me as part of the food scene in the 757, or even from the places where Shirleen's food career had flourished.

A search of the name filled up the screen with links and images, but a quick scroll proved most were quite wrong. The search results were filled with people that were too young, not involved in cooking, or even just seemed too ordinary. Grimacing at the wedding announcement that celebrated the union of Janice Brown and Carson O'Neal, I could only sigh. The name was fairly common, but I had the faint hope I might find a slim lead first.

A new email alert popped up from Adrienne Blake. She wrote mostly about earlier this morning. She was chipper, and didn't directly address the incident, although she did say that the WVHB team was able to get all they needed and her team even got some clips to cross-promote. Then she spoke about how much she enjoyed working with me, and that there might be an opening soon at Kitchen Atelier. If I was interested, I should let her know.

If I was *interested*?

Was I not interested in my daydreams coming to life?

I liked working with Shirleen, but it was always going to be a temporary project. It should be temporary, because I kept crossing the line between professional and personal, and it wasn't just because I was getting into her business with this murder investigation.

It was a certain nephew of hers too who was tipping the scales on my decision.

My phone buzzed and an unfamiliar number flashed across the screen.

I hesitated, but then picked up the call.

"Hello?" I asked.

"This is Davis Packer," came an assuredly familiar voice. "Is this Keisha Scott? I got the number from Austin. I wanted to chat with you. I heard about the show today. I've got a friend who works on *The Dish*, they mentioned what a wonderful job you did today."

Adrienne had said similar to me both in person and in her email, but this left me a bit uneasy, because I didn't understand why he was calling me.

Wouldn't he be looking to talk to Virgil instead?

"Well, I have done a few promotions with Shirleen before, mainly in the background. This was a little different as I was featured."

"You did well, very well. See, I've been developing a new TV show. I told you a bit before. Originally the idea was to do short-form media. The more I thought about it, there still is an appetite, pun intended, for longer form TV, and you'd be great for it. You're young, with fresh ideas, and the amateur cook thing is a great angle. Your association with Shirleen could even convince producers."

Convince producers, when it was often unfairly whispered that Shirleen was difficult to work with? I wasn't sure how putting me as the star of a show would help, other than the fact they could probably pay me less.

It was a stepping-stone to somewhere, just like how my sister started out doing science communication by doing social media posts for the botanical garden she was doing her fellowship at. Something so small and silly gave her the first step to her dreams to do it as a career.

This could be the same.

Yet my heart didn't leap as it did from Adrienne's mere suggestion of a role.

"I'm not sure about a TV show," I said. "I'll have to think about it."

"Yes, think all you need. No need to make any decisions. Nothing gets decided until next year anyway. Just wanted to let you know about it. You're a rising star, Keisha Scott, even if you don't realize it quite yet."

Police Underbake the Investigation into the Death of Ruby Walton

By Maxine Roberts

The family of Ruby Walton have called on the police to renew their investigation into her death at Tully Manor. In a recently released statement, they declare the police have not done enough to get to the truth of the celebrity chef's sudden and untimely death. Ruby Walton is thought to have died from an acute allergic reaction from a sample of cake. Deemed an accident, her death was seemingly brushed aside. An inside source at HBPD suggests the investigation was rushed to get a hungry public some answers – the best the understaffed PD could manage. While there are calls to arrest Shirleen Foster, who had a complicated history with Ruby Walton, the evidence is not there to prove her involvement. Witnesses state there was a verbal altercation shortly before Ruby Walton's death, but other statements insist that Shirleen Foster was genuinely shocked and pained by the event.

One question remains: why then was Shirleen Foster held as the likely suspect? Mere hours after Ruby Walton's death, Detective Dimaandal detained Shirleen Foster and released her without charges given there was only circumstantial evidence.

Namely a slice of Christmas cake.

Among the more strident voices protesting this attempt to frame Shirleen Foster as a murderer is her nephew, Virgil Sullivan, whose podcast *Death by Christmas Cake* lays out a compelling argument that there's more to Ruby Walton's death… perhaps even foul play by an unknown third party. Hinting at details and suspects the police have overlooked for a tidy solution, the podcast aims to provide answers that Ruby Walton's family and the public deserve to have.

And as a source close to the action says, "Maybe the podcast can find what the police can't."

Chapter 20

When I saw Maxine's article the next morning, I was glad that I currently wasn't talking to Virgil. For even if I wasn't named, it was obvious I was the one that Maxine quoted and worse, she spun my comments to deeply imply the podcast was going to perform miracles. (Not that it couldn't, but I didn't want that printed!)

Although the podcast was out in the wild, I wondered if this article, and the not-so-minor frenzy it had caused demanding answers (aided no doubt by little Emily), would have Detective Dimaandal tuning in even sooner.

The detective had been very adamant about us not investigating and staying out of police business… but I hadn't gotten a call from the police about my little gift of the cake carrier either.

Maybe the podcast was going to cause a fuss, but I wanted the attention. This investigation wasn't going the way I planned, but I wasn't wrong in thinking something was there. As my dad said, when it came to birdwatching, sometimes to see a bird you needed to make some noise. Finding a murderer might be no different.

Although that didn't stop me from fretting most of the morning that I would get another call from the Hunton Bay police department with several demands for my time and attention. It was with some relief the morning passed without such a call and I made my way to the studios of WVHB for the appointment with Sunil to view the archives.

Virgil had arranged everything days ago, and I almost expected to have the whole meeting canceled after our fight, but it remained unaltered, except that instead of him joining me in the archives, I arrived by my lonesome.

"You picked an excellent time to visit," Sunil said, when he met me in the lobby as he nibbled on a sugar cookie in the shake of reindeer. I could hear strands of holiday music and good cheer about having a party during business hours pouring in from a meeting room.

"You told me to come at this time," I said, as I accepted the proffered visitor's pass.

"That's because it's when you're least likely to attract attention," Sunil teased. "Especially now since you're famous."

"Oh, don't be silly," I said. "I'm no more famous than you are."

"Right now, but one day, all that will change!" He glanced back behind me, with a curious expression. "You came alone. I thought Shirleen's nephew would..."

"He's sick, and couldn't come," I said quickly.

Accepting this with a nod, Sunil took me through the hallway, away from the party, to a back room in the studio archives. Reminding me of a library research room, the shelves were filled with boxes and binders, plus rows of filing cabinets lining the wall.

"No wonder I had to come here – nothing is digitized. Should I expect VCR tapes? Do you know where anything is?" I asked.

"I do, and especially all the Shirleen Foster files," Sunil said. "We had a Make-a-Wish kid in here not too long ago, who might just be Shirleen Foster's number one fan. She had me in here looking at everything on file, and when I didn't want to show her the outtakes, she sat there and glared at me until I did."

I chuckled, thinking this had to be Emily. "What were the outtakes about?"

"Behind the scenes stuff, for a documentary that was pulled and never finished. This footage came to the collection because someone heard we keep all of Shirleen Foster's media work here. A family member of the person who was doing the documentary sent it."

"Janice O'Neal?" I asked hopefully.

"No." Sunil sat in chair before a computer and went searching. "Paul Olson. It's not complete. I suppose it was cut because Shirleen didn't want to see it complete, which I understand, after looking at it."

"Was it unflattering?" I asked.

"Why don't you see for yourself?"

Sunil selected a recording, and on the screen was a younger Shirleen cooking in her first kitchen in Norfolk. She had made a mistake and was laughing as she corrected it. Given her hairstyle was no different than it was today, I couldn't tell exactly when this occurred until a little boy toddled into frame, carrying a small footstool. He put it next to the counter and climbed up to stand next to Shirleen. Her smile brightened as she slid a bowl over to him and they continued to cook together. The film jumped between different clips, mostly showing Shirleen around her house, cooking or working on a cookbook, and even answering letters to various friends and acquaintances. I didn't get all the names but none were Janice O'Neal. The next scene was in a radio booth, at the old WVHB studios, where little Virgil quietly sat with a coloring book while Shirleen answered questions from her callers.

It seemed all fine and normal, when suddenly Shirleen jumped up with a shout. Virgil looked up. Shirleen pasted a smile on her face, moved him to an empty chair, and put headphones on him. She hurried out the room, and the cameraman followed, bouncing and shaking, into a hall full of people. In the knot of bodies Ruby jabbed a finger at Glenn, her words lost in the fray as the camera bounced around.

"Stop it, stop it," Shirleen cried as she came between them. "What's going on? You're not supposed to be here!"

"You can't stop it, not this time," Ruby pushed Shirleen aside. "I don't know what you're thinking!"

"Let me explain–" Shirleen stopped and suddenly pivoted, looking directly into the camera, and barked in her most foreboding tone. "Stop rolling!"

The screen went black, and I blinked as the screen changed to another video. "That's all we got. Boring, isn't it?" Sunil said.

"For a sick kid eager to learn all about their idol. But not for me."

"And someone else it seems." Sunil swung his chair around to face me. "I've been thinking lately, maybe there's something odd going on. Ruby Walton dies and then old clips surface on the internet, some of which can only be gotten here."

"So, someone stole it?"

"No, they made a copy. That's why the clips look even more dated than they truly were. You can't tell on the small screen, but on something bigger you see it was recorded using an external camera. Someone snuck in here and used something, maybe a cellphone, maybe a camera like the one you carry around, and copied the footage they wanted."

"Without being noticed?" I asked.

"This is public radio," Sunil said, as if that answer sufficed. "We do our best, but what can I say? We're not going to have someone guarding the archives. We can barely get coffee."

I pointed to the screen. "I know you can't tell me who sent it, but can you tell me exactly when this happened?"

"Is it important?" Sunil brightened. "Wait, if I tell you, can I get on the podcast?"

In answer I took out my phone and hit record. "When did someone contact WVHB in the hope of getting information about Shirleen Foster that they couldn't find elsewhere?"

Sunil cleared his throat before he dropped his voice an octave to say, "The first email arrived on November 23rd. I replied in early December, but the respondent didn't show the high interest of the first email. Between those messages, footage that can be only found at WVHB made its way to the internet. While I cannot share with you who sent the message, I can say it was not someone that our logs show as a recent visitor. Although," Sunil added with dramatic effect, "it's not the first time someone has given a wrong name to hide who they are."

"Excellent work, Sunil," I said, stopping the recording. "I didn't know that part, so that's definitely going in. Let me know if anyone contacts the archives looking for information about Shirleen."

On the way back to collect my bicycle I sent the audio clip to Virgil and a voice note summarizing what I learned.

As I was unlocking my bicycle, my phone buzzed.

Oh, he wrote back, *we're still doing this? I thought you quit.*

In my eagerness I had forgotten my rash words.

I scowled, ready to shoot off a quip of my own.

But then remembered. This was about a murder, and sometimes pride had to be sacrificed.

You won't solve this without me, Sullivan. I replied. *I figured out where the old clips came from. They're local.*

Virgil's reply was swift. *I figured they were. That solves one minor mystery, but I'm left with another, how did they know in the first place?*

I mused over this question as I made the final preparations for the holiday party with my friends. I had cooked most of the food the day before, having finally settled on a menu: a mix of dishes I'd grown up with, plus the new ones my friends introduced me to. I had sides that were tributes to the friends that couldn't make it for the party and, of course, I was making a cake – my specialty, the Caramel Pecan Delight, a cake I knew I had to make for the family I had gathered around me.

I had just taken the cake out when a message from Romy flew across my phone, saying she was freezing on my doorstep. I opened my kitchen door to her and Jamal.

"You're supposed to be next door," I said.

"We're here to help," Jamal replied, and added as he swept his gaze along my food-splattered clothes, "and to make sure you enjoy the party this time around."

"Wowzers," Romy said, spotting the laden bamboo trays on the counter. "You have outdone yourself, Key. This is a feast. Can we really eat it all tonight?"

"That's why containers exist," Jamal said. He placed a hand on my shoulder. "You're too kind to us, Key, but you should have just done something simple. We like your food, but like you better."

"I had fun," I said. "And I think I managed to make a dish everyone can eat this time."

My front doorbell rang and I hurried into the hall, hoping to catch my cats before they would get underfoot. I wasn't expecting a delivery, but found a package waiting for me anyway.

"I have brought my famous–" Shirleen declared and then stopped to stare at me. "Goodness gracious child, it looks like you went to war with your oven! You did need help after all! Good thing I did not come empty-handed, but you should have called me and I would have come sooner."

I grinned despite the rebuke. She showed up after all! "I'm finished for the evening, actually. We'll be dining next door, but where are…" I began, only to realize she wasn't holding anything.

I mentally kicked myself into an icy river, as Virgil stepped out from around the car with a stack of several foil-wrapped pans in hand.

I may have only extended the invitation to Shirleen, but it had gone to Virgil anyway, as how else would his aunt get here?

Not thinking of that, I considered as he walked up to my door, was an oversight.

"Hello, Kelsha," Virgil said quite coolly. "Where should I put this?"

I eyed the stack. It was already going to be a tight fit getting everything on the table without these additions. "In the kitchen, it's right down the hall."

As they headed in, I grabbed the curious Decker and Poppy before they could make their great escape. With a gentle nudge, I urged Lola into the next room, corralling my impish trio.

"Stay there," I warned.

I hurried back into the kitchen to make introductions… only to find that I didn't need to.

I figured my friends would know who Shirleen was. I mean, she was famous after all. But as I arrived Romy and Jamal chatted with Virgil like they were old friends.

"When you said you were busy," Jamal chortled, as he initiated a complicated handshake with Virgil, "you should have been specific!"

"Same to you," Virgil retorted. "You never said what you were up to tonight!"

"It's the same thing every week, dinner with friends. I suppose I should have been more specific."

As I entered the kitchen everyone turned to me, and I tried to not show my confusion as I cleared my throat. "You know each other already? I thought I had to make introductions."

"No need to," Romy added brightly. "Virgil's my new best friend for actually being able to move the piano I got from my grandfather into my new apartment."

I blinked, staring up at Virgil, vaguely recalling Romy telling me this last year. "The moving company who performed that small miracle is yours?"

"And mine," Jamal added. "I'm a part owner of Moving Champions."

"You are?" I said as my head spun at this news. "Jamal, you never said anything about owning a moving company."

"Because he runs the day-to-day, I'm just the idea guy," Jamal remarked. "But I did the most important part, I made the logo." Jamal's gaze settled on me filled with glittering mischief I had long learned to be wary about. "You know, Keisha, I didn't realize you knew each other, would have saved me the trouble of trying to make introductions."

"Introductions for what?"

"Oh, that small favor you asked me."

Jamal shot me a peculiar glance and my face warmed as I remembered that at the beginning of fall, I asked him to introduce me to any of his single friends to bring as a date to my college roommate's wedding. He had obliged, saying he knew just the guy, only to follow up a short while later saying he'd have to think of someone else. That his friend wasn't dating as far as he knew but was too hung up on a girl, and that Jamal didn't want to waste my time with a hopeless romantic. I went stag to the wedding, had a blast, and promptly forgot about it all as I was busy working with Shirleen and avoiding her annoying nephew.

But if Virgil was Jamal's friend, did that mean…?

"Amazing we all know each other!" Romy beamed. "Funny how life goes, isn't it?"

"Or shows how small this city is," I said quickly, trying not to look at Virgil. "I need to get the rest of the food ready."

"Not so fast." Jamal grabbed me by the arm. "*We* will get everything ready."

"Go get dressed for the party," Romy encouraged, "and let us help."

She shooed me away, as did Shirleen.

"Heed your friends, Keisha," Shirleen declared as she plucked my planned menu from the table. "A good hostess doesn't do everything. They delegate and delegate well."

Thus shoved out, I hurried upstairs to change out of clothes spoiled by splatters of sauces and oils. Instead of the outfit I had laid out earlier, I pulled on a gold sequin party dress with a swooping neckline and trailing bell sleeves and a hemline that fell to my knees. I had been outmaneuvered so well, it seemed that this time I wouldn't be going back and forth into the kitchen, so I could glam it up. Sliding on a bracelet and earrings I seldom wore, I gently teased my hair from its twists into a halo of curls.

After the excitement of the past few days, I wasn't sure I wanted to put on this party, but I had pushed through anyway, throwing myself into menu planning, especially as my friends told me how much they were looking forward to it. My mother had died the day before Christmas, and my grandmother passed in the embers of Thanksgiving, so I welcomed any chance to add joy and celebration to this time of the year, especially with those I loved dearly.

With my camera in hand, I bounded into my front room to grab my coat, when I realized I wasn't alone.

Perched on a chair, Virgil dangled a fishing rod before Lola. He nearly dropped the rod as I entered, and my cat loudly vocalized her disapproval before he began bobbing it once more.

"You start playing with her, you can't stop until she's had her fill," I said. I spotted the open door to the next room, although my other two cats were nowhere to be seen.

"You look nice," he said. "I mean not– I didn't mean…"

"I'll take that as an insult," I joked with a smile, and he grew flustered with each passing moment. It looked well on him, nearly as much as the soft cable knit sweater he wore. "It's fine, I don't get a chance to dress up often. Don't like getting my good clothes spotted with food."

Virgil cleared his throat with an effort. "From the way your friends talk, you hide in the kitchen at big gatherings."

"I'll tell you a secret," I said. "I'm very shy in a group. You get to see me at my best."

"I never doubted that."

Lola lost interest in the fishing rod and stalked away. Virgil still twirled it around as he spoke. "I was told to stay back to make sure you don't add anything else to the table. Pascal said it will collapse and we will have to eat on the floor."

"He would say that," I replied, not asking why Virgil got tapped for the task, when he was more or less a guest. I glanced at my camera thinking of the last time I had it in hand, in the gazebo halfway across town, and in a moment where it felt like we were almost friends.

"You owe me an apology for what you said at the taping," I remarked. He flinched at my abruptness, but I continued unabashed because playing coy wasn't working. Clearly being direct was for the best. "I was rude and insensitive, but you didn't have to get snippy."

"I wasn't snippy," Virgil said, but when I frowned he added, "but I was rude. I've gotten used to protecting Aunt Shirls, especially about her private life. There's been trouble, even with those she worked closely with before."

"I'm not trouble," I said. "I can help. Especially if it's about a murder – it is my specialty after all."

"I don't think you mean it like that," Virgil said, "but lesson learned about pushing you out. I'm sorry."

Accepting this apology, I seriously asked, "What are your food preferences?"

"Everything?" he answered, quite confused. "I grew up eating anything my aunt made."

"Yes, but even Shirleen has her preferences."

"If you made it," Virgil said softly, "it's all good to me."

He meant it too.

I swallowed hard, at a loss for words. No one has ever said that before. Sure, they'd try a new dish I made, or joke that they'd take a bite just to see, but I had gently pressured them first. For the truly adventurous eaters, it has less to do with me and more to see what would surprise their palate.

Virgil was different. I had seen him not just sample my food, but eat until there was not a crumb left behind and be disappointed there wasn't anything extra.

Anything, he said. And I knew he meant it, and in more ways than one.

Walking into Pascal's front room I found he had been busy since I had been over here last. Although he always decorated for the holidays, Pascal had truly decked the halls with off the chart jolliness. There was a battalion of nutcrackers on the side table guarding a jar of candy canes, wreaths in every window, pinecone-studded garlands around door frames, and small pots of poinsettias on each step leading upstairs, and a miniature Christmas town on a side table, where a small train ran through. The air was scented with bright pine and spruce, some which came from his Christmas tree and the rest from flickering candles. Dozens of Christmas cards were also taped on the archway to his living room. Overlying each other like the finest feathers, they held wishes for the holidays and other thoughtful notes from Pascal's friends, old students, his relatives, and others I only got a glimpse of in his life.

His Christmas tree was framed by the cards, and the glittering white lights made the handcrafted glass ornaments shimmer. Presents were under the tree and while some were merely decorative, not all were. I spotted my name amongst the bright colored gift tags, as well as Romy and a few of my friends who were planning to be here on Christmas Eve.

"It's really quite decorated," Virgil remarked.

"He goes all out every year, and look," I said pointing to the figurines of angels cutting it up as they played saxophone, trumpet, and electric guitar on the mantel. "I got these for Pascal two years ago, and went hunting in thrift stores in five different states. His wife found the piano playing one, and I knew I had to complete the set for him."

Virgil didn't move an inch, his gaze resting on the decorations Pascal had strung up along the ceiling. I followed his gaze, and spotted the large clump of mistletoe dangling in the direct center of the room.

I edged around it like it was a sword dangling overhead. Virgil mirrored me as we shuffled our way into the dining room where everyone was waiting for us.

I had planned for a dinner of eight.

Myself, Eden, Romy, Jamal, Pascal, Shirleen, plus Jessica and Sunil. Adding in Virgil was hardly any trouble, as I always planned for an extra two or three at the table. However, I was welcomed by the sight of ten other people who usually joined in for the dinner most weeks, plus some extra guests that included often-mentioned partners, children, and two strangers.

I lost count, stunned as they grinned at me.

"Surprise!" Pascal said as I stared at more people than I had prepared for. "Now it's a true party!"

"There's so many!" I whispered, still trying to do the math. "I didn't prepare enough food for everyone!"

"What are you talking about, Keisha?" Jessica laughed. "There's so much here, I can hardly see across the table."

"Plus, those of us with the tricky food preferences brought extra," Shauna said, who hadn't been around since August. She smiled widely at me, as she jiggled a toddler on her hip. "For tonight, Keisha, enjoy the gift of good company!"

"The food is made," Eden added, as she and Romy escorted me over to the table. "Just enjoy it!"

"We want you to because… well, we're all here because of you," Romy added. "You started these dinners and brought us all together. Tonight this party is about you!"

I smiled, trying not to cry even as the full weight of the sight before me sunk in.

All the people I had come to know over the years, were they all here for me? These people I first met as strangers, and got to know all their fears, desires, wishes, and hopes over various dishes and meals. Many I saw only once a week or every few weeks. I fed them and heard their stories about ploys and work, love lives, and family drama, and watched how they got promoted at jobs, dealt with being fired and laid off, brought new romantic partners each week, got married, got divorced, had children, lost pets, traveled the world, and brought me back souvenirs and recipes. While not everyone gathered into this place were my closest friends, these were all people who added flourishes and texture to my life.

So, I sat down with them and let myself enjoy the good food and even better company.

Pascal had a house made for entertaining, with a large spacious dining room. His late wife had made sure there were several large tables that could be combined into one grand table, with enough sets of dishware for even a large party. Even the small children's table under the twinkling lights of the Christmas tree wasn't a little card table, just a smaller table no less respectable than the main one.

Pascal floated like he had jet boots on, reveling in his hosting duties, hopping up to assist as needed. When he couldn't do, Eden or Sunil did.

I was left sitting at the table, nursing my cider, directly across from Virgil. He was so expressive in his pleasure as he sampled everything on the table, I found myself watching him more than anyone else.

His answer about food preferences still rattled in my mind. Why couldn't he give a straightforward answer? Say he didn't like fish, tasted soap when a dish had cilantro, or turned his nose up at asparagus? How could he say that if I made it, he liked it? How irrational and unreasonable… and it made me want to try to prove him wrong.

I would have ample time to try, it seemed.

As it turned out, *all* my friends and acquaintances had gotten to meet Virgil as he helped move them from an apartment to a house, a house to an apartment, and other places they found home. In addition to helping Romy and Eden with their recent moves, he put Shauna's father's things into storage, helped Carly and Jan move their son to college, and was there for CJ as he moved seven times in the past three years. His company, Moving Champions, had been behind it all and had been mentioned more often than I realized.

"I still don't understand how you didn't know about it," Jessica said as she leaned across the table, with something quite close to a smirk. "Jamal's been telling everyone about the moving company for *ages*."

I shrugged, trying to deflect. "I just tuned Jamal out."

"Rightfully so!" Romy teased.

Jamal huffed, but Eden playfully nudged him. "You do talk too much. The only way Keisha would listen to you is if you get a podcast. Or maybe have her take pictures."

"Speaking of Keisha taking pictures," Jessica jumped in. "The ballet school is putting on our winter recital. There are sections to highlight the different classes, plus a play."

"My kids are in the lead parts." Clark beamed from down the other end of the table.

"I don't know about going," Jamal drawled. "Is it *The Nutcracker* or that Dickens story where a rich man actually gains a conscience?"

"The play is actually something new," Jessica said, ignoring his joke. "Keisha would love it. It's a murder mystery."

"For kids?" Pascal cried, quite aghast.

"Yes," Jessica said, "they picked it too! It's fun and very lighthearted in a way. The story begins when a snowman is found melted."

"It does sound like fun," I said. "How long is it running?"

"Into the next week. You should come," Jessica encouraged, as if that wasn't the goal of this conversation from the moment she brought this up. She gestured around the table, a hair away from launching into an aggressive pitch to support the arts. "Bring someone along with you – 50% of our ticket sales put books into hands of children."

"Is it just ballet?" Virgil asked.

"Oh, there's all sorts of dancing," Jessica said, "but don't worry, our goal is to make ballet accessible to everyone. I hope to see you out there, you said you love a good mystery."

"Just like Keisha," Jamal chimed in. He winked at me, and I grabbed my cider to down the rest of the drink.

I shifted around to different parts of the table, taking in conversation with all the friends and acquaintances I didn't get a chance to see often. Their week had not been as interesting as mine, but they were happy to tell me about it, as it meant no one was asking me about Ruby.

After dinner, most of my friends had settled around Shirleen. Some were subtle about it, but Jessica, who never was chill about anything, pressed Shirleen for tips and advice. While many of the dishes on the table were clean by the meal's end, Shirleen's food vanished the quickest, with fights occurring to get the last bite.

Not only was there less food now, but fewer people as well, as those with the youngest kids departed. I went around the room saying my goodbyes and thanking them for coming out. I had just seen Clark out when the lights dramatically shifted, so only Pascal's holiday lights were left as the brightest illuminating source.

Romy appeared through an open doorway, and there were groans and remarks around me that didn't make sense until I saw the microphone in her hand.

"You won't go to karaoke," Romy spoke into the microphone, her voice amplified by the portable karaoke set, as she looked directly at Jessica who was hiding behind her hands. "So, karaoke has come to you! The sounds of the evening will be festive offerings. No overtly religious songs, no *Jingle Bells*, and Keisha is not allowed to utter a single note of Mariah Carey!"

As heads swiveled to me, I placed a hand to my chest in pretend shock, which only caused more laughter to erupt.

"I get why Keisha isn't allowed to belt, but why no *Jingle Bells*?" Shauna asked.

"It's not a Christmas song or even winter theme, it was performed originally as a minstrel tune," Virgil said.

His words got people murmuring, and CJ, who always liked to stir up trouble, asked, "Do you really know that's true? Or are you making it up?"

Virgil shrugged. "I made a podcast about it. Give it a listen and argue with me later."

CJ blinked, and then recovered with a nasty sneer. "Oh, there's going to be a later? Guess Shauna was wrong, you *are* awfully close to Keisha!"

Romy aggressively turned on the karaoke instrumental, and spoke right into the microphone with an exaggerated cry. "CJ, did you just volunteer to go first? Why don't you kick things off?"

"Yeah," Sunil jeered. "I think I heard him too. CJ, get on up there and sing for your supper!"

Hounded by this encouragement, CJ sauntered up, milking the people chanting his name as he grabbed the microphone. "I'll do better than that, I'm going to win!"

As the machine cranked up, CJ launched into a rousing rendition of *Rudolph the Red-Nosed Reindeer*. Virgil moved to stand behind me. "How," he asked as he leaned in closer so I could hear him clearly, "does one win karaoke?"

Tilting my head back, I could see his eyes twinkling with amusement.

"By making sure no one wants to follow you." I pointed to myself. "I should know. You're speaking to the reigning champion. Although it's not a competition by any means, they're mostly amateurs."

"Compared to you?" he joked.

"Not to toot my own horn, but I'm quite excellent. I'll probably sing a solo. Most karaoke nights I usually do a duet with Jamal, but he has a rule about overt Christmas songs, and you can't win by singing *Let it Snow*."

"Are you sure?" Virgil remarked.

"What, are you going to prove me wrong?"

He laughed as he held up his hands as if to ward me away. "I'm not getting involved in this!"

"Suit yourself."

"What are you going to sing, since you're banned from singing the most overplayed modern Christmas song in the world?"

"I was never going to sing that one," I protested. "I have a classic up my sleeve, the best Christmas song ever."

"*This Christmas* by Donny Hathaway," Virgil declared.

"Yes!" I beamed. "What other song is there?"

"I'm sure others may disagree, but they are all wrong!"

I didn't get a chance to prove my boast. My friends kept beating me to the microphone. Each time I got up to get it, it was snatched from me. Which was only a little annoying as it meant I could sit there and quietly critique the performances with Virgil. As it turned out, he had an ear for music and just as many opinions on everyone's choices. We traded thoughts about Jamal channeling Ray Charles for *Winter Wonderland* and how Romy delivered a rather soulful *Silver Bells*. Shauna faked us out with *The Dreidel Song* before doing *My Favorite Things*. Then Eden took her turn, with an R&B inspired take on *Run Rudolph Run* that she had clearly kept in her back pocket for tonight. Jessica and Sunil were the only ones who wanted to follow up, with a comedic take on *The Most Wonderful Time of the Year*.

Pascal and Shirleen got up front and did a duet of *What Christmas Means to Me*. They looked rather cozy as they did so, with Pascal playfully putting an arm around Shirleen when she accidentally flubbed a lyric.

I looked over at Virgil, curious to see what he would make of this. But he had vanished.

I twisted around looking for him, and spotted through the swinging kitchen door Virgil pacing around with a phone to his ear.

I slipped away to join him, catching fragments of his words. As I entered, he turned to me and gestured for me to come in.

"Detective Dimaandal, we're just working off speculation and observations. It's just a little podcast I put together as it seems to be part of the story of the cookbook…"

As I neared, Virgil turned the phone onto speaker mode.

"We're not sharing anything, because we're not working together," Dimaandal crossly shot back.

"Did you get the cake carrier we found?" I asked. "It was in a gazebo in Port Walker Point. My note told you where it was and–"

"You shared your pet theory that it was the opening play of a setup, yes, I got your note, Keisha," the detective snapped back. "You just gave me a platter. Where's the cake?"

"Wasn't there," I said cheerfully, knowing she couldn't say we weren't helpful now. "There should be enough to test for poison. You might want to think of running toxicology once more; I'm pretty sure it was missed initially that Ruby Walton was injected with potassium cyanide."

"Or maybe even ask who did the report, because that's not something easily missed," Virgil added into the deadly silence over the phone.

"Why potassium cyanide?" the detective asked.

"She said something about almonds," I began and before I could expound Dimaandal sighed.

"For the last time, stay out of this investigation. I can't stop you from putting out a podcast, but you're making it difficult for my team to find answers. And if there is a murderer, all you're doing is making yourself a target."

The detective hung up without even a goodbye.

"Well, that's not going into the podcast," I said. I peered over at him. "Did you just accuse the police of a coverup?"

"Something must be going on for such a thing to have been missed," Virgil remarked.

"That's your lawyer instinct," I teased.

"No, just common sense." Virgil dropped his phone onto the counter and turned to look at me. "You know it's odd to frame it so, but I really enjoy conducting the investigation with you. It's nothing like what I expected, and I had a lot of expectations."

His smile started to fade to something that was harder to interpret, and bizarrely the echo of Jamal's words floated around us.

Jamal had tried to set us up before and, while that hadn't happened, I met Virgil anyway, only to sour on him almost at once when I caught him recording me without permission. I was still sore about it, and his words from the other day, but I couldn't deny that most, if not all, of the reason why I had been so angry in the first place, then and now, was because there had been a vibe.

I was pretty sure I wasn't the only one who noticed.

"Keisha, would you–" Virgil began.

"Yes," I interrupted.

"Would you like to hear the cut of the next episode?"

"Episode?" I echoed, not expecting this. "For the podcast?"

"Of course, I've been working on the next few ones, I got up to six figured out since it's all the setup for our investigation. I just didn't want to release it yet… after that article by Maxine Roberts."

"I didn't give her a direct quote!" I cried, "She took my words out of context–"

"I know," Virgil assured me. "But that means there's more attention and people actually want to hear the next episode. I finished up the next one mostly, but I wasn't happy with how it was coming along, something… was missing." He looked directly at me as he said the last bit, leaving little wiggle room about what he meant otherwise.

"It's probably an obvious detail you overlooked," I quickly retorted, unsettled by this admission. "Despite all the notes you made."

"Which is why we should take care of it while we have a moment."

"You want to work it now?" I hastily turned to the mile high stack of dirty dishes, suddenly very desperate to find a task to keep me occupied. "The party is still going on."

"It's winding down," Virgil said. "No one will miss you."

"What would my friends think if vanish on them?" I could feel a blush creeping into my face despite my best efforts. "They already think I invited you here, when I only ever asked Shirleen."

"But," Virgil replied quietly, "you aren't disappointed."

As I was strongly considering if I had misread the invitation he just extended, his phone buzzed.

As it was lying on the counter between us, I got a glance at it too.

An unknown number popped up, alongside a picture of Virgil and myself at the gazebo in Port Walker Point peering out at the water.

As it faded two messages appeared on the screen:

YOU DON'T EVEN KNOW WHAT YOU'RE LOOKING FOR

SO STOP BEFORE SOMEONE ELSE DIES.

Chapter 21

Showing Virgil the pepper spray hidden in my hand sanitizer bottle, the covert comb that had a knife inside, and the stun gun flashlight, did not ease his concerns about us being stalked.

"I also took boxing classes," I said, moving into a defensive stance with my fists raised. "You're talking to someone who has a plan for every situation of being followed, chased, or pursued, by foot, bike, or car. I'll be fine. Also don't forget you're in the picture and stalkers do not discriminate by gender. You live alone but I have a neighbor who's always looking in and have enough friends that if enough hours go by they get worried."

"Keisha, we should–"

"Don't say stop the podcast and investigation. Because if I've learned anything from video games, if you run into trouble, you're on the right track."

Virgil bit back a smile. "All I was going to say is that we should mention this to Detective Dimaandal. Especially if you got a text from the stalker too."

Rummaging around for my phone revealed that I did. It came from the same number but the message was slightly different, as this stalker threatened me with the loss of a new opportunity.

"That's odd," Virgil said.

"No," I said as I stared at the screen. "I've gotten a couple of job offers recently. Adrienne Blake from Kitchen Atelier floated a chance I could get a job there. It's not guaranteed, just talk, but it could easily vanish. Don't take this the wrong way, but I don't want to work for your aunt forever."

"I don't either," he murmured. "Tell me more about Adrienne Blake. Isn't it a bit sudden to offer you a job like that? I mean, you were very good at the taping, but isn't it strange?"

"Why? She was nothing but helpful."

"She was talking to my uncle," Virgil said, "and she moved in quickly when that woman fainted."

"She was efficient," I protested.

"Why did the show have to suddenly move to Kitchen Atelier? I never got a good reason. It's like someone wanted you to be on the turf that they knew."

"Don't add her to the list of suspects just because she offered me a job," I scoffed, but then frowned as I remembered something else. "Davis also offered me a TV gig."

"Davis?" Virgil blinked. "As in Davis Packer?"

I nodded, "I'm not that keen on it, but it's another opportunity. I'm not sure how this stalker found out." I took a screenshot of the text, and then opened a new message.

"Who are you and why are you bothering me?" I muttered as I typed.

"Is that wise?" Virgil asked.

"Probably not." My finger hovered over send. "Aren't you going to stop me?" I asked.

"Why? You know boxing and jujitsu and can kill a man with a spoon," Virgil waxed. "You know what you're doing."

"You're darn right I do," I said and hit send. "We're being followed. That means we're on the right track."

I waited for him to refute this, but Virgil nodded. "You're not wrong there. I've been thinking about what the cabbie said about the blue car and the writing desk. I think I've noticed every blue car since then, wondering why Ruby had been so worried about it. I wish we had more to go on."

"Have you been looking for the writing desk too?" I asked, recalling his great interest in it. "The cabbie didn't tell us where Ruby got it from, but I was able to trace a few recently expired ads. It must be at her house, but if only we could poke around just to be certain."

"You know, I had the same thought." Virgil grinned. "Here's where things get really lucky. Ruby's daughter Gayle finally contacted me about moving the items in her mother's house into storage using my moving company. If the writing desk is there, I'll have plenty of time to look."

"Can I come along?" I asked, eager to find what secrets that desk might hold. "You can't go snooping without me!"

"Sure, come along," Virgil said, as an easy and a rather pleased grin unfurled. "You just gotta wear the company shirt!"

In sneakers, a baseball cap, and one of my less-nice wool coats, I strolled out of my place the next morning when a truck bearing the Moving Champions logo pulled up in front.

"I was going to meet you there," I said, bounding over.

"No need for that, since the office is so far away." Virgil tossed me an orange T-shirt with the logo – an Atlas-like figure holding moving boxes instead of the Earth – splashed across the front. Virgil wore a sweatshirt version of the shirt, and despite the cold had pushed up his sleeves to expose his forearms. "I was busy uploading the next episodes, so I didn't get a chance to check, but did you get any other strange messages?"

"Not yet." I settled into the cab, dropping my bag onto the floor next to his equipment. Wiggling out of my coat, I pulled the tee over my long-sleeved shirt. "I won't have to actually move anything, will I?"

"Two of my guys will be there, they're taking the other truck. Should get there before us, I think."

"Two trucks," I said. "Is it that big of a house?"

"We're doing two separate trips: one to storage and the other to the daughter's house. It's usually extra but a chance to get inside to find that desk more than makes up for it."

"Why does the writing desk bother you?" I asked.

Virgil frowned. "The effort. Why did Ruby go through so much effort for a desk? She went to collect after all."

"Maybe because it's tied to something else. You got my note about the documentary I saw, right?"

"I did."

"What if," I suggested, "Ruby hid something in the desk?"

"I wouldn't be too surprised. People leave all sorts of things in drawers," Virgil replied. "Maybe that's why I want to find the desk. I have this feeling something important is inside it."

"Maybe your subconscious is telling you it's important," I said. "You were around your aunt's work a lot when you were little. Maybe you witnessed something from that time – that could be the key."

"I was about five, I don't remember everything."

"I could hypnotize you. I heard that works."

Virgil laughed, and when he saw I was serious he continued to laugh as we drove across town to the place Ruby Walton once called home.

Riding up the long winding treelined drive, I decided on the spot I might have to think of judging cooking in the future because Ruby had done quite well for herself. Her house was more like a small manor, with a screened porch on the side. Tucked in the back of her neighborhood, there was a quiet dignity to the cream-colored house surrounded by cherry trees. In the loop up front, a slightly larger Moving Champions truck waited. Hopping out, I was soon introduced to the cousin duo, Pat and Jack. Although they were different ages and different genders, I couldn't tell them apart, for they were similar heights and builds, and seemed to take pleasure in my confusion.

"You don't need to tell us apart," Jack or Pat said. "Unless you'll be hanging around to help the boss with the podcast. Then it matters."

"How wise," I said.

"Jack tends to be," Virgil said sternly to the pair. "Keisha isn't here to help with *Moving Day* but will help document the items we're moving."

"If the client has questions, can we have her answer them?" Pat asked.

Virgil looked between the pair, and Pat grinned as if trying to pass it off as a joke. "Find me first before you do that," Virgil said.

A small SUV pulled into the drive, and Gayle stepped out, with a pre-teen at her side.

"Sorry," Gayle said, "the orthodontist ran a little late. Thank you so much for coming. You got the list I sent of where things need to go?"

Virgil nodded and discussed the logistics with her. A few things were marked for where they would go, but Gayle would be in the kitchen if there were any further questions.

"Most things are in boxes, but there are a few smaller things that need to be packed. Mostly in my mother's office."

"I can handle that," I volunteered.

Gayle turned to me, but either my baseball cap was doing the job, or I hadn't left that much of an impression on her, for she didn't appear to recognize me. "That would be wonderful. Everything in her office is going to my house. I wanted to take some time to go through her old papers. Just shove it all into a box and I'll take care of it later."

Virgil got some extra boxes from the truck and he walked with me to Ruby's office, leaving his employees to manage upstairs for now.

The house's rooms and hallways were stacked with cardboard boxes, but Ruby's office still was set up as if she would return. There were plants on her windowsill, a paper calendar with her holiday plans in vivid red ink, portraits of her family on the bookshelf… and a desk that held stacks of neatly arranged papers and books.

"Is this the one?" I asked as Virgil went to it. He was already shaking his head as he rounded the heavy, L-shaped desk.

"This is not a writing desk. It's a desk, but not the right type. It's too big. A writing desk is just a desk surface, with maybe a single drawer. This has too many compartments and drawers. It's not the one we're looking for."

"Of course not, that would be too easy," I grumbled.

I brought one of the boxes over and began to place the contents into the box. "When I moved into my grandmother's house, it took me ages to settle things. To figure out what to give away, what to keep, and even what to store away."

I opened a drawer and poked around the contents. "This is fast."

"Ruby was in the process of selling and moving in with her daughter," Virgil said. "There wasn't a rush. The new owner won't be arriving until spring. They were getting started, Gayle just wanted to accelerate the work. Although we may have to redo it, as an inferior company did the packing."

"You can tell that by looking?" I asked, flummoxed as the boxes appeared quite ordinary to me.

Virgil scowled at the sealed box as if he had X-ray vision. "They need to be repacked," he said, "but there isn't time for that."

Ever the professional, he had packed up three boxes before I could even fill one, but I was taking my time to snoop. Seated at the desk, I skimmed paperwork looking for familiar names or places that indicated who Ruby had been eager to meet that night. I found nothing of interest. Most of the papers on the desk were related to the move, plus works related to the church she belonged to, and her plans for a new charity.

It was only when I tugged open a drawer that I found something worth all this digging around. Ruby's purse from that night was in there. It had been organized, as whoever put the contents back was able to get everything to fit inside it, including the notebook. It was the same one I saw protruding that night; the cover was marbled and had a curled corner where it had been dropped.

With a pulse of excitement, I pulled it out.

Inside was not a detailed agenda or even a journal conveniently spelling out everything, including who might have murdered her. Instead, it was the one thing that still surprised me.

They were recipes.

I was only familiar with her collaborations with Shirleen, so I couldn't confirm that Ruby made them, but I knew these weren't any she'd done with Shirleen before. There was a very innovative spin to some, and the inclusion of trendy ingredients, like ube or kale, pointed to a modern approach.

The next page had a list of book titles, some were circled or crossed out as she riffed on several different themes related to cooking techniques. So, it *was* a cookbook that she was shopping around!

The last page with any writing was a short to-do list. Most of it was typical errands but one thing stood out:

Fire agent.

What sort of agent, I wondered. It couldn't be a real estate agent, perhaps the agent that helped her book TV appearances? Did she have a literary agent? I kept turning pages looking for answers, and then a ticket to this year's Whisk and Kettle Fest fluttered into my hand.

I had gone as Shirleen's plus one to the event. As it was my first time in Nashville and at the festival, overwhelmed was the word that covered most of my memories. I didn't remember seeing Ruby. Not that Ruby couldn't attend, but there hadn't been a whisper of her even being in attendance.

I was checking the list of attendees when Virgil came around with a box of books under his arm. "Are you not done yet?"

"Packing, no. Snooping, yes," I said. "I found the notebook she had that night. It's full of recipes and had this ticket stuck inside. Ruby was at Whisk and Kettle this summer."

"How is that a surprise? It's the biggest event of the year, why wouldn't she be there?"

"I didn't know she was there, and in years past there was some mention of it."

"Maybe she just went to speak with Winifred Chan."

"That is a good guess," I said. "There was something that's been nagging me about Winifred since the funeral."

"Not quite a guess." Virgil leaned over my shoulder to point to the calendar that was propped up right before me. "Considering it's also on the calendar."

On the square for the night of the party, Ruby had written. "Speak to WC at S's party/ Follow up on talk we had at Whisk and Kettle."

"I hate you," I grumbled as I took a picture of it.

"No, you don't," Virgil taunted, absently brushing past and he went back to packing.

I took pictures of the notebook and the rest of the contents of the purse and then went back to shuffling through the desk and pulled out a manila folder. When I opened it, I found a contract for *Whisk it All*.

I skimmed it at first, until my eyes fell to lines marked heavily in red, where Ruby or someone else had circled the end date of the contract: August of this year.

August. That would have been when Ruby finished up taping her show. Did that mean Ruby was out of a job? Would that explain why she wanted to fire her agent?

The next page had a series of numbers scribbled on it.

I had just started taking pictures of the contract when the door opened and one of the cousins ran in.

"Boss! You got to see it! It was like this when we got there, I swear. We didn't do a thing. I swear!"

"Slow down, Jack," Virgil said. "What's wrong?"

"One of the windows upstairs is broken, and it doesn't look like an accident!"

Virgil handed over the box of books to Jack, who staggered under the sudden weight. He hurried up the stairs, and I followed right behind, my heart thumping in my chest.

Pat was in the doorway and a perfect mirror to Jack's panic. The cousin stepped aside as Virgil hurried past.

I felt a strong chill before I even crossed the threshold. I shivered as curtains fluttered in the air. Once upon a time this was a bedroom for one of Ruby's children, given the old posters of celebrities and singers still clinging to the walls. Boxes were stacked in here, as well as a coat rack, old exercise equipment, golf clubs, and mountains of shoe boxes.

As I stepped around all of this, I was able to get a clear view of the window. A hole slightly bigger than a dinner plate was in the glass, it was jagged and uneven. Shards were sprayed across the window and the floor, and even some of the boxes.

With so much of the space turned into storage already, it was hard to move, but there was a small pathway to a far wall, where a writing desk stood.

Mostly.

A bent golf club lay on the floor, next to the split and shattered remains of a white writing desk that was cracked open like an egg.

"Oh my," I said, taking pictures with my phone. "What was it like when you got here?" I asked Pat. "Was the door closed or locked?"

"It wasn't locked," Pat said. "It was stuck real good. Jack had to put a shoulder to the door to pop it open."

Virgil went to the window and peered out but didn't take a closer look. "Let's go inform the client," he said to Pat. "She never mentioned this in the brief and it looks new."

As Virgil left the room with Pat, he silently gestured around the room to me, as if I needed further instruction to snoop.

Snapping more pictures freely now, I glanced at the window, looking for signs of watermarks or mud. I saw neither but thought there might have been a nick in the paint. A bare-branched tree was near the window, but the branches were too thin to hold a human's weight. This was the back of the house too, facing the woods.

I went back to the desk and hit record on my phone. "The writing desk we were looking for is right here in Ruby Walton's home. It seems Virgil was right to think that there was something interesting in it. I stand before a desk that has been smashed open with a golf club. It seemed the aim was to open a locked drawer. The handle has been tossed on the ground, and I can see scratch marks around the keyhole from an attempt to pick it open. The drawer is broken into three pieces, and it looks like whatever was inside is gone."

I pulled on my gloves to nudge aside some larger splinters. "There are a couple of buttons, both different sizes, one is wooden and the other black. There is a strand of red ribbon. A scrap of paper with a few words – it's in blue ink. I can make out only part of the words: 'Icy and fair'. And a receipt." I picked it up, barely making out a logo for a grocery store, and the impression of an address. "It's for a small health food store, that was local to the area, but closed a long time ago. The contents have been tucked in here for a long time, so what value do they have?"

Hearing footsteps in the hallway and voices growing louder, I hastily stood up, but kept my phone recording as the door opened.

"I can't believe this!" Gayle cried, unable to settle her gaze on either the window or the desk. "To think someone would do this! Was this the only thing you found?"

"So far," Virgil said. "We'll take a look around."

Gayle clutched the strap of her purse. "Will we be safe here? The intruder isn't still here?"

"I don't think anyone is hiding," Virgil said. "When were you last here?"

"My brothers and I were here the day after the funeral." Gayle looked around with growing remorse. "We didn't come into this room though, and no one's been here really since Mom died."

"Home security?" I asked.

"We took it off," Gayle said with regret. "We've been coming in and out, and with no one here and most of the important things – Mom's jewelry, photographs, some keepsakes – moved already, I didn't see the point." Gayle took out her inhaler and quickly pumped medicine into her lungs. "I need to call the police. This could be related to Mom's death!"

I wish she hadn't connected that bit quite yet, as I wanted a closer look, but neither Virgil nor I stopped her as she dialed.

However, Virgil did manage to get Gayle out of the room to make the call.

I had only moments so I bent down once more by the ruined desk and scooped up the scattered pages the intruder left behind. Shoving them into my jeans pocket, I hurried to join everyone else as we waited for the police to arrive.

I sat perched on the edge of the couch with the other two movers down in the den, when a police cruiser pulled up in front of the house. The pair of uniformed officers announced themselves, and Virgil went upstairs with Gayle telling what they knew of the broken window.

"They came fast," I remarked to Jack and Pat as the footsteps faded away.

"Why is that, is it because this is a rich ZIP code or something?" Pat muttered.

"Or maybe it's because of the murder," Jack said. "You know that's gotta be why! This house belonged to the lady that got killed!"

"We're here because I have questions," Detective Constance Dimaandal announced as she stepped into view.

Her trench coat flapped around her, as she swept in. Not like a storm but a foreboding wind that intensified as it landed on me.

"You're here." she sighed. "Why am I not surprised?"

"We don't know anything," Jack declared and gently pushed me forward. "She's the one with all the answers!"

The detective didn't smile at me. "I sure hope she has them."

"Jack, you and Pat can take a break in the van," Virgil said. "We can't touch anything until given the all-clear."

"Don't leave the property, I have some questions about how the room was found," the detective added.

As the cousins departed, Dimaandal turned toward us like a school teacher ready to discipline her unruly students.

"Still poking around I see," Dimaandal said.

"This is a job," Virgil stated unconvincingly and pointed to the logo on his sweatshirt. "I'm helping Gayle move her mother's possessions."

"Who happens to be Ruby Walton. What a very convenient way for you to snoop." The detective's eyes moved to me. "That you're helping with."

"I'm just helping because he called in a favor," I quipped.

The detective snarled. "I knew you two wouldn't leave this alone! I thought saying a few things would put it to rest, because young people have too much going on to do something so silly as investigate a murder." She glowered at us, leveling the full force of her frustrations. "Or making baseless claims that there is corruption in the police station."

"You heard the podcast," I joked.

"Yes," Detective Dimaandal said, as if the very word pained her. "I listened to your little podcast, and while you haven't shared everything, you are also gathering information in areas we overlooked. I'm not condoning what you've been up to, but I must admit, you dropped the episode just as we were about to put a warrant out for your aunt's arrest. The uproar it caused got it canned. Though you were starting to look like a next likely suspect. My junior officer logged a tip related to you, Virgil. Don't fret though," she languidly remarked, "I'm your alibi for last night."

Virgil swallowed. "What do I need an alibi for?"

The detective raised an eyebrow and stood in silence for a very long moment and we arrived at the only possible conclusion.

"The tip blamed Virgil for this?" I asked.

Dimaandal nodded. "The tip cited that Virgil was going around looking for a writing desk that was in Ruby Walton's possession."

"How do you know the break-in was last night?" Virgil asked.

"This is not my first time coming out to this house," the detective said. She reached into her coat for an envelope. "This is a copy of the autopsy. I am showing it to you because you were right, it's potassium cyanide."

I reached for the report, but the detective pulled it back. "What didn't make the podcast? When I listened to the dialogue you shared before the scream happened, you were already concerned. What else did you cut out?"

I looked at Virgil, who shrugged as if to say there was no reason to keep hiding it. "Keisha and I overheard someone in the hallway plotting trouble for my aunt."

"You mentioned threatening texts, but why not this?" the detective asked.

"It seemed no one was taking it seriously, and the threats were toward Shirleen and not Ruby." I looked over warningly at Virgil, hoping he wouldn't mention the photograph of us at Port Walker Point. Dimaandal was just on the edge of giving her blessing about investigating, letting her know we were being followed would dash our chances.

"I assure you, we are taking all threats seriously." The detective leveled me a stern stare. "While I won't say you've been helpful, your input has brought about interesting turns of events. Nor am I saying you should continue, but bringing tips helps. Not only were you right about this," she said as she handed me the sealed autopsy report, "but you were also right that this investigation was a rush job. My superior was told to make an arrest as quickly as possible because it could affect tax credits. If it wasn't for the family speaking out, we'd be having a different conversation. Also, your podcast didn't go unnoticed either. Be careful." The detective swung around, her coat swishing behind her. "There's a dangerous game going on."

On those dramatic words, she left us to join her team upstairs.

We stood there in silence waiting for her footsteps to retreat.

"Tell me you recorded that," Virgil said.

I held up my phone, with a grin. Turning off record, I opened my photo gallery and handed him the phone so he could look over the pictures. "Do you think someone took the golf club to the desk?"

"Looks like it. The club is a heavier one, and the desk looks pretty fragile. I think just about anyone could smash it apart. It's how they got in here that's the issue."

"They just used a ladder," I said. "Last night was the new moon, making it ideal. There are no near neighbors and no alarm system running because people have been in and out of the house. They also knew this beforehand, so they could plan. The only question is if they meant to create the scene we saw or not."

"It does look like someone took out their frustrations on what they couldn't find in the desk." Virgil kept scrolling until he stopped. "I went too far," he remarked blandly.

I snatched back my phone without looking. Spurred on by previous conversation, Romy had sent a few photographs taken during her momentous move, featuring Virgil and some of the crew from Moving Champions, posing around the piano – and it came with colorful commentary. Very colorful commentary, as Romy was not shy about making her opinions known.

"How long do you think the detective will be here?" I asked. Honestly, I wasn't even curious, I just desperately wanted to change the subject.

"Not long, but I don't think we're getting back up there anytime soon. I think they're going over everything."

"Hopefully with a fine-tooth comb," I said. "Although I may have gotten all the important details." I waved some of the slips of paper. "I still have to make sense of them though."

"Make sense of what?" Virgil cried. He pointed to the paper with such excitement. I had misread the name in my haste, and saw it for what it was now: Flair Spotlight.

"Austin's company," I breathed. "Why is this here?"

"That merits finding out."

"But how? I stroll up to his office? He's very annoyed with us if you recall."

"You still have an excuse, you never got back your peppermint bark tin."

"A *good* excuse," I said.

"Just try it," Virgil suggested, "because he wasn't even supposed to be at the TV shoot, until he insisted."

Excerpt from *At the Stove with Shirleen*

Shirleen Foster: *Okay caller, what is the problem you placed at the back of the stove to simmer?*

Deirdre Mayfield: *It's about my neighbor. We have lived next to each other for nearly fourteen years. Our youngest children are about the same age, and our older ones less than two years apart. We've traded having parties at each other's home and combined our backyards for cookouts for the neighborhood. Now things haven't been the same since she's gone back to work. I don't mind that part, but it's what she's asking me to do in the meantime. To cook or check in on her children, and even her husband, when she's running late. I've done it before when her sister was sick, but this is different. She's even taken to passing off the food I've made as her own.*

Shirleen Foster: *Well, I know a thing or two about friendship problems. You're talking to me, which means you aren't ready to talk to her yet. Before you do, decide what you are really upset about. Is it only what she's asking, or the fact she's taking advantage of your friendship? After so many years you take for granted that a good friend will always be there. Friendships tend to take a hit for the other relationships in our lives, but it's the one with the most choice, for to keep friendships in bloom we must always keep choosing them and not with fear. It sounds to me that this is just change upsetting things. You need to talk before this festers into something worse. My advice: find some time together to catch up, and find out what else is going on in her life as you relate your feelings. Having something tasty will help. If you don't have a recipe with shared history, I can recommend these cinnamon rolls that pair well with just about anything…*

Chapter 22

Virgil ended up being right on two accounts.

First, as kind as the detective was to give us the autopsy report, Virgil didn't get the all-clear to finish packing up the house. She told us to return later, maybe tomorrow, maybe next week, as the investigation was ongoing.

As I expected this, I wasn't too annoyed by this prediction.

However, I was very vexed, peeved, and overall quite put out when Austin responded to my quick text about coming to collect the tin that had held the peppermint bark.

I was waiting in the moving truck while Virgil gave direction to his employees, so I was unrestrained in my grumbling as he returned.

"Austin replied to me right away. He's in his office and says that if I want the tin, I can get it today if I like. That's not suspicious, is it?"

"If you're asking, you already know the answer," Virgil twirled his keys, exposing how pleased he was at being right. "Are we headed there?"

"We?" I replied. "I think I'll be fine on my own."

"Because you can defend yourself with a spoon and a tube of lip balm that has pepper spray in it," Virgil replied.

“I could,” I asserted, but sensing his jesting was more of a gentle parry, I countered, “but I’d rather not, so I guess you could come along.”

We went straight downtown to Austin’s office. On the weekend the streets were empty enough, that parking the moving truck was hardly trouble at all, though Virgil parked it on a side street just to be safe.

I had come here only once before and remembered having to be buzzed in as no one was manning the front desk for the coworking space.

I forget how loud footsteps echoed in the empty building, and I wasn’t quite ready to admit that that Virgil was right for the third time that afternoon. It would have been foolish to come alone, especially as the light spilling out of Austin’s office was the only illumination in the dimly lit narrow hallway.

“No rest for the wicked I see,” Austin said as we entered his office.

“It’s a busy time all around,” I said.

The tin that I had given him was in the middle of his desk, within easy reach. Austin nudged it forward to the very edge as I entered, and he kept eyes on the tin like it was a curled-up viper.

“Here I thought you would be out there investigating for your little podcast. I can’t believe that’s what you’ve been up to.”

For once Austin was not staring at one of the monitors on his desk.

Austin looked as if he had aged overnight, fine lines had sprouted across his face and there were heavy dark circles around his eyes. Guilt, or perhaps something else?

“It all seemed rather curious how Ruby died,” Virgil said straddling the line of many truths.

"You just had to make podcast about it. Do you know what happened?"

"We've just started," I began.

"But you know something, more than the police it seems." He pressed his hand against his desk. "You noticed things that night."

Next to me, Virgil shifted in his chair. "We saw many odd moments that night. Did you?"

"No." Austin's words were clipped and short as he reflexively shook his head. "I didn't."

"Are you sure?" I asked. "Because you dashed off while I was talking with Winifred and Shirleen."

"That has nothing to do with Ruby or anything else. I have other clients, and one had just insulted the Muslim and Jewish communities with a badly structured joke. It's a fire that hasn't died out ever since."

"But you ran outside," I said recalling what the cabbie had told us about his view that night. The person that had been outside the manor had to have been Austin. And I was starting to think my guess wasn't that far off that mark.

"It was the only way to get some quiet." Austin paused. "I went outside the ballroom first, but there was so much noise I stepped outside."

"Then you saw something?" Virgil asked. "What did you see?"

Austin swallowed his next words, and then squirmed long enough I thought he wasn't going to say a word. Then he said, "While I was on the phone with my client. Someone dashed into the nearby corridor, pushing a cart. I thought it was one of the servers. She wasn't dressed like any of the help that night." He looked at us as if we could absolve his guilt. "I didn't think it was important, just another thing going wrong."

"When did it happen?" I asked. "Did you hear the scream?"

"I heard a crash near me," Austin spoke slowly as if recalling a dream. He looked at us nervously as he continued, "maybe I heard a scream too. But I dashed outside as it was right near me. The woman was gone, but there was something left on the ground, it looked like crumpled decorations from the party. They were wet and sticky, and at first, I was upset that the staff there threw it out like that. Littering is a crime, you know."

"So is murder," Virgil remarked.

Austin gulped. "You think… a murderer left that there? That the woman I saw… did she, could she…" He fumbled around his desk for a drink and pulled out a water bottle and gulped down several swallows.

"We only have your word for all of this," I said as I watched with each trembling word Austin remove himself from the list of suspects.

There was no proof beyond this word, and as he explained he threw out the crumbled decorations and fabric, there wasn't even that piece of evidence that left him innocent without a doubt.

Yet there was a call log with his client, and we could easily prove he had been dealing with the minor crisis for the better part of two weeks.

"I didn't even know Ruby would be there that night. She didn't even mention it to me."

"Why would she?" Virgil asked.

"We were having a few chats," Austin turned to his screen. "Meetings related how to package her publicity for the new season of *Whisk it All*. I visited her earlier this month. In addition to that, she was very keen on hiring me for a new project, although she never quite said what it was. I'd asked of course, but she said she'll tell me later when everything is settled."

"You knew about her feud with Shirleen, and yet agreed to work with her?" I asked.

"It wasn't like I'd be working with them both," Austin said. "It was still just conversation. I suppose," he said, "it's not very useful is it?"

I took back the snowman tin, as Virgil assured Austin, "You never know how these small details make a difference."

"Which I suppose is why I wanted to see you now," Austin said to me. "This podcast of yours has given me several headaches, but someone needs to find out what happened."

Discussion about Austin's removal from the suspect list and the tailspin it sent our investigation in had us going around in circles on the drive back. Austin was the wild card we both were pulling for, as he had ample time to set things up, and perhaps enough reason to commit a murder or two. But his words as well as his reaction seemed too genuine to keep him in serious contention.

"Although I admit he never struck me as someone who knew his poisons," Virgil remarked, "but I liked the idea mainly because he didn't want me to do the podcast. The one I meant to do originally, about the new cookbook."

"He was? That's news to me!"

"Austin likes being in control but I suppose that's why…" he began before he suddenly cried, "Oh no, I drove back here instead of your place!"

"It's fine," I said. I had suspected we were headed back to Shirleen's house, and I hadn't minded since I wanted to keep talking to him. We lost a suspect, but today brought us closer to a truth that had been nipping at our heels. "I probably should check in with Shirleen. I haven't seen anything about the recipes I'm to work on this week."

Entering the house, the front hall was dark, but Shirleen's sensible sneakers were lined up by the door and her clutch purse dangled on a nearby hook.

This wasn't too surprising. On the days that Alberto wasn't here, the curtains were drawn and Shirleen only turned on the lights in the rooms she was in. However, it was quiet, and I couldn't even hear the echoes of her favorite soap operas, just the gentle hum of the heater.

Shirleen wasn't in the kitchen, but there was a mess of wet papers on the counters and a pair of desk fans attempting to dry them. In fact, every space that could be spared was covered in wet papers, enough to make up a whole book it seemed. The air was damp, the buzzing fans oddly echoed in the room, and the lingering drip from the sink's faucet didn't lessen my concerns about how this scene took shape in the first place.

"Aunt Shirls?" Virgil called. Just as he was about to bound out, the kitchen door swung open and Shirleen appeared.

"Back so soon, Virgil, I thought you'd be gone longer." Shirleen walked in with a shawl draped over her shoulders. Her frown faded as she spotted me, and she smirked. "I see you two have finally made up! Although it looks like my nephew has dragged you into his work. Funny that you should do him a favor when I got the sense he made a mess of things."

With a laugh I looked down at the Moving Champions shirt I still wore. "This was for something else."

"Your investigation into Ruby's death has you moving boxes?" Shirleen remarked as she sat down in a nearby chair.

"It does when it takes us to her house," Virgil said as he eyed the drying papers. "Gayle asked me to move a few things for her."

"Hoping for a family friend discount," Shirleen huffed.

"I may have sweetened the deal to snoop. Did you know that Ruby got a writing desk recently? An intruder came in and smashed it. As far as the police can tell that was the only thing disturbed in the house."

Shirleen blinked.

"A writing desk?" she asked.

I held out my phone to show her the pictures and she snatched it from me as she zoomed in on it, looking not at the broken parts, but the legs of the table.

"That was hers!" Shirleen cried.

I had been hoping for a reaction, but I felt electric hearing these words. "Her desk?"

"I gave it to her as a gift when she started writing. She got rid of it a long time ago, or so I thought."

"She tracked it down recently," Virgil ventured.

"For a reason," Shirleen surmised. "She may have left something locked inside. I know I used to be afraid of doing the same thing. When I got divorced, I made sure to turn out every drawer just in case I left behind an important paper."

"Ruby must have done the same," Virgil said.

"I wonder what she left in there, because it wasn't anything she needed urgently." Shirleen mused as she handed me back my phone.

"Do you have an idea how long it was?" I asked.

Shirleen tapped her chin in thought and then pointed at Virgil. "He was still in middle school. Ruby had moved into her new house by then, and the writing desk didn't make it. That's all I really remember."

"That's more than enough," I said looking at the image once more. I thought of what Austin told us about the mysterious project Ruby had been working on. It had to have been in the desk. Did it make it an old project or a new one?

"Virgil, I need you to visit the storage unit." Shirleen's abrupt words brought me out my musings. "This time no putting it off, you need to go as soon as you can."

"Is it about the old decorations or this book you dunked into water?" Virgil pointed to the drying pages. "What happened?"

Shirleen sighed as if she had been waiting for this. "I was juggling recipes. I had the book propped up on the shelf while I was doing something else. I turn my back to get a pot then the book fell over. I was trying to recreate an old recipe and now I lost them all."

Despite the attempt to dry the pages, they were illegible; the ink was smudged, the pencil was long gone, and the pages were curled and brittle. The cover was still intact so I knew this was her brainstorming notebook where she had put her ideas in first as she played around with ratios and ingredients. A notebook like this had saved her professional standing with fellow cooks as it showed her process and evolution of her recipes.

"This is quite bad," I said, "but is it a good time to tell you I made a copy?"

Shirleen clasped her hands together with glee. "Did you? I didn't know you took such extensive pictures!"

"I wanted to refer to them as I studied the recipes. I captured everything you had lying around."

"I'm glad you did."

"I can share it with you and print out a new copy."

"No rush," Shirleen said, "I just need to find one particular recipe and share it with Winifred, since she's been asking about it."

"Winifred Chan?" Virgil asked.

"Who else do I know by that name?" Shirleen scoffed.

"Did Winifred want to see a certain recipe?" I asked.

"Yes. I don't know why – to be sure, perhaps? I must have made it sound enticing. It's just a jambalaya..."

I opened it up on my laptop as she described it, and went to the images I had saved of the original notebook. Maybe because I knew that Ruby had tried to meet with Winifred several times over, this seemingly innocent request had my heart thumping as I flicked through the digital notebook.

Timing was everything, so for Winifred to ask now about the dish... it meant something, didn't it?

Virgil had caught the wave I was traveling upon as he came to my side to watch as I flicked through the images.

It was a good thing he had, for I wasn't certain how else I would react when I landed on the recipe Shirleen was looking for.

Nothing was the matter with the recipe. It was perfect, five stars, I could tell from a glance.

It was the attribution next to it that gave me pause. Scribbled in the corner it read, *original tweaked from Janice O.*

Chapter 23

I knew Shirleen had a weak heart from a long illness, so I let Virgil talk me out of asking her directly why Winifred might want this particular recipe, and thus raising the real possibility one of her friends murdered the other.

"If we can't ask Shirleen, then we'll need to talk to Winifred," I told Virgil as he walked with me to the light rail station.

"I don't have an easy way to do it, I already spoke to her, and she's too sharp. Any reason I give to speak with her again she'll see through and she was already very reluctant to speak with me before. She's still sore that I tricked her. I hadn't seen her in ages so she didn't realize who I was, until I slipped it in at the end. She won't talk."

"Then we'll have to ambush her," I suggested. "She lives in Revere Hills, doesn't she?"

"The last I heard." Virgil frowned. "Where are you going with this?"

"My friend Romy is in a caroling group that hits up the ritzy neighborhoods. They're going tonight, and if I call her now, I can get her to change which neighborhood they're planning to visit!"

Virgil complained at first about joining the caroling group, because he thought it was one of the groups where they dressed like repressed Victorians. I assured him that nobody dressed up, although people were encouraged to wear Santa hats or get some festive accessories. Somehow this group also had many people who used Virgil's moving service, making his presence easily welcomed. Between that, and Romy assuring me there was a dire need for a mezzo-soprano, we were absorbed into the caroling group as soon as I pulled on a red and green striped hat.

"We aren't going to be walking all over the place, are we?" Virgil said, holding up his songbook as if it could stop his voice from traveling as he followed the group, who were on their third round of *Deck the Halls*. "I mean, how much did you tell Romy?"

"I told her whose house we wanted to go to, and that we'll slip away afterward," I replied, "but she wanted to get her money's worth out of us. They weren't planning to come to this neighborhood until later this week. Took a lot of fast talking on her part."

As if speaking her name had summoned her, Romy drifted back to join us, with a devious smile that made Virgil groan.

"I'm helping you, so you got to help me out," Romy said. "It's a 'no drop' caroling group. We commit to an hour of this and get drinks afterward. It'd look bad if you guys ditched us early." She raised her eyebrows so high they nearly vanished underneath her fluffy snowflake beanie. "Unless you want people to think you snuck off to have a little fondue canoodling."

"Never say that again," I groaned.

Romy pouted. "I thought it was a fantastic pun!"

"I'm with her on this one," Virgil agreed. "Don't say that again."

Romy only grinned. "Either way, I'm glad you came tonight for caroling, even if it's a ruse for a murder investigation and you're going to interrogate a sweet old lady. Afterward, please come out to the coffee roaster." She added far too eagerly, "I'll be a good alibi."

"I'm sure we won't need one," I said.

"We hope," Virgil murmured.

Winifred knew something and ambushing her gave us a slim chance of finding out what. I kept thinking of the notebook that Ruby had shoved into her too-small purse.

She had come to see someone at the party. I remember her telling me that. And the note we saw in her calendar suggested this was the plan. It didn't seem that she got a chance, since at her arrival she had been intercepted by Shirleen, by me and Virgil, and probably others.

When had Ruby met with Winifred Chan that night? Knowing that they met at Whisk and Kettle Fest didn't make such a meeting urgent, even if the prominent and influential editor could change a person's fate with a stroke of a pen. So many things had occurred at Whisk and Kettle, drifting about the conference I had heard business deals get brokered over coffees, books and TV shows get pitched while in line to the next panel, and I heard whispers of the latest news before it spread everywhere. The biggest surprise had been that Shirleen's updated cookbook had been THE news of the event. I was of course happy that it was. My big break had been part of it all. The flurry and frenzy afterward wasn't what I expected, though. Or how it changed everything else around the cookbook. Many people had reached out to talk to her. They had been shocked, and while some had been delighted, others had been quietly peeved. In fact, I still remembered how the shifts in attitudes around people I thought were friendly had begun. Lucia had been one of those shifts and there had been others as seen at the different parties I attended with Shirleen over the course of the weekend. For many it was subtle, but others could barely hide their disgust. Back then, I had been less than charitable with these reactions. Shirleen had been a curt and rather gruff boss, but now as I got to know a bit more about her and the circumstances in her life, I could see things much differently.

As we were walking up to the next house, I was so lost in the fog of my thoughts that when someone grabbed my arm, my other elbow intuitively went for the solar plexus.

Virgil grunted behind me, and managed to whisper, "You need to step back, this is Winifred's house."

I stepped out of the warm glow of the lights on the porch to hide behind one of the other men, who were tall enough that they could mostly block me.

Winifred came out with a big grin as the caroling group regaled her with a few songs. I had always seen her dolled up, but without the makeup, she looked like her slightly younger sister.

"Wonderful, wonderful," she clapped, "thank you so much! Which group are you with again?"

"The Hunton Bay City Orchestra," the first violin said. "If you enjoy the singing, you'll enjoy our remaining concerts for the holidays."

As the group departed, Virgil and I stepped back to let them go. Romy winked and whispered good luck.

Virgil turned on his microphone, as we stepped onto the porch.

"Do you have a moment?" I called out to Winifred.

"Yes, is there a charity–" she began, only to stop when she recognized us. She shoved her hands into the pockets of her sweater, and I swear I could see ice form across her features.

"Why are you two here? I'm busy," Winifred said. "It's nearly Christmas and there's so much to do."

"It'll only take a few minutes," I said. "Just a few quick questions."

"To talk about Shirleen for your podcast?" Winifred said rather crossly. "I already did that."

"About Ruby Walton," Virgil said, and she stilled.

Virgil let the pause settle over all of us as he added, "We know you met with her several times before she died. A few comments you made suggest you might know some things, and we aren't the only ones who find that interesting."

Winifred hesitated at the door, her dark brown eyes conflicted, then another voice broke the silence.

"Might as well let them in. Even if Shirleen hasn't sent them, she'll find out anyway."

As the voice registered, I saw the *Starry Night* bag resting on a side table, and then saw Margot as she stepped forward.

Accepting defeat but keeping her pride, Winifred opened the door, and urged us to join them.

She had a real Christmas tree, and the smell of fresh pine was overwhelming as I entered the hall. Displayed in the front room, so it was the first thing you saw, the cool white light danced along golden ribbons and the miniature snowcapped town that sat underneath the tree.

Margot, settled amidst this elaborate decadence in homespun clothes, didn't quite fit, but at the same time I wasn't surprised to see her here. Especially when I saw the tumbler and drinks on the table, next to a stack of old books, photo albums, and a few weathered magazines.

They sat across from us on a couch, but divided us between two stuffy armchairs.

"My husband will be back from his club in about an hour, so I want you gone by then," Winifred said.

"Keeping secrets?" I asked.

"No, trying to keep you out of trouble. He'll call the police on you for harassing me with false accusations."

"No one is accusing you of anything," Virgil said.

"We've heard your little podcast," Margot leaned back on the couch, rapping her fingers along the tumbler. "You're looking for the murderer to keep Shirleen's name in the clear. I respect that, but you're looking in the wrong places."

"Like coming here," Winifred added.

"We're just trying to get information," I said. "You met with Ruby about a new cookbook. We found a notebook with some new recipes."

Winifred picked up a tumbler but didn't drink. "Ruby was exploring new horizons. Waterhouse Productions didn't renew her contract. She had wanted to stay as a guest judge at *Whisk it All* as the money was good, but didn't want to commit to full-time again. When her agent tried to play hardball, it went badly."

"How badly?" Virgil asked.

"Ruby fired him on the spot," Winifred said, "but she didn't say much more than that. She was always rather coy about money and business. Embarrassed too I think, as she fired an old agent to get this new one."

"Any idea why, after everything, she went to you?" I asked. "Was she going to write a column again as part of her new horizons?"

The older ladies shared a glance, before Margot answered. "She was, even if it meant dredging up the past."

I had a question ready for this, but Virgil leaned in first, the microphone jostling in his pocket. "Is this where Janice O'Neal comes in? Your old friend."

"Yes."

"Can we meet her? Her name keeps coming up. Most recently with the jambalaya recipe my aunt just sent you at your request."

Another look passed between the ladies. "No, you can't, she's passed," Winifred said.

I nodded, expecting this, and looked at the photo album on the table. "A picture then would be great."

Without a hint of complaint, Winifred opened an album, turning to a page that included not just the fabled New Year's Eve meeting, but a snapshot of Shirleen and Ruby's shows, both together and solo. Winifred tapped an image of much younger versions of herself, Margot, Shirleen, and Ruby.

"There she is," Winifred said.

"There's only four of you," I said, before I realized her finger placement was deliberate.

It was right on Ruby.

Just as I connected the dots, Virgil whispered, "She's Janice O'Neal."

"Ruby changed her name when she got married. She grew up in an abusive household and cut ties with everyone, save her little brother, who she brought with her," Winifred said. "Before then, she wrote as Janice in a food column at a small newspaper that no longer exists. I think she even wrote to Shirleen back then, but she never told her."

"Why not?" I asked.

"Because," Virgil answered instead, "Ruby's background. There have been questions for years about how much of her early history was true or exaggerated, like her tales of studying in Italy, or working with Leah Chase. After a certain amount of success, it didn't matter. Get caught in one lie, the questioning begins."

"Ruby took her secret to the grave," Margot said.

"Yet you're asking about recipes now," I said refusing to get further sidetracked. "What were you planning?"

Winifred didn't quite smile. "We are doing the same thing you are: looking for who might have killed Ruby and why. Admittedly we can't romp around town, but it's clear something happened in the past and even our faded memories might hold a clue."

"Do you know why Ruby went looking for her old writing desk?"

"From what I gathered, she wanted to find the recipes she had been working on at the time," Margot said. "She asked me about them, because I had a few tucked away. Ruby even came to see me at August Towers, more than a few times, as if I had recipes tucked away in there."

"She asked for a few from me as well," Winifred said, "but not in great detail. I knew she was looking and that it related to a cookbook. But I don't see where it fits in. Why would someone kill her over a cookbook? I can't make sense of it."

"Unless it comes to the other theory you suggested in your podcast, framing Shirleen." Margot said. "I think that's even more likely. Shirleen is a dear friend, but boy does she have a long list of enemies and rivals! We've been putting together a list." Margot pulled out a slip of paper, covered in names, many that were already on my murder board. "Perhaps your rude interruption has some benefit. Why don't you take care of this?"

"If you need anything, call me next time," Winifred added. "We might have different methods but they all lead to the same result."

With a list, some pointed advice and encouragement to return if we had more questions, Virgil and I left with more answers than expected.

"Well, that takes them off the list," I said, as we walked, streetlamps lighting our way out the neighborhood. "Neither Winifred nor Margot are involved in any of this."

"You didn't seriously think…" Virgil turned to me in surprise. "They are some of my aunt's closest friends!"

"True, but they knew something quite key – that whoever is behind this has a history with both Shirleen and Ruby. This list just proves it, and there are a few matches to what we found already. Oscar Fantom and Lucia rank as top suspects for motive, opportunity, and deep history," I declared. "Just a few notches down is Davis who has history but not clear motive, and your mysterious Brandon Morton. If only because it's been so hard to contact him. I don't know why you've been trying so hard. He hadn't showed up in our investigation as a major suspect."

"Brandon Morton worked on the documentary about my aunt that got canceled. It seems the dream has not died. He came unexpectantly to the party – the announcement of my companion podcast gave him hope that Shirleen was open to the documentary idea."

"He's not the only one that got new hope," I murmured. I tugged at the zipper of my jacket. "Davis was talking about a new show with her."

"He has?" Virgil said. "He hasn't mentioned it to me."

"Would he?" I asked and then thought of a better question. "Has he asked you before?"

"Only when he thought I could influence Aunt Shirls in any fashion. I don't know why everyone thinks I can. She doesn't listen to me."

"No," I remarked, "but she does consider you."

He snorted, and shoved his hands into his coat pocket. "I doubt she does. Aunt Shirls still goes for a walk the same time every morning and she barely looks both ways before crossing the street. She thinks no trouble will come to her when I need her to be on the lookout for that blue car that the cabbie mentioned."

"What he told us was very vague. We need a make and model." I said. "We don't know if it's just a sedan compared to a sporty hatchback. Or if the windows were tinted and you can't even make out who's driving in daylight or night, and if they drive with no lights on."

Virgil frowned. "That's very specific. Have you seen a blue car recently following you around?"

"Very recently," I said hoping my expression wouldn't give away the slight tremble in my voice. "Right now. Don't look back," I urged, and he began to twist around. "Let's keep walking until we're out of the neighborhood. The shops aren't far."

I had spotted the car when we first left Winifred's house, but didn't think much of it until we turned a corner and a car kept inching behind us. Maybe whoever was driving thought with the growing gloom we wouldn't notice. But even without a steady diet of true crime podcasts, I was always aware of who might be following me.

I kept my gaze on the brighter lights of nearby restaurants and small shops, where at a coffee roaster, Romy was likely waiting for us.

At one point it seemed like I was just making it up. The car had turned right when we turned left, but as we crossed a couple more streets, the same car appeared, idling on a street corner opposite of us.

We walked right past without turning to give it a closer look.

I didn't know enough about cars, only that it was a four-door sedan. It had North Carolina tags, and I only saw the first three letters of the license plate as shadow obscured the rest as it moved on.

Sounds of shoppers were getting louder, and then a different car, a jeep driven by some college students blasting Christmas music, sped past us.

I grabbed Virgil's arm and tugged. I just meant to urge him to hurry, but the car was like a gun going off at a track meet.

We ran.

I don't think either of us really had an idea of where we were going. I hadn't been to this neighborhood more than once, and Virgil had not come in this direction often. The streets were a series of connecting lines, and given we were headed in the right direction, we burst out into a side street near a noodle shop that claimed to serve the best yock in town. I probably could have kept running, but there were too many people on the sidewalk, and I slid to a short stop. I might have slipped, but I was still holding Virgil's hand somehow, and his weight was a counterbalance that kept me from falling. He pulled me in close, especially as someone carting a mass of presents walked by.

"I think we're good," Virgil said breathing softly, still holding my hand in his. "We lost whoever it was."

"Did you get a good look?"

"No," Virgil said, "did you?"

"A little." As I began to describe what I saw, he shook his head. "Not here, let's go meet up with your friend. We have a lot to talk about."

Romy, dear friend that she was, just sat at the table nursing her ginger tea at the roaster. She hadn't been waiting for long, but it felt like ages since we had seen her. While I didn't intend to tell her anything, something in my face alerted her at once, and she refused to leave until I had told her what happened.

"Did that sweet old lady try to poison you?" Romy demanded.

"No, we realized she's not involved in Ruby's murder. But while we were leaving, we might have been followed, again."

Unlike my other friends who exploded with questions, Romy was a listener. She sat there listening as we explained the threats, the photograph of us snooping around, and my laments that I only saw part of the license plate.

Romy just shrugged as she finished her tea. "Then you should ask for help. Eden knows cars and has contacts due to her work as an EMT. I can also help trace who sent the picture and even the messages."

"What are you, a hacker?" Virgil scoffed.

"No, a software engineer with too much time on her hands," Romy said. "Photographs have metadata and if this person isn't that clever, I might have something to work with."

"You can do that?" I asked. Hearing the offer for help was a weight lifted off my shoulders. What was it that Shirleen told me at my party? *Good hosts delegate and delegate well.*

I'm not sure investigations and looking for murderers could compare to dinner parties, but the difference surely wasn't that great, was it?

"It helps that you guys have a list of people who caught your eye for this," Romy said. "It'll narrow things down."

"Then that's what we'll do. We trace the messages, find out who's following us, find out anything else related to the agent that screwed Ruby over, and what else am I missing?"

"Wrapping presents," Romy said.

"Presents?" I echoed and then remembered with a groan. "The Friends of the Library!"

"We have to wrap presents for the library and we're making a small party of it," Romy explained to Virgil. "I think Eden will be there, and so will Jamal. You should come, it'll be fun."

"I have a few errands to run," Virgil said with true regret. "I might not be able to get there until later."

"No need to rush," I said. "We'll hardly be done no matter when you get there."

Chapter 24

My words ended up being more prophetic than I would have liked.

While I had intended to wrap presents first and then tell Eden and Jamal about being followed by a blue car last night, the opposite happened. Stacks of presents remained naked of their wrappings and ribbons as Eden reached out to her contact who could track cars with only a sliver of information.

The contact Eden had wasn't police, and she was cagey enough about telling me about the less than legal aspects of this contact that I let things alone. In contrast, Romy didn't mind me sitting nearby as she worked away on her laptop tracking down the unknown phone number using systems that were legal for her to use, but not in the way she was using it. Through a complex process I couldn't quite follow, she found that while the number that had been messaging us was a dead end, the photograph wasn't entirely stripped of its metadata and left enough breadcrumbs to lead to a phone number.

I thought of calling it, but wanted to wait for Virgil just in case it ended being someone he might be more familiar with.

In the meantime, Jamal kept asking questions about the case, with increasing incredulity. With his help, I brought my so-called murder board to the main room, although I spent more time explaining it to them than understanding how the case had shifted.

As morning turned to afternoon, we tackled the presents in a rush, but didn't get very far. Each ring of Eden's phone that wasn't her contact with news on the car disrupted our flow. Jamal and Romy asked to listen to the raw interview recordings Virgil had given me for notes, but I had to pause them every few minutes to explain. In the end, very few presents got wrapped, we got through only two and a quarter of the interviews, all my cats got into the present-wrapping supplies, with little Poppy nearly getting wrapped up in a box because Jamal thought she was a sweater. Two hours later, we took a short break to munch and hydrate, and there was still a mountain of toys, clothing, and more to wrap.

"You should have done this in stages," Romy said, as I lamented this over a sandwich.

"Or, here's an idea," Jamal suggested. "You should not volunteer to help when you know you're busy this season solving a murder! I know she's your boss and there's strange things going on, but you don't have to do this. I mean, you're being followed! Is all this worth it?"

"Yes," I said, "because I wouldn't be this close to finding out the truth otherwise."

Eden's phone rang and this time it was her contact.

"He found the car," Eden said. "It's a lease. The name on it is Orion Brown."

Romy was quicker than me, having looked it up on her phone the moment Eden said it. "Is there anything more than that? Orion Brown hits a lot of different names. Can't tell if it's a person or a company."

"I'm getting different results as well," Jamal said, looking up details on his phone too.

"Same here," Eden added. "I'm getting constellations, suggestions I meant Charlie Brown, and a bunch of noise."

We went back to wrapping presents as the interview recordings played on. I noted a contrast in the ones Virgil conducted before and after Ruby's death. I took special care to see how they spoke around Shirleen, and while I had listened to them several times by now, this time I heard something I hadn't before.

I stopped the recording, and went to call Virgil so quickly I forgot to disconnect from my Bluetooth speaker.

"I was about to call you," he answered before I could speak. "I'm outside your place."

Ignoring the snickering from my friends, I hung up and dashed over to my front door room to glance out the window.

Virgil hopped out the car and gave a little wave before he popped open his trunk. For a wild moment I thought he had brought a gift to wrap, until as he got closer, I realized the box under his arm was a very beat up moving box.

Keeping an eye out for my cats, who had followed me into the hall, I opened the door wider for him and let him inside..

"You finally went to the storage unit?" I asked.

"I wish I'd gone earlier." Virgil shuffled in with the box, pausing only to leave his shoes by the door before he headed into my den. "My aunt has so much stuff in there she forgets everything she shoved away. When her divorce went through, she got rid of everything my uncle left behind, even the things she could have used, just to get it out of her sight."

Virgil placed the box on the table. Briefly greeting the others, he opened the box, and removed several smaller boxes of carefully wrapped ornaments. The ones on top had been made by him as a child, with a delicateness of age that made the popsicles, straws, pinecones, and tinsel appear fragile as a dinosaur bone.

"Is this what you wanted to show me?" I carefully picked up an ornament of a very young Virgil with missing front teeth beaming in the middle of a snowflake.

"Not these," he said pulling out a box wrapped in paper, "but this. These were the ornaments Aunt Shirls was thinking of and wanted to put her hands on."

On the box, it simply said, *from Ruby*.

A mix of wood and ceramic, they were kitschy, sentimental, and filled with inside jokes, as there were a surprising number of pickle ornaments.

"These are ornaments Ruby gave her?" I asked, picking up a small chicken with a Santa hat perched on its head.

"Aunt Shirls likes to collect ornaments, and people have given her enough for a dozen trees. Most are still at the house, but this is one of the two boxes she put away."

"Not a good sign for your childhood ornaments," Eden said.

"These are the worst ones," he brushed off, "and the other boxes have more, plus the ornaments from her first Christmas with my uncle. But that's not the only thing put away." Virgil reached inside and brought out another box.

He pulled out what I mistook for a photo album, but it was a binder for an unbound book. A cookbook, I realized, as I turned the pages for appetizer, entrees, and soup dishes. I skimmed them at first, flipping through the recipes, but when I spotted a familiar phrase, I flipped back. I had been staring at

Shirleen's recipes for months now and knew all the little turns of phrase she slipped in. It wasn't surprising that this was her cookbook, but as I turned back to the front, I still found myself shocked to see it attributed to Shirleen *and* Ruby.

I stared at it, not believing what I saw. "They never wrote another cookbook again," I said to Virgil.

"One that was never published as it quietly died when their falling out happened," Virgil said. "Aunt Shirls had me tearing up her attic looking for it, because while she remembered putting it away, she didn't get rid of it entirely."

"Did she know that Ruby had plans with her copy?" I asked.

"Now she does," Virgil replied. "I called her while I was at the storage unit. She says she didn't think a cookbook of hers warranted murder, but stranger things have happened."

"You really think her death was due to this?"

I wasn't really looking for an answer, and Virgil just shrugged, before he asked a question in return. "Have any of these recipes been used in the other cookbooks?"

"I'll have to look." I turned to the title page, "'*Thyme to Savor*,'" I read, "'*recipes from our home for yours*.' Looks like it was, although more traditional Southern cooking, riding on the soul food trend. It would have been good." I scanned the table of contents, seeing the names of traditional dishes. "It's focused on Northern Soul. Which is mostly Philly, Detroit, Chicago, and a few other places. This one looks familiar." I pointed to a page. "But it's not from a cookbook. It's from Ruby's notebook."

"Are you sure?"

"I've got copies of the notebook on my murder board."

I held up the book against the printed images I took. "It's the same," I declared.

Virgil tapped his chin. "The same because she made a copy." Then he snapped his fingers. "I know what was in the desk! This manuscript! They had their own copies to work with. When things went sour, Ruby shoved it away, and didn't think about it until recently."

"An old cookbook," Jamal said, "that's what this centers around? That's enough to get you chased around by a strange car?"

"Apparently," Virgil said.

"We found out about the car," I said. "It's a lease held by Orion Brown. Does that ring any bells?"

"It sounds familiar," Virgil said after a long pause. "I can't remember who said it or when. I've been talking to so many people, all the conversations blur together."

"Then it's on the tapes? Full disclosure, we did not get through all of them," I said.

"We can listen to the rest," he said easily enough. Then, with a cough, he remembered the others, who were watching us as if there wasn't anything better to do. "What about the phone number?"

"I figured that out earlier. I thought Key might have let you know," Romy teased. "It's simple. I found a number attached to the phone that photograph was originally taken with. We haven't called it yet."

"Then let's call," Virgil suggested.

"On it," Romy dialed at once, and switched to speakerphone so we could all hear.

It rang and rang, and clicked over to voicemail. With a chirp the automated mailbox said, "You've reached Lucia Espinosa. I'm not here right now but if you leave your name and number…"

I wished I could have been surprised to hear that voice, but as I listened, the more the pieces fell into place.

"I'm glad I didn't call then," Virgil murmured. He turned to the board, and pointed to Gloria, the other professor at the culinary school. "Lucia started working at Hook around the time Aunt Shirls turned down tenure." He left the thought unfinished as Virgil asked me. "Want to head out to Hook College? Unless you still have things to do."

"Go on ahead," Jamal encouraged before I could answer. "We're nearly done with all of the wrapping anyway. Go have fun."

"And go catch a murderer," Eden chimed in.

Enthusiastic as they were, I had a trickle of dread as we once more headed to Hook College. Exams had brought a solemn silence to the campus, and it was more of a hope that Lucia would be in her office. There wasn't a way to check, but we got lucky.

Lucia was in fact in her office, intently grading papers.

She greeted us at first, thinking we were students, until she realized otherwise.

I couldn't tell if she was going to demand we leave her office, but I knew that the thought certainly crossed her mind. "What brings you back now?" Lucia grumbled.

"A few follow up questions," Virgil said, as I got out my phone and dialed the number.

A phone rang and Lucia's eye darted to it before she answered Virgil. "Questions about what?"

"Did the announcement of the new cookbook come as a shock?" he asked.

"Hardly." Lucia relaxed. "Anniversary years are a big deal – look no further than the *Joy of Cooking*."

"Then were you surprised that after working and knowing her for so long, my aunt tapped a stranger and newcomer to help? Or maybe surprised is the wrong word?" Virgil said. "How about angry enough to send murderous threats?"

Her mouth fell open. "I don't know what you're talking about!"

I dialed another number, this one being the number the threats had been sent from. The phone didn't ring this time, but her purse vibrated violently. "Better watch out, I'm telling you she must die?" I said. "That's just one of the messages you sent to me and others. Such a silly thing to do, but something that worked before, when Shirleen was up for tenure. Who did you send them to? Did Ruby get them too? You know that there's a murder investigation. It turns harmless pranks into serious threats."

"I never sent Ruby anything–" Lucia burst out, one hand slamming on the desk. She realized what she admitted with a gasp. "I just wanted to scare Shirleen." Her voice was small as she sat back down. "I didn't want anything to happen to her, or Ruby. I only made those calls in the first place because I'd had enough drinks to make it seem like a good idea. You're right, I was mad. I didn't spend all those years working with Shirleen to not be considered a co-author."

"Why did you think it would work?" Virgil said.

"It worked before," Lucia admitted. "She almost had another show twenty years ago. But someone called the station and left a death threat, and that was enough for her to walk away."

"Then what about this?" I showed her the photograph taken of us. "You've been following us around?"

"The park is by my neighborhood. I saw you out there. I knew you were poking into what happened with Ruby. I was only trying to discourage you before you got onto his radar."

"Whose radar?"

"Oscar Fantom," Lucia said. "He was also upset about Shirleen's new cookbook, and other endeavors. Not enough to kill," she added quickly. "He was planning a nasty surprise for Shirleen at the party. That's why he agreed to DJ, so he could be there to cause havoc. He's very vindictive like that. I didn't realize how much when he first came to me about it, since he knew from a previous radio interview how unhappy I was. He had nothing to do with Ruby's death, I swear."

"We're going to need more than that," I said.

"Much more than you're telling us," Virgil agreed.

Lucia pulled out her phone.

"I thought this might prove useful one day, but I didn't think I'd be sharing it with the likes of you," Lucia said before she tapped the screen, and then voices echoed from the device.

"The guests will be arriving soon, so get that out of sight!"

"Don't worry, we won't start until Shirleen is here. Trust me, she'll get more than she bargained for!"

This was the conversation Virgil and I heard the night of the party. I could now hear her, but the second voice left me stumped until I realized it was Oscar Fantom; his voice was less flamboyant and more muted when he wasn't putting on a character.

"That's the voice from the hall," Virgil said. "We overheard you!"

"You see, it was a silly plot and a worse alliance," Lucia said. "I blamed Shirleen for my failings and a prank to scare her made sense. But then Ruby died. I have nothing to do with Ruby's death. I swear, you can have this right now."

"Did the prank have anything to do with cake knives?" I asked.

"I was going to have the knives switched out," Lucia said. "Oscar had gotten some poor quality ones. The effect was to throw her off her game when they cut the cake in front of the crowd, so she would lose her temper and goodwill. It didn't happen."

"Because someone died," Virgil said. He shook his head, more baffled than anything as the confession continued. "I don't understand this. What was there to gain?"

"It was never about what I could gain," Lucia said. She bowed her head over her desk. "I just wanted to see her lose. She could have helped me, and she overlooked me to give an outsider a leg up."

Ignoring this jab, I asked, "Was it just Oscar Fantom you were working with? What about Orion Brown?"

Lucia frowned. "I don't know anyone by that name. What, is Oscar up to something else? He swore he was going to leave it alone. Is this where you call the police?"

"No, what is there to call about? A few threats? A prank that never happened?" I said.

"Maybe if Oscar Fantom is up to something, it might be a good idea to make a report yourself," Virgil rumbled.

We left her in the office, hopefully wrestling with her moral compass. We took the long way back to where Virgil had parked his car.

"This is staff parking," I observed.

In silent agreement we walked along the lot. While there were a few blue cars, none matched the North Carolina plate Romy had found or even had the similar look of the one that followed us.

"She spotted us by chance," I said, as Virgil drove me back to my place. "She is our threatening caller but not the one that followed us that night."

"Was she your pick?"

"I'm not sure I have a pick. Having one makes you assume and overlook all the evidence."

"But assumption gives direction."

"We know it's related to an old cookbook. Ruby was the intended target."

"I think the framing of my aunt was on purpose too," Virgil said. "The threats were unrelated, but the timing was right. Like Lucia and Oscar, someone else got stirred up. Someone who would take this change adversely." Virgil went quiet for a long moment, before he said, "There's Davis, who's tangled up between them, but I don't know why he would do it. He wants to do a show with Aunt Shirls, why do anything that would land her in jail, or worse?"

"He's also the only one left on our list. Unless we were too hasty to remove others." I sighed. "What if we're going about it the wrong way? The who is important, but have we considered why and how?"

"Don't we know how?" Virgil said. "The poison was in the cake."

"According to the autopsy," I said. "I wondered how much of Lucia and Oscar's shenanigans impacted everything."

"That they were up to something is more than enough for me to want to report them," Virgil grumbled. "Bad enough they were planning trouble, even if it came to nothing. Those threats made things so complicated."

"Then tell the detective about it," I replied. "I don't know if it'll lead to murder, but Oscar Fantom seems to be cooking up more trouble."

"Is it still possible he poisoned Ruby?" Virgil pondered. "We have a short list of suspects that was whittled down, and when we removed the most plausible, we're left with the less plausible and outliers, and maybe even someone we overlooked."

"Anything's possible," I replied. "We just have to consider all sides."

My place came into view and when he stopped the car, I hurried to get out.

"Wait, Key," Virgil began.

I let the nickname pass unremarked as I turned back to him, struck by the impulsive drive behind his words. "Yes?"

He licked his lips and then said rather weakly, "You're going to the dance recital for Jessica's students?"

"I planned to," I replied, confused as I had expected another question. "Though I'm surprised you are. Not to say that supporting my friends is bad, but did she bully you to get you to attend?"

"I wouldn't call it bullying, but I got tickets. I thought of going but then Brandon Morton asked me to meet him at a nearby café."

"You still don't have to go to the recital."

"If you're going, I might as well," Virgil said. It was too dim in the car's interior, but somehow, I just knew the tips of his ears had turned pink. "We can talk about the case, after a full night to mull over it."

"Maybe even find who or what Orion Brown is," I added, brightly. "See you then."

Chapter 25

A full night's rest didn't yield any more answers than before I went to bed, but I had an email from Adrienne Blake sitting in my inbox. She had sent over a link to the show we taped.

I played it right away, knowing it wouldn't be too bad. In the clip, the woman who fainted thinking the eggnog was poisoned wasn't shown. I was even more glad that none of the aftermath was in the comments.

Adrienne didn't mention the potential job offer, but I wished she had because there was another message from Davis. He had followed up inquiring about what I thought about the television gig.

The more I read of it, and about the promised salary I could get, I realized as if struck by a falling tree that I didn't want the job.

I didn't like how it was supposed to be a vehicle for Shirleen and now it was about me.

It seemed like an odd shift where I wasn't even sure what I did to deserve it, or if there was more to this offer.

Putting it aside for now, I grabbed my camera to head out to the ballet school.

Even though ballet wasn't my thing, I had planned to go anyway to take photographs with my camera. I'd done so for the past few years, and gotten some rather lovely pictures that ended up in advertisements for the school.

It was on the top level of the community arts center, sharing the building with the local theater and improv groups. Since I got there early enough, I was about to scout out a good spot to take pictures of the stage.

I was still figuring out the best way to show off the stage props, when Jessica came up to me carrying a stack of programs. In her leotard, dance skirt, and tights she looked almost like she was about to take the stage with her students. "There you are, you must have snuck by me!"

"Worried you won't get your free publicity?"

"I thought you lost something." She gestured to where Virgil was making his way over, but his microphone had gotten him cornered by some of the students who thought he was here to interview them. "Is this a supportive friend thing or a murder thing?" Jessica asked.

"Murder thing afterward, and we're supporting you first?" I replied.

Jessica handed me a program with a curt nod. "As long as your murder thing isn't happening during the recital, it's fine."

She handed a program to Virgil as he made his way over and greeted the other people starting to fill the auditorium.

"What's your freelance rate?" He waved to a family, who waved back. "I just told them that I'm doing a podcast about the community center, and that you're taking pictures for the local paper."

"Buy me coffee," I said, "but that's your fault for having the microphone out."

"Always be recording," Virgil said as he sat down next to me. "You never know what's in store."

According to the program there were several performances that afternoon, starting with the children's ballet, where five year olds spun and turned around for the adoring crowd. The second act was the snowman murder mystery, which was far cleverer than I would have thought at first. The last performances brought in the adult actors and dancers, with a mix of dancing and short skits. I went around taking pictures, and then I nearly dropped my camera.

On stage was the woman who had fainted on Kitchen Atelier's soundstage.

She didn't recognize me, but her face and the beauty mark were seared in my mind. As were my questions about why she had fainted in the first place.

I couldn't ambush her, so I settled on lingering near the stage, taking pictures of the dancers long enough that Virgil came over with his microphone turned on and blinking.

"Is that…?" he asked in a rush.

"Yes," I said. "I'm pretty sure that's the woman who fainted at the taping." I walked right over to the stage. "I'd like to get a photograph. What's your name?"

"Kate Higgins." She turned, twisting around to get what must be her better angle. "What is this for?"

"Just some general publicity photography," I said. "I wanted to make sure the community arts center is well covered for the event. You were a standout," I lied, hoping to encourage her. "Although I feel like I've seen you before."

She puffed up. "You may have. I have been on stage for quite a few productions."

Virgil snapped his fingers, his voice brightening in enthusiasm. "Yes, that's right. I think I saw you in…"

"*A Christmas Carol*. As Party Guest Ethel," Kate said. "I was also in the chorus for *The Nutcracker*."

"Of course, that's where we saw you," I cried. I made a show of thinking rather intently. "There must be something else. I know, you were at Kitchen Atelier this week. You made a great performance there."

Kate's face, which had been perfectly composed, collapsed into panic.

I'm not sure if she recognized us, or at the very least me, who had been on camera that day, but her reaction showed all was not forgotten.

"I can't stay too long, I have to get back," Kate began.

"We'd like to hear about your performance at Kitchen Atelier," Virgil said.

"I don't know what you're talking about," Kate said. "I got a free ticket. It was fun."

"Until you collapsed because you were poisoned," I said. "Excuse me, I thought you were poisoned. You were very convincing, enough that everyone panicked around you."

She swallowed, and her eyes darted around like a cat facing a stream of rushing water. "I don't know what you're talking about. I felt faint."

"Witnesses were convinced you were poisoned," I said.

"Well, I thought... I felt..." Kate blustered. "I was told..." She clammed up. "I don't have to tell you anything!"

"Then we'll just have to tell the police you were faking to ruin Shirleen Foster's reputation which is defamation and slander," Virgil said.

Those weren't the right things to call the matter, but Kate either didn't know or was too panicked by his authoritative tone.

"I was hired to play a part," Kate cried. "I wasn't faking!"

"Isn't that the same?" I asked.

"I was paid," Kate said, "and the money they gave me, trust me, you wouldn't turn it down so easily. I wasn't to do anything really, just pretend a little. I almost didn't do it, since there was hardly any space, and the floor was rather gritty."

"Who hired you?" I asked.

"I don't know, it came from my agent at Orion Brown."

I gasped as did Virgil at the name. But luckily Kate was too preoccupied with telling her stories to notice how we exchanged glances with the other.

"...although it might have been someone pretending to be my agent," Kate concluded.

"You didn't check?" Virgil asked.

Kate lifted her chin, even as her voice shook with principled outrage. "A job is a job," she said. "And the money left me no further questions."

"What if you had to do much worse?" Virgil said. "I'm hoping to shine a light on such terrible things."

Kate's eyes flickered to the microphone. "Are you a reporter?"

"I have an investigative podcast," Virgil said, sidestepping the truth. "If you're willing to tell us what happened, we may find some interest in your story. Because it's very interesting, the person who asked this job of you."

"It is." Kate's eyes shone once more at the prospect of attention. Although that was uncharitable of me. Given her panic, she knew something was wrong, and this was her first chance to tell someone without judgment.

"Let's move to somewhere quieter. One of the practice rooms, I think?" I suggested.

Set up in one of the rooms, I got to witness the most eager person we'd interviewed so far. Kate was hungry for the next great opportunity, but she also wanted to tell her story. For all her flourishes and original evasions, she knew something wasn't quite right.

"I have been at the agency for two years now," Kate said. "I have gotten a series of small parts, mainly in local commercials and theater. I've gotten consistent work mainly because the agency has expanded: it used to be a one-man unit, but now there are several other agents looking into all sorts of markets. Actors, writers, musicians, podcasters… I can get you their contact information if you like."

"I'd appreciate that," Virgil said. "How do you usually get jobs? Or gigs?"

"I get assignments," Kate said, "through my agent. Usually it's emails or text, or when she gets excited by phone. However, this one for the show was very strange. It came from a company email, the one usually for announcements, but it was meant for me alone."

"Has that been the only time that's happened?"

"Only then. I figured it was just a new system. When I asked my agent, she had no idea what I was talking about. So she went and asked Mr. P."

"Mr. P?" Virgil echoed.

"The boss. The owner of Orion Brown. He said it was fine, and some hiccup in the system."

"You didn't think it was odd?"

"I was only told about the act. I didn't even realize who that Shirleen lady was until afterward. Or what happened to her friend. If I knew, I might have asked more questions before taking the job."

That wasn't good enough for me, as there was one piece she hadn't told us, either purposely or not. "Who's Mr. P?"

"Mr. Packer," Kate touched her lip with a frown. "Mr. Davidson Packer."

"Davis Packer?" Virgil ventured, the tightening of his grip on the microphone the only trace of the shock that was washing over me like torrential waves.

"Yeah, do you know him?"

"Not as well as I thought."

With more precise details, we found the website for the Orion Brown Talent Agency and, more importantly, a page where Davis Packer peered out at us, as a talent agent for "anyone wishing to make their mark on their world". With Ruby's name on his list of clients, we gathered the elusive puzzle piece that made us see how all the other pieces slotted in.

"I thought he was a producer." I tried to accuse Virgil of this lack of knowledge, but he appeared as surprised as I was about this news, even more than me.

"He was, when he worked with Aunt Shirls. Maybe because I was too immersed in her past, I didn't check to see what he was doing currently."

"Producing didn't pan out the way he hoped," I said, as we approached the bookstore where Virgil was to meet Brandon Morton. "If he really was her agent and she wanted to fire him about the contract…"

"Then he just shot up to the top of the list."

Brandon Morton sat in the café side of the shop, working away on his laptop.

Just like Virgil said, this was the man who had been right there when Ruby had collapsed. He had helped best as he could, despite just being nearby. He was older than I had realized, but he had the still trim look of someone active in his later years, radiating such vigorous health that his gray hair wasn't the first thing you noticed.

Brandon looked up warily at me at first until he relaxed when Virgil made introductions.

"Now I know why you look familiar," he said as he greeted me. "You're working with Shirleen."

"I hope to keep working with her as long as I need to," I said.

"I hope so as well," Brandon replied quite grimly. "Terrible thing that happened to Ruby. I don't think I can tell you any more than what I told the police. But I did bring my footage." He slid a flash drive across the table. "I recorded most of the event. The police looked at it, but they didn't find it too interesting. You can't really see Ruby or who she was next to. Shirleen is barely on it, because it had been set with one layout in mind, but the room had been changed around so it got the wrong angle."

"Still, I appreciate you bringing it," Virgil said. "Why were you interested in doing this documentary about Shirleen?"

Brandon stroked his chin. "Everybody loves a comeback story. I was hoping that working on her other cookbooks gave me an advantage. Your podcast," – Brandon gestured to the microphone – "made me think I had a chance."

"She didn't even want a book written about her," Virgil said.

"Which was why I was hoping by taping the party I could make my case, a pitch, so to speak. Show off what I can do and she might agree. But the footage I got won't work." He looked hopefully at Virgil. "I admit I wanted this meeting solely so I could appeal to you."

"I can appeal to her for you," Virgil said, "but no promises."

"Don't expect any." He checked his watch. "I'm afraid I'll need to cut this short, but keep the footage if you like."

Brandon gathered his things and left us, and Virgil slid around to the empty chair, pulling his own laptop out of his bag.

"Don't get your hopes up," Virgil cautioned as he turned the machine on. "The police saw nothing on it."

"They didn't know what to look for," I said, bringing my chair closer.

Virgil plugged in the flash drive, and soon we were watching the party from a different angle.

"The servers were wearing red that night, you see them?" I said. "There's six of them. For a few moments here there are seven. When I was in high school, my sister and I stopped going to a local grocery store. The employees there wore yellow shirts and after too many times of being asked by strangers to help them find the beans or salad dressing, my sister and I vowed never to wear yellow while shopping there. Because when people see uniforms, they see that and nothing else. Which is what our seventh server did," I said, as Davis walked to the refreshment table carrying a tray. He had worn red like the rest of the event staff, but his red was slightly different. He stopped by the table, and picked up a glass, and placed down another one before walking away. Ruby came back around and picked up the same glass Davis put down, sipping it before walking off the screen.

"Davis," Virgil whispered. "It was him. I didn't think he would be that clever."

"I don't know if it was clever, but he's a producer. He knows how to pitch a good story. We have the pieces. A victim, a suspect, old grudges, and shared history. Detective Dimaandal said the only reason Shirleen wasn't arrested from the start was because it seemed too pat. It was so pat it overshadowed everything else. Which is why we thought the poison was in the cake."

Virgil rewound the recording. "We were all wrong, because it was in the glass."

"Which makes much more sense with potassium cyanide, as the salt easily dissolves in water. The liquid spilled on the cake, so there were some traces."

"You really do know your stuff," Virgil said.

I shook my head. "I'm not good at this. Davis came to us directly to tell us a few things. He distracted me with a job offer. He wanted to listen to your recordings. He wanted to know a lot of things about what we're doing, and I never thought how odd it was."

"Because we don't know why he would try to frame my aunt. He was talking about getting Shirleen a job, a job he turned around and gave to you."

"Maybe because he liked knowing there was no other option," I said. "You were talking before how all this is a reaction to the cookbook announcement, and you were right! I remember how cordial Davis was at the cookout I met him at. After Whisk and Kettle, he turned cool and chilly. I was surprised he was invited to the party. I just never saw him enough to make it a concern."

"Did Gerald Hopkins seem like a serial killer to the quaint town of Saylor's Rest?" Virgil asked.

"No, because no one expects the dentist as a murderer," I said. I focused back on the slightly blurred image of Davis.

"I think we got enough to tell the detective," Virgil said.

"She saw this already and dismissed it. We don't have enough evidence to give her something, but Davis has been waiting for an answer to his job offer. I'm going to meet him."

"Not by yourself!" Virgil hissed. "If he really did this, you shouldn't speak to him alone!"

"It's the only way I can. He won't talk to you since he'll suspect you'll be recording. Even if he doesn't suspect that, he'll think you'll run off and tell Shirleen."

"You work for my aunt," Virgil said, as if I needed reminding.

"The longest someone worked for your aunt lately is eighteen months. She just added to my workload, why wouldn't I have bad things to say about her, just like everyone else? I could probably even spin that I only came on the podcast because I was trying to save my job. We have only one shot here," I said gruffly. "We don't even have solid evidence yet and we need that. I'm going to reach out to him and set up a meeting."

Virgil drummed his fingers against the table, until he finally said, "If he doesn't bite? What then?"

"Trust me, he will."

"But going to his office? If he has any inkling that you suspect him, it'll be trouble." Virgil's protest was cut short by the twin buzzing from both our phones.

"Sunil and Jessica are at the train station." I flipped open the group chat with my friends, unsurprised to see that Virgil had now been added to it. I scrolled past the images Sunil had snapped at the train platform of Jessica still in her ballet costume with luggage at her feet. "Why does Sunil say he'll see you at Lost Pirate Cove? Did you make plans or something?"

"Oh, it's where I'm scouting next for the local history podcast. I usually put places where I'll be next as a teaser, on the account's social media page–"

"You shouldn't be doing that," I interjected.

"It causes buzz."

"No, that's how the murderer – Davis – knew where to leave that cake carrier he stole. You said you'll be at Port Walker Point soon. So, he planted it there."

"That's a guess," Virgil protested, but didn't argue further.

"He has an eye on you, because if he can't get to Shirleen directly, you're the next best thing."

"I don't care, you're not going to face him alone." Virgil began again.

"I never said that," I interrupted, "Only that Davis shouldn't see you."

Chapter 26

My message to Davis regarding my interest in this new TV show was simple and vague, yet immediately he agreed to a meeting on Tuesday.

Despite my efforts to gently steer him to a public place, we were to meet at his office across the river in Portsmouth, and he picked mid-morning.

He also made it clear that he expected only to see me.

It was an unneeded but telling detail, and one that punctured my bravado about meeting Davis. But it was too late to change my mind.

Davis mentioned more about the TV show, and for the first time I saw just how immensely vague about the project he had been, to a point that I still didn't even know what it would be about. I had never strongly considered his offer, so I hadn't looked at it closely, but now that I did, I was glad for my indifference.

I couldn't believe he thought I wanted such a job, but then I must have seemed so desperate, overwhelmed by all the work Shirleen had handed me, and uncertain what would happen once the cookbook wrapped up.

No that it mattered anymore. I just needed Davis to believe me for a little while longer.

I walked alone into a large office building. I wasn't worried that it would be empty so close to the holiday, but the presence of several people did relieve me a bit. Christmas had exploded across the front desk in wrapping paper and ribbon, as the woman at the desk put together a few last-minute gifts.

"I'm here to see Davis Packer, we have an appointment," I said.

"Yes." The woman jumped up, dropping a roll of tape on to the desk. "You must be Keisha Scott."

As she picked up her phone to call ahead, I caught sight of a maintenance man gathering supplies from a nearby closet. The boxes jingled, and the office manager called out for him to be careful.

"We had to get someone in to paint due to some last-minute damages," the office manager informed me, as she replaced the phone back into its cradle, "so if you hear any strange noises, you can ignore it. But you shouldn't be bothered too much as Mr. Packer's office is at the end of the hall."

She meant it to be reassuring but it was opposite for me, especially as I walked down the hallway with her and saw how many offices weren't occupied, as the glass panels on the doors revealed equipment collecting dust.

"Is there a party going on?"

"No, just lucky people who wisely saved up their PTO." Her smile was slightly self-mocking. She knocked on Davis's door and announced me.

"Here she is, Mr. Packer," the woman said. "Call me if you need anything."

Davis looked up from his papers. "I will, thank you Amy."

As the office manager left, Davis rose from his desk. "And thank you for coming, Keisha. I am so excited that you wanted to hear more about the show. I know we're going to do wonderful things. Follow me, I have a presentation ready."

He left his office, and took me to one of the meeting rooms down the hallway. A meeting room with a door that had no window panels.

"Take a seat," he said and gestured to take my coat. I gave it to him, and pretended to not notice as he gently shook it as if a microphone would drop out of it like gumdrops.

He dimmed the lights, and turned on his computer. "I'm glad you wanted to hear more of my pitch. Things have been shaping up nicely."

"What would I be doing again? Besides cooking, of course." I made a show of emptying my purse to find my notebook and pens. I took out my phone, accidentally flashing the screen so it was clear it wasn't recording a thing. I even left it face up on the table so the odd messages from my friends would keep coming in. All those notifications and messages that set my teeth on edge proved that my phone wasn't being used for recording. With each little update, Davis relaxed like the smug snake I always knew him to be.

I wasted a few minutes chatting with him about the show, working my way to the subject.

"It would be my recipes?"

"Your recipes? Why yes, of course," Davis said. "Your recipes would be perfectly fine."

"Oh that's a relief, you wouldn't try to force me to use others."

"You mean like Shirleen's?" he asked.

"Well, I have only gotten people's attention through her."

"Oh, but you're so much more," Davis said. "You have a lightness and an approach that will do well on the screen.

Your clever take on food would be rather interesting and what people will want to see."

I nodded. "I expected as much. I'm glad, in a way, that this is coming together. Shirleen is..."

"You don't have to mince words," Davis chuckled. "I know her quite well. Better than most, I can say."

"Shirleen is very demanding, and for good reason," I said with some hesitation. "There were some days it was very hard to work with her. I'm happy that'll be put behind me."

"Which I'm glad to be part of," Davis said.

I sat back in my chair, hoping I sounded at ease. "Is that what you told Ruby?"

Davis blinked. "Pardon?"

"About the new show?" I said. "I was thinking about the concept. And then I realized it never suited her to begin with. This conversational angle the show would take would work much better with Ruby. She was who you offered it to in the first place."

He stilled. "What are you talking about?"

"You were her agent. You started working with her when she began booking TV spots. She trusted you because of your past, which was her greatest folly since all you've done is cause her to lose opportunities. Some by pure accident, others very much on purpose. You offered her a new show. You haven't produced anything new for decades, and your last hits had included Ruby or Shirleen. Shirleen, at the time, was all but retired, so you went with Ruby. Just when you were hammering the details out, Shirleen's big comeback happens. You pull back from Ruby to try to go after Shirleen. Shirleen refuses and won't listen to your arguments. You think, no problem, Ruby was interested before. But now, surprise, surprise, Ruby isn't ready to play, and has decided to do what she really wants: write her first solo cookbook."

Davis said nothing, watching me with narrowed eyes. I wavered slightly as I continued. "The night of the party, you weren't supposed to be there, but Naomi had invited several people she shouldn't have so you were able to slip in. Shirleen wasn't as upset about seeing you there as she could have been, which would have clued me in… but it was too late."

"You're right." Davis turned on the lights.

As they flicked on, he stood before me with a small pistol leveled at me.

"You're absolutely right, Keisha, it would have been too late for anyone to stop the plan I set into motion."

"You poisoned Ruby," I said.

"I did," Davis said smoothly. "There was so much going on that night, I was able to move about without trouble, and make sure that enough evidence pointed to Shirleen. All you need to do is give a suggestion, and the rest will fall into place."

I sat there, letting his words sink in around me. "You're actually admitting it."

His smirk slowly filled his face. "There's nothing you can tie me to."

"Not without proof," I said.

"Which you don't have. If there was footage of me, it would have been released earlier. And if you raise the issue, you'll just cause trouble for yourself. You know this, which is why we're talking here, instead of a windowless room with plexiglass between us."

I swallowed hard, against this logic as much as the pistol he still pointed at me. "Why did you do it?"

"I saw a chance. Ruby was going to sue because of the contract and it would ruin me and my business. Around the same time, Shirleen made her big comeback. I haven't been able to produce a show in years because of Shirleen, she made sure none of the most talented chefs would work for me. Shirleen is the reason I had to become an agent in the first place, she had snuffed out so many chances for me, just to be petty. When I got the invite to the party, and then heard Ruby would be there and that Shirleen would be there with her cakes, I knew I had to act. She deserved it, don't you agree?"

"No!" I cried. "No one deserves that!"

I reached for my phone, and his arm jerked as a click echoed in the meeting room.

"You touch it and I'll shoot you," he said. "I don't want to do it. I rather not, as I just wanted to talk. But I will if I need to."

Without a word of protest, I lifted my hand away from my phone.

"It's upsetting," Davis continued, "that you've thrown your lot in with Shirleen. I was hoping you would see things my way. Otherwise, I wouldn't have bothered with breaking into Ruby's house."

"Weren't you after the papers in the writing desk?"

"I was, but the greater appeal was to get Shirleen's nephew arrested. There's nothing she wouldn't do to protect him. But not even she could make a good argument if there's evidence pointing toward him."

"No one would have believed that," I boasted.

"Don't be so certain." His eyes glittered. "I might not have the best reputation in the business, but who do you think the police will listen to first, me or any of *you*?"

I surged to my feet, forgetting about the gun.

But in the moment I nearly did, a shrill fire alarm echoed across the building, and this time I really did forget about everything.

"What in the world!" Davis cried, as he spun.

I didn't waste a single word. I snatched my phone off the desk, and I ran, yanking my coat off the coat rack so hard, it toppled over.

I glanced back as I ran, wasting precious moments. But instinct pushed me to make certain.

Davis had moved around the table, but he didn't fire the gun. In fact, it was lowered.

But he wasn't chasing after me, but letting me go with his last taunts at my heels, confident he outmaneuvered my amateur detective work.

Although the office manager claimed most of the staff was gone, it didn't seem like it now.

What had been empty was now filled with people in either business casual or holiday sweaters, trying to elbow their way to the stairs or the nearest exit despite calls to remain calm.

But the fire alarm shrieked, badly echoing in the hall, and the sound only provoked so much anxiety within me – even though I knew there was no fire.

I let myself be swept up in the knot of the crowd, not even being annoyed when I got poked or prodded with a bag.

Eventually I managed to get out the building amongst this panicked knot of people. It was a bit tricky to slip away, but I ducked around with some effort seeking a certain clump of trees.

"What is the point of making a meetup spot if you can't remember," Virgil remarked as he pulled off the maintenance cap.

"There was a lot going on," I replied. "I thought you were going to give me a half hour before you pulled the fire alarm?"

"The timetable changed when you moved into a windowless room," Virgil remarked. "Especially after I found this in Davis's office."

Tucked into a reusable sandwich container was a small amber glass bottle, with a research facilities label on for potassium cyanide. It wasn't empty either as the white powder shifted around as Virgil turned the container over.

"Where?" I asked.

"Bottom drawer in his desk. I couldn't find any package, and I almost missed it because he had it tucked inside several corporate cups. I hope you didn't eat or drink anything he gave you."

"I know not to do that." I glanced over my shoulder and through the trees at the building.

The fire alarm had stopped, but a fire truck and an ambulance had arrived. "But you weren't wrong to pull the alarm early. You had great timing too, because by then I got everything I needed." I opened my purse to pull out my camera.

I had left the lens in place, but the camera itself was still on, just switched to video so I could record.

I held it up triumphantly.

"Wait until you hear what I got!"

Interview: Keisha Scott

Virgil Sullivan, voiceover: *Keisha Scott is the recipe developer for* Season by Season Revisited. *She is perfect for the role, as she studied Shirleen Foster's cookbooks from a very young age, approaching cooking with a flair and thoughtfulness that showed up on her blog,* Waffles, Shirleen's Way, *which got her the gig in the first place. Inquisitive and curious, she's at the very beginning of her cooking career and no one's more excited than her to see what's next.*

Virgil Sullivan: *Let's start with a question that's been burning in my mind. Why call the blog after the waffle recipe? Shirleen only put out one and it's rather basic.*

Keisha Scott: *Exactly. She had one waffle recipe credited to her, across all the cookbooks, all the advice columns, and shows. She uses the same one, but modifies it, making it savory or turning it sweet depending on who's she's making it for. For me, to use her recipes was to see that they can adapt and change to meet the circumstance. The whole blog was about tweaking and adjusting, especially the more I learned what suits my tastes. Working with Shirleen, or even her recipes, isn't about following her tastes, it's about discovering what can be yours.*

Chapter 27

The sound quality from my camera wasn't ideal, but Virgil managed to amplify enough that it was clear it was Davis speaking.

We played it for Detective Dimaandal that very afternoon. A quick message brought her to Moving Champions' office, in a Christmas sweater that looked like tinsel and confetti had thrown up on it, and jingled riotously to the amusement of the elementary schooler that came along with her. The child looked enough like her, I suspected it was her son, especially when the detective placed headphones on his head and had him sit in a corner with a video game as the recording played.

She listened to the rest with a stormy expression that didn't abate once it was turned off. "I should have you both arrested for interference and recklessness."

"Davis wasn't going to shoot me," I began. "Not while we're still in public."

"That sort of thinking nearly got you killed. And you," she added sharply to Virgil. "Falsely pulling a fire alarm is a felony, not to mention you masquerading as another company's employee – and what gave you the idea in the first place?"

"My friend looked into their company's schedule–" I began, only for the detective to declare: "I don't want an answer, I don't need to know the details that come with their own trouble!"

"Yet you came here when we said we had news," Virgil said.

In reply she retorted. "I only came here to make sure you hadn't put yourself in even more danger. I don't care if what you did found anything of value, even if you did something remarkable."

"You said remarkable," I cried, delighted at this slip of hers.

"Don't smile, don't look pleased," Dimaandal snapped. "Just be glad your luck did more than get you out without a scratch. I'll take a copy of the recording and this little bottle you found. I'll also put eyes on this Packer fellow. I recommend you stay with a friend, Keisha, just to be on the safe side. I look forward to listening to the podcast you are building about this case – but hold off publishing anything too concrete, until you get word."

"Will you call us?" I asked.

"No." The detective grinned, with seasonably appropriate jolliness. "But you'll know."

An abundance of caution had me mainly at Shirleen's house working my way through recipes claiming I was trying to finish up one last chapter of the cookbook before Christmas. I don't know if Shirleen believed me, but she popped in less frequently as Virgil was assisting me with the pans, bowls, dishes, and other prep work.

By the evening I had made one cake, a pot roast, potatoes three ways, jambalaya, a pie crust, fried rice, a rather experimental eggnog cheesecake, and enough carrot ribbons to wrap around a tabletop Christmas tree.

"This is not in any of her cookbooks," Virgil said as he dangled a carrot ribbon between his fingers.

"It's a garnish." I snatched it back, onto the plate. "And you said you're helping."

"Helping to keep you from tapdancing on the ceiling," Virgil said, "not whatever this is."

"Restrained panic," I said.

"Not what I would call it." Virgil slid the cutting board and the remaining carrots away from me. "You've made three nights' worth of meals, let's not make it four."

"Why not?" I said. "There's nothing else to do."

My phone started rattling before I could further make my case. A slew of messages poured in from my sister, so quickly I couldn't even make out what they were. I was about to check them when Shirleen stomped into the kitchen.

"Is this your doing?" Shirleen demanded, shaking the phone at both of us. "Why didn't you tell me?"

I could barely make out the screen, but I could see the most important part of the headline:

Davis Packer arrested for the murder of Ruby Walton

"I knew something was going on but not this!" Shirleen cried. "I cannot believe you kept this from me."

Virgil turned to me, hoping I would say something, but I looked away.

I had assumed he'd broken the news to his aunt, like any sensible person would.

Without me to save him, Virgil turned back to his aunt with a sheepish grin. "It wasn't on purpose."

"When were you going to tell me, Virgil?" Shirleen asked. "Or did you plan to let me hear it in your podcast?"

"Well," he began, and Shirleen flicked the back of his head.

"Wrong answer, my love!" she grumbled, then without a change of expression, she leaned over to embrace him from behind, pressing a kiss to his cheek as she squeezed him. "You're lucky I put up with your nonsense."

"I know," Virgil said simply.

"And thank you, Keisha," Shirleen said to me. She didn't extend a hug, but gave me something far more valuable: the highest esteem sparkling in her eyes. "I had my doubts, as you're no sleuth, but you have a talent in this to match your cooking."

"It shouldn't be a surprise," Virgil said. "Mystery solving and cooking make the perfect pair."

As it turned out the public was *very* willing to take our words over Davis's. Not only was there a recording with Davis confessing the broader outlines of his plan, his threats came out loud and clear. When there were doubts about how this recording came about, other testimony arrived from those who knew Shirleen the best. Like from Winifred and Margot who spoke about Davis's devious plot and hinted at previous plans or Malcolm Demetrious Freeman speaking on the strange things he noticed the night Ruby died. Even Lucia released a statement of what had occurred that evening. She didn't publicly confess to the small role she played in the threats, but she did come around to tell Shirleen the truth.

I hadn't been there for such a meeting, but Virgil said his aunt was hardly surprised at the news, for Lucia was probably the only one who would target her in such a way.

As for Oscar, who had been more vicious in the planning of his prank, he had gotten fired from the radio station, turning long simmering rumor into fact. If a small anonymous tip had sped things along, I wasn't about to admit to anything anytime soon.

Although the year was winding down, it appeared things were just ramping up around Shirleen. Given the splash the arrest made, it was no surprise that people were clamoring for interviews.

It was also less of a surprise that Austin decided to capitalize on everything by squeezing in one last book event for the year. The bigger surprise was Shirleen not only agreeing but inviting *Wake Up, Hunton Bay* into her home for a Christmas Eve breakfast.

I arrived while the stars were still quite vivid overhead and barely had coffee made before the news production staff descended upon the house and its kitchen, bringing not just lights and film equipment, but additional Christmas decorations – including a few more wreaths and angel figurines, plus mistletoe discreetly hanging in the foyer.

As Shirleen made omelets and pancakes with the hosts, she talked about the origin of her first cookbook, and the others that followed, highlighting the breakfast cookbook, which arose due to her nephew coming into her life.

Watching her dazzle, I couldn't believe how this little scene almost didn't happen. Just before she started filming, Shirleen had been taken over by a spell of nerves that didn't go away until Virgil was summoned from his bed, still half-asleep, to the house.

"Don't you think she made a remarkable recovery?" I said to Virgil, as we stood in the foyer watching on one of the extra screens. "The moment you got here, her nerves were gone. It's like you're her lucky charm."

"No, she's plotting." Virgil yawned. He downed his coffee and was eyeing mine with great interest.

"Plotting?" I echoed.

"Yes, because congrats are in order. She told me Kitchen Atelier just called you in for an interview."

"It's too early for congratulations," I protested.

"You are nearly perfect for the job, and if you don't get that one, there are dozens out there ready to woo you. So Shirleen is plotting."

He wasn't making any sense so I handed him my coffee, hoping the caffeine boost would help. "To get me a job?"

"Most likely. Smile," he added as he chugged the rest of the coffee.

I turned to see that Camera One had spun over to us.

I smiled on reflex, until the camera turned back to Shirleen and the morning hosts. "Plotting?" I asked again, though I had an inkling what he meant now as Shirleen looked as pleased as a cat presented with a fat fish.

"Watch out for the mistletoe," Virgil said over the rim of the coffee mug.

I looked upward to find we'd been standing underneath it the entire time.

I didn't move away, nor did he, as we eyed this teasing plant whose presence was not as innocent as it might seem.

But as my eyes caught Virgil's, it was with shared understanding that this little plant held only the amount of power we wanted to give it.

My name was called, by someone from behind me, and I turned rather numbly, confused at first, until I saw Eden, Jamal, Romy, and Pascal crowded behind us.

"Aren't you supposed to be up there?" Jamal asked. "We came to see you on TV. I should have stayed in bed a bit longer if you're just going to be hanging around."

"I will be up for the cake segment later," I said.

"Oh, good," another voice called from behind my friends, "we aren't late!"

My friends parted like curtains to reveal my father and sister sitting on their wheeled luggage.

I stared in stunned silence for several moments, before I flew to them both, hugging Aisha and then my father. "What are you doing here?" I asked. "Dad, you're supposed to fly in tomorrow! Aisha, we were coming to see you! Why are you here? Why are you both here now? What about Martha's Vineyard?"

"We're still going," Dad said. "I was just curious about what's been going on here."

"Why didn't you call me?" I cried.

"I did," Aisha replied without shame, "but when you didn't answer, I figured it would be better to surprise you. Plus, Dad was curious about what you've been up to." Aisha tacked on a cheeky wink, that left me greatly concerned about what she was going to say next.

"Your sister contacted us and we helped her arrange how to get here without you knowing," Eden said. "You were so busy it was almost too easy."

"We figured a good surprise wouldn't hurt you!" Romy added.

"Since your father's allergic to your cats, Keisha, he can stay at mine," Pascal offered.

"Glad to see my Key has so many good friends," Dad said. Then he looked directly at Virgil, who was suddenly wide awake, as if he'd drowned in a whole bucket of coffee.

"Dad, this is Virgil Sullivan," I began awkwardly, stumbling on what else to say. All the things I would have said a month ago didn't seem quite enough.

My father made no pretense as he met Virgil's polite smile with a scrutinizing stare. "One of your friends," Dad said, so deliberately I could only glower at my giggling sister. What had Aisha told Dad this time to make him want to shift all his carefully made plans around?

"Do you like birdwatching, Virgil?" Dad asked.

Virgil, oblivious to both the overwhelming doom behind this question, and how Eden, Jamal, and Romy were all silently telling him to say no, cheerfully replied, "Yes, I enjoy it very much."

"Excellent, we'll go out Christmas morning, before the girls get up. Meet me at Port Walker Point just before dawn."

"You don't have to go," I began, but one of the production assistants walked over and tapped me on the shoulder.

"You're up," he said, and put a mic on me before I could get a word in. Joining Shirleen and the morning hosts, I was introduced not merely as a recipe developer, but as an important voice for *Season by Season Revisited*.

"Today, I'll be making one of the Christmas cakes featured in the book," I said, and then looked down at the ingredients on the table. My voice wavered as I looked back at Shirleen, for this was not what we had planned. Instead of giving me an answer, she only smiled, and I continued. "This one holds a special meaning," I said, looking past the cameras to where my father and sister were watching, along with my friends, both old and new. "For me, it's not Christmas until I have a bite of Caramel Pecan Delight."

Afterward, once all the filming was done, I found Aisha badgering Virgil about the podcast.

"I want to know if I made the podcast!" she cried. "Please, just one little hint."

He shook his head with far too much pleasure. "Just listen to it as it drops, no spoilers!"

Aisha pouted. "You're no fun!"

"It's all about the journey," Virgil said.

Aisha still huffed, but her expression altered as she spotted me. "Well then, I'll get spoilers from my favorite sister."

"Don't even think about it," I warned her. "I won't crack that easily."

"Oh," Aisha said, "I haven't even begun to try..." She cackled and then called over to Romy, "Hey, Romy, I heard we're going to karaoke tonight! Shall we team up to blow Key out of the water?"

Left alone, I sighed. "I must apologize for my family. They're a lot."

"No, it's fine," Virgil chuckled. "It sort of explains everything about you."

"Because it's Christmas, I'm taking that as a compliment," I grumbled. More sincerely, I continued, "You don't have to go birdwatching with my dad. He's an ornithologist, which means he's a serious birder. He's always looking for fresh blood, since all my friends are wise to his ways."

"Then I'm glad that he asked," Virgil said.

"You might regret it."

"I won't," he assured me quietly and in such a manner I let the matter drop. "After the TV people roll out, Aunt Shirls and I are off to Moonhaven. Although Jamal and the others invited me to come to the dinner with the rest of you, it might be a tight fit and I figured it's probably better to give you this now."

Virgil went to the hall closet and got out a bag. I had started protesting that he needn't give me a gift, even before I saw it was the same bag that Naomi had given him, just with different tissue paper.

"Gee," I said dispassionately, "you really shouldn't have."

Virgil waved the bag in front of me until I took it.

As I shoved my hand inside, I expected a mug or a riff on the many themed gifts I'd been given in the past that revolved around cats, bicycles, and cooking. Instead, however, I pulled out the smaller of his two microphones, with a bow attached to it.

"Merry Christmas, Keisha," Virgil said. "It's been an interesting few weeks and I think you've proved you need one of these with you."

"I didn't get you anything," I said softly as I held it, seeing not just the microphone but the promise of something else behind it. "Why are you giving me this?"

"I've been thinking of doing a spin-off for my local history podcast," Virgil said. "There are all sorts of true crime stories, cold cases, and other mysteries about. I thought it might be fun to investigate. Maybe even try to solve a case or two."

"Sounds like a pretty big project," I said, pretending I didn't know what he was asking. His words held not just a promise of continuing the investigations we were conducting but something equally as delightful.

That like a yeasted bread that needs time to rise and rest, we were far from done.

"Exactly," Virgil said. "I can't tackle it all by myself. I'll need a partner."

"I'll have to think about it. We'll talk about this when I get back from my trip." I remarked. Emboldened by the warmth in his answering smile, I turned on the microphone and sang, *"What are you doing New Year's, New Year's Eve?"*

Acknowledgments

Over the last few years I've gotten very interested in podcasts, and ones centered on food media were my top listens. There's so much we can learn about people through food, because food shapes our society in every way we can imagine. Especially the recipes: whether crafted with care, found in a cookbook, seen in a social media post, or taken off a label of a box of oatmeal or a bag of chocolate chips. Recipes can tell us many things, but they can be missing a few things too. My mother famously has a bread recipe that no one else could replicate, until we realized that she neglected to share the other steps she takes – steps that weren't included in the original recipe as written!

Like a well-run kitchen, this book benefited from a great deal of support from many different quarters:

As always major thanks to my family, to my mother for the pile of cookbooks and bakeware she shared with me, my father for spreadsheets on what to cook next, the recipes my sisters shared or tried, and to my little niece who got me thinking about what recipes to share.

Thanks to Jennie Goloboy who always helps me know when to strike for a good opportunity.

Thanks to Ella Chappell for guidance and enthusiasm as I worked and Jo Harwood and Dan Hanks for some excellent notes that prodded me in the right direction.

A big round of thanks to the team at Datura Books: Caroline Lambe, Niki Igbaroola, Kai Misquitta, Christiana Spens, Olha Yezhova, Chris DeVeau, and more. Thanks for all your support in getting this book prepared and shared out to the world.

To the writers I shared drinks and meals with over the past few months as we talked craft and beyond, thanks for the support and encouragement in more ways than one!

Major thanks to the foodie podcasts the tantalized my ears over the years, *The Sporkful, Gastropod, Proof, Gravy, and Your Mama's Kitchen.* Inspiration truly is found everywhere and leaves me hungry for more.